3544400394...
PB MAT SF
Matthews, Susan R. author
Blood enemies
WITHDRAWN

"Out, [...] the alar[...] through [...] narrow h[...] children?

"Three here." One of his men came out of the black corridor, a child hardly more than a baby under one arm, dragging another by a handful of a night-dress, the child so stunned with such an awakening it seemed sleep-walking. "Diter's got the oldest, we should go."

"I'll cover," Fiska said. He was the raid leader. His position in the hierarchy demanded he share the grim realities of their work, and be seen doing it. He had to maintain his position. It was the only way to make sure that these atrocities would be avenged, that the Angel of Destruction would itself be destroyed before it had a chance to send out roots and establish itself in the new worlds of Gonebeyond, to rule there by blood and terror.

Someone else was there. Somebody's older sister, or somebody's young mother, coming out of the room behind Diter as Diter hurried by with a young boy clinging trustingly to his neck. "Noll?" There was an edge of hysteria in her voice. "Noll, where's the baby, where's Ida, did your sisters get out, who has the baby?"

Diter was gone. Fiska backed out into the street again, blocking the interior from view. *She came at me with a piercer,* he would say. He fired; she fell. He was a good shot. She was safely dead, but the others, were there no others he could save?

**BAEN BOOKS
BY SUSAN R. MATTHEWS**

The Under Jurisdiction Series

Fleet Inquisitor
(Omnibus includes *An Exchange of Hostages,
Prisoner of Conscience, Angel of Destruction*)

Fleet Renegade
(Omnibus includes *Hour of Judgement,
The Devil and Deep Space, Warring States*)

Blood Enemies

Fleet Insurgent (forthcoming)

To purchase these and all other Baen Book titles
in e-book format, please go to www.baen.com.

BLOOD ENEMIES

The Under Jurisdiction Series

SUSAN R. MATTHEWS

Thompson Nicola Regional Library
300 - 465 VICTORIA STREET
KAMLOOPS, BC V2C 2A9

BLOOD ENEMIES

This is a work of fiction. All the characters and events portrayed in this book are fictional, and any resemblance to real people or incidents is purely coincidental.

Copyright © 2017 Susan R. Matthews

All rights reserved, including the right to reproduce this book or portions thereof in any form.

A Baen Books Original

Baen Publishing Enterprises
P.O. Box 1403
Riverdale, NY 10471
www.baen.com

ISBN: 978-1-4814-8334-6

Cover art by Kurt Miller

First Baen printing, April 2017

Distributed by Simon & Schuster
1230 Avenue of the Americas
New York, NY 10020

Library of Congress Cataloging-in-Publication Data

Classification: LCC PS3563.A8538 B58 2017 | DDC 813/.54--dc23
LC record available at https://lccn.loc.gov/2017003339

Printed in the United States of America

10 9 8 7 6 5 4 3 2 1

3 5444 00394624 0

CONTENTS

This book is dedicated to the Intemperate Muse, according to his Excellency's good pleasure; and to my wife Maggie, who has been putting up with me, and the "Under Jurisdiction" series, for nearly forty years now.

I dedicate this seventh novel in the series
Under Jurisdiction to the readers who have taken
a kind interest in my story since my debut novel twenty
years ago; with special thanks to independent
booksellers all over the world.

GETTING HERE FROM THERE

Twenty Years Under Jurisdiction

"Blood Enemies" is the seventh novel in my series "Under Jurisdiction," which debuted in April, 1997. There's been a lot of story between then and now; let me try to summarize what you might like to know before you head into this one.

My protagonist, Doctor Andrej Koscuisko, arrives at this novel after a troubled career as a State-sponsored judicial torturer—a Fleet Inquisitor—and years spent in struggling against the very system he exemplifies, earning him the reputation of a renegade of sorts.

When he graduated with honors from a prestigious medical college's school of surgery, his father told him it was time he did a stint of service to the State—the Jurisdiction Fleet—before he took his place at the head of the Koscuisko familial corporation. That's traditional; and Andrej comes from a very traditional culture, rather parochial compared to worlds under Jurisdiction taken as a whole. He's an important person in his extended family, and by extension in his system of origin—the Dolgorukij Combine. He's the inheriting son of an old, rich, profoundly influential family; the posting he takes to render service unto Caesar must reflect the prestige of both his family and the Combine entire.

There is only one posting that's acceptable to his father, under the circumstances: that of Chief Medical Officer on board a Fleet cruiser-killer class battlewagon, traveling from system to system keeping the peace, monitoring compliance with Bench rules and regulations, supporting the rule of Law and the Judicial order.

There are, however, significant drawbacks to the posting. Fleet serves an old system of government, its authority—and tax base—threatened by its increasing inability to maintain civil order and serve the common weal of an ever-expanding number of worlds under Jurisdiction. The government is getting a little anxious, increasingly authoritarian; and has instituted a formal—and increasingly ferocious—program of state-sanctioned torture as an instrument of social control.

As can be expected of a system of government based on law and order above all else, the Writ to Inquire, and everything it entails, is documented and controlled at every imaginable level. Candidates for the Writ must be accredited physicians, qualified medical professionals. As might also be expected it's not all that easy to find people willing to embark on a career as a professional torturer, especially people drawn exclusively from the medical establishment; so when the Bench grants the Writ to

Inquire it also grants the rank-position and perquisites of Ship's Surgeon to all of the Bench's torturers: Chief Medical Officer, Ship's Inquisitor.

Andrej fought the assignment as fiercely as he could, but filial piety is the founding principle of the Dolgorukij social order. Andrej's family—and Andrej's position in it—make his behavior a highly visible reflection on the respectability, even the morality, of the entire Koscuisko familial corporation. In the end he does as he is told.

Then it gets worse, because during his orientation course of training and indoctrination Andrej makes the life-shattering discovery that there's a savagery within himself he's never experienced before.

Along with this unexpected passion for torture, and an unexpected genius for using it to find things out and punish transgressions, comes an almost equal genius for getting sideways of people in authority: for making trouble, just trying to find a scrap of decency and justice within the cold hard iron system of Judicial inquiry.

Andrej's a stubborn man—he was raised to be an autocrat, after all—and one would almost say that he makes enemies more easily than friends, especially enemies in high places who are accustomed to people doing as they're told with deference and dispatch.

Over the course of years Andrej keeps trying to do the least harm, struggling to control the expression of his native will for dominance in Secured Medical as he does so. The more prisoners are referred to him, the more field assignments he's sent on, the harder and harder it becomes for him to hold on to his psychological balance; but he never stops fighting Fleet, the Bench, himself.

It can't go on forever and it doesn't. During the course of the novel "Hour of Judgment" Andrej finally determines on the only course of action left to him. He won't be Bench torturer any more, even though refusing to perform his statement of work is mutiny. Even a Ship's Inquisitor—granted Bench immunity from sanctions for almost any crime—is vulnerable to a Tenth Level Command Execution.

If there's anyone who knows what that can mean it's Andrej Koscuisko; but if he's going to die, there's someone who needs to die first, and Andrej's just the man to make that happen.

The Bench has chartered a very small number of special agents, Bench intelligence specialists, to read between the lines—wriggle between the cracks—serve the rule of Law as individual operatives with powers of extraordinary discretion. One of them, Karol Vogel—the protagonist of "Angel of Destruction"— has been losing his faith in the rule of Law for years; and it's his own innate sense of justice, rather than any concern for Andrej, that leads him to protect Andrej from the consequences of his crime.

Vogel also shares with Andrej the fact that someone highly placed in the Bench administration is determined to see Andrej dead, for reasons totally unrelated to the murder of Captain Lowden. Partially because Andrej needs to consult a specialist for help, partially because Andrej needs to see his lover and his child safe and protected when the time comes that his crime is discovered, Andrej goes home—for the first time in years—to take care of business.

While he's there he meets unexpectedly face-to-face with an old, implacable, and by now insane enemy from his earliest days at Fleet Orientation Station Medical, who reveals to him the existence of a plot to frame the entire crew of the Jurisdiction Fleet Ship *Ragnarok* for a nonexistent mutiny to cover black-market racketeering at high levels of Fleet's administration. In order to ensure that he gets the proof on Record in his capacity as a Judicial officer Andrej has to get back to the *Ragnarok* as soon as possible, narrowly avoiding being murdered himself on his way.

They almost don't let him back on board, reasoning that a man who has as much to lose as Andrej Koscuisko— who is, after all, a Judicial officer—is unlikely to back their plans to remove the ship to some safe haven while the legal niceties of the situation are sorted out. He convinces them that he is on their side, taking an unusually active role in shooting their way out of a trap.

Now the *Ragnarok* has committed "mutiny in form," and Jurisdiction's Fleet is distracted by political developments adverse to the rule of Law and the Judicial order. This is Andrej's chance to steal the bond-involuntary Security slaves with whom he's forged a strong mutually supportive relationship over the years.

Bond-involuntaries are a special class of criminals condemned to participate in the process of Inquiry under extreme coercion from an implanted governor in their brain; all that Andrej has to do is pull the governor, and then smuggle them all out to a safe haven in the sanctuary of Gonebeyond space. It's an illegal and complex surgical procedure: but he's Andrej Koscuisko.

Everything runs about as well as Andrej could have hoped until the very last, when Andrej's Chief of Security—Brachi Stildyne—realizes that there's one thing Andrej hasn't arranged: someone to accompany the Bonds who knows why they act the way they do, how to protect them from their own savagely thorough conditioning, what they need to un-learn to be free men again.

Before Andrej Koscuisko Stildyne didn't know what "love" was, let alone unrequited sexual passion that matured over time to selfless dedication. Now Stildyne goes away into Gonebeyond with Andrej's troops, and when Andrej realizes what Stildyne's done and why he did it, Andrej realizes that he owes Stildyne the biggest apology of his life.

So Andrej follows them into Gonebeyond. That doesn't exactly work out as planned, because he got Karol Vogel to take him, and Vogel has parked him at Safehaven Medical Center where he's been in protective custody—more or less under house arrest—ever since. Safehaven needs doctors, especially ones with Andrej's experience and surgical qualifications; Andrej needs protection, because Gonebeyond is full of people with very good reasons to want him dead.

He and his Security-in-exile, Stildyne included, have exchanged brief, necessarily impersonal, messages over the past year; but Andrej is determined to make his apology face-to-face.

As the action of this novel opens, therefore, we find him at Safehaven trying to get away, and his life—as well as that of Stildyne and the stolen bond-involuntaries—about to get involved, by accident, in a desperate mission to locate and destroy a Dolgorukij terrorist society determined to cleanse Gonebeyond of ethnic impurity in the name of the Holy Mother and the Angel of Destruction.

Seven novels, over twenty years. Man! What can I say? When Harper Collins published "An Exchange of Hostages" in April, 1997, I knew I had a lot more to get done before the story was over. There was a complex personal story to work out with Andrej Koscuisko from start to finish, and an entire dystopian government to replace.

There were significant unalterable events in the time line, even then: someone Andrej loved had been killed in an assassination attempt; Security Chief Stildyne had a long painful road to travel from being a casually brutal survivor of unspeakably mean streets to becoming a human being capable of concern and empathy; Andrej himself had not one, but two really significant moral conflicts to resolve.

Those were the fundamentals of my story as I understood it, twenty years ago. There've been refinements, evolutions, and complications as the novels have gone by. There are things I wish I could go back and tweak, with the benefit of 20-20 hindsight. I wish I'd made more notes as I went along. I wish I'd gone east, rather than west, with some non-load-bearing plot element or other. I wish I'd written that line differently, or used a fresher adjective, or added a paragraph, or deleted one.

The novel you're going to be reading or listening to is one that I've known was waiting for me all along, though it doesn't look much like I thought it was going to on my first way through. I think it kicks butt harder, further, and faster than any of them since "An Exchange of Hostages."

I take a tremendous amount of pride in this book. I hope you find it's worth the read.

BLOOD ENEMIES

ENEMIES

The Under Jurisdiction Series

CHAPTER ONE

Night Raiders

She was alone in the dispatch center in the middle of the night when the chirp of a status message alerted her to incoming voice traffic. "Freighter *Byrnie*, with traffic. Mavrine of my heart, Mavrine of my dreams, have you saved any apples in your stores for your one true love?"

Mavrine grinned. Teasing, he was, but she loved the sound of his voice, even badly distorted by the antiquated transceivers that were the best they could manage at Haystacks. Antiquated, but free. Everything in Gonebeyond space was salvage, including their freedom itself.

"Not for you," she said. She'd meant to tell him before, but his last visit had been too short. Less than a day. She couldn't keep the news from Cheber any longer. Everybody else could wait until she started to show. Then they would be married, Nurail-fashion, since it would be

3

obvious that the union was a fertile one. "I need to save all the apples I can. To boil up, you see, when the time comes. To make applesauce."

Silence, from Cheber. She smiled again, broadly and happily. There'd been blood feud between her people and his, once upon a time; but it didn't matter. The Covenant that governed what passed for community in Gonebeyond, out beyond the acid-sharp claws of Jurisdiction that had done its best over the years to kill them all, that Covenant was an end to feud. *History stops here. No one may pass who will not pledge an end to all old hates and retribution.*

"Fit for the toothless," Cheber said, thoughtfully. At last. Hope in his voice; hope, love, wonder, gratitude. "Oh, Mavrine. Oh, darling.—And oh, here's the spin coming up, I can still turn back."

He was making his final approach to the vector, then. Mavrine thought about it. "No, the news could come out too soon. And I'll need supplies." There hadn't been a baby since last year. Children were held almost in common, at Haystacks; they had so few. "There'll be cloth for the wrapping, for one."

"I'll hurry," he said. His signal was beginning to break up, to lose coherence. "—soon as I can. A daughter."

"I'll be waiting." But the blip that was Cheber and the freighter *Byrnie* was almost gone, into the black void of the vector at Broder Hoops. "Haystacks Station away, here."

"—away." Pushing away from her boards Mavrine stood up and stretched, slowly, luxuriously, lengthening her limbs to their fullest reach. She'd been disappointed that he hadn't had more time, but the job had been tightly scheduled, five of the largest cargo containers to be offloaded pending further retrieval; and away to the next job. Now Cheber knew he was working for three.

The fire alarms went off. They were always going off. Mavrine grimaced in annoyance. She wanted time to savor the memory, what she'd said, Cheber's reactions; but a person couldn't think with the klaxon sounding.

It was better that the sensors should mistake the faint traces of wood-smoke in the air for a real fire than that they should fail when they were honestly needed; and there was a fog on the river—she'd come to work the night-shift through the fog, acrid, moist, heavy, pressing the wood-smoke from the residential section down to the earth and trapping it there. No help for it. There'd be no thinking for her until she'd reset the alarm.

Locking her communications down she made her way out of the dispatch building and outside. Smoke hit her lungs like a lead weight; she staggered forward, doubled over with coughing. Not a false alarm. A real fire. The fog and the smoke were so thick she couldn't make sense of where she was, completely disoriented before she'd taken three steps; she couldn't so much as find her way back to the door.

Through the roiling clouds of smoke-blackened fog Mavrine could only just glimpse a scene of horror, fire red and golden in the night. Fighting her way forward against the smoke Mavrine dropped to her knees, remembering her training; the air was a little less choking, near the ground. She could think.

The station was on fire. She couldn't gear up because she couldn't tell where the fire-suits were, since she couldn't find the dispatch building. She knew she was mere steps away, but she had no hope of finding the right direction in the disorienting haze of fog and smoke. She couldn't help fight the fire. She had to find the collection point instead. That was a different alarm.

The klaxon shut off, suddenly; pressing her face to the ground Mavrine pulled her shirt up over her nose and mouth, waiting for the ringing in her ears to subside. There. The signal-beacon from the gather-place. No. There. Where? The fog distorted sound, muffled it, she couldn't tell which of the signals she heard was the right one, which ones mere echoes.

Someone was here. Someone seized her by the arm, pulled her to her feet, urged her into a run. Stumbling, she fell, choking on the smothering fog; her rescuer dragged her along. She helped as best she could, her eyes swollen, her tears burning now-reddened lids and smoke-seared cornea.

Then they were clear. They'd gained the fire-safe collection area, open to still-foggy skies but shielded by the vapor-barrier airstream wall that deployed in the presence of smoke. Mavrine lay gasping on the clammy ground, hoping for a rescue inhaler. None was offered. She could hear shouting, but it was confused. Screaming. Laughter.

Laughter? Blinking to clear her eyes as best she could Mavrine struggled to her knees, trying to make sense of what she was seeing. People in rescue suits, but she didn't recognize them, not even the suits. Someone took her by the hair, bending over her from behind; she felt the cold burn of a knife against her throat and it hurt, but why?

The knife bit no deeper. Someone had come, putting out a hand to stop Mavrine's attacker from finishing the assault. Her rescuer pulled off his face-mask and crouched down on his heels, looking up at whoever it was behind her; said something, but not in any language Mavrine could recognize. She didn't recognize the man either. Then he spoke to her reassuringly in Standard, humor and what seemed to be kindness in his voice.

"You bear a child," he said. How could he know? Had he been monitoring communications? What, who, had been in the containers Cheber had just delivered? "We release it from its shame. We send you into the embrace of the Holy Mother."

He had an accent that Mavrine thought she recognized. Dolgorukij. There'd been traders at Haystacks from the Dolgorukij Combine, recently. They'd been eager to make contracts, interested in everything about Haystacks Station. Launch-field capacity. Population. How many children; they'd brought sweets and pastries.

And suddenly Mavrine knew, even as the man pushed her so hard that she fell over onto her back on the cold hard ground. Night raiders. Devils from beyond the Broder Hoops.

Hard unforgiving hands wrenched her knees apart, held her down, tore through her worn clothing with sharp knives. She could smell raw wood, the resinous perfume of the straight-growing evergreens in Haystacks' woods; the man spoke to her again, and his words were beyond horror. "Out of respect," he said. "Your suffering is shortened. The child wins respite, for its mother."

The knife cut deep between her legs. But the pain

could not be compared to the pain that followed it, unimaginable, relentless. She screamed and screamed and screamed, because she understood. The smell of wood. The sharpened stake. The forest of the dead, it was a story, only a story, no grotesque savagery in the history of all the feuds ever sung in Nurail weaves had ever approached this.

"But not too shortened, because there is a point to be made, after all," the man said. She was surrounded by obscene laughter. Someone strapped a rescue inhaler to her face, finally, air and—stimulants. *Your suffering is shortened*, he'd said. *But there is a point*.

They raised the sharpened pole with her on it and fixed it into the ground, all of her weight bearing down on that sharp point and tearing slowly—oh, so slowly—up into her body.

And then they went on to the next prisoner.

Through the black smoking Hell of homes burning in the night Fiska—Fisner Feraltz—worked his way ever more deeply into Haystacks' residential blocks, weeping as he went. "Out, out, everybody out! Fire! Fire!" Shouting over the alarms in accented Standard Fiska shouldered through a door left unsecured into the thick haze of a narrow hall. How many people lived here? How many children?

His team spread out to his left and right, searching; setting incendiaries as they went. It didn't take long. All they had to do was tear the children up out of their beds, and drive them away from ruin and destruction. It was for the Holy Mother to decide which of the children would survive their ordeal, but no one else was to be allowed to live.

"Three here." One of his men came out of the black corridor, a child hardly more than a baby under one arm, dragging another by a handful of a night-dress, the child so stunned with such an awakening it seemed sleep-walking. "Diter's got the oldest, we should go."

"I'll cover," Fiska said. He was the raid leader. His position in the hierarchy demanded he share the grim realities of their work, and be seen doing it. He had to maintain his position. It was the only way to make sure that these atrocities would be avenged, that the Angel of Destruction would itself be destroyed before it had a chance to send out roots and establish itself in the new worlds of Gonebeyond, to rule there by blood and terror.

Someone else was there. Somebody's older sister, or somebody's young mother, coming out of the room behind Diter as Diter hurried by with a young boy clinging trustingly to his neck. "Noll?" There was an edge of hysteria in her voice. "Noll, where's the baby, where's Ida, did your sisters get out, who has the baby?"

Diter was gone. Fiska backed out into the street again, blocking the interior from view. *She came at me with a piercer,* he would say. He fired; she fell. He was a good shot. She was safely dead, but the others, were there no others he could save?

At least one of the souls in this house was dead before the fire ate them, or worse. He had to hold on to that. The Angel of Destruction understood that he might agonize over what he'd done; he could confess his pain and be absolved, though he dared not admit to any merciful murders. *Yes, any decent man would feel as you do, Feraltz. And you are a decent man. The Holy Mother understands your sacrifice in Her service.*

Five years working his way back into the Angel's ranks. Five years winning trust and confidence. Now all he had to do was live somehow with what he had done for a few more weeks. Cousin Stanoczk would come. Fiska would transfer the data he'd collected so carefully, so secretly, to the man who would be his rescuer; names, locations, resources, access codes.

For now there were more houses to burn, more children to harvest, more people to save from death by slow torture if he could. They would be avenged. He would not fail.

The Holy Mother knew indeed what he did, what he had done, and why. When he had completed his task she would be merciful, and grant him peace.

General Dierryk Rukota. Artilleryman; guilty of being inconvenient to have around for people engaged in black-market arms sales; former commanding officer, now subordinate officer, of Captain Jennet ap Rhiannon of the Jurisdiction Fleet Ship *Ragnarok*. Renegade and mutineer, almost by accident.

In his long career upholding the rule of Law and the Judicial order he'd been places he hadn't wanted to be, done things he'd regretted having to do, seen things he would rather not have seen. But nothing like this. This was different.

There was a little boy in his arms, an emergency blanket tucked around his trembling body, waiting for his turn. It was a beautiful day. The autumn color of the dying leaves in the lush and gracious woods was restful to an eye accustomed to the flat textured grey corridors and muted neutral tones of shipboard life. The sun was high in the sky, her gracious warmth cheering the air. There was a perfume of wood-smoke in the air, overlaying a terrible base note of roasted flesh.

Autumn and dying leaves meant cold at night. The little boy had been driven from his home in his sleepers, loose long-sleeved shirt, loose trousers, no slippers on his cut and bloodied feet. They could have made a fire, but the only survivors were too young to have been taught, and had no fire-kit. And were in shock.

Three days, "Two"—the *Ragnarok*'s intelligence officer—had said. Three days without food or shelter. He couldn't stand the silence. He had children, though he hadn't seen much of them over the years. He liked children. That was one of the reasons his wife had chosen him to be their father.

He started to rock the little boy gently in his arms, murmuring an old play-rhyme soft and low. *Yup shah, nar shah, podiyai, podiyai.* Flinging his arms suddenly around Rukota's neck the child buried his face against Rukota's shoulder, and began to scream; and there was nothing Rukota could do about it.

Dr. Mahaffie beckoned. Oh, good. It was his turn. No words; Rukota held the child, and Dr. Mahaffie examined him as best he could a traumatized patient screaming in inarticulate desolation. Gille Mahaffie was Ship's Surgeon now, since Koscuisko had gone off on his own tangent. They knew where Koscuisko was, of course; but he'd provoked the Captain, and Safehaven needed Koscuisko more than the *Ragnarok* did.

"Think we have something to work with, here," Mahaffie said, and beckoned for one of his orderlies to come take the child away. Now that Mahaffie had completed his examination it was safe to give the child medicine to counteract the shock, to dampen the memory of what the boy had seen—at least until the boy gained strength to survive. It was hard for Rukota to let go. He wanted to hold on to the frightened child forever, but it was too late to protect the little boy, and nothing Rukota could do could change that.

"Report, Doctor?" Captain ap Rhiannon suggested, to Rukota's considerable surprise; because he hadn't known she was there, and she was usually hard to miss, even if she did only come up to his shoulder. He was a tall man. She was better-looking. Her voice sounded a little strained, underneath her calm professional presence; that was new.

"Statistics from Langsarik Station suggest twenty-six children under the age of ten years Standard, your Excellency. We have nineteen. There were twenty, but one too near the end to salvage." That would be the one Rukota had found in the first sweep, the one they'd found clinging to the blood-stained sharpened stake on which its father had died.

Ap Rhiannon hadn't shown signs of stress before—a base level of outrage and anger, yes, but crèche-bred Command Branch had no pity in them. Trained out of them at a very early age. "How is staff holding up?" she asked, formal and almost aloof. *It's the fourth time for us, now*. She didn't have to say that part out loud for Rukota to hear it.

"Tahumos was worse," Mahaffie said. "As I gather." The *Ragnarok* hadn't been first on the scene at Tahumos; they'd been mapping new vectors in Langsarik space, and the mining station at Tahumos had been in Sesscomb's area of responsibility. It had been ugly at Tahumos, but it had been ugly for someone else.

Ap Rhiannon nodded. "Carry on, Doctor." She looked up briefly to meet Rukota's eyes; so he followed her respectfully as she walked up to the crest of the ridge. They could see the ruins spread out in front of them, from fire-gutted warehouses to food depots still smoldering. And peoples' homes. They'd collect the bodies, and count them up as best they could to make sure no one was missed.

They'd do that once they'd found all of the children. The raiders always left the younger children behind: either to die of cold and shock and dehydration or to live in torment with their memories for the rest of their whole lives. "There's something familiar," ap Rhiannon said, musingly; and introspection was unlike her. "I just can't get what it is."

"We *have* seen Chorb," he reminded her. "Palladure before that." But ap Rhiannon shook her head.

"I've never walked the settlement. Until now." She was scanning the remains of the ruined houses, frowning. "I felt like someone else, somehow. As though I was in a different body. Not this one." She tapped the chest-plaquet of her over-blouse as she said it as if for emphasis, thumb and five fingers gathered into a loose fist.

Six digits to a hand made her a category three hominid, and Rukota had typed her as Versanjer, in his mind. The Bench took the orphaned offspring of its destroyed rebels to populate its crèches. They had to be processed very young, or their indoctrination didn't take. How old had Jennet ap Rhiannon been? Was it possible that she remembered?

"They're not going to get away with this," Rukota said. "We'll find them. Someone will find them." Because raids like this, terrorism on this scale and consistent over time, meant organization. Needing bases of operations and supply lines. Meant someone somewhere knew something. But Gonebeyond space was full of unmapped vectors leading from who knew where, going to who knew where; in the year since the *Ragnarok* had chased after Andrej Koscuisko's stolen bond-involuntaries the *Ragnarok* had just begun to scratch the surface.

"I'm going to want Koscuisko when we do," ap Rhiannon said. To execute the murderers? Or simply to find out everything they knew, one way or another? Because nobody was better at that than Andrej Koscuisko. Everybody knew that.

Even though the Captain herself had closed Secured Medical, had mandated drug assist for any interrogations Koscuisko might be called upon to perform under her command, General Rukota could find it in his heart to wish Tenth Level Command Termination for the people who had chased that little boy into the woods and left him there, cold, starved, bereft, to live or die alone and terrified.

⊕　⊕　⊕

The patient—a man named Lens, fit, mature, well-muscled, not over-fed—sat in the embrace of the diagnostic chair, waiting for Andrej to finish studying the flimsies. There was something about the referral that didn't add up.

"My apologies," Andrej said, lifting his head to address his patient. Lens had traveled all the way from Fintack out near Carlin Station to get here, an eight-day trip at the very least; and there were all the right chops for a properly executed medical referral, from Carlin Station's clinic all the way up to Safehaven Medical Center. "Aortal adhesion can be difficult to image on a consistent basis. I'm just finding the bloodwork inconsistent with cardiac tissue degeneration."

It wasn't his field. They had a cardiologist at the hospital, but only one, and it was Racklin's off-shift. Since there were few calls for neurosurgery at Andrej's level he spent most of his duty time as a general practitioner. Lens had been first in line, this morning; waiting when Andrej had come in, in fact, diagnostics and lab-work in hand.

"May I see?" Lens asked, his curiosity clearly engaged. He reached for the diagnostic flimsies as he spoke, but how would Lens be able to interpret what he saw?

Standing side by side with Lens, Andrej pointed at the data-plot that confounded him. "Here's an index line for the standard range of healthy cardiac muscle. These are your results from this morning. High to average, yes, but yours should be somewhere up in this range."

Lens slid his rump out of the diagnostic chair and stood up, leaning in close, tracing the line to which Andrej was pointing with his finger. "Here, d'you mean, Uncle?"

Lens had to shift his weight to reach, turning square to Andrej's side. Suddenly Andrej knew that something wasn't right. But it wasn't "Uncle." "Uncle" was simply something that Nurail called men in a position of authority, and in his case Andrej believed it was at least partially so they wouldn't have to say his hated name.

Before Andrej had a chance to think it through Lens caught at Andrej's shoulder to stab him. Andrej grasped Lens' intent just as Lens struck, so he was already turning to defend himself—as Stildyne had taught him—when he felt the knife.

It didn't stop Lens, but it saved Andrej's life; the knife slewed wide to its mark, tearing the fabric of Andrej's clothing—Infirmary white duty smock, under-blouse— and slashing him to the skin from his chest to his belly.

Not fair, Andrej thought. He hadn't had combat drill for a year. If Stildyne were here Stildyne would have kept him current on hand-to-hand. If Stildyne were here Andrej would have better Security, professional Security, to watch his back. How many was this, three, four almost-successful assassination attempts, in the year he'd been at Safehaven?

Lens stepped forward, trying to maintain close assault range. Andrej did a quick pivot, turning his back to put his elbow into Lens' stomach just below the diaphragm. He had to be mindful of Lens' diagnosis, which reduced his options. But why should he care? Lens was trying to kill him. He'd thought they were slacking off. He should have known—

Known better. Lens staggered forward after Andrej, catching Andrej's duty whites by the back. Andrej went down hard onto his back on the floor. Cold hard floor. It needed mopping down; he'd have to say something about it, at the next staff meeting. "For Anders," Lens said, pinning Andrej to the ground. "For my father. My uncles. My mother, my brother—"

All Nurail, of course. That was the problem with being Andrej Koscuisko in a hospital full of Nurail. How many years had it been, since the Domitt Prison? Not enough. And of course Andrej had done more than just bring Nurail to a horrible death, but that had been the job description. Ship's Surgeon; Ship's Inquisitor. "Security!" Andrej called, but not as strongly as he might have wished. "Security—"

Center of gravity. That was Chief Stildyne's voice in Andrej's head. *Not yours. His. Give it a good kick.* If Stildyne hadn't come away into Gonebeyond space Andrej wouldn't be here. He owed his Chief of Security the apology of his life, and no Nurail would-be avenger was going to stop him.

Kicking out for Lens' knee Andrej hit him hard enough to get a good loud grunt out of the man, something that they should be able to hear clear out in the waiting area. So where were Security? Not in any hurry. That was where.

Andrej got clear while Lens was still trying to regain control of his leg, and scrambled to his feet. Flexing his foot toes-upward he got a solid strike in, the hard heel of his boot against the hinge of Lens' wrist; the knife clattered off across the floor harmlessly, coming to rest beside the bottom shelf of one of his cabinets.

Watch yourself. That was his own voice in his internal

ear, now. *This is a patient, not a prisoner. Concentrate.* Andrej smelled blood, his own blood, soaking the front of his duty blouse. It hurt enough to slow him down; and Lens had another knife in his shirt-front. Well, of course. What self-respecting assassin would come in armed with only one weapon?

With a look of desperate determination Lens got to his feet, bracing himself against the diagnostic imager and sending it crashing across the floor.

Red rage possessed Andrej with overwhelming strength. That was valuable equipment. It would be hard to replace, because Gonebeyond was outside of the established trading communities of Jurisdiction space and had no access worth speaking of to anything like adequate markets. People coming into his Infirmary to kill him Andrej understood. People vandalizing the equipment, however, he would not tolerate.

Taking Lens by the throat Andrej dragged him to the floor where he could hit him. Being hurt made people angry; Andrej knew that he could do much more harm than most when he was angry. Because he knew how to hurt people, he was very, very good at it, and he knew how to take pleasure in the act. He'd done without for years now, two years, more; but an addiction of such power did not go away just because Andrej had withdrawn from the execution of the Question.

"Like to make a mess, do you?" he snarled. "Come in here and throw things around, you fish-eater, you contemptible excuse for an assassin—" He hit Lens in the face, and dazed him. Lens was trying to get up, but Andrej wasn't having any of it. Andrej was dimly aware of sounds coming from the door, now, people apparently trying to get through without destroying the door at the same time. He ignored them.

With a brutal twist of Lens' wrist Andrej wrenched the knife out of Lens' hand. He knew about knives. Now. Where was he going to needle in; which excruciating pain would best express his outrage? There was a nerve-bundle at the back of the Nurail jaw that—if tampered with—set off an entire constellation of agony so sharp that a man could not even find the breath to scream. So nobody would hear a thing.

What did Andrej care if they did? Didn't they already know who he was, what he was, didn't they let him live only on sufferance to start out with, and because they'd all sworn to put away the destructive fury that was blood-feud—howsoever merited—as the condition of being allowed to join Gonebeyond's refugee communities?

And all at once Andrej missed the freedom of Secured Medical. Oh. How he missed it. Lens was down, gasping for breath, helpless; and the anguished expression on his face was the first taste Andrej had had of the drug of his addiction for more than two years.

No. He was not going to forget who he was. He was not going to give a single shadow of a nod to the wolf of his addiction. He was a doctor. He would make it work. He would preserve the only thing that was left to him of common decency, after all these years.

It was safe to get up, now. His patient wasn't going anywhere, and Security were rattling around at the thin steel-framed slider of the clinic room's door. The door was a joke, for security purposes. Had it not been for the stalloy honeycomb that formed its core it would be about as convincing a barrier as a piece of the cellulose-fiber toilet paper that the administration provided for his use. "Doctor Koscuisko, sir—"

Wearily Andrej started to limp across the room. Someone surprised him by kicking the door in, with decision and dispatch; and a man Andrej thought he recognized stepped over its splintered remains into the room. For a moment Andrej was confused: the figure seemed familiar, but the uniform was not. Langsarik colors. Did he know that man? Didn't he?

Then the kicker-in-of-doors opened his mouth and spoke. "Good-greeting," he said, and Andrej knew who it was in an instant. "Respectfully inquiring whether the officer is in need of assistance?" Robert St. Clare, Nurail, former bond-involuntary Security slave. The man for whose life Andrej had made his first—not his last, but perhaps his most significant—compromise with his honor, all those years ago.

"Holy Mother," Andrej said, surprised out of noticing that his body hurt and his head was spinning. "Robert. Where have you come from? It astounds me to see you."

"Very good to see you, sir," Robert said cheerfully, the relative informality of his language delightful to hear after all these years of dealing with the constraints a governor imposed on a man's comportment. "I was in the neighborhood, thought I'd drop by. Have I come at a bad time?"

Andrej shook his head, extending his hand. He wasn't going to embrace Robert, because the color of his blood would clash with the Langsarik rose-gold of Robert's uniform. "No, it is merely a day in the life." Security were piling into the examination room; there was a body on the floor. They probably needed to know what he expected them to do with it.

Andrej pointed. "Refer this one to Racklin, priority cardiac. He may need surgery." Lens was still a patient, after all, unless the medical referral had been created out of whole cloth. "And call the janitors to wash the floor. It's filthy."

Now more than ever, what with blood all over it. There were two gurneys at the door trying to get in, with several apparently exasperated orderlies trying to muscle them through; two? Yes, of course. One was for him. "Come along with me, Robert, tell me all your news. It is so good to see you."

There'd been times in this past year when he'd thought he'd never see Robert again. There'd been times when he hadn't been sure he wanted to, for fear of the awkwardness between them. "There's a lot to tell," Robert agreed. "But it looks like you may need to be glued first, your Ex—sir."

Because he'd been cut with a knife, and was possibly about to fall over. Sitting down on one of the waiting gurneys Andrej surrendered himself to medical necessity, his mind full of grateful wonder at Robert's welcome presence in Safehaven.

Robert St. Clare bent his head down close to the cyborg bracing on the desk in the narrowly focused circle of light, listening as he worked. "I want that imager checked and back on line tomorrow morning," Koscuisko was saying. "And the cabinets secured. We almost lost the last sefta-rem in Gonebeyond."

It was Alderscote "Beauty" Sangriege, Safehaven's provost marshal himself, who sat on the other side of the desk in Koscuisko's quarters, arguing. "But we didn't. You had the problem under control, well done, by the way. We're going to need a new door."

"So post some Security in clinic, while you're organizing one. To remind them that there should be some," Koscuisko said, irritably. Koscuisko was clearly annoyed and in pain—Robert could sympathize completely, the alcohol was filthy, apparently distilled as it seemed from seaweed and soggy cardboard—but Koscuisko and Sangriege apparently had a relationship that contained some elements of cordiality, howsoever deeply buried.

Robert had heard about Koscuisko, and Beauty Sangriege, and Chonniskot Dawson. There were no Nurail in Gonebeyond space who had not heard the story of how Andrej Koscuisko had saved the life of the only surviving child of the war-leader of Darmon in a refugee relocation camp. How he'd declined to raise an alarm over some anonymous prisoners escaped from Limited Secure; how he'd treated their wounds, struck off Dawson's chains, and walked away absent-mindedly. Fit of pique over abuse of prisoners outside of Protocols, it was said.

"There would have been Security," Sangriege said, in what seemed to Robert to be a patient and reasonable tone of voice. They called him "Beauty" because he was scarred; clear across the face, from top to bottom. He'd been a pretty man once, by report. Even now he could boast of a fine head of hair, iron-grey and curling. "It seems they were distracted by a call from someone in passenger receiving, out at the launch-field. A curiosity, some Nurail visitor in Langsarik colors, and asking after the souvenir shops."

Well, he couldn't come all this way without bringing back scenic views or saltsea stickies for the others, could he? Yes, there'd been a sufficiency of mid-meal idlers in front of the clinic building when his mover had dropped him off. They'd known who he was. The only Nurail Robert had heard of wearing Langsarik colors was one of "Black" Andrej's notorious bond-involuntaries, the ones Koscuisko himself had stolen from the Bench and sent away into Gonebeyond.

Beauty's remark could not be allowed to pass without a response. Robert spoke up. "That would explain how a man could walk up to clinic at mid-day unchallenged, I suppose," Robert said mildly. "With a stinger in his boot, in case he decided to kill somebody." The point being, of course, that with respect to Safehaven's Security, there didn't seem to be much.

He couldn't spare much time to enjoy the moment, however, because he had little enough time over-all and cyborg bracing was delicate equipment. Safehaven had its own med-tech maintenance department, but apparently Koscuisko hadn't felt quite confident that if he asked them to have a look at the thing it wouldn't come back hurting him worse than before. As a sort of a Nurail joke. He was going to have to disappoint Koscuisko, even so; there wasn't much Robert could do with something this complex. He didn't have the rating.

Robert hadn't been there when Koscuisko had injured

his hand; that'd been after Koscuisko had had them all smuggled away. Apparently there was some residual nerve damage, and a cyborg brace—a cobweb-light net of wires across the back of Koscuisko's right hand, whispering encouragement to the nerve receptors through the skin— didn't maintain itself forever.

"He'd sworn to the Covenant," Sangriege said to Koscuisko, clearly not about to dignify Robert's remark by acknowledging it. Robert hadn't meant it entirely seriously. Security would have known that Koscuisko stood in no danger from *him.* "Nice little conspiracy, this time, six people involved at least by preliminary count. We apologize for the knives, though. I'll have the duty officer beaten, d'you want to watch?"

"Beauty, if I wanted a man beaten I'd do it myself, and see it done properly." An established joke between the two of them, Robert guessed. "But I want my equipment back and my dose-cabinets secured. I don't care what Robert did to your sin-soiled and heterodox door."

"Anything to keep the peace, and way ahead of you." Beauty stood up. "It'll be done by morning. Until next time, then, Doctor. I'll see myself out."

Robert wished him well of the endeavor. Large portions of the non-clinic areas in the hospital—dormitory and mess, among them—were clearly still under construction, raw-poured flooring and sheeted unglazed windows and all. A man could be hard-pressed to find his way around it day by day.

The door into Koscuisko's modest suite of rooms was a hinged sheet of pressed cellulose with a hair's-breadth layer of veneer that closed behind Sangriege's back with a faint and almost embarrassed sigh. Robert put down the micro-hook and reached for the jeweler's weld, discouraged. "Tell me everything," Koscuisko said.

They hadn't had much time to really talk since Robert had arrived. There'd been the entire examination, clean up, and close up to accomplish. Koscuisko's wound was long, though shallow; it had frayed muscle and scraped bone, and those were muscles and bones that moved every time a man took a breath. There was no help for it hurting; a man had to breathe.

Where to start? "Your people landed us at Ripen Secht, in Langsarik space. Some cousins of yours were waiting for us there." Malcontents—the slaves of Saint Andrej Malcontent, the secret service of the Dolgorukij church—were apparently all called "cousin," though from what Robert had gathered the exact word used rhymed with "three rungs lower than stale shit." "Not the officer's Cousin Stanoczk. He came later."

And they'd all thought it was Koscuisko come to see them, at first, because of the superficial similarities between the two men at a distance. Stildyne and Cousin Stanoczk had something going between them, though, so Robert had got comfortable with how much Cousin Stanoczk could remind a man of Andrej Koscuisko.

It had been Cousin Stanoczk who'd explained that Bench specialist Vogel had brought Koscuisko to Safehaven for safekeeping. They'd gotten pulse-messages back and forth over the past year, but always too short. "We wanted leaving to ourselves, and they did. In a week or such that thula, you remember, the Malcontent's, turned up on the doorstep with a cheerful red ribbon tied around its center of gravity and a note that said to 'please take care of my ship.'"

The thula was an elite scout-courier, and it was carrying a main battle cannon just like the one on the *Ragnarok*. It almost made a man homesick to see it. "Then we went to support a depot at Surchanic Station. It was a good place for us, privacy, and we could make ourselves useful. Stildyne helped. He knew where we'd been."

Under governor, that was. It'd been a lot to ask of Security Chief Stildyne, voluntary self-exile into Gonebeyond space with a crew of men he couldn't be said to know—not with the governors removed from their brains, and long years of trained self-censorship at constant risk of punishment to get over somehow. But Stildyne had come. Because Koscuisko had asked, and there wasn't anything Stildyne wouldn't do for Andrej Koscuisko. "Here," Robert said, holding out the cyborg bracing for Koscuisko to take. "I've done what I could. Try it on."

Koscuisko fit the brace over the back of his right hand and tapped its core gently to engage. Robert watched Koscuisko's face carefully, and there were the uplifted eyebrows and slightly relaxed forehead of pleased surprise, so it was better, at least. But there was still some sort of a regret that hadn't gone away from Koscuisko's expression.

"All of this time I have been wondering how I am to explain myself to Brachi Stildyne," Koscuisko said. "When I realized what he had done, and I, I had not so much as told him. I ran out of time. I do not excuse myself, Robert."

Wait one, Robert told himself, startled. "You sent him with us," Robert said, daring Koscuisko to say any different. "Why else would he have come?" Stildyne had never said anything about it. Suddenly Robert knew why.

"Because he thought better of me than to have sent you away with no adequate arrangement." He couldn't see Koscuisko's expression well enough to evaluate it, but Koscuisko's voice was bleak. As well it should be, Robert thought, resentful for Stildyne's sake. "And apparently wished to avoid making less of me in front of people he knows I love, or you would not ask that. And for all this time I have failed and failed again to get away from here. It has not been for lack of trying."

Sent here for safekeeping; kept here ever since, under Safehaven's formal protection. It made a sort of sense: if people with the most collective cause to wish him dead could stand security for his life, there was scant chance they'd let anybody else enjoy the pleasure vengeance was supposed to bring.

"We've been kept busy." That was true. "Or we'd have come to see you sooner. But we've just been called to Langsarik Station, and I found a ride." Someone had to stay with the thula or they'd all have come, so Robert had snuck away by himself. "Last-minute opportunity. I've been wearing the same boot-stockings for three days now."

Koscuisko could extrapolate about the rest of Robert's underwear as he cared to or not. But it was a good opening, so Robert stood up. "And now, I'm sorry, but I've got to go, or I won't get back in time to make muster." He was cutting it close, but he knew how to do that and make it work. Now more than ever he wasn't going to let Chief Stildyne down.

"I've disappointed you, Robert," Koscuisko said. "I

have earned your disapproval fairly." Robert didn't want to part on these terms. It had been a year. He had a speech, he'd rehearsed it. He hadn't had the chance to tell Koscuisko at Jeltaria, where he'd sent them away. All that practice, wasted.

"We're free men, your Excellency." He'd wondered all this time what he was going to call his officer of once-assignment; Koscuisko, Excellency, Anders. Now he didn't have the time to think twice, and the familiar words just came out of his mouth. "You did that. Everything else is just brambles in the fleece."

It seemed to help; sighing, Koscuisko stood up—very carefully—and offered Robert his hand. "It was good of you to come and see me, Robert," Koscuisko said. "I hope to see you all again. Soon. I'll beat Sangriege's watchers and get away, somehow. And then I will have words to say to all of you, if you consent to hear them from me. Especially Stildyne."

"Keep you well until then," Robert nodded, clasping Koscuisko's hand in his own for one brief but heart-felt moment before he let himself out to get back to the launch-fields. There were two days and more between here and Langsarik Station on freighter transport; and he had plenty to think about.

Whether or not he was going to let Stildyne know that he knew Stildyne's secret. And whether he was going to tell the others.

Tired and despondent in spirit Andrej Koscuisko walked down the corridor toward his quarters; slowly, because he was sore from his neck to his knees. It had been a quiet day. He'd had several days of relative leisure to brood on what Robert had said. Stildyne hadn't told them? Andrej had thought that he couldn't be more ashamed of his behavior; he'd thought wrong.

Stildyne had once wanted him. Andrej knew that. Then Stildyne had invested himself body and soul in Andrej's struggle to stay whole, complete, one fully integrated hominid soul, as Captain Lowden brought all the pressure he could to bear on Andrej, sending him prisoner after prisoner for interrogation, always demanding the most severe sanctions he could impose for the crime accused.

Andrej hadn't seen Stildyne changing. But he'd realized that Stildyne had changed, making himself over into a man who could win Andrej's trust. Andrej missed Stildyne, and he hadn't had a good game of tiles—or a good argument over one—since he'd got here. But it was so much more than that, he had exploited Stildyne's passion for him shamefully and shockingly, and to find that Stildyne had let Andrej's gentlemen believe he'd come at Andrej's request was absolutely the last straw.

He had seven failed escape attempts under his belt. It was time to try for eight, and make it work. He had a plan. He'd been testing it. It wasn't quite ready, but Andrej couldn't wait, he had to try, he had to try now—no matter how much his ribs hurt. What analgesics the hospital held in stores had to be reserved for people with more urgent need of it than he had. He was looking forward to self-medication with the liberal internal application of alcohol, but as he neared his quarters his attention snagged on something wrong and he slowed down.

The door wasn't exactly closed. *Oh, good*, he told

himself, disgusted. *Another one. And in my room this time.* Shouldn't Security be twice as vigilant about assassins today, after their recent embarrassing lapse? He should call them, and put that question to them exact. He should turn around and go the other way. He should not raise his voice and call out to let them know he was coming and that he knew they were there.

"Whoever you are, it's all been tried before, so go away and don't bother me." *And all Saints damn you to Perdition for humorless catechists*, but he didn't have time to voice that thought. Security was already here, it seemed, one of the squad leaders coming out of Andrej's room as Andrej spoke. No, of course he didn't have any privacy. He was only the Chief of Surgery at this hospital, that was all.

"Sorry for the inconvenience, sir," she said. Her diction was a little slurred—though it remained difficult for Andrej to tell the difference between some of the thicker Nurail accents and actual drunkenness. "No other place handy to stash these for you, just at present. Beauty said you wouldn't mind."

What she didn't sound was threatened, so nobody was likely to be lurking inside his door with a mind toward murder. Andrej closed the distance between them. She was tipsy; but her breath didn't smell of the local drinkable, or of imported drinkable, or of refined propellant, or even of wodac which these people could hardly drink anyway because it took a lifetime's practice. No. Her breath smelled of cortac brandy, the elite beverage of choice of the Dolgorukij Combine.

Where had she come by that, when he knew perfectly well that he didn't have any? And what personal visitors could he possibly have, apart from the ones who were trying to kill him? The women didn't count; their interest in him was merely instrumental, and none of them tried to kill him yet. Weary him to death in pursuit of the children he owed to replenish the weaves he had vandalized, perhaps, but that was different.

"Thank you, Miss Terend." She blushed at the implied rebuke of his formality; or maybe it was just the flush of alcohol. "That was very thoughtful of you. Who is within, if I may ask?" He didn't wait for her reply, because by her frown of concentration she was having a little trouble remembering. Pushing the door open wide Andrej stepped across the threshold, and took stock.

His outer room was full of people and a familiar fragrance of home, comprised of food and drink and the subtle combination of nervous people with wool and Aznir whiteloomed flax. It took years off Andrej's shoulders just to take a breath, even as it filled his mind with perplexity.

Here were five people in respectable merchanters' uniform. There was a tall stack of crates against the back wall at his right, three wide and five high, like those in which flasks of cortac brandy were customarily shipped. Against the near wall at his left someone had brought a sideboard from somewhere—wallboard on two trestles, perhaps—and draped it in snowy linen, loading it with dishes redolent of home cooking; cold red-root stew, a succulent roast in the Borevitch style, a modestly modernized rhyti server, a stack of dumplings, a pyramid of honey-soaked nut-cakes.

The strangers in his room lined themselves up, four across, at perfect attention. The fifth man went down on one knee in front of them, lowering his head respectfully to fix his gaze one hand-span in front of the toe of Andrej's cloth-booted foot.

"Good-greeting," Andrej said, because it was safe and it would give him a moment to call the correct phrase to his mind. He'd been long from home, except for a visit cut short more than two years ago. The only time he'd seen his son Anton. "I see you come to me from some distance; speak."

If these people were family within five degrees of kinship, the leader would stand up. If within fifteen degrees, look up. If the leader was a petitioner with no existing relationship who'd come to either beg a boon or propose a business arrangement, he'd either bow lower over his knee or prostrate himself at length.

This one did none of those things: so he represented a family member within the fifteen degrees of kinship, but not one with exceptionally privileged status. Or else he was just being very, very careful, because he was up to something.

"Prosper all Saints to his Excellency's purpose," he said. He had a lovely accent, and the phrase was High Aznir, the half-archaic dialect taught only in the most elite cultural circles and increasingly less spoken even there. "We are sent with greetings from his Excellency's brother next-born and second eldest. My name is Pravel Plebach. Your servants here before you have the honor to represent Iosev Ulexeievitch Koscuisko in embassy to his Excellency, praying to be remembered to you."

Andrej felt an instinctive twitch of disdain, confused in the moment between the agreeable novelty of having Azanry show up so suddenly in Gonebeyond space and the contempt he had for his brother Iosev's character. Plebach was clearly sensitive to his employer's disgrace; it explained the posture he maintained, even though Andrej's brother was well within the privileged five, not fifteen, degrees of kinship.

"Stand up, Pravel Plebach." Under these circumstances, Andrej felt that a little relaxation of etiquette was in order. It wasn't Plebach's fault that Iosev had married twice. "Set yourself at ease, and refresh yourselves." The traditional tribute-gift of food and drink was meant to serve a man and his whole household, so there was plenty to go around.

The supper the hospital had provided was sitting in its heat-keeper on Andrej's desk, a sliced meat sandwich with a something brown sauce, a dish of local greens braised in fat and vinegar to break down the fibrous toughness of its stems, a carafe of something hot steeped out of something's ground-up roots. They fed him as well as anybody here, and better in some ways. They gave him cream and sugar for his rhyti; when they had cream, when they had sugar, when they had rhyti.

Plebach stood up because he'd been told to, slowly, clearly concentrating on avoiding any hint of presumption. "Thank you, lord prince. Your kitchen has provided for us generously." That would be the hospital center, Andrej supposed, so if Plebach's people had gone there at all Plebach was lying. Their own ship's mess clearly offered the better meal, going by the one they'd brought him. "May one speak?"

The problem with Andrej's brother Iosev wasn't that he'd married twice, not in itself. It was that he'd used the traditional and most binding form of marrying the mother of inheriting children with the full four sacred-art-thous, as Dasidar had married Dyraine in the great ancestral epic of the Dolgorukij nations. A man could only do that once.

Iosev had taken two sacred wives, concealed of necessity from one another; an act of contemptible betrayal. The wife from the inferior lineage had killed herself for shame once Iosev's betrayal was discovered, leaving her child a bastard born of bigamy. Iosev had tried to refuse recognition to his daughter, but Andrej's mother had put an end to that. The baby was her grand-daughter; while Iosev she only barely acknowledged as her son, the shame of what he had done was that great.

"Not yet, Plebach, I mean to fix a plate. Partake with me." The smell of home cooking was a distraction. It was a traditional courtesy to share the tribute-meal they'd brought; still, the offer seemed to have surprised Plebach, possibly— Andrej thought—in light of Iosev's bad odor. Andrej put five cream-rolls on a plate and held it out for Plebach to receive. One each. He was hungry. Taking some red-root stew to start Andrej sat down behind his desk and pushed his hospital-provided supper to one side with a mental apology.

He ate his dish of stew slowly to give Plebach's party a space of time in which to eat cream-rolls, which they were now obliged to do. It had been too long since he'd had homely fare, though he didn't particularly like cold red-root stew.

This was delicious, however. The bone-extracted stock was rich with gelatin, the tang of the fermented juice was subtle, the sweetness of the roasted root pureed into the broth was complex and fully rounded in the mouth, and the herb that seasoned it over-all was popular nowhere else in known Space, sharp and challenging in the nose and on the tongue.

When he set his dish aside Plebach was waiting for his attention once again, with a subtle relaxation to the set of his shoulders that spoke of considerable relief of stress and anxiety. Perhaps Plebach had made up his mind that Andrej was not going to have him flogged. "Now," Andrej said; and Plebach stepped forward toward Andrej's desk, pulling a wrapped packet out of the bosom of his sober merchanter's blouse.

"For three years the prince our master has been embarked on a special enterprise, one focused on developing markets in Gonebeyond space. For the past year he has been resident at a station near the Neshuan vector, devoted to that cause."

Andrej frowned, concentrating. "Neshuan," he said. "That vector access lies in Langsarik space, does it not?" He'd seen some patients in critical care not very long ago, rare survivors of an attack by night raiders at a mining station. Hadn't they come in on Langsarik ships?

"It is as his Excellency says. Hoping to find his Excellency graciously willing to set aside a portion of the injury done his Excellency by his actions, he begs to be allowed to show his work in the service of the Blood of his Excellency's father and mother, and hope for favor."

Extending the packet Plebach bowed deeply. Andrej knew that Plebach would not straighten up again until he accepted it, and people leaning over his desk howsoever respectfully intruded into his personal space. So he accepted it; and turned it over in his hands once or twice, for examination.

It was an old-fashioned documents-case packaged in leather, containing a letter written in ink on thick paper. There was no monogram on the paper, no proud seal on the packet—Iosev was presenting himself humbly indeed; as well he should.

There was a great deal of formal verbiage to be got through in any such letters, and Iosev's handwriting was very careful and therefore of a relatively large size because of all the flourishes that had to be gotten in. The ink was good. Andrej was reminded suddenly of the last letter he'd gotten from his son, from Anton Andreievitch, and it wrenched his heart.

Concentrating on the moment Andrej read the letter through. The message underneath its pretty phrases and archaic construction was straightforward enough; *you're my brother. I've worked hard to redeem myself. Let me show you. We're kin.*

Refolding the letter Andrej laid it down on the desk in front of him, regarding it thoughtfully. As the oldest and inheriting son, he'd had less to do with his brothers and sisters than they with each other. Still they were his family, his blood relations; they'd be in his care.

He too had violated the rules of his caste. He'd bred a child to a woman not his pre-contracted wife. He'd the appalling poor taste to marry its mother rather than the Ichogatra princess inheritrix to whom he had been promised. He'd argued with his father, and come shockingly close to actually flouting his father's will before he had bowed beneath the weight of tradition and filial obedience and submitted to becoming an Inquisitor.

He'd never violated a sacred vow. But he had other crimes to lay against his account, which in the great balance outweighed any mere moral turpitude and a light handful of innocent lives. Could he really stand in sanctimonious judgment, and not be guilty of the rankest hypocrisy?

There was something else. Neshuan lay off Langsarik Station; Robert had said the thula was there. Was Pravel Plebach the last thing he needed to complete his plan, to make his escape? The last time he'd tried, he'd gotten all the way out to the new launch-fields outside the city and stayed at large for nearly a day and a half before they'd found him.

Only his inability to successfully stow away on any of the freighter-tenders, small transports, or couriers had defeated him that time. Now here was Pravel Plebach with an invitation, and presumably a ship. Andrej didn't have to go so far as to see Iosev. He only needed to get to Langsarik Station. Once he could but find Stildyne and the rest of his people he wouldn't care if Safehaven fetched him back as soon as they found him.

He saw a flicker of guarded optimism in Plebach's face. "*Chornije's* freighter-tender is berthed at the old launch-field, scheduled to depart within eight Standard hours," Plebach said. "We travel by way of Langsarik Station to the entrepot at Canopy Base. Dare we hope for his Excellency's condescension?"

Andrej made a quick calculation. There were no patients currently in his surgical queue. Also no ships incoming with medical transport, not that he'd heard of. Safehaven could easily spare him for a few days. If there were any speakers of High Aznir on staff at Safehaven it was news to Andrej; he could be blunt, because he was not speaking Standard.

"I am kept very close, here," he said. "Report some incidental laborer tardy. Have a mover on stand-by." That the ship was at the old launch-fields was a stroke of pure luck. The old launch-fields, the original launch-fields, were less than an hour's walk from Safehaven Medical Center. He would have to walk—a mover in the street in the small hours would be sure to draw attention to itself— but walking was no obstacle. "I will come with you, if I can get away."

"We will unfailingly perform to his Excellency's specification," Plebach assured Andrej solemnly. "And go to prepare a cabin. Have we your leave to go?"

"With all Saints to put this purpose forward," Andrej agreed, fervently. They left the food behind, of course, because a food-gift once tendered was not to be carried away. Andrej knew what to do about that. It would be his good-bye party, if only he could make it work this time— and all signs seemed to be in his favor. He keyed his talk-alert.

"Canteen? Koscuisko. Someone's left a great deal of home cooking in my quarters, if you would care to come get it before it gets cold. It may serve to supplement the board, for fourth-meal; and there may perhaps be something welcome to quench the thirst, amongst the soups."

Something to drink, in other words. They could have it all, when he was gone. Now all he had to do was wait for shift-change, and review his plans, and hope all Saints would look with favor on his enterprise.

CHAPTER TWO

Discordant Notes

The time was now.

Andrej cast one last look around his quarters. He'd left his meal on his desk, but no one would think twice about that; everybody would have heard the story of Pravel Plebach's embassy, before long. His bed was half-made-up as though he'd merely gotten up early and gone down to the clinic to relieve his boredom—which he did from time to time, if only to set precedent for just such an occasion as this.

He had a hospital-issue jacket and a cap that he'd drawn from stores during the cold months of the past year. In the right costume he could pass as Nurail, short and blond; it had worked for him before.

He'd told Robert the plain truth. He'd kept on trying to escape, to make his way out to the launch-fields east of the old city, to find a ship to hide in. This time he only needed to get to the small old launch-field, down by

Safehaven Head where the river ran huge and serpentine with mud flats and rocky islets into the bay. They would be waiting for him; he wouldn't have to find a ship. He might never have so good a chance as this ever again.

Opening the door to the outside corridor by slow degrees Andrej listened, carefully. He didn't expect company; the Nurail women who came to him by night to demand a child of his flesh usually came earlier, before he'd gone to bed. It took the drug he required to perform under such circumstances longer to take effect when they had to wake him up. So he was safe for tonight: miscalculation meant the risk of premature discovery, but he had to take the chance.

He'd studied the scheduled rounds of the night-watch carefully. His investment paid off: he saw no one as he went up the unfinished staircase to the next level, as he slipped through the loosely strung construction barriers to make his way across the unfinished floor of the new outpatient surgery wing to the other side. Into the construction staging area. He wasn't interested in pallet-stacks of pressed cellulose wallboard. He had another target in mind: the evacuation ramp.

He keyed the door to the emergency escape ramp to its "administrative" status and pushed the gates open. If he moved slowly enough, at a normal pace, the lights would stay low and the klaxons would not sound. The evacuation ramp knew that people had to walk it periodically for inspection. Someone in facilities administration might have noticed when he opened the door to get in, but it would have been a transient alert blip, easily overlooked, of a moment's short duration.

Now he was outside, ground level, closing the doors as carefully as he had opened them. This was the warehouse area, but at night there was only the watch; no deliveries were made after dark, because lighting was at a premium. A security fence, yes, but foot traffic came and went through a simple latched door beside the now-closed vehicle gates. Nothing of value in these warehouses could be removed by a man on foot.

Strolling casually through the exit Andrej latched the chain-link barrier behind him, forcing himself to move with casual insouciance. No hint of a hurry. No suspicion of suspiciousness. There was no alarm.

The fog from off the river was his friend. It lay like snowfall in the streets, hushing the sound of Andrej's footsteps into a whisper. He kept to the shadows as he moved through the empty streets, hurrying now that the sight of a man moving briskly to get to where he was going would arouse no questions in anybody's mind if he was seen. The streets of Safehaven were dark after dusk, to save the drain on municipal resources; when the night was clear a man could see the stars overhead in all their brilliance, undimmed by light pollution.

It was a peculiar feeling to be out alone by himself, and he liked it. At the hospital a man was never more than a raised voice away from other people. On board of a ship someone was always there. At home on Azanry there was always someone waiting near at hand to hasten to his will, because he was the inheriting son of the Koscuisko prince and had been from the day he'd been born. Princes were never alone.

Short-haul cargo handlers frequently were, however,

because they were transient labor, hired and let go as they were needed. Shoulders hunched as if against the clammy chill to further conceal his face Andrej approached the launch-field's access control, hands in his pockets. If he could get past the night watch's guard station he had won.

"An's Groshan," he said, standing on the fog-wet pavement at the access control station's window, looking out toward the launch-lanes. One of Safehaven's moons was full, ghostly in the haze that lay so thick it even blurred the face of the officer of the watch at the window. "Late to report, they'll dock my wages for sure. Freighter *Chornije*, and what kind of an uneducated name is that, I mean to ask."

He'd had a year to study Nurail accents, and—perhaps more important than that—Nurail syntax. The music of the Nurail habit of speech, even when speaking Standard. The officer checked her log-screen; Andrej gave himself a little shake, as if remembering a somewhat tedious trifle of administrative protocol, and unfastened the collar of his buttoned-up jacket to reach inside. "Ah, sorry I am, officer, my docs—"

He had documentation, too. He'd had to do the forging himself, but he was not without resources. He had to be sure of the calibrations of his sensitive surgical equipment, so he had to check it for himself from time to time, so much was only expected. And he was universally welcomed to the task, because it was boring, so people left him alone.

Anders Groshan. "Anders" was the Nurail of Andrej, and "Groshan" started on a note that was a bit like Koscuisko. He'd chosen carefully, as an extra bit of precaution against the habit in a man's mouth of saying his own name when people asked him. *My name is Andrej Koscuisko, and I hold the Writ to which you must answer.* But that was over now. History. Never again.

And there was no need to produce his documents, after all. The officer waved him through. "That they will, and serve you right," she said. "Out of my light. I've a watch to keep, here." He nodded gratefully, moving away, but she wasn't looking at him, closing out the record of his passage with a strike of her official identity-chop.

So he was in. He was through. And there, some little distance away, Andrej could see—through a brief clearing of the fog, a breeze footing up fitfully from the bay in the early morning, the tide had begun to turn—a freighter-tender, and a mover trundling over the tarmac toward him. The duty officer had let *Chornije* know that its tardy crew-member was on his way. Was it the right mover, though?

Andrej thought about fading back into the shadows before the mover could reach him, dreading the sight of one of Beauty's Security at the pilot's station. Had it been too easy, getting this far? No. He wouldn't run away from disappointment if it came. He'd have the Port Authority's people up to his room and get them all stinking drunk on cortac brandy, just for the vengeance their hangovers would provide him. They would have earned a drink from him. Time and again . . .

But not this time. The mover drew near, slowed. No one got out; why would they, for a lowly short-haul cargo handler, and an untrustworthy one at that? But someone was sitting next to the driver: and that someone spoke.

"Prosper all Saints to his Excellency's purpose," the someone said. High Aznir.

"And the Holy Mother hold us in her heart." He got in. The mover turned around. Back down the launch-field to a freighter-tender, waiting, ready to depart. He had done it at last. He'd gotten away from Safehaven's protective custody.

He was going to have his chance, after all this time, to say what he needed to say to Brachi Stildyne; and propose a solution to the problem that was between them, after all these years, with guidance from Dasidar the Great.

The conference room in the management suite at Canopy Base was as luxurious as money could make it, money which had in part come from the patron who sat at the head of the great table receiving Deputy Sorsa's report. "Deputy" was such an innocuous word, Fiska mused. Sorsa owned the Angel's mission in Gonebeyond, and everything that went with it.

"Let me see the record of your work, as you speak." The lord prince Iosev Ulexeievitch Koscuisko—second son of the Koscuisko prince—gestured commandingly with his hand, and Sorsa's office administrator made haste to bring up the mission briefing on Haystacks. Edited, of course. Fiska himself was one of Deputy Sorsa's servants—but at a much more privileged level. He'd worked his way up, earned his place, claimed his position. Deputy Sorsa's trusted aide. Complicit in so many atrocities: but the game was worth even such a price.

"Just as you say, lord prince," Sorsa said, with the calculated deference that was perfume and pleasuring to

Iosev Ulexeievitch. The prince did not seem to realize the contempt in which Sorsa actually held him. But Iosev was of the Blood, for all his failings; from one of the oldest, finest, purest of all Aznir families. Sacred blood.

"We arrived at dawn. Here you see Haystacks before the righteous vengeance of the Angel of Destruction descended on the ungodly, to make of them a lesson and remove their taint."

The visuals had been recorded by an undercover agent amongst the crew of an innocent trader. Haystacks had been peaceful, thriving. They had traded in sweet apples, fresh fruit, cider, preserves, dried apple-flesh. And he, Fiska, had been part of the savagery that had destroyed it.

"A fine place to plant the Holy Mother's sacred mission," the lord prince said, approving. As a physical specimen he was utterly magnificent: tall as an Aznir ever got, a beautiful silky black beard shining with a gentle curl and perfumed with censing wood, a deep calm voice like that of thunder over the hills. Fiska remembered thunder, though not hills. His had been a trading family. "They could have lived in peace, and prospered. And yet they were defiant."

Magnificent in his person, as compelling in his presence as his father. And yet not the prince inheriting; that was Iosev's older brother, Andrej Ulexeievitch. Andrej was *the* son of the Koscuisko prince. All of Andrej's brothers were merely secondary. All that Fiska had heard of Andrej Koscuisko pointed to a man of considerable intellect; quite unlike his brother Iosev, though suffering from an immense moral burden. *From which grant him respite, Holy Mother.*

Fiska had no such blessing to wish on Iosev. Iosev was a bitter, jealous man, whose life had as it seemed had been ruled by resentment of the fact that he had not been born first. "The lord prince knows what grace the Angel extends in the Holy Mother's name," Sorsa confirmed. "And yet Her offered mercies were rejected."

The Angel hadn't bothered to make any such offer. The lives of unbelievers were as weeds in the field, to be plowed into the earth beneath the remorseless weight of the Holy Mother's cultivation engines. Iosev didn't see. He didn't understand. Fiska didn't think Iosev was an evil man, unless the level of willful blindness required to look on such sanitized images and not suspect the harsher truth behind them amounted to an active malignancy of mind.

"There was resistance," Sorsa said. The briefing had advanced, muddy images from a smoke-filled nightmare. "Treacherous, but futile. You know how much mercy the Holy Mother holds in her heart for all men, lord prince. Your servants can only pray that She accepts the waste of these outlandish lives as sufficient penance for their sins, and grants their children sweet peace in the life to come."

The "sweet peace" of servitude. The "sweet peace" of slavery, to reward a brutal death by torture and fire. Once Fiska had understood, believed, echoed such sentiments with fanatic conviction. He was better, now. The Holy Mother was not so cruel a caricature as this.

Iosev re-settled himself in his great arm-chair of heavy wood, carved with his family's device: the mountain hawk of Chelatring Side, the Koscuisko familial corporation's mark. "You need not glaze over the truth with me, Sorsa," Iosev admonished him, condescendingly. "People were killed. I know the gravity of the task. I know the weight of your work."

Sorsa bowed his head, solemnly; and advanced the record of Haystacks' agony. "Thank you, lord prince, I am fittingly rebuked. We left Haystacks cleansed. As you see." Fire. Smoke. Burning homes. Iosev seemed to honestly believe that there had been survivors, and not just the children. Fiska envied Iosev that blindness.

"Feraltz was there, that day," Sorsa added. Fiska was sorry to be called out, but he understood Sorsa's gambit— and knew what part he was to play. "Report to the lord prince, Feraltz. I know you were at the forefront of the fight, risking your life for the Holy Mother."

Fiska bowed. It required no effort to put on a somber face. "We cleared the residences one by one, lord prince, at gunpoint. We left no home unsearched. The Holy Mother granted us the strength and the resolve to work Her will."

He didn't have to lie outright. He could have, and Iosev Ulexeievitch would not be any the wiser; but Sorsa would have cautioned him, later. A man was not to deny what he had done for the Holy Mother, whether or not all men were fit to know the truth whole and entire.

Iosev nodded, gravely, wisely. "We will do what we must," he said. "These people must be stricken from the earth, these places sanitized and made ready. It is a hard task, I know that, Feraltz. Only a true son of the Holy Mother can understand how difficult it is for you to be so mercilessly stern. You serve well. You are to be commended, and with all my heart I thank you for your sacrifice."

At sunrise Haystacks had still been burning. There

would be no survivors. There was no sign of the forest of stakes, or tortured bodies. Who could imagine that Haystacks' people would not have resisted to the end? Iosev Ulexeievitch. Either Iosev had honed the art of willful blindness to an overwhelming degree, or he was fundamentally stupid. "I am humbled by your gracious condescension," Fiska said, with his head bowed respectfully. "Thank you, lord prince."

Until Andrej Koscuisko had married his concubine with the full four sacred-art-thous, Iosev had apparently cherished a secret hope that his elder brother would be killed in the line of duty, and the inheritance fall to him as out of the Canopy of Heaven. The Angel had been recruiting Iosev for years, making good use of his weaknesses; carefully, slowly, but also daringly, placing its counselors within the very heart of the Koscuisko familial corporation, right under the nose of the Malcontent. The enemy.

When Andrej Koscuisko had named an heir, when the Koscuisko prince—Alexie Slijanevitch himself—had raised the bastard son of a mere gentlewoman to his feet on the broad steps of the great hall at Chelatring Side and called the ten-year-old boy Anton Andreievitch, inheriting son of the inheriting prince, then Iosev had given himself to the Angel heart and soul.

"Thank you, Feraltz," Deputy Sorsa said. It was his dismissal. Fiska heard Iosev talking as he left.

"And how many stations have been cleansed now in Gonebeyond space, Deputy Sorsa?" The door closed behind him before he could hear the answer. He knew the answer. He didn't need to be reminded.

Fiska had met the Malcontent Cousin Stanoczk, who had once been Iosev's cousin. Was no more, because the slaves of the Malcontent became non-persons when they put the red ribbon halter around their necks. But Fiska knew that Cousin Stanoczk's family blood was every bit as good, if not as wealthy; and Cousin Stanoczk was anathema to the Angel of Destruction, while Iosev was a benediction of the Blood upon the Angel of Destruction and all its works.

Cousin Stanoczk was coming here, disguised as an even greater catch for the Angel's blood-soaked mission. Fiska could turn the data over to him, surrendering the burden of his dangerous enterprise at last. Cousin Stanoczk would take the data, and with it the Malcontent would destroy the Angel of Destruction, and even perhaps Iosev Ulexeievitch Koscuisko.

It could not come soon enough for Cousin Fiska.

His name was Cousin Stanoczk, called Stoshi; called other things by people to whom the slaves of St. Andrej Malcontent were the lowest form of Dolgorukij life. Paradoxically the contemptible status of the Saint's possessions—the once-people who formed the secret service of the Dolgorukij church—were the freest of all Dolgorukij, not bound by duty, religion, convention, morality. That alone could be enough, for some.

Stoshi had seen in his life many miracles for which thanks were due and gratefully rendered to the Holy Mother of all Aznir. The Langsarik pirates had successfully escaped their doom, one engineered by a terrorist band of religious fanatics long believed extinguished. To Stoshi the

Malcontent had given the freedom to walk the world without lying about who he was in a culture wherein a man who desired other men was a depraved and criminal soul, a shame and a judgment against his family.

They had been tracking the shadowy and elusive terrorist organization—the so-called Angel of Destruction, to speak the name of which was as to spit— ever since it had surfaced at Port Charid some years ago. Its savagery had been such that even the ferocious Chuvishka Kospodar of nightmare memory had been forced to repudiate it; now it was at work in Gonebeyond.

The Angel was Dolgorukij. It was for Dolgorukij to deal with them. For years the double agent that the Malcontent had placed within the Angel's ranks had been working his way into a position of increasing responsibility, gaining access to its inner workings. Now it was time for Cousin Stanoczk to extract Fisner Feraltz—the Malcontent Cousin Fiska—from the term of his purgatory, and his information with him.

Now everything was ready. All the pieces were in place. Now Cousin Stanoczk stood in Hilton Shires' office and faced a man with whom he'd once worked closely: the first test of the imposture required to rescue Fiska and the fruit of his labor.

"Good-greeting," Shires said. He was a man in his thirties, responsible, respected, a man with a wife and children and an aunt with whom the Bench intelligence specialist Karol Vogel was in love; one of those men whom intelligence and ability made charismatic, perhaps the more so—not less—because his ears ran a little large to the Jurisdiction standard. "Ah, your Excellency, is it?"

"No, it is not 'your Excellency,'" Stoshi said firmly. "In fact it would be best, Provost Marshal, if it was nobody at all." Andrej Koscuisko had been raised a Dolgorukij autocrat, and could be blunt. *I am master here. We will pretend that it is not so, and yet it is.* "The courier, she is here, I understand, along with my—with its crew?"

There was more to this interview than a test of Stoshi's ability to play Andrej Koscuisko. The Malcontent's thula *Fisher Wolf* was an elite courier ship of exceptional speed and maneuverability, capable of carrying very convincing armament. The Saint had given it over into the custody of the former bond-involuntary Security that Andrej Koscuisko had stolen from the Bench, and when they'd come to Gonebeyond, Security Chief Stildyne had come too. He would be the second test: because he'd been one of Cousin Stanoczk's admittedly numerous lovers almost since the moment they'd met.

The Angel of Destruction was expecting Andrej Koscuisko at Canopy Base. Arriving on *Fisher Wolf* with its crew of Koscuisko's assigned Security slaves—and Chief Stildyne—would strengthen the imposture, and provide a significant advantage if something went wrong and they had to get away.

Stoshi had spent weeks in hiding here at Langsarik Station perfecting the final elements of his imposture. Chemical masking of the color of his eyes from dark brown to mirror-silver grey. Bleaching of hair follicles to present a lighter shade of straw; partial depilation of body and facial hair, beard and torso, to match the genetic expression of an Aznir variant sub-racial characteristic. Temporary surgery to change the pitch of his voice.

When he and Andrej had been children they'd delighted in fooling their teachers—at a distance, where the color of their eyes would not give them away. Also preliminary information indicated that the Angel of Destruction's hospodar in Gonebeyond had never met Andrej Koscuisko, and Andrej's brother Iosev hadn't seen him for years. So the thula *Fisher Wolf* was ready. Stoshi was ready. He would go to Canopy Base in the person of Andrej Koscuisko. He would bring Fiska and his treasure-trove of data out with him. But first he had to get past Hilton Shires without arousing Shires' suspicions.

"*Fisher Wolf* awaiting your orders." Shires had clearly taken no offense; his tone was perfectly genial. "As per instruction. For planning purposes only, are there parameters you care to disclose, of any sort?"

Stoshi shook his head, but not as Cousin Stanoczk would have done in his proper person. He was wearing an armature cloak that would help disguise his figure until he reached Canopy Base, but Andrej's body language had required careful study. He passed well enough for Hilton Shires—he could see it in Shires' face. But Shires didn't know Andrej as Security Chief Stildyne and the thula's crew did. Nor was there anyone under the Canopy of Heaven more familiar with the differences between Andrej and Stoshi than Brachi Stildyne.

Just as well they all knew how to mind their own business. He would keep to his cabin. If Stildyne suspected, if Robert St. Clare—who'd been with Koscuisko for nearly twelve years now—thought there was some deception going on, they would carefully observe the boundaries of duty, and keep their questions to themselves. Stoshi was counting on that.

"You must accept my regrets." Andrej spoke more formally than Stoshi did. Stoshi kept company Andrej never had. "I can offer no insight. You will call for transfer to the ship?"

"Transport waiting," Shires said, with a cheerful note of mild resignation in his face. "I wish you good travel." Through the open door of the Provost Marshal's office Stoshi could hear a familiar tread approaching: Stildyne. "Thank you, Provost Marshal," Stoshi said, so that Stildyne would hear the tenor rather than the bass, the "I-give-you-good-greeting" rather than the "Stildyne, shall we not go to bed? Never mind, here is a desk."

Some of the most cunning of souls had given themselves to the service of the Angel of Destruction. Stoshi could not give Stildyne more than a moment's pause, here and now, before they arrived at Canopy Base, or Deputy Sorsa—the Angel's hospodar—might catch a hint of what was going on in Stildyne's mind. The Malcontent did not know how long the Angel had been watching Andrej, or from how closely at hand.

There was no question, however, that the Angel wanted Andrej Koscuisko's cooperation very much. There was scarcely a more pure line of descent outside the Autocrat's own blood-lines; and one of their mutual several-times-great-grandfathers had been the insanely racist Chuvishka Kospodar himself.

Stildyne had paused on the threshold, all appreciably-taller-than-Stoshi of him, the expression of masked delight on his ruined face with its misshapen nose and its scarred eyebrow and its narrow eyes quickly veiled over at the sight of the armature cloak. Stildyne had not seen Andrej for a year, because the Nurail would not let him leave Safehaven. An armature cloak was a signal and a warning. *I may be your officer of once-assignment. You are to make no assumptions. I trust we understand each other.*

No warmth, no hint, no shared trust or companionship. Stildyne would be used to that. "Your courier package," Shires said to Stildyne. "Safe journey, safe return."

Without a word Stildyne stood aside to let Stoshi go before him. Stoshi paused in the doorway. "I do not explain," Stoshi said to him, over his shoulder. "When we are returned I relax a degree of formality. Not before."

Stildyne gave him the bow as precisely as though he'd been a bond-involuntary himself, conditioned under the malign influence of a governor to suffer an excruciating correction for any hint of less than perfectly disciplined behavior.

There. The first test, passed. The crew of the thula would be next; and then Canopy Base, and Deputy Sorsa, and the single most dangerous mission Cousin Stanoczk had ever undertaken: for the freedom of Gonebeyond space, and the final destruction of an ancient evil. He dared not fail.

Their passenger was safely loaded, *Fisher Wolf* en route to the Neshuan vector. The passenger had declined to specify where the vector spin he'd given them would put them on the other end; but that was only of minor perplexity, compared to the much larger issue.

The officer. It had to be. Stildyne knew Andrej Koscuisko; he'd been Koscuisko's chief of security for years, now, ever since Koscuisko had been posted to the living Hell that Captain Lowden had made for him on board the *Ragnarok*. Been responsible for Koscuisko's physical training, to the extent that Koscuisko would tolerate being dictated to—which he actually did quite well, and which Stoshi had told Stildyne was a token of respect for Stildyne's position.

Seen Koscuisko at work in Secured Medical, seen him blind staggering drunk with an ecstasy of dominion when he'd established lordship in the torture-rooms; blind staggering drunk with near-lethal quantities of overproof wodac when he'd come out of Secured Medical and started to remember that he was a doctor and a man who had been decent and kind, once of a time.

Koscuisko was wearing an armature cloak. Stildyne could understand that. Safehaven had held Koscuisko close, all of this time they'd been in Gonebeyond. One memorable evening Stildyne had heard a Nurail gossiping about Koscuisko, about his escape attempts, about how no under-tall Inquisitor was a match for the Nurail port authority. Stildyne had made plans to divert the thula to Safehaven to see Koscuisko for himself, at the first opportunity. Maybe the Langsariks, the Nurail, knew that perfectly well; maybe that was why Stildyne hadn't been able to find the opportunity.

Once they'd reached *Fisher Wolf*, however, once Koscuisko and Stildyne were on board, Koscuisko hadn't said a word, but headed straight back to the aft cabin he'd occupied the last time he'd been aboard. On the way from

Azanry back to the *Ragnarok*, that had been, strapped into a stasis-mover, because his wound had been extensive and painful. He'd shut the door.

He'd sent text messages once or twice since to deliver instructions, direct to Pyotr's coms, and not one word more than he absolutely had to. Maybe he was ashamed, Stildyne thought. That would be all right; it had been uncharacteristically unfair of him not to tell Stildyne that he'd arranged to send his troops away into Gonebeyond. With headaches, psychological ones at least, where their governors had been.

But nothing. By the second time Koscuisko sent his orders out they were all on edge, anxious, resentful. Koscuisko had no right to treat them as shabbily as this. He *had* had the right, once. Bond-involuntaries were condemned criminals under Bond, governed by means of a cyborg device in their brains that knew exactly how to inflict atrocious pain for the slightest infraction and that— being what it was—had not the slightest reservation about doing so.

Koscuisko had been their officer of assignment, serving him in Secured Medical a significant part of their punishment. If they'd come to trust him to be humane— at least with them—it only made his current behavior the more perplexing.

Then there was Robert. He went further back with Koscuisko than anybody. Robert had been watching Koscuisko intently, if covertly; so had they all, Stildyne included. Once Koscuisko's second message had been duly logged and noted, once the course alterations had been laid in, Robert spoke.

"Privacy barrier in effect, Hirsel?" Robert asked. Moodily Hirsel swung around in his clamshell to toggle some switches; then, scowling, turned back again to face into the room, where everybody was looking at Robert, now. "That's not him."

Maybe not the most comprehensive thing to say, Stildyne thought; but it got the point across. That didn't mean he was going to take Robert on faith alone. He didn't like Robert. Well, he did like Robert, he hoped Robert would never remember what Stildyne had done to him at Port Burkhayden, and his major complaint about Robert for years had been only that Koscuisko loved him. Which wasn't Robert's fault, any more than it was Koscuisko's fault that Stildyne hadn't known what emotional pain was until he'd fallen in love with Andrej Koscuisko.

"So, yeah?" Lek demanded. "That's where you went. You knew we'd figure it out. What happened?"

"It is, I did. Himself was in the middle of a fight, when I got there. People always coming around to knock on his door and kill him, from what I gather. He thinks it's very boring."

"Ghost, then," Garrity said. He was a man of few words. Spitzstaten by origin; phlegmatic by nature.

Robert shook his head. "Two things. One is, he was cut, and it was long and hard. Across the ribs, almost all the way down. Man can't walk so pretty for a few weeks, after that, and an armature cloak isn't going to cover it, not as soon as it's been. And the other thing. I came away from Safehaven, made it back in time, didn't I? Chief?"

They called him "Chief." They always had; but now it

was his role, and not his rank. Crew chief. Coordinator. He couldn't tell them what to do, and they didn't need him; but they were a team, with him in it, forged by force of circumstance, united around the central issue that was Andrej Koscuisko and whether they could keep him sane, in their own best interest. If you could call it sane. And alive; Koscuisko was unquestionably that. "True," Stildyne agreed. "Had started to wonder, but only started. So?"

"So I made it in record time as an unregistered passenger on a fast ship. Nobody else logged into Langsarik Station afterwards, nobody that came across the vector from the Nurail quadrant, from Safehaven. Right? Nobody? Koscuisko didn't have time to get there before me, not when he was at Safehaven when I left. So. Not Koscuisko. Good effort in getting us to believe it is, though, and why would that be, I'd like to know."

"Cousins." Stildyne was in a better position than almost anybody here to answer that question. But he wasn't going to think about "positions," not with Cousin Stanoczk in mind. Some of his favorite positions—

"About the only other person it could be," Robert said. "So he's working something big, and he can't take us into confidence. That means it's important for us to believe he's the officer. Do our best to pretend he's the officer. You're going to have to figure it out, Chief, we can all do resentful compliance with lawful instruction received, but you need to be all hurt and confused. Er, I mean, pretend. And in your way."

"I get you," Pyotr said. Pyotr was the oldest among them, in terms of the number of years he'd been under

Bond. "He wants us to think he's Koscuisko. So he wants us to be angry. I can do that."

Stildyne could do that too. He had as much cause as any of them; more, perhaps, because everything they had done for Koscuisko out of self-interest, he had done for love. "Angry, check," Stildyne said. "Resentful. Deeply emotionally hurt." He'd clock the first man who showed him the faintest hint of a smile of disbelief, so it was just as well nobody did. "I'll take care of that part, in particular."

Good. Done. "Privacy barrier is not in effect," Hirsel said. Better if Koscuisko didn't notice that the wheel-house had suddenly gone mute.

"Carry on," Stildyne said, and went to find a berth to lie down and pretend Koscuisko was Stoshi for an hour or so.

"I am replete," Andrej said, setting his linen napkin down with finality. "Not a single morsel the more, no. I have not feasted like this since I last dined at banquet in the presence of the Autocrat's Proxy, at Chelatring Side."

"You honor us, lord prince," Plebach said, with evident sincerity. He'd eaten almost nothing himself, watching Andrej anxiously moment by moment while transparently doing his best to avoid being caught at it. Plebach had no cause for concern; the cooked meats were superlatively sauced, the soup was poetry, the raw dishes were perfection and the breadstuffs were such as had risen up to torment him in his dreams after one too many meals of the best Safehaven had to offer.

At Safehaven they all fed from the common mess. He

wouldn't have had it any other way. And the quality of the ingredients available rarely rose above the mediocre, but that was not the core of the matter. It was only that in Safehaven's kitchens Nurail staff cooked Nurail fare for Nurail, and Andrej wasn't.

"It is your kitchen-master who honors me." King of the cooking-fires. Prince of the plates. Wizard of viands, and magician of meals. "Would you call for him, so that I may in person convey my gratitude? Before I convince myself that to fail to finish this last slice would be a sin as well as stupidity, and burst thereof."

Plebach seemed to hesitate. It couldn't possibly be concern about the dessert; no, the apple pastry was such as all Saints might lust after.

And there was cavene, served with cream that could only have come from dairy cattle fed a much richer browsing than available almost anywhere but Azanry. Cavene wasn't Andrej's usual choice of beverage—he was a rhyti man, when drunken oblivion was not on the schedule—but he ate and drank what was put before him in another man's house, so he'd had cavene. To go by the combined effect the flavors made in the nose and mouth the kitchen-master had made the choice to serve cavene deliberately and well.

What was Plebach's hesitation, then? "I will gladly present his Excellency's compliments," Plebach said. "Our Waclav will be anxious, though, conscious of his work-dress. If his Excellency please, perhaps he might be excused the meeting."

No, Andrej did not please. Appreciation for this dinner could not be adequately communicated second-hand.

That the miracle had been wrought on a modest freighter in transit only made the accomplishment more notable. "Please, Plebach, I should very much like to speak to him directly. I'd be glad to go and visit the galley with you, if that is more convenient?"

Plebach shook his head, beckoning for the waiting server at the door. "Not at all, lord prince. Waclav will wait upon his Excellency's pleasure presently." Andrej couldn't quite identify the emotion he sensed in Plebach; Plebach clearly had reservations of some sort, but Andrej could think of no reason why that could be so. Dinner had been flawless.

That perfect apple pastry was sitting right in front of him, all but pulsating with magnetic force. The server had gone to fetch the kitchen-master. But Andrej could help himself very easily; the freighter's dining room would not seat more than five or six at once. And the pastry was so very good.

He hadn't tasted that sweet peppery corns-of-incense spicing, so subtle it was almost only smelled rather than tasted at all, since he'd been home. Corns-of-incense was in short supply even on Azanry, because the climate had changed over the centuries and the shrub—which had to be naturally grown, to be perfect—was exquisitely sensitive to terrain, soil acidity, prevailing winds, and the minerals in the rain-water.

The server was back, escorting the kitchen-master, who was wearing a clean white smock. He had a familiar face that Andrej recognized in principle, though they'd never met before. Waclav wasn't as tall as Lek Kerenko, but his face was broad, his nose was prominent: a good face, strong features, Sarvaw chin. Waclav. Of course.

"You have done me the honor of calling for me, sir," Waclav said to Plebach, who had not turned away from the table to face Waclav when he came in. "I hope the meal has been to your satisfaction." The language was polite, but Waclav clearly knew the meal had been more than merely that. No man of so much artistic brilliance would stoop to false modesty.

"Indeed so," Plebach replied, turning his head at last. Waclav was one of his crew, and familiarity bred— familiarity; there was no real need for Plebach to take special note of his kitchen-master, Andrej supposed. "Our guest has asked for you, Waclav, to speak of his appreciation for your cooking."

"It has been an honor to prepare your meal, lord prince," Waclav said. "Greater still, that it has won your approbation."

Waclav was a master of his art by demonstration, and yet seemed less than confident of Andrej's approval. "Whereas for my part I consider it to have been an honor to consume it, kitchen-master." There was a shadow of disapproval in the room that Andrej didn't understand. "I haven't eaten so well out of my father's own kitchen, and every dish you sent us has been so fine that I only regret I couldn't eat twice as much of it."

"Very gracious of the lord prince to say so." Waclav bowed deeply. "The quality of ingredients is key, of course. I only strive to stay out of their way as much as possible."

"And yet somehow I suspect you could make a meal in even Safehaven's mess with cold-meal mush and spent malt that would be fit for the mothers of princes. Thank you, kitchen-master." He was the senior in rank, and got the last word. Waclav bowed once more, and Plebach dismissed him with a nod of his head.

When the door had closed behind Waclav, Plebach set his chair square to the table once more, shaking his head. "I must confess myself to you at once, or risk reproach," Plebach said. "He is the best of cooks. But unredeemed."

It took a moment for Andrej to grasp what Plebach meant. In the worst days of Aznir atrocities on Sarvaw, when the savage Chuvishka Kospodar had so passionately pursued his intent to destroy everything that did not yield and submit to him, children were "redeemed"—allowed to live—only if an Aznir among the occupying force would claim to be the father, or if testing proved genetic admixture.

So Waclav was of pure Sarvaw stock, in the minority. There was no Aznir trace in his blood line to redeem it from its ethnicity. It was a shame that no one of pure blood had raped one of Waclav's ancestresses: that was what Plebach meant.

Andrej laughed once, but in sheer perplexity more than anything else. It had to be a joke. An offensive joke in the poorest of taste, one made under the influence of the kind of drunkenness a truly superlative meal could induce; but still a joke. And yet it took Plebach just a moment too long to take Andrej's cue and laugh too. Plebach had meant what he'd said.

It soured Andrej on Plebach, though it couldn't sour the excellence of the meal. Plebach had been nothing but polite to him, deferential, attentive; and it had flattered

Andrej's ego, especially after a year living amongst people whose respect was grudging and granted only reluctantly to his own art and ability as a doctor—not a man, not a soul, not a person.

Wasn't Plebach just the same, though, if from a different direction? Plebach's respectful deference was paid to Andrej not as the man he was, but as the inheriting son of the Koscuisko prince. And Andrej himself was the several-times-great-grandson of Chuvishka Kospodar, on his mother's side.

"A man who could give us such a meal stands in no need of redemption, in my eyes," Andrej said. Race prejudice was everywhere, even in the house of Andrej's father. And still that word, "unredeemed," was token of an ancient and particularly ugly kind of prejudice, one he'd never thought to encounter in earnest. "Please spare me the hearing of such language in my presence, Pravel Plebach. You will excuse me. It has been a long day."

He'd already seen his lodgings; the best cabin on board, no doubt, and every luxury provided. The room was not to blame for the ugliness of that word, the reminder of the most shameful hours in all of the history of the Dolgorukij Combine—even with so broad a range of atrocities from which to choose.

"Langsarik Station within three days, lord prince," Plebach said, rising quickly to his feet to bow respectfully. "May I express a hope that his Excellency will rest well."

"I do not doubt it, Pravel Plebach." Maybe he had over-reacted. Plebach was his host; Andrej was indebted to him for making Andrej's escape possible, at last.

"Already I look forward to my fast-meal. Thank you, Plebach, and good night."

Plebach could hardly be in sympathy with the blood-soaked agents of the Angel of Destruction, to speak the name of which was as to spit, whose horrific crimes had been condemned by the Autocrat and the Holy Mother of all Dolgorukij. The Angel was dead; the Malcontent had killed it.

Did Iosev know what manner of man he trusted with his letters? The question made Andrej uneasy, and he went to his cabin with an unquiet mind.

During the years of his career as a Bench intelligence specialist, Karol Vogel had seen many strange sights; and the conference room within the administrative center at Poe Station was definitely one of their number. It wasn't that he didn't know these chairs, the table, that carpet; he'd been at Poe Station, on and off, for two years.

But now that they'd been hastily pulled together in a single room—the best from all of the conference rooms on Poe Station—the effect was a little surreal, in Karol's estimation. And looked much better than he'd thought it would, for which he was grateful.

There were five Pashnavik warships on the viewing screen. *Ragnarok*'s littermates, Prosser in traffic management had called them, when they'd made their first appearance coming off the Janghan vector; and it was true that the *Ragnarok* had been built at the Arakcheek shipyards. But the *Ragnarok* had been a Jurisdiction Fleet ship, an experimental one at that, and these beauties were Dolgorukij. Which was a problem.

"Delegation from Combine Home Defense Fleet Ship *Direwolf* on the ground," the dispatch officer said, the excitement of the moment scarcely disguised beneath her professional diction. "Estimated time of arrival conference area in twenty."

The image of the warships drawn up on the Line where the struggling young government had decided to establish the symbolic point of entry into Gonebeyond space faded into the one of the receiving apron on the launch-line, where the courier had landed. Beautiful courier, too; Karol wished *they* had one.

Several officers were disembarking; Karol studied them with interest. Dolgorukij were handsome people, healthy, with a good opinion of themselves. The Home Defense Fleet's uniform was very pretty. The senior officer looked familiar to Karol, from a distance; *no*, he told himself. *Couldn't be*. All Dolgorukij looked alike. That was all.

It wasn't true; there were many ways to look Dolgorukij, from the tall dark-haired way to the short blond way, with many stops in between. "What's that they've brought?" Torribee—the Port Authority on-shift—asked, pointing. Karol squinted. Oh. Nice. "They come bearing gifts," he said. "Rhyti and pastries, at least. They must have scanned our kitchens."

Torribee snorted; *as if we had a choice*. Karol nodded in agreement. Five Pashnavik cruiser-killer class battlewagons. They could have swept past the little terraformed asteroid that was Poe Station without a second glance; Poe Station had nothing with which to stop them but the Line itself, and that was only a conceptual barrier.

Under Jurisdiction commerce codes, however, there was no crossing the point of entry without authorization. For a small craft, unauthorized entry—usually by way of an out-of-the-way vector, at an unmanned station—meant smuggling, of one sort or another. But a Home Defense Fleet's battleships crossing the Line without clearance could only be an act of war.

The problem was that Gonebeyond space was no-man's-land, a largely uncharted and poorly mapped galactic field with nothing but the occasional colony of refugees from the Bench for population. It wasn't a recognized political entity; not yet. He meant for it to be one, a politically autonomous government on equal footing with any other in known Space. Once upon a time Bench Intelligence Specialist Karol Vogel could almost have made that happen by fiat, but those days were gone.

"Just remember," Karol said. "I'm not even here." He wanted to keep out of this, at least in public. A Bench intelligence specialist was one of a very small and elite group of independent agents granted Judicial powers of extraordinary discretion, answering to the First Judge alone. To speak up would be as much as to say that he was in charge: and he didn't want to be in charge.

Terrible things happened when Bench specialists decided they should be in control. The last one to come up with that idea had destroyed a political system that had been stable for eight hundred years; and under the new confederacy model there was no longer any single final Judicial authority, so what was a Bench intelligence specialist any more, anyway?

Mags Imbrole—their Provost Marshal—was here at the door, now, with a courtesy team of station Security to escort their visitors. Karol stood up, but Torribee remained seated—protocol. Mags preceded their guests into the room, standing behind her designated chair alongside Torribee and Karol so that the Dolgorukij would know where to sit; but there were introductions to be made first.

"Good-greeting," the senior officer said. The rank markers on the man's uniform were impossible to misinterpret, at close range. "Thank you for receiving me. I am Leo Ulexeievitch Koscuisko, Combine Home Defense Fleet *Direwolf*, commanding. I have come to ask you for my brother back."

And, oh, but Karol wished the Flag Captain of the battle group on their doorstep had not said those words. Captain Leo Koscuisko. One of Andrej Koscuisko's brothers. And him with a flimsy from Beauty Sangriege at Safehaven, *regret to have to admit Andrej Koscuisko unauthorized absence from duty*. In other words, gone missing. Still there was nothing in Captain Leo's opening statement that could excuse being rude to him; and there were people quietly and stealthily setting up a massive beverage station against the wall, just inside the door.

Torribee stood up and bowed his head in polite acknowledgment, as though he had been a diplomat all his life rather than a refugee clothier with a side in people-smuggling. "You are welcome, Flag Captain," Torribee said. Karol was impressed; Torribee must have checked the rank markers whilst Karol hadn't been looking. "Please. Be seated. Explain to me, won't you, what it is about a man's brother that would merit the dispatch of five warships to hunt him down?"

Surely Torribee knew, Karol thought, suddenly. Of course he knew. He'd been on the floor in communications when Karol had gotten the message. Torribee sat back down; Mags and Karol sat down; Captain Leo sat down. "My officers," Captain Leo said. "My executive officer. My logistics officer. My command coordinator, my navigation officer." Then they sat down, too. "Will you permit my caterers to offer a beverage, Port Officer Torribee? I am at a disadvantage. There is awkwardness."

"I like bean tea." Torribee was still being polite. "Thank you. But first explain this awkwardness you are experiencing."

Captain Leo nodded—a little reluctantly, to be sure. "Very well. The son of the Koscuisko prince is my brother, if I may put it in such blunt terms in Standard." Because the correct language in Aznir in this instance was "my lord the prince my brother, eldest and second born," or words to that effect. "He is to be a man of some influence within his system of origin, and he is also a Judicial officer. These things combine. I will explain. Ganitsje, the report?"

By all means explain, Karol thought. But he didn't say anything. For one, it wasn't his place—he wanted to keep all lines of authority, explicit and implied, focused on Torribee. For another, he was the man who had ferried Andrej Koscuisko into Gonebeyond space this year and more gone by.

Koscuisko had been parked at Safehaven ever since, gainfully employed in a socially useful position. What had gone wrong? All right, so they hadn't found a spare month to pull the thula off patrol duty to reunite Koscuisko with his people. *I of all people*, Karol told himself, *should have known better than to underestimate Koscuisko's ability to get out from underneath things*.

One of Captain Leo's officers pulled a web-sheet out of his blouse, a gossamer hologram reader that opened into a whisker-thin folio and anchored itself upright to the middle of the conference room table. As Captain Leo spoke a data-stream started to spool up into document format, translating itself from common Aznir into Standard almost seamlessly.

In the course of the past year, all over Jurisdiction space, Ship's Inquisitors have been disappearing.

There was a background docket attached. Ganitsje tapped his index finger on the table twice, and it bloomed into a list onscreen. *Judicial officer Hompirna, Jurisdiction Fleet Ship* Rendaccet, *missing after down-station leave. Judicial officer Gith, JFS* Forticar, *found dead in Port Saraband four months after failure to return from temporary posting, cause of death traumatic decapitation. Judicial officer Sternalle, JFS* Nimrod, *missing en route to ship of assignment after home leave.*

The names kept scrolling, but there was a helpful table running along the top of the page with a running tabulation: number of Ship's Inquisitors assigned, inactive, retired; normal attrition indices on suicide and death by misadventure or natural causes; number missing; number found dead under circumstances either suspicious or consistent with adverse third party intervention.

Murdered Inquisitors, eight, and Inquisitors were

usually better protected than that. But the number of Inquisitors missing, either from active duty or retired registration rolls—forty-six, and that was an astonishing figure. There were a limited number active Writs assigned. A certain number went missing year by year as Inquisitors sought escape from their job duties or the attendant notoriety; but never on this scale.

One of the caterers had circled around behind Karol, offering a flask: bean tea, strong, fragrant, beautiful. Poe Station was between supply runs. All they'd had for weeks was on its fourth steaming. The second caterer set a tray full of condiments down noiselessly between Karol and Torribee—cream, Dolgorukij beet-root sugar, Washima grass sugar, sliced citrus wheels from at least three distinct cultivars. Karol pretended not to see the platter-full of pastries that was laid down beside that. He was supposed to be concentrating.

Criminal organizations may have been involved in several of these disappearances. Significant extralegal activity may currently be exploiting the unmapped vectors of Gonebeyond space for escape and evasion, and the creation of safe havens.

It could have been the chance translation of a phrase. Or it could have been diplomatic code for "and we know where Andrej Koscuisko is, too." Or even "you've lost track of him, haven't you, and such men above all should not be lost track of." Karol decided against that last potential meaning, because it would be impossibly awkward otherwise. A man had to stay positive.

You will therefore proceed to Poe Station in Gonebeyond to make face-to-face contact with our beloved

*nephew Andrej Ulexeievitch Koscuisko, and from him
there obtain such evidence as will satisfy you that he is
safe, content, and not suffering distress or restraint, or
under duress of any kind.*

"You see this last," Captain Leo said, and pointed. "I
am directed to request of you access to the person of my
brother, to prove by the evidence of my own eyes that he
has not joined the ranks of disappeared Inquisitors. I have
further orders which require me to initiate a search for
him myself, if he cannot be called here to Poe Station."

Captain Leo apparently took his rhyti black, which was
unusual for a Dolgorukij. He took a few moments to sip
his rhyti now, giving the implications of what he had just
said time to mature and perfume the air.

So he'd been sent to find his brother. Karol could
appreciate that, in light of Andrej Koscuisko's unique
status. Prince inheritor to the Koscuisko familial
corporation, one of the oldest, among the richest, in the
Dolgorukij Combine. Judicial officer still in custody of a
Writ to Inquire, with Ship's Inquisitors apparently
evaporating at a worrying rate.

Now Koscuisko himself had evaporated from
Safehaven. Captain Leo's orders required him to cross into
Gonebeyond space to find him, and with an unwritten brief
to bring his brother back out and away with them, probably.
Poe Station couldn't stop Captain Leo: they didn't have the
ships. But once allow an autonomous warship to enter
Gonebeyond space and there would be no stopping
everybody else who might want to exploit Gonebeyond's
resources under cover of presumed rights to protect, even
repatriate, its refugee nationals.

Which would be a clear violation of the sovereignty of Gonebeyond space, and a betrayal of all who had fled into Gonebeyond in the first place, and the end of any hopes for building a new form of government to replace the Bench model. One that was based on the common weal, not the despotic rule of Law. Government by consensus, not coercion.

Torribee's options were extremely limited, but they had to do something. There was only one solution Karol could deploy at such short notice. Putting down his flask of bean tea with just enough of a chime against the table's surface to attract Torribee's attention, Karol made eye contact. Torribee in turn nodded; *Yes. Go ahead*.

"Unacceptable," Karol said. "Completely out of the question. I suggest a compromise. I will personally escort Andrej Koscuisko here, to Poe Station, to meet with you in this room. You will provide bean tea for the duration of your stay. Eleven days. Your concurrence, please."

Perhaps the status of a Bench Intelligence Specialist was uncertain, now that there was no longer a unified Bench. Nobody, including Karol himself, knew whether he could still topple governments and deploy whole Fleets. Nobody could say he couldn't, until he tried and failed. Until then psychological inertia was on Karol's side.

Captain Leo set down his flask, and stood up. "Thank you, Bench specialist," he said. "We return to *Direwolf* and wait. Permission to stand off at Poe Station for eleven days, Administrator Torribee?"

Andrej Koscuisko had disappeared from Safehaven. There were a limited number of ships he could have left on, and one of them was a Combine hull en route to

Langsarik Station. Karol would go to Langsarik Station and track Koscuisko from there. He didn't have much time.

"Granted," Torribee said. "Good bean tea, Captain Koscuisko. Thank you, and good-greeting. I'll have someone see you out." *That was that, then*, Karol told himself. He found Andrej Koscuisko and brought him to Poe Station, or there would be war, with a destructive impact for Gonebeyond far beyond what would probably be a minimal casualty list. Not one that Gonebeyond would win, so it was up to Karol to make sure it didn't get started.

"No time like the present," Karol said; and carried his flask of bean tea with him out of the room and down to the launch-lanes for a courier, with the briefest of detours to his quarters to pick up a change of underwear.

Langsarik Station was clean, cheerful, bustling with traffic. Freighters in geosync orbit. Freighter-tenders going up and down, freight to warehouse, offload cargo, load the next. Andrej Koscuisko stood on the tarmac beside the tender that had ferried him down from *Chornije* to Langsarik Station's launch-fields and frowned at the faint stink of scorched thermal shielding in the air. Neither launch-lanes nor freighter-tender were in perfect repair.

"And gave no word?" Andrej repeated, though Provost Marshal Shires had just said as much. Shires nodded, arms folded casually across his chest: *that is the sad fact of it*. It had been a significant mark of respect for a man of Shires' rank to come out to the launch-field to speak to Andrej personally. All the more important for Andrej to honor the courtesy, but he was bitterly disappointed.

"His Excellency is welcome to lay over until their return," Shires said. "Perhaps a few days in clinic, to relieve any potential boredom while you wait."

He was sure he could find plenty to do in the clinic here. But if he stayed, Safehaven would be sending for him back; they'd accepted guest-responsibility for him, and couldn't be faulted for wanting him where they could see him. The wound Andrej had sustained from the last assassin ached from his breast-bone to his nether beard even now, for all the supportive medication *Chornije*'s medical stores had made available to him.

"Thank you, Provost Marshal. I am conscious and appreciative of the opportunity, but I feel I must go on." He couldn't see an alternative. He'd escaped from Safehaven's protective custody to seek out his people and see Stildyne: Stildyne, whom he had not made privy to his plans that year ago; Stildyne, who had gone into exile for no other reason than to help Andrej's gentlemen learn how to be free men again. "Might I respectfully request someone let them know I came looking for them, should they return before I can get back?"

Under Jurisdiction a bond-involuntary who'd lived out his term of penal servitude received months of care to undo the conditioning that had ruled his life for thirty years: even with the governor removed it could continue to poison a man's life, to be in constant apprehension of pain.

There were no such facilities in Gonebeyond. Andrej had coordinated with his cousin Stoshi, who was

Malcontent; but Stildyne hadn't known—though he might
have guessed—and Stildyne had taken on the task, to be
a steady point of reference, to leverage the years of his
acquaintance with Andrej's bond-involuntaries to help
them begin to live again. Over the years Stildyne had
earned their trust. Had he not earned Andrej's, after all
that he had done?

"Glad to oblige," Shires said. "I'll leave you to return
to your ship, your Excellency."

He wasn't going back to Safehaven. There was no help
for it: he would have to return to *Chornije*, he would have
to tolerate its racist crew, he would have to visit with his
contemptible brother Iosev. Once that was done he could
require they return him to Langsarik Station: and hope
that the thula—going by *Fisher Wolf*, now, apparently, a
Malcontent hull if ever there'd been one—had returned,
hope that he could find his way to wherever they were if
they had not.

Halfway across the launch-field on the way back to
administrative offices Hilton tapped Kazmer Daigule on
the shoulder with a wordless suggestion that they pull up.
He'd had an ulterior motive for asking his friend Kazmer
to drive him out to the launch-lanes; Kaz and Koscuisko
had history together, of a sort. Though it had been years
ago, it was still worth appealing to. "So, Kaz," Hilton said.
"Curious. What was it like, seeing him again?"

He couldn't share the problem of two Koscuiskos,
because Kaz didn't have the need to know. But he *could*
use Kaz's help to confirm identification.

That two men who self-identified as Andrej Koscuisko

had stood in his office within the space of three days was without question. One of them had taken a very expensive piece of machinery and a crew of peculiarly circumstanced men and made for the Neshuan vector on a mission, destination unspecified.

Which of the two men actually was Koscuisko was another question, but people couldn't be allowed to walk around calling themselves Andrej Koscuisko all over the place; it was a killing offense to impersonate a Bench officer, under Jurisdiction, and even here in Gonebeyond it seemed clearly something that should be discouraged. Especially when the officer impersonated was a Ship's Inquisitor, in custody of a Writ to Inquire.

"Strangely anti-climactic." Kazmer sounded triumphant, in a quiet sort of way. "Always wondered whether I could look at him and not come over all a-quiver. Even though he never laid a hand on me." Kazmer had been taken with a freighter full of contraband from a warehouse in Port Charid that had been raided, its crew tortured and murdered.

Koscuisko had been seconded to run inquiries. Kazmer—who had ties to the Langsarik pirates, and certain that he would be forced to falsely implicate his friends—had thrown himself on the mercy of the Malcontent at their first, and only meeting. Koscuisko—fortunately for Kazmer, for all of them—had turned Kazmer over to the Malcontent Cousin Stanoczk, under a "religious exception" for jurisdiction over Dolgorukij nationals accused of Bench violations.

Nobody knew what might have happened if Koscuisko hadn't done that, if Koscuisko had pushed for a confession, if Koscuisko had made Kazmer name some names. It hadn't been Langsariks. Nobody was under any illusions that that would make any difference to an Inquisitor on the hunt for collaterals. "Sure it's him?" Hilton asked. Because that was the point, though Kazmer wasn't to know. Kaz nodded.

"Yeah," Kazmer said. "No question in my mind. I go back there sometimes, you know, time to time. I don't think I've ever been so afraid in my life." He'd set the mover in motion; it seemed to Hilton that there was weight off Kazmer's shoulders that Hilton—maybe Kazmer—hadn't even realized was there.

"Glad it's over, then," Hilton said. Sincerely. "Coming to dinner? Faron's making dumplings. Modice's recipe, Faron's been practicing, don't tell. It'll be."

He had to let Karol Vogel know. And he had to be very careful how he went about doing it, because of the sensitivity of the two-Koscuiskos problem. "Wouldn't miss," Kaz replied, bringing the mover to a stop in front of one of the side-doors into Hilton's office complex. "We'll bring greens braised in bacon fat, thick vinegar."

Pondering his problem Hilton climbed the three flights of stairs to his work-room, to compose a message that would get Karol Vogel's immediate attention without leaking any compromising information if the encodes should chance to fail.

Too many salamanders in water-feature, come as soon as you can. There weren't any salamanders in the water-garden Vogel had been building, off and on, for Flag Captain Walton Agenis.

Salamanders.

That should do the trick.

CHAPTER THREE

The Masque of the Inquisitor

Now after four days' travel and two vector transits they'd arrived at Canopy Base. Cousin Stanoczk sat in the luxurious confines of Deputy Sorsa's own office, watching the monitor screens. He knew who Sorsa was; Cousin Fiska as well. He'd been the man who had taken Fisner Feraltz into the Malcontent's custody: though not the one who had made the breakthrough, who had reconciled Fiska to the workings of the Holy Mother, who had restored the integrity of Fiska's soul.

There was also here the launch-master who was to have taken possession of the *Fisher Wolf* once its crew had vacated the premises; it was not a bad thing to have Canopy Base put on the wrong foot, to make them scramble to overcome an unexpected set-back even before "Andrej Koscuisko" had been shown to the quarters that had undoubtedly been prepared to receive him.

"Explain to me," Stoshi said, allowing a sliver of

impatience into his voice. "You permitted the Sarvaw to lock ship's comps?" Kerenko had done that on arrival, before clearing out of *Fisher Wolf* to let the cabin refresh team come in. "I wish to understand how this has been allowed to happen."

"We failed to correctly predict this obstacle." The launch-master's tone of voice was almost cringing. "In truth we should have expected it, even of a Sarvaw. If his Excellency had only given an instruction—"

No, he couldn't let that pass. He was Andrej Koscuisko. He was expected to be over-lordly, insensitive. These people had never met Derush, and, to be fair, Stoshi's cousin Derush could do lordly, haughty, and imperious with a natural flair that was in itself beautiful to behold in its perfect arrogance.

"You do not attempt to lay your failure at my feet," Stoshi snarled. Lek Kerenko had denied Sorsa's people access to *Fisher Wolf*, and Stoshi should have anticipated that for his own part, because it could only be seen as a provocation—and, if Lek wouldn't surrender his comp-keys at once, insubordination. "Explain in immediate terms how you will redeem yourself, and return control of *Fisher Wolf* to me. To us."

If Stoshi had thought to warn Lek to segregate his permissions-queue, to show no evidence of ship-lock in the clear, the thula's failure to respond to Sorsa's people might have been covered as a simple malfunction of some sort. Stoshi hadn't made the arrangement. His mind had been over-full of Fiska's dangerous situation and the challenges that faced them both; which explained the lapse, but did not excuse it.

Tiny slips. Infinitesimal mistakes. That was all it took to destroy an enterprise; but the Malcontent did not despair. The Malcontent never despaired, because the Holy Mother—against all of the teachings that had grown up around Her divine law—held the Malcontent in Her heart. And had given the least respectable, the least saintly of Her saints a sacred charge.

Deputy Sorsa rose to his feet, and bowed. "It was my miscalculation, lord prince, which I cannot regret more deeply. We will break the secures. The thula will be ours."

Stoshi couldn't wait. He had to have immediate access to the thula in order to be sure he could get away with Fiska, and with Fiska's information; without raising suspicions in Deputy Sorsa's mind if possible, but get away they must. On the *Fisher Wolf*. With its state-of-the-art communications to transmit the information, in case they could not escape. He had to have the thula. If he could talk to Kerenko—

He couldn't afford to wait. He had to do something now, something decisive, absolute, brutal, and arrogant. Something the Angel of Destruction with its warped interpretation of the world might expect from Andrej Koscuisko.

"I see no reason why I should be made to wait for your people to accomplish this," he said. "I do not doubt their quality, but I see a much simpler solution. Bring Kerenko to me. I will speak to him. You have someone on staff to assist should a correction be required, I would imagine?"

Sorsa did. He supplied a flourishing black-market trade in the pornography of pain. Stoshi knew; Andrej would only be making an educated guess, though it would come out a demand. Kerenko being Sarvaw, there was the real chance that he would refuse to deliver the thula, the Malcontent's thula, to even Andrej Koscuisko, without coercion or constraint; so there had to be some pressure brought to bear on the problem.

"Indeed we have, lord prince." Deputy Sorsa sounded only a little surprised; and gratified, in a sense. Yes. This was as Deputy Sorsa expected Andrej Koscuisko to behave. Deferential and polite, Sorsa waited; Stoshi stood up.

"Then you will please arrange an interview, Deputy Sorsa, and permit me to remove this unexpected obstacle. A small enough return for your effort in bringing me here. But let me first bathe, and change my clothing; and perhaps a glass or two of cortac brandy, to recruit my energies."

In all the years that he had worn the Malcontent's halter, he had not sent a man to torture. Not a man he knew. Not such torture as was evidenced in Sorsa's black-market entertainment recordings, Inquiry under Bench protocols. "If the lord prince will come with me," Deputy Sorsa said. "We hope to have arranged the prince's accommodation to his satisfaction."

There was a first time for everything.

There was no price Cousin Stanoczk would not extract, no price he would not pay, to see that Fiska's mission did not fail, to bring the years of Fiska's collected information back to the Malcontent. So that there would be no more raids in Gonebeyond space. So that there would be an end to trade in torture, terror, horror, and the ancestral hatred that had so stained the Dolgorukij

Combine in generations past. So that the Angel of Destruction could be stopped, once and for all.

Sitting at his ease with his legs stretched out in front of him Brachi Stildyne contemplated the gather room to which they'd been escorted several hours ago, on arrival at Canopy Base; and collected his thoughts. If Robert St. Clare said that their passenger wasn't Koscuisko, he wasn't. And Robert had; and Stildyne had had plenty of time to work things out. Therefore Stoshi was working an angle. Therefore it was important to concentrate on Stoshi being Andrej Koscuisko.

When they'd arrived on Canopy Base, Stoshi had exited the thula wearing the armature cloak; so he'd presumably withheld his identity from them—as he had— and they'd be expected to resent it. There was bound to be some controversy over the fact that Lek Kerenko had locked the thula down. When the signal came at last— after several hours spent reducing the very generous buffet the establishment had provided to a tidy array of empty plates—it was only what they all expected.

"With your permission." The phrase was clearly formula, by the bland and uninflected tone of voice in which it was spoken. "May one intrude?" The door— which had been locked—slid open; and there was a man standing at the threshold. Dolgorukij by his cheekbones and his dress, but tall and dark, rather than the short blond sort with which Stildyne was more familiar.

"What's the story?" Stildyne replied, draining his glass—he'd decided to stick to cavene, under the circumstances—with borderline politeness. "We'd like back on the thula. There's some stand-down maintenance we'd like to be working on." There almost always was, but it didn't matter. The point was made.

The man at the door coughed politely into a loosely clenched fist. "An issue has arisen which prevents us from returning you to the *Fisher Wolf*. Which of you is Lek Kerenko, please? The son of the Koscuisko prince has requested a word."

"Would be me," Lek said, standing up and dusting the knees of his trousers to remove persistent traces of powdered sugar from the plate of pastries he had annihilated. "Glad to oblige. We'd all like a word with his Excellency. And we've been locked up here for some time. An oversight on your part, doubtless, because otherwise it's inhospitable, and yet I see bread and milk, salt and sweet proferred together on this table."

The man at the door paled, scowling. *Advantage Lek*, Stildyne thought; he'd struck a nerve. "We regret your detention," the man said, sounding like he didn't regret it at all where selected people were concerned. "Which is required for the security of the courier's mission, and for your comfort and protection. We have no Sarvaw here, Kerenko, and desire no incidents. Please come with me."

Suddenly and absolutely Stildyne very much didn't like the sound of that. Koscuisko's family had embraced Lek, if only as a curiosity. That had been due in no small part to Koscuisko's insistence that it be so; but Stildyne had learned more about Sarvaw and Aznir Dolgorukij since that visit. Canopy Base didn't want Lek contaminating its racially pure halls and walkways with his Sarvaw-ness.

Stildyne stood up. "Maybe if you could explain the nature of this issue," Stildyne suggested. "You may not need Kerenko at all. What's the problem, exactly? And be specific."

But the man at the door, having once allowed himself to express annoyance, would not oblige this time. "I regret that I have no personal knowledge of the details." It didn't matter; Stildyne already knew what the problem was. They couldn't get in to the *Fisher Wolf*. "I am an administrative staffer, not maintenance crew. I was directed to request this person's presence for an interview with his Excellency. May we go?"

Out of the corner of his eye Stildyne caught a flicker of finger-code from Godsalt. *Stinks*. The man at the door had carefully avoided actually stepping into the room— so he'd been warned to avoid becoming a hostage. Maybe he was over-thinking this, Stildyne admonished himself. Maybe the courier package just wanted to explain. But every survival instinct in Stildyne's body was barricading itself against the idea.

"Permission to accompany?" Robert asked the man at the door, politely. "I have a private message for delivery to his Excellency on arrival, ears only, entrusted to me by Langsarik Station prior to our departure."

It was an ingenious lure. Robert wasn't Sarvaw; he wasn't even Dolgorukij. There was no risk of additional contamination. The man at the door seemed clearly perplexed, but intrigued as well. "Very well," he said. "Come with me."

The man's Standard accent was very good, but his reality was clearly one narrowly focused on a parochial

Dolgorukij model. What did traditionally minded Dolgorukij do to people who tried to pass as their betters, especially when their betters were the inheriting sons of princes in charge of entire familial corporations?

"I haven't heard of any message," Stildyne said, to further the play. He added his own bit of finger-code for Robert's benefit: *Careful.* "I trust we can expect their prompt return."

It was still possible that there was nothing sinister going on; still possible that Lek and Robert would be right back with Cousin Stanoczk to explain everything. He was going to have to trust them on this one. Lek's nod spoke volumes, in bond-involuntary: *I don't like it either but they'll probably insist.* True, Stildyne thought. If they wanted *Fisher Wolf* badly enough they'd just find a way to take Lek, one way or another. Maybe it was better if Lek didn't go alone.

"I doubt it not," the man at the door said. Backing out of the doorway into the corridor beyond he gestured with an open hand. "This way, please." Were those Security in the corridor beyond, fleetingly glimpsed through the rapidly narrowing angle of the door as it closed behind Kerenko's departing back?

"The thula is probably just fronting some attitude," Godsalt said. Stildyne knew that Godsalt didn't believe that. "You know how it can get about its favorite pilot." Reminding them all that there was another pilot.

Pyotr could fly the thula in Lek's absence, just not as well, and with less of that effortless response from the machine itself. Stildyne didn't know how long it might take Pyotr to get the thula's attention. Would Koscuisko know that? Maybe. Did Cousin Stanoczk know that? Almost certainly.

What was the game? Why was it in play? Why had Cousin Stanoczk come here? And who exactly was it who wanted to see Lek, bearing in mind that "Excellency" was a courtesy title in the Dolgorukij Combine as well as the standard form of address for a Ship's Prime officer in the Jurisdiction Fleet?

"Right," Stildyne said. There was still at least a chance nothing was wrong, if one that grew smaller moment by moment. "Isn't that a tiles-and-tokens set?" Yes, in a games cabinet, to one side of the depleted array of savory breads and sliced meats. "I'll give the first comer a nice juicy handicap."

And they'd huddle together and plan, in bits and pieces of finger-code, until either Robert and Lek came back or they went out to retrieve their fellow crew and get away from Canopy Base, and Cousin Stanoczk with them.

The ceilings were considerably higher than those of the Jurisdiction Fleet ships—*Scylla* and *Ragnarok*—on which Robert had spent the years of his life under Bond. The lights were bright, full-spectrum; the floors and walls were spotlessly clean. And still somehow Robert had no doubt that he was on his way to Secured Medical—a civilian version, perhaps, but with the same purpose. There were even five men in escort, like Stildyne with a team of bond-involuntaries.

"In here," the man who'd come for Lek said, with a queer dip of his chin. To Robert it looked as if a polite nod had been in progress when the man had suddenly remembered that Lek was Sarvaw. "The son of the Koscuisko prince will see you now."

So in they went. Two of the Security posted themselves at the door; the others stood at attention-wait behind Robert and Lek. Robert looked around. It was a nice office, with a display screen in place of a picture window; a view from the high towers of what might well be Chelatring Side high in the mountains on Azanry, the seat of the Koscuisko familial corporation since before there'd even been one. He'd stayed behind the once Koscuisko had gone home, but he'd seen vistas.

There was a great heavy desk of carved wood with a rhyti service and a plate of pastries; and there behind the desk was not-Andrej Koscuisko, leaning over the gleaming surface of its glossy expanse of polished wood and smoking a lefrol.

Robert remembered that they were supposed to be angry at Koscuisko, and declined to salute. Why should they, after Koscuisko's outrageous treatment? One of the Security cuffed Lek hard across the back of the head, so that he staggered forward. The security here had lovely uniforms, blue and black, the white raised collar of their under-blouses showing. Robert knew the pattern. It looked just like one of Koscuisko's.

"Respect your officer," the senior security man—the "Stildyne," Robert decided—said mildly. Lek regained his balance; Cousin Stanoczk in his Koscuisko disguise twitched the index finger on his not-occupied-with-holding-a-lefrol hand, and the Stildyne stepped back. Saving Robert an equivalent cuff, Robert supposed, and was grateful.

There was another man here as well, seated in an armchair between Robert and the desk. That was a signal of privilege, sitting in the presence of a ranking officer; station management, then, or some equivalently important personage. He didn't look anything like Andrej Koscuisko, narrow face, pointed chin, severely trimmed brown hair, maybe taller. Not talking. The man who'd fetched them here whispered a word in the man's ear before excusing himself with a bow; Robert suspected he knew what it was about.

"Now, gentlemen," "Koscuisko" said. "I need the thula. I'm sure you acted out of habit merely, Lek, and it is a prudent habit warmly to be recommended, but it does not my purpose serve. You will therefore provide to Deputy Sorsa the command access keys immediately. Tell *Fisher Wolf* that I its full cooperation require."

Looked like Andrej Koscuisko. Sat like him; smoked like him. Didn't speak like him, not exactly. The officer only reverted to Dolgorukij syntax when he was drunk or agitated; Robert had just refreshed his experience on that score.

This was Stildyne's lover Stoshi, the Malcontent agent who'd been their interface with Gonebeyond space; and he unquestionably had his own very good if currently unfathomable reasons for the imposture. One of Robert's subtle secret intents was to put that imposture forward.

"I respectfully decline, your Excellency," Lek said. He didn't have to work at pretending to be a properly trained bond-involuntary. All he had to do was fall back into the habit. It hadn't been that long, not compared to the length of time they'd been under Bond; Robert was the youngest, and even he was more than twelve years into his sentence. "The thula is on loan. I may not surrender control without appropriate authorization."

Bond-involuntary for *get skint*. Maybe it was "get finned," in Dolgorukij. Cousin Stanoczk leaned back in his chair. "Mister Kerenko. Can you have forgotten so soon?" He made a very convincing Koscuisko; the mild reproach in his calm clear voice raised the hackles at the back of Robert's neck. "You belong to me; to me your service owe. I direct you. Provide the access keys to Deputy Sorsa, and do not fail to cooperate fully."

No evasions, no omissions, no passive aggression. Lek shook his head. "This troop regrets—" and Cousin Stanoczk stood up with the feral menace of a natural-born predator, slapping his hand down on the desk with such force that the flask of rhyti at his elbow rattled. Robert was impressed. Cousin Stanoczk had been practicing.

"You do not dare to with me temporize," Cousin Stanoczk snarled. "Have you so soon forgotten? You know better than to think I will overlook your insubordination."

It was possible that Lek had actually lost color in his face. "I know you stranded us out in the middle of nowhere without so much as a schematic." No "your Excellency." Lek's face had gone dead white, but that was as likely to be suppressed anger as fear. "Twelve hours' warning. If it hadn't been for your Cousin Stanoczk we'd have had nowhere to—"

But the Stildyne himself hit Lek, this time; much less gently than before, laying him out flat on the floor. "You do not link that name and mine," Cousin Stanoczk said.

"That is a filthy Malcontent. It insults me to be in the same breath."

It was true that Koscuisko had frequently described Malcontents as "filthy," but never in that tone of voice. When Koscuisko called his cousin a filthy Malcontent it was a term of familial endearment. Robert decided it was his turn to provoke; if they forgot he was here, it would foil his plot.

"But that's exactly what you did," Robert insisted, helping Lek up from the floor. "Abandoned us." More truly than Lek realized, but Robert had no intention of revealing what he now knew about Stildyne. "How long have you been at Safehaven? Never once bothered to ask us out for mid-meal."

Cousin Stanoczk dismissed this with an impatient gesture, a short sharp wave of his hand as if brushing aside an annoying insect. "Lek, I direct you once more." The door had opened behind them; Robert heard the little sigh of the slides, and felt the subtle difference in the air current at his back. "I do not care to expose one of my own to unpleasantness if it can reasonably be avoided. Nor need I. Doctor Mathin will act my agent, if you make it necessary."

Robert didn't recognize the man who came forward, but the uniform was unmistakable—Jurisdiction Fleet. He knew the precise shade and saturation of the color, the black that was unique to the uniform of an officer of Ship's Prime rank. There was the section marker pinned to the left breast of the uniform blouse; Medical. This was bad. This was very bad.

Only one medical officer held the rank of Ship's

Prime. Only one medical officer wore a section marker
that was lined through with a narrow thread of crimson:
Ship's Surgeon, and Chief Medical Officer. The Ship's
Inquisitor.

"*Fisher Wolf* is not mine to surrender." Lek was
frightened, and clearly didn't care if everybody knew it.
No man knew better than one of Andrej Koscuisko's
bond-involuntaries what the presence of an Inquisitor
meant to a man who refused to obey "instruction lawful
and received." "It belongs to the Malcontent; the
Malcontent alone determines its use. Not you, your
Excellency."

Cousin Stanoczk sat down slowly, his regret—and his
resignation—evident. He doubtless had few illusions
about what Lek faced. And would still send Lek to be
tortured? How high were the stakes, if Cousin Stanoczk
was willing to do that to Lek? "I'm sorry you insist on
stubbornness." He sounded utterly sincere. "But I am not
without resources, and I will have the access codes."

Robert couldn't allow that. Cousin Stanoczk really
wanted the thula—or at least Stoshi wanted Sorsa to
believe he did. But *they* were going to need Lek to fly the
thula, to escape. Robert knew what had to be done,
though it wasn't any easier to face for being necessary.

"Doctor Mathin is widely acknowledged to be a hack
and a waste of his training, never mind his engendering,"
Robert said, loud and firm. It wasn't true; he didn't know
anything about Mathin. But he needed to get everybody
to focus on him, instead of Lek. "Good luck with *him*,
Koscuisko."

He meant his insolence to remind them he was here,

and capture their attention. It seemed to work. The
deputy turned his head to address Cousin Stanoczk with
a conspiratorial air. "He claims to have a message for you,
lord prince," Sorsa said. "For your ears only, to be
delivered on arrival. Does it please your Excellency that
we should hear it?"

Clearly, they should hear it. If Robert had been
entrusted with a message for Andrej Koscuisko, Koscuisko
could hardly decline to take the bait. Cousin Stanoczk
raised his eyebrows. "Is this true, Robert? You may speak
with freedom, Deputy Sorsa has my full confidence."

"That's as may be." This was going well. He'd set the
trap; now all he had to do was spring it, and catch himself
in the snare. "But you don't have mine. Threaten Lek
Kerenko? I'll be keeping my message for myself, thank
you."

The Koscuisko closed his eyes, as if in pain. "Be
careful, Robert," he said, so like Andrej Koscuisko that it
wrung Robert's heart. When he opened his eyes to meet
Robert's, cold and deadly, Robert caught the slimmest tail
of grim agreement there, *I know what you're doing and
why, and I'm sorry.* "Be very sure. I will not hesitate to
demand this information."

Now there was only one more thing they needed.
Robert could only trust Cousin Stanoczk to provide it, and
stood silent, mute, stubborn. The Koscuisko sighed. "Very
well. Doctor Mathin, take my Robert instead, and inquire
after the message he refuses to me in open defiance of his
lawful orders. Take also my Kerenko. If your demonstration
is sufficiently convincing, some unnecessary suffering may
be yet be avoided."

And there it was. They'd be kept together. Robert would go first. It didn't matter if *he* was incapacitated; Lek was the one whose skill and knowledge was crucial to a successful escape. Robert had no illusions about what he faced, but he had a hidden advantage; there was no secret message, and all he had to do was avoid mentioning that fact for as long as possible.

It'd be like his student exercise all over again. He'd failed, then, there, Fleet Orientation Station Medical, so many years ago; but he'd been much younger, and it had been Andrej Koscuisko with the whip. Whoever Mathin was, he was not Andrej Koscuisko. Things could be worse. There was hope.

Security seized him and bound him, hurrying him out of the room closely followed by a similarly trammeled Lek. Robert met Lek's eyes for an instant only, but it was long enough for men who'd been under Bond together. Lek knew what Robert had done. He knew why. He was no happier about it than Robert was.

Fervently hoping that Stildyne and the others would find a way out for them all—sooner, rather than later—Robert followed Dr. Mathin down the beautifully high-ceilinged and clean and well-lit corridor to face the Question.

Command and General Staff, Jurisdiction Fleet Ship *Ragnarok*; sooner or later—First Officer Ralph Mendez thought, taking a deep draught of jarvic—they were going to face reality, and start calling themselves the Jurisdiction Fleet Renegade Ship *Ragnarok*. Maybe once Jennet ap Rhiannon was dead, and old age would have to do it.

She sat in the captain's chair as solidly as if they were stem and stalk, and equally prickly. "Wheatfields," the Captain said. Over the year they'd been out here in Gonebeyond mapping vectors for sheer distraction there'd been a certain degree of relaxation in her military discipline that crept out from time to time; she no longer called her staff by their departments, rather than by name. "I want a global reset, all chronos, Intelligence. Tick them all back by twelve, can it be done?"

"Two" was late again. Ship's Intelligence was on her own time; she'd developed a bad habit of tardiness, but the Captain had apparently not found a way to let Two know she'd noticed it. How did you even know when you had a giant bat's attention?

Wheatfields—Serge of Wheatfields, Ship's Engineer—contented himself with a grunt of assent, leaning back in his chair with his arms folded over his chest. Wheatfields had to lean back. The only chair that Ralph knew of that fit a man of Wheatfields' height had been specially made for his station on the Engineering bridge. There might well be another in Wheatfields' quarters, but Ralph had never been invited in.

Now scuttling through the slowly opening doorway into the officers' mess here she was, Two, her great leathery wings folded and her strong little feet clawing at the decking like a mad gower-lizard on the wrong piece of rock.

"I am sorry!" she said. Or her translator said. They'd given her a female voice, because she was a female bat; her natural voice was far too high for most of them to hear, and what the translation interface might be was anybody's guess. She talked twelve words to the one in Standard, and complained from time to time about how slow they all were by comparison. "You have not noticed any insufficiency of time, because of the interest of what I have here which removes all other thoughts from your mind. Look. See."

With one flange of her left wing on the table for leverage Two climbed up into her chair, where she would stand for the duration. On the Engineering bridge's observation deck she hung upside down, her position of choice: but the officer's mess was not configured for bat. She didn't have her data-interfaces dangling from the ceiling all around her perch, not here.

With the next flange down of her left wing she set about clearing a space, picking things up, putting them down. The vestigial fingers at the last joint of her wings were remarkably strong and agile. "Excusing this, you were done with that yes of course yes. You are amazed at this picture." Flipping a little data-cube through the air so that it landed in the middle of the now-cleared table she chirped at it, and a white plotting-grid as big as a bedsheet unfurled to cover the table.

Mendez stared. He could see data-points, yes. Codes. Notes scratched into the record; but nothing in Standard. He cleared his throat. "You're going to have to walk me through this one, Two, what are we looking at?"

"Yes, thank you," Two said. "My handwriting is bad, it is the fault of your styli. Captain. Here are patterns. These are ten raids from the same donor, of which we know. Here is the latest one. Haystacks." Out once again with the huge flange of one wing, lifting it high overhead to avoid sweeping everybody on her side of the table to the ground. Even half-folded her wing stretched halfway across the room; still, her nail-tipped fingerlet tapped one spot with precision.

"I have made this map with vector analysis, because there is otherwise too much dimension. So you see. We came to Haystacks by Veronash. Langsariks, to Hougli over Driccen. The Nurail patrol to Oak Leaf though Seringa, here; and so forth."

Ap Rhiannon had leaned forward. It certainly looked to Ralph as if she was seeing something, but ap Rhiannon had the advantage in extrapolating from two to three dimensions, because the crèche-bred weren't taught to read or write—beyond the bare necessities—and were less bound to the flatness of screens. Ralph came from a more literate culture; and the stark topography of the Santone desert prejudiced a man toward working in two dimensions, and calling it good.

"We've been through the Driccen vector," ap Rhiannon said. "That's where we found Sandringam. We mapped five other lines off Driccen, didn't we?"

Two nodded, but it was Wheatfields who responded. "We got entry pings back on four of them," he said. He'd sat up to get a better look. Mapping a vector was a highly speculative activity; no one sent an actual ship through without some idea of what was on the other side, except by accident. The *Ragnarok* used probes. If there was a ping-back, the probe had successfully crossed an exit vector into space . . . somewhere.

"Look," Two said. "Here. Here. Here. We have just received a data packet from Langsarik Station, for the first time we have the news on all of these other places which I have mapped. Look here. Observe."

She couldn't look herself, not very far. She relied on her astonishingly precise echolocation for anything further than the far wall; that was only good for actual physical objects, of course, but she knew where her data-points were, and stabbed at them with increasing vehemence, as though they offended her personally. "Probe sent here, from Archilan, no answer. From Gwalli, no answer. You can see. Put them all together, and it is clear, yes? We should go here. We should look."

Tracing a vector transit across a silent route line, intersecting a silent route line from another vector. Contrary to her usual habit Two hadn't relaxed back against the seat of the chair in which she stood to wait for her translator to catch up. Leaning forward, left wing braced against the table, right wing pointing to the map, Two kept her eyes fixed on the face of Jennet ap Rhiannon, waiting. Pointing to the intersection of hypothetical vectors.

Ten raided systems, ten slaughtered populations, more than ten silent route lines off recently mapped vectors, but ten of those silent routes could reach a common terminus. The night raiders could be there. They might not know which vectors had been recently mapped. They might not have taken the *Ragnarok* into account at all. It was an experimental ship. It had enhanced pattern analysis capabilities; and it had Two.

"Which one's closest?" ap Rhiannon asked. "Serge?"

He'd already parsed it out in his mind; Ralph could see that. Of all Ship's Primes, Wheatfields had the most difficulty with the sight of traumatized children. Children were so rare, so precious to a Chigan, that they were held in common within lineage groups; and no man knew which of the clan-mothers' offspring might be his get by donation of genetic material—not even if it was that most precious of all Chigan children, a fertile girl. Ralph knew some of the terrible things Wheatfields had seen in his life and survived with apparent imperturbability. He'd only learned quite recently that a child crying could reduce Wheatfields to paralysis.

"We're en route for Janghan," Wheatfields said. Poe Station was facing some sort of a confrontation there, and had called for all available hulls. "We could detour through Sekles to Marleborne. Risky, though, your Excellency. Could scratch the shield-membrane if we dropped vector in the wrong place."

Probes didn't ping back for a number of reasons. If the vector debouch wasn't clean the probe would be destroyed as soon as it dropped vector. Maybe it hadn't dropped vector, at all, but was trapped in transit for as long as it took to get to the other side. Some took years to traverse. They had no way to tell exactly why a probe went silent: but if Two's newly correlated data could lead them to the night raiders, Ralph thought it might be worth the risk of annihilation to find out.

"We're the JFS *Ragnarok*," ap Rhiannon said. "We get second helpings of risk for fast-meal or we're irritated for the rest of the day. I'll do it. Ralph, get me a suitable message for Poe Station. Serge, divert to Marleborne for vector transit. Brief your sections, any questions? Go."

She stood up, so they stood up; Ralph, Wheatfields,

Mahaffie who was Ship's Surgeon in Koscuisko's absence, General Rukota who was Ship's Weaponer by default even though there was no such rank on a ship of the *Ragnarok*'s rating. Two was already standing, but she folded her wings, coming to attention. They bowed; ap Rhiannon nodded. She left the room; Ralph left the room, and the rest in order of precedence, Wheatfields, Two, Mahaffie. Ralph's second-in-command came last, Lieutenant Seascape, the second senior Command Branch officer on board.

They all wanted those night raiders. They'd do whatever it took to find them. "Fighters on line, Lieutenant Seascape," Ralph said. "Make yourself sure of the kill-rounds. Bring your sections to alert status." Once they found the raiders, they would bring them to account—before the next raid. Before any more such raids, ever. Before a single child the more was left with a smoking corpse for a parent.

It couldn't happen quickly enough for Ralph Mendez.

Robert evaluated Mathin's work-space with a critical eye. More room than in Secured Medical; more monitors than Robert was used to seeing, though, making themselves obvious, hanging from the ceiling and arrayed along the walls. Which did the *Ragnarok*'s Judicial record several times better.

Lek they tossed into the central of an array of open-faced cells along the left-hand wall, where he'd have the best view Robert supposed. There was a sleeping-bench in there, Robert was glad to see, but no wash-basin; Lek would have to rely on the wait staff for drinking water.

Hydration was important. They were going to need Lek's brain in prime working order. But so would Canopy Base, at least until Lek gave up the codes; so that would be all right.

"Quite different from your usual, I can see," Robert said to the torturer. Mathin didn't respond. Robert waited patiently as Security stripped him naked. He didn't bother to resist; it was Mathin he had to annoy. He'd been looking for an excuse to requisition new underwear anyway.

A familiar stalloy grid came down from the ceiling to anchor on the central post, and that part *was* like a Jurisdiction torture room. Security fastened him to it— well up off the floor, so that the weight of his body fell full on his chains. Robert tried again. "What brings you here, if I may ask? Since we're to become better acquainted, and all. Why not still with your ship of assignment, which would be—ah—"

One of the Security slapped him hard in the face, which was no more than he'd expected. Mathin didn't pay any attention to that; he'd opened up a rolling cabinet that held an instrument kit that Robert recognized, and was sorting through his screws and clamps, sharp pointed things, fire-points and shock-rods and all of the technological tools of torture.

No whips to be seen, that was an interesting detail. Whips took skill and physical effort to deploy effectively, and not just any man could lay a driver down and make it count. Andrej Koscuisko had the eye and the taste for it, and had mastered his craft well and early. Robert knew. He'd been there.

"I'll ask the questions," Mathin said. "You'll answer

them. And that's all I need to hear from you." It was a very vulnerable feeling, to be naked and pinned to an upright grid in the center of a room surrounded by people in a bad mood. Robert had to get something started, anything to take the edge off his unavoidable and in his opinion entirely reasonable and well-founded apprehension. Not to say fear.

"I've heard that before, you know. From the officer himself, and it was a long time ago, but you never forget something like that. Memorable occasion. I was lucky to survive the experience, let me tell you."

"Yes?" Mathin was lingering over a little box tucked into his kit; it didn't seem to be standard issue from what Robert remembered, but every Inquisitor had his own little off-schedule favorites, he supposed. "How did that work out for you?"

Mathin's voice was level; he was making an evident effort to seem uninterested. But Robert could tell he'd piqued Mathin's interest, just as he'd hoped. "I told him everything he wanted to know, and a good deal more besides."

It hadn't been his fault. It had been the first hint anyone had had about Koscuisko's empathic streak, which had laid the truth-sense on him. "What about yours?" Robert asked, after a moment's silence to let the point sink in. "Was it assault on a Bench official? Maybe the onagosha smuggling ring? I was supposed to give him willful destruction of Bench property to the disadvantage of the Judicial order."

He'd caught the man. Raising his head sharply Mathin turned away from his kit to stare. "What are you talking about?" Not a very good Inquisitor, obviously. He was handling this all wrong.

"Fossum, your Excellency, surely you remember." A tiny bit of flattery. Men who weren't the keenest dog in the gather-run could be susceptible. "Fleet Orientation Station Medical. The fourth level exercise, that's designed to go to fifth."

He'd been just out of orientation, as green as they came. That was part of why he'd been there in the first place. He'd been very young, and vulnerable to conditioning. Robert pushed the point home, trying to express disbelief with the subtlest of undertones of contempt. "What, you didn't know the 'prisoners' they send you aren't? We were all bond-involuntaries on first assignment. I was Koscuisko's."

The point was to dangle the famous name in front of Mathin's nose, letting him know that Robert was uniquely qualified to compare him against the benchmark standard. "You're babbling," Mathin said, disdainfully. "It's fear." But Robert could tell that he'd successfully introduced an element of uncertainty, setting Mathin off-balance. "Do you really expect me to believe you were tortured for training purposes?"

Implying, of course, that whatever Mathin had done to his own "prisoner" to gain the selected confession, Robert had already been through it. It would make Mathin more determined to get Robert's collapse as proof of his own expertise. *See what this man has already endured, and I had him anyway.*

"Only because it's true, your Excellency. Bond-involuntary. I couldn't lie to an officer to save my life."

An outrageous claim, since he *was* lying, but he wanted to find out as much as he could about what Mathin did and didn't know. "Then I won't be needing this, will I?" Mathin asked. Picking up the little box in his kit he stepped up close to where Robert hung in chains, opening it, raising it to Robert's face where Robert could get a good look at it.

There was something there, a tiny device with a single baleful glowing red eye, a cyborg spider with whisper-thin legs. Robert knew what it was. It was a governor.

Panic terror seized him, and he was helpless against it. He remembered. They'd taught him the basics in preliminary orientation, enough to know how things were to be done. Then they'd implanted the governor. Then they'd put him through his basic drills again, and he'd found out what the merciless torturer in his brain would do if he faltered for even a single instant to respond correctly to lawful and received instruction.

The orientation that followed had made the preliminary conditioning seem like child's play: discipline had to be perfect, especially when what he was required to do were things few souls under Jurisdiction could be made to do of their own free will, or even the strongest sense of misplaced duty.

Koscuisko did his own dirty work. For that alone—Robert had learned—his fellow bond-involuntaries would have loved him. Yes, there were people who liked it. They didn't make very good Inquisitors, not really, because brutes were just brutes, not men of intellect and understanding like the officer. They only hurt people.

Yes, the officer was capable of experiencing

transcendent ecstasy in Secured Medical, a passion more than merely sexual whose fulfillment shattered him—first with the joy of the ravening wolf; then with guilt and horror. But Koscuisko found truth where lesser Inquisitors found only pain-blinded and meaningless compliance, confessions that were worth no more than to validate the Judicial order.

Before Robert had learned anything about Koscuisko he'd had to learn the requirements of his job. The dancing-masters had taken him through it all again and again, until the understanding of what he was supposed to do, and the knowledge of what would happen to him if he didn't, had been seared into his soul with pain and terror.

Once they'd been satisfied with his conditioning they'd put away their training aids, and let him find out for himself that there was no further need for any external stimulus to punish lapses or infractions, that the governor itself would rule him from then on. He'd learned quickly. He'd had no choice.

Just the sight of the hellish thing was enough to bring it all back, to force him to stifle a fear-filled moan, to prevent him from turning his face away. *You will never turn your face away from a superior officer unless you have been instructed to do so. If it is a brutal rape, if it is the laying bare of living flesh, if it is a white-hot firepoint at eye-level, you will not turn your face away.*

Moreover. You will perform the brutal rape, on instruction. You will lay bare the flesh. You will endure the firepoint, you will use it according to instruction against even your fellow bond-involuntaries, if that is what you have been told to do. No hesitation. No hint of revulsion. You'll do as you are told, or you will have no one to blame but yourself for the consequences, which will be sure and swift and certain.

"Well, then," Mathin said, with evident satisfaction. Turning away he put the governor back into its box. Was it even a real one? Robert wondered, grasping at windblown spider-silk for something to manage the agony of his terror. "Maybe later. Unless you answer thoroughly and truthfully. Just don't forget that it's there. I know your governor's been removed, you see. I can change that."

He'd been told that what the officer had done to him at Fossum had set his governor out of calibration. It was still an imperfect technology, after all. Apparently his governor had started to die at Fossum and at Burkhayden it had gone critical. The surgery there had removed the governor, which hadn't killed Robert only because it was too far gone itself.

There was an answer for his terror there, however. Andrej Koscuisko could pull a healthy governor and not kill his patient. Andrej Koscuisko had: five of them, from Pyotr through Garrity, before he'd sent them away into Gonebeyond. Implanting a governor was a risky procedure that required the best neurosurgeons under Jurisdiction, and Mathin wasn't one of them, or he wouldn't be here. The most Mathin could do was kill him. Mathin wouldn't dare. So there was that.

That had been well-played on Mathin's part, even so; Robert revised his initial assessment accordingly. Belonging to Andrej Koscuisko for all these years could make a man complacent, arrogant. Mathin didn't have to be the torturer Koscuisko was to make Robert scream. He wasn't to be underestimated.

"If I could ask, your Excellency." *Careful, Rabin*, he told himself. He needed time to manage the insane rush of fear that had overwhelmed him when Mathin had shown him the governor. "How does a man of your rank come to be here, when Gonebeyond isn't under Jurisdiction?"

Mathin snorted contemptuously. "You should know better and you do. But I'll tell you. You won't remember it anyway." The effect agony could have on short-term memory was well understood, even by Robert. Traumatic amnesia. Except when there wasn't any, and a man re-felt his agony over and over until he wished he could die of it. Robert had tried it both ways. "I was recruited. We weren't getting paid, not once the confederacy was announced."

That had been more than a year ago. There would be no single authority to enforce taxation and revenues to support Fleet; each Judiciary was its own polity, now. That was what made political development in Gonebeyond possible: the fact that Jurisdiction was preoccupied with its own problems.

Mathin was still talking, though. Robert didn't want to interrupt. He needed all the time he could get. The room was unpleasantly cool, and his own weight on his shackles was starting to wear on him. "I'm getting paid *now*," Mathin said. "By people who know what I'm worth. The base salary's not bad, but the real money is in royalties. I'll be getting a very nice bonus out of you, nothing personal."

"Commercial enterprise?" Robert asked, startled out of his strategy. Was that why there were all of those monitors? Torture sessions were on record because whatever a prisoner said was legal evidence, and for use as intimidation. At the same time very illegal copies were also circulated by specialty consumers with peculiar tastes, as long as they had enough money. Did Canopy Base record its torture exercises to supply a niche market? Did they generate on demand?

"Now they've got Andrej Koscuisko." Mathin had decided on a shock-rod, Robert was sorry to see. "If he was half the man they say he was he'd have those comp-keys on drug assist, so I guess we know his secret now, don't we?"

Professional jealousy. It was ugly to see, but Robert understood it perfectly well. Stoshi was playing for time, but what was more to the point, they'd want "Koscuisko" to select the drugs, and Stoshi couldn't. Because Stoshi was making it up as he went along, just like the rest of them.

Stepping closer, looking up into Robert's face, Mathin raised the shock-rod to eye-level, so that Robert could have no doubt of its identity. "I should ask him to recommend a protocol," Mathin said. "Seeing that he's a such a very big deal. But I can't take that chance. I'm not going to end up like Sternalle." Robert didn't recognize the name, but he thought he got the idea. "And for you that means—"

Mathin nodded at the Security guard posted at the door—to turn on the monitors, perhaps. "I hold the Writ to which you must answer. You have information I require, and you're going to surrender it to me sooner or later. Depend upon it."

Actually, no, Robert had no information. That was precisely the information he was not going to give up. He'd only let the secret slip by accident, all of those years ago at Fossum. He'd been absolved of willful sabotage, but the exercise had failed; if Koscuisko hadn't made the bargain he'd struck with Fleet, Robert would have died there, and horribly.

Mathin was waiting for a response—possibly for dramatic effect. Defiance, maybe. Protests, pleading. Robert expected he'd get to a bit of pleading a little further on. He could be more annoying right now by not giving any response at all: so he didn't. He did his best to take the pressure off his arms and legs by flexing the muscles of his thighs and shoulders, hoping Mathin didn't know about Nurail and crozer-hinges.

The moment stretched as Robert stared into Mathin's eyes, knowing perfectly well that Mathin wasn't the man Koscuisko was, letting his knowledge put an edge to insolence. Grimacing in exasperation Mathin switched on the shock-rod and set to work.

CHAPTER FOUR

On the Brink

Chornije was a tidy little freighter; fifteen souls on board, Andrej had been told, its own shuttle, and characterized by a degree of luxury he'd all but forgotten. It was almost too easy to relax into the remembered privilege of his childhood and feel the prince inheritor once again. Standing on the observation balcony at the rear of its wheelhouse Andrej watched the activity on the station below them, Plebach at his side.

Canopy Base, this is freighter Chornije. *VIP visitor for the second son of the Koscuisko prince. Please advise, slip for passenger shuttle.*

Something seemed to not be going according to plan; Plebach seemed confused, anxious. "*Chornije*, this is Canopy Base. Identify VIP for the record, please." Plebach glanced at Andrej and then down and away, clearly embarrassed. Andrej would just as soon not have so formal a record of his presence here; but there was no reasonable way around it.

Catching the comm crewman's attention with a little cough Andrej raised his voice. "I am Andrej Ulexeievitch, firstborn and inheriting son of the prince Alexie Slijanevitch Koscuisko. I have come because I was told that my brother third born and second eldest Iosev Ulexeievitch has invited me. Yes?"

Gratitude, from Plebach. Andrej had no reason to make things unpleasant for the young man just because he was an elitist of a particularly unpleasant sort. In fact, knowing Plebach was a racist made it easier, in a way, to accept his many courtesies. It was nothing personal. He wasn't Andrej Koscuisko to Plebach. He was a standard of ethnic purity in abstract, who existed only as a carrier for his pedigree. What Plebach would say about all the Nurail women who came to his bed demanding a child to replace the ones he'd stolen from the weaves Andrej could only imagine.

Canopy Base fell silent, apparently waiting for the voice-ident to run through; illegal access to Jurisdiction security files, clearly, but this was Gonebeyond. Andrej used the time to admire the station's well-ordered transit lanes, its neat warehouses, its general air of prosperity and bustling commerce. There was plenty of traffic; that raised a question.

"In what do you trade, here?" he asked Plebach. Before Plebach could answer, however, Canopy Base came back on line. *Canopy Base is honored by the presence of the inheriting son of the Koscuisko prince. We beg forgiveness for the fact that a mechanical problem unavoidably delays your landing. We sincerely hope to be permitted to bow before you in a very few hours, if it please his Excellency.*

A few hours? Andrej saw no evidence on the base below of any problems, but at this distance it would have to be an explosion before he'd see it. Or a fire. "Deputy Sorsa," Plebach explained low-voiced. "The station manager. I'm very sorry, your Excellency, I don't know what the delay could be."

There was no sense standing here, then, and it would only add to the general stress and confusion if he did. "I shall want a tour, and a briefing," Andrej said. And not from any mere Pravel Plebach, either. "I will go wait in my quarters."

It didn't matter. He wasn't looking forward to seeing Iosev, and the frustration of having found his way to Langsarik Station only to find the thula gone—with no scheduled time of return—lay in his chest heavy and cold still.

He knew how to get back to his guest quarters by himself; he neither needed nor wanted Plebach's help. He'd had as little of Plebach's company as he could reasonably manage. It had been unpleasant to encounter the ghost of an old atrocity; but the library had been good, the food uniformly superlative, the water hot and in plentiful supply and the wardrobe they'd pressed on him— suspiciously perfectly fitted, suitable for a prince travelling without retinue—was unquestionably an improvement over the one he'd brought with him into Gonebeyond.

Was he morally complicit in racist elitism if he wore its clothing? It was good to have new linen. Now that he knew Iosev had a base here maybe he could arrange a regular supply of life's little necessities. Rhyti. Lefrols. Undergarments.

Strangely enough, given the experience of his days on board, a rhyti service and an accompanying side-table towering with savories and sweets was not waiting in his cabin when he got there. That made him smile; the delay in landing had clearly set the entire mechanism of the ship off-balance. Someone signaled at the door almost immediately, though; waiting for him, perhaps. "Step through," he called; and who should come in but the kitchen-master, Waclav? Pushing a trundler, but otherwise quite alone.

"His Excellency's pardon," Waclav said. "May I be permitted to serve the lord prince on this occasion?"

"Oh, and welcome, kitchen-master." This was the closest anybody had come to actually talking to him—rather than at him, from several steps away, and with a bowed head—for days. After a year of living with Nurail Andrej had found the contrast to be extreme, and both gratifying and irritating by turns. "Might I hope that you would take a flask of rhyti, with me?"

Waclav smiled and shook his head, as if to say *we both know better but thank you for asking*. "His Excellency is princely indeed, but I dare not presume. I've made a shallow basin of soup, lord prince, homely stuff, not worthy to be set before you, except perhaps for nostalgia. Does his Excellency condescend to permit me?"

All he really wanted was a cup of rhyti. But he wasn't going to argue with an artist of Waclav's caliber any more than he expected subordinate staff in Safehaven to argue with him about psychopharmacology, not that it had ever stopped anybody. "I'm in your hands." The rhyti service was ready there, waiting. Sitting full across the now-closed doorway; blocking it, in fact.

Spreading a pristine linen cover over the cabin's table Waclav set a shallow dish and a soup-spoon down, a white napkin; and lifted a jug from a lower shelf of his trundler. When he poured Andrej saw it was a cold summer soup made of crisp pale green water-gourd with its cool dense flesh, garnished with soured dairy cream. He could smell its perfume, seasoned as it was with an herb that grew like a weed in the hedgerows of home and formed one of the staples of Dolgorukij home cooking.

"I'm delighted," Andrej said almost completely truthfully, lifting his spoon. Of the summer soups he liked best the fruit and cream soups, because they indulged a man's sweet tooth—or perhaps more accurately, a boy's sweet tooth. But since Waclav had made it . . . "I can't wait to—"

Waclav held up one hand, *no, wait*, and Andrej paused obediently, spoon in hand. "With your permission, lord prince," Waclav said, taking a cruet from the same shelf. Ah, yes. There was frequently a savory garnish.

Sitting back in his chair Andrej watched with happy anticipation as Waclav poured a careful stream of thick bright red liquid onto the creamy white green-flecked surface of the water-gourd soup. Red was a surprise; red-root base was usually the keynote ingredient of winter soups instead, roasted and grated and married to a slow-cooked smoked joint of a roast hog, salty and rich in gelatin.

The pattern was a little odd, asymmetrical, but Waclav was taking great care; so Andrej watched intently as Waclav poured, leaning close over Andrej's shoulder. Things took fewer letters to write in old Aznir script than in Standard, and that was what Waclav was doing. Writing. Mal-con-tent.

A red ribbon in his soup; and "Malcontent."

Waclav could hardly wear the Malcontent's halter among people already contemptuous of him for simply being Sarvaw; but Malcontents were never so dangerous as when they were undercover. The Saint had no prohibition against deceit and blackmail, as long as it served the Saint's purpose: as many incautious young Aznir had learned to their cost.

"There, lord prince," Waclav said, stepping away from Andrej and admiring his work with evident satisfaction. "If his Excellency would be graciously pleased?" To destroy the pattern immediately, before anybody noticed there was one. Cabins could be monitored. Stirring the red ribbon into the soup Andrej set to with haste and dispatch; not surprisingly, it was delicious.

"Once again you astonish me with the excellence of your cooking, kitchen-master Waclav." *Cousin.* "Your use of kivass is not at all what I would have expected, but adds so much to the flavor. I cannot face a future without such cooking. Have you not brothers, nephews, cousins perhaps, that I might recruit to help me forward, and comfort me in adversity?"

Waclav shook his head. "His Excellency is gracious indeed, but I dare offer no such impertinence. Do you care to finish? Two more bites only, lord prince, and then

I should get back to the galley before I'm discovered where I ought not to be."

There was more soup in the dish than that. Andrej had stirred it well to ensure that its compromising message disappeared, so he knew the depth of the plate; but he took two spoonfuls and sat back, shaking his head with an expression of wonder that required no dissimulation on his part.

Two more bites only. Somewhere on Canopy Base, two other Malcontents. Now the only question was why Waclav had told him; but there was a limit to how much information could be contained in a dish of soup. "I'm in your debt," Andrej said, patting at his mouth with the napkin. "And would not for all the world put you at risk of discovery, so it must be good-bye, I suppose."

"Thank you, lord prince." Waclav was deploying the rhyti and pastry with a smoothness that disguised its speed. "Please sip the rhyti carefully. It's an old urn. Sometimes there is foulness that can only be spat out."

Rhyti. Fresh napkins. A platter of beautifully arranged pastries plump and fragrant and tempting to gluttony. The soup-bowl was gone. Waclav took his pastry-trolley to the door. "And I'll be out of your way, lord prince, thanking you again." Opening the door he checked the corridor, quickly but casually, before he backed out of the cabin. "I hope to have the honor of serving you again, at some point in the future."

Alone in the cabin Andrej drew himself a flask of rhyti, thinking hard. There were Malcontents here. Keeping a close watch on Iosev, who had proved wanting in character? That wouldn't take more than one. Two more,

Waclav had said—Andrej thought—and that he'd be seeing Andrej again. But did he mean on *Chornije*'s return trip, or something else? And what did an old urn have to do with it?

Perhaps Waclav meant to warn Andrej about his brother, or maybe it was nothing. Stoshi sometimes said things with deep and hidden meanings; sometimes Stoshi talked shameless nonsense; and frequently it was hard to tell which was which.

He sipped his rhyti, checking the cup carefully for dead spiders or dog excrement. Taking up a fat jam-filled purse with delicately crisp pastry petals Andrej picked it apart, leaf by toasted sugary leaf; eating it slowly, he concentrated on committing Waclav's exact words to memory, to be contemplated further when he reached Canopy Base.

Stoshi sat in Sorsa's office, again, with a lavish tray of pastries at his elbow, watching the live feeds from the torture-room. That was Robert St. Clare, hanging there by his wrists from the ceiling, blood running down his naked chest. Robert, whom Stoshi's cousin Andrej—Derush—loved, whom he had ransomed from death by slow torture at Fleet Orientation Station Medical with his honor. Robert had a lovely singing voice. Stoshi hated to hear him scream.

"We hope our interpretation of your will has been correct, lord prince," Sorsa was saying. "Indeed it serves two portions on one plate, to approach it in this manner." Cousin Fiska was here as well, bending close at Stoshi's ear, *would his Excellency care for another cup of rhyti.* Stoshi nodded.

"It is indeed so, Deputy Sorsa, the approach I would have taken exactly. Well done." Sorsa wanted him to watch. Sorsa meant to recruit Andrej Koscuisko. Stoshi couldn't be sure Derush would not succumb to the temptation, which was only one of the many good reasons to keep Derush absolutely out of it. "Drug assist communicates so little threat, and we are talking about Sarvaw. It is much more effective, I find, with an ancillary portion of blood and screaming."

Lek Kerenko, that was another brace of pheasant entirely. However it had happened, Lek and Andrej's son had made a connection heart-to-heart, the stuff of sagas; Anton Andreievitch wrote to Lek regularly, and Lek did his best to answer promptly. Soul spoke to soul; nobody had foreseen it.

Which brought Stoshi back to the point that neither Derush nor Anton Derush's son would forgive the peril to which he had exposed Lek Kerenko. Anton Andreievitch had never met Robert St. Clare; but he would forever resent Stoshi on Robert's behalf out of loyalty alone, *you have brought to torture a man my father loves, and are to be contemned entirely therefore.*

Something, it seemed, had distracted Sorsa; something on his desk feed. He glanced at Fiska; Fiska hurried from the room with a glance in Stoshi's direction, but Sorsa gave no sign.

"Smell of blood," Sorsa said, musingly. "Yes, sometimes nothing else will do. With respect, lord prince, have you any thoughts, on what this supposed message might be?"

This was a warning. Stoshi heard it clearly. "Indeed I

do not, Deputy Sorsa, I regret. I have not seen the man for more than a year, now. Why would Langsarik Station have entrusted a message to such a one, rather than to me direct? I cannot understand the meaning of such a choice."

Fiska was back. He was pale. Bending down close, Fiska whispered in Sorsa's ear; Sorsa nodded, Fiska left the room again. "Nor can I understand why he would refuse you the message," Sorsa said. "Oh. Unless. Unless in fact you were not the son of the Koscuisko prince at all, and he knew it, because he knows his master and that you are not he."

He was discovered.

But he had reviewed all the contingencies imaginable, he and his superiors, over the years that they had been planning this; he had recovery strategies in place for almost everything. What had betrayed him?

First he had to pretend that he knew nothing of what Sorsa was talking about. Then . . . but first things first. "You fail to communicate," Stoshi said, in a mild and moderate tone of voice. "It is misplaced humor, no doubt. Explain."

Here was Fiska once again, with Station security. "I should have guessed when you refused to see Iosev Ulexeievitch," Sorsa said. Not *your brother*. So Stoshi's ruin was absolute. "I should have gone for voice-ident on arrival. I have rectified that oversight."

And he had his answer. Clearly enough. Sorsa stood up with a convulsive movement of decision. "You are not the son of the Koscuisko prince, because that man has only just arrived from Safehaven on one of our own ships, and all Saints attest to his identity. But there is a cousin of the son of the Koscuisko prince, a Malcontent, a pollution of the Blood. You are he. Take this filthy piece of shit away, search him against self-slaughter, and shut him up close."

What? Andrej? Derush, Drushik, here, here at Canopy Base?

"I owe to Iosev a debt of gratitude," Stoshi heard Sorsa say to Fiska, as Security bundled him out of the room. "Granted he lied to Plebach. But had he not, Plebach would not have brought Andrej Koscuisko to us here, to save us from disaster."

Iosev had gone behind Sorsa's back, then, to bring Andrej to Canopy Base, whether to demonstrate his own influence with his brother, to take credit for recruiting his brother to the cause, or both.

If they gave him to Mathin on drug-assist Stoshi had no fear of betraying Cousin Fiska. He had training. He could not overcome the effects of a speak-serum completely, but unless Mathin made choices characteristic of an Inquisitor as skilled as Andrej himself nothing Mathin could threaten him with would defeat the resistance strategies Stoshi had learned and practiced. He would die. There was a good chance, a solid chance, a very-much-better-than-reasonable chance that he would die horribly, but Fiska would be safe.

And if they dared to involve his cousin Andrej—

He could afford no room in his mind for what he might have done to Derush. He had to plan, adjust, try to find his way clear to salvage the work of years. Or they would both die, he and Cousin Fiska, their long agonies a source of revenue for the very enemy they had risked so much to bring down; and the Malcontent would have to start all over.

Fiska stood to one side as Security took Cousin Stanoczk away, stunned, shaken to the core of his being. How could this have happened? And what did it mean for his mission, his data, was it all to come to nothing after all, and he and Cousin Stanoczk both to die at the hands of the Angel of Destruction with their bellies cut open and their entrails pulled out of their bodies, used to create the obscene wreath of living flesh that was called the Kospodar Garland?

Sorsa studied the closed door once Security had left the room. Fiska couldn't read Sorsa's expression, but Sorsa could read his well enough, it seemed—what Fiska could afford to show, shock, perplexity, concern. All reasonable reactions for a loyal lieutenant when a Malcontent was suddenly discovered in the midst of their organization.

"Very troubling," Sorsa said. "But not a disaster, Fisner, the Holy Mother guides us and protects us now as always. I'm humbled by her care. This is a blessing on us all."

Well, maybe. "It was your caution with Iosev Ulexeievitch that saved us from reflecting poorly on the Holy Mother," Fiska said. Sorsa hadn't notified Iosev of "Koscuisko's" presence; at Cousin Stanoczk's request, yes, but there wouldn't have to be any embarrassing retractions. "And yet Plebach has deviated from his chain of command, it would seem."

Sorsa waved this off. "Yes, admonish him, but gently—only make sure he doesn't know that Iosev didn't have my knowledge and consent. Leave it at the feet of the Holy Mother. Sit, Fisner. Help me think this through."

It was a privilege to be asked to sit, a greater privilege to be invited to strategize with his superior. Fiska sat down, and said nothing.

"Koscuisko doesn't know there was a Malcontent imposter here in his place, because Plebach doesn't know. Nor does Iosev. Sanitize the duty rosters, Fisner, make sure no one who had to do with the imposter has any sort of contact with Koscuisko. That's a start."

He'd explain to them, of course. Fiska knew better than to worry that one of the station's personnel would engage in any sort of gossip with Koscuisko; but an extra layer of security was always good practice. "The crew of the thula," Fiska said, because Sorsa would wonder if he didn't. "Currently dismantling the ready-room and down to the foundation walls, we were going to have to move them soon anyway. Do they join their fellows in Mathin's work-room?"

Sorsa grimaced. "In confinement, yes. Let us not call it Mathin's work-room, though, I have doubts about whether we will have his services at our disposal for much longer. The son of the Koscuisko prince will question our management of the predicament we were in, perhaps rightly so, but—"

Something had just struck Sorsa's mind, forcibly. "But. If only. This is a fantasy, Fisner, I must caution you that it can never be spoken of. But just to imagine. Andrej Koscuisko, and one of his own people, even on drug-assist.

We will have the thula. And the proceeds could keep Canopy Base running for months, just that."

They could have something even better, and though Fiska could not quite face the direction in which the interim step inevitably led it was so obvious that to not give it voice would be to give Sorsa reason to wonder. "If I may put words in your mouth, Deputy Sorsa, with your permission. You propose that Koscuisko be allowed to express his indignation against Mathin in close contact. His anger will serve to weaken his resolve."

That was part of the planning package, yes. First was to associate Koscuisko with Canopy Base for its significant propaganda value. Next, though, was to gain his cooperation, Andrej Koscuisko, who held perhaps the single most notorious Writ in known Space. The exact approach to successfully recruiting Koscuisko as the Angel's top Inquisitor was still in the definition stage, but perhaps using Mathin would break the ice . . . and then there was Cousin Stanoczk.

Looking up at the ceiling Sorsa puffed up his cheeks and forcibly expelled the air, his eyes moving between overhead light-spots and decorative accents without coming to rest on any one thing in particular. "We must have everything the Malcontent knows, as soon as possible. If the imposter fails a scheduled contact the Malcontent may take fright and shut its operation down."

As it would, once Fiska could get the watch-word to Cousin Waclav. Wishka. Fiska concentrated on Sorsa, speaking on, to hide his thought, lest Sorsa see some hint in Fiska's eyes. "We have to act before they know we have their man. And yet the Holy Mother has brought

Koscuisko to us in our moment of need. It is a sign, Fisner."

Sorsa had heard much about Andrej Koscuisko from Iosev, Fiska knew. But also Sorsa had made a careful study of the son of the Koscuisko prince—for his bloodline, as the father of the next heir; and for his special skills. Sorsa knew the nature of Koscuisko's addiction. Koscuisko's once-commanding officer, the corrupt Captain Lowden, had put a great deal of money into his retirement accounts based on his unique access to strictly controlled records of Inquiry. Koscuisko had a weakness. Sorsa believed he could exploit it.

Now Sorsa straightened in his chair, stood up. So Fiska in turn rose to his feet, respectfully. "Go to Iosev Ulexeievitch, Fisner," he said. "You are astonished and deeply impressed, stricken with awe at what he has done for us, what he has pulled off. I myself will have gone to see to the greeting-ceremony, and everything that has to be made ready—at a moment's notice, unprepared as we were for this great event."

That wouldn't take Canopy Base long; they'd had the reception ritual prepared, standing by for Cousin Stanoczk's permission to reveal his presence to Iosev. "In the mean while I will speak to Mathin," Sorsa said. "Then I will appear, to congratulate the lord prince on his accomplishment."

At which point Fiska would go make sure everything was in order, the ceremony, quarters refreshed and stripped of any hints of the imposter, station staff assembled and briefed. It would take the launch-field several hours yet before the thula was completely concealed by a temporary maintenance structure; because if Koscuisko saw *Fisher Wolf*, Koscuisko would want to know why it was here, and where his people were.

But underneath it all, the planning, his double role, the scene he would have to play out with Iosev Ulexeievitch, there was the single fervent prayer running through Fiska's mind, over and over. *Holy Mother. Show me the way to rescue the Saint's enterprise from His ancestral enemy. And your servant Cousin Stanoczk, from Andrej Koscuisko.*

Chornije's passenger shuttle had landed; Plebach had bowed Andrej to the passenger debarkation ramp. Andrej stepped out onto a thick plush carpet of deep rich blue edged with silver, the colors of the Dolgorukij familial corporation, as blue as the sky above the Chetalra Mountains, as white as the feathers of the agile bird—the mountain-soarer—that nested amongst the towers of Chelatring Side, a symbol of Koscuisko's valor.

The carpet was wide enough for three men to walk abreast, but Andrej was the only man privileged to tread on it. A part of him accepted that as his natural right; no one here was of sufficient rank to share the foot-path of the Koscuisko prince. He was not yet *the* Koscuisko prince; his father was alive, and in good health, as far as Andrej knew. He was, however, the inheriting son of the Koscuisko prince, so Plebach and his officers walked humbly behind, and on bare tarmac.

Canopy Base was an attractive place, very nice to look at after the messy work-in-perpetual-progress that was Safehaven Medical Center. He could see elevated pedestrian walkways, landscaping; and there were easily a full eight veserts from the launch-field to the outermost rim of the containment dome—a small city, but a city nonetheless.

Less attractive was the sight of the man who knelt at the far end of the blue carpet, head bowed, with a rope around his neck and a sheaf of grain still on the straw laid out before him. *I am your slave, your beast of burden.* It was the stuff of Dasidar and Dyraine, when Dasidar's brother Brabicam had sued to be forgiven for his revolt against his lawful lord.

Dasidar, the first Autocrat, to whom the Koscuisko familial corporation—and every other family with pretenses to greatness and power, within the Dolgorukij Combine—traced its origin, had let Brabicam live, and given him a troop of lancers as a token of his forgiveness. It had ended badly.

Andrej had expected a family visit, nothing more. Iosev was forcing a public reconciliation instead. Andrej was tempted to turn around and go right back up into the ship, let Iosev kneel as he might. As Iosev's people, however, all of the station personnel were duty-bound to kneel at the first sign of obduracy on his part; and stay there, on their knees, night and day, until Andrej raised Iosev up and kissed him.

Andrej didn't want to kiss Iosev. Iosev had been bitter and resentful from the day he'd been born, jealous of Andrej, greedy for his perquisites. Andrej had never understood why Iosev had come out the way he had. Surely the person with the most reason to resent him was their sister Mayra, the oldest of his father's children, who if she had been born Ichogatra rather than Koscuisko might well have been Princess Inheritor.

But Brabicam's people had not been at fault, as the famous stanzas of the seneschal Cedargris—on the pain of an ill fate that had bound them to an unworthy lord— so poignantly expressed. Canopy Base's people might have no idea what Iosev had done, in the past. So what was the harm, Andrej asked himself, in giving Iosev his moment? Nobody who had eyes to see would be misled.

Stopping a haughty five paces in front of where Iosev knelt Andrej put his hands on his hips in the time-honored attitude of lordliness, and waited. If Iosev wanted to do this, he would have to do it right. As the moments passed he could see Iosev glance around him, head carefully bowed—he'd shaved the back of his neck, of course he had, to emphasize his submission—as if trying to understand why his grand gesture was not going off.

Finally, Iosev put his hands palm-down to the carpet on which he knelt, leaning forward to take some blades of straw into his mouth. *I am a beast in stables in your house.*

Since it was what had been written, Andrej was to unbend from his icy and outraged dignity, rushing forward to lift his brother to his feet. He rushed with all deliberate speed; there was no hurry. "'You are my brother beloved, valiant and noble.'" If Dasidar said so. And he had. "'Rise, to sit at my side and eat at my table, and let there be no distance between us, from this time forward.'"

Now he had to kiss him. Andrej made it quick. It was awkward for Iosev, too, as well, since Iosev was significantly taller, a great broad-shouldered black-bearded man who would have made a splendid picture in the clerical robes for which he'd been intended, but from which his moral turpitude had barred him.

"'Conscious of my fault I humble myself at your feet, deserving only shame and punishment,'" Iosev said. There was the strangest note of resentment in his voice, as though he blamed Andrej for following the script, or maybe felt Andrej hadn't raised him up quickly enough. That was humorous. Iosev had set it up; Andrej was only playing it out.

Had Iosev imagined that Andrej, either overwhelmed with emotion or forced into a corner, would rush forward all anxious to embrace and forgive? "'Your acknowledged fault we set behind us both.'" Not really. An innocent woman's disgrace and suicide could not be glossed over; this charade changed nothing. Andrej had always liked his other brothers better.

None of his other brothers were moral deficients, that was true. Andrej and Iosev shared that quality between them, and if Andrej's moral crimes were sanctioned by the Bench they were more personal and immediate than anything Iosev had ever done. "'Let us go in, and dine together. We will talk about the future, not the past.'" Good. That was done.

Andrej declined to go off arm-in-arm with Iosev, however; he'd done what he had to do to spare the station staff prolonged embarrassment, but he wasn't required by tradition to pretend that all was forgiven between brothers. For every exegesis that hymned this moment as one of trusting accord and perfect fellowship there was an equal and opposite point of view. Andrej didn't have to believe that Dasidar spoke ironically, with full fore-knowledge of betrayals to come, in order to suspect that Dasidar had had his reservations all along.

Bowing deeply, Iosev invited Andrej to precede him toward the open door of the receiving building beyond. He'd be meeting Deputy Sorsa, Andrej presumed, and there'd be an elaborate reconciliation meal. He wasn't hungry. He didn't have to eat any of it. Words were words, and now they'd been said.

He wasn't sorry to have tasted Waclav's cooking. But apart from that shamelessly sybaritic pleasure, this entire excursion had been an absolute waste of time; and the only thing that reconciled him to the tedious necessity of being polite to Iosev was the chance of seeing Stildyne and the others on his way back to Safehaven, as soon as he could leave.

A man couldn't think when he was in so much pain. And Robert had never been particularly good at thinking. "Tell me what message you were to deliver," Mathin said.

Won't, won't, won't. Because there was no message. How long had this been going on? A day? Two days? He didn't know. Too long, one way or the other.

"Tell me the message, and you can rest." *Be so good as to state your identification, and the crime for which you have been arrested.* "What do you hope to gain by resistance?"

A man's mind sought reason, rationality, order. Pain called to pain. He saw his father fall, his chest all blood. He saw his brothers murdered, shot in the head one by one as they knelt on the edge of the open grave he'd helped them dig. He'd seen the Pyana soldiers, laughing at the sport of it all.

They'd had a warrant, with Bench endorsement. His family had been in violation of article something, subsection something, but it didn't really matter. Enemies of the state, killed while resisting arrest, or trying to escape, or inexcusably and blatantly and shamelessly being on their own land living their own lives when somebody else had a better use for one and no use at all for the other.

"Your suffering is pointless. You know you'll tell me the truth, eventually. They always tell me the truth." Not so. Inquiry had never had much to do with the truth. The point was to extract confession to a pre-determined crime, in order to validate the rule of Law and demonstrate the inexorable nature of judgment and punishment. Koscuisko was one of the few of them who ever actually got the truth, and it was because—

He lost the thought. He needed to say something; he needed to keep Mathin engaged. He couldn't think why, but he was sure there was a reason. "Doubt it." It took concentration to speak. "Your pacing. All wrong."

"My apologies," Mathin said; and there was a searing heat deep in the joint in Robert's right knee that made him scream aloud. "How's that? Better?"

Neural rasp. It inflicted a precisely targeted agony that quickly taught a man how sincerely he wanted to avoid it, by any means possible. Koscuisko had used a shock-rod, and a rope; he'd felt his way deep into the joint in Robert's right shoulder, the extra joint, the crozer-hinge, and torn it out of its proper alignment with his bare hands. Robert didn't think he'd screamed then, but he'd never forgotten the pain.

"Don't worry." Mathin was still talking. "No damage done, yet. Tell me now, and you needn't be crippled for the rest of your life. Work with me, here." Robert couldn't afford to think about how much it hurt. He had to do this. He'd known worse pain even than this and survived.

On the night when Captain Lowden had been assassinated in Burkhayden, Robert's governor had started to die, which according to its programming meant taking Robert with it as painfully as possible. That's what they'd told him. Robert didn't remember much, and he'd never been tempted to try.

That gave him a vague unfocused hope that that he wouldn't remember this pain either. He had to concentrate. He had to keep Mathin away from Lek. They needed Lek; no one else could save them. No one else could pilot the thula the way Lek could. No one else had the codes.

The pain in Robert's groin was brilliant, white like the noonday sun, sharp as vinegar. Robert lost track of things. When he came back up for air Mathin was talking, but Robert didn't try to understand what Mathin was saying because he already knew he would not be interested.

He couldn't stop the spasms in his body, reflexively pulling away from the rasp even though it was no longer there. He felt pressure against his skin where his thigh hinged into his hip, and knew what was going to happen. Was this what it had been like for him in Burkhayden?

The intensity of his agony bridged the gap of years, connecting pain to pain, travelling back in time. He was there. Security detail, the Danzilar prince's garden party, the *Ragnarok*'s Lieutenant Wyrlann drinking and laughing.

That was the man who'd raped a female bond-involuntary in the service house so brutally. Koscuisko had been dispatched to repair the vandalism, because Burkhayden and all the Nurail in it were to be rented to a rich man from the Dolgorukij Combine—one of Koscuisko's cousins, in fact—and the contract required the Bench to make good on damaged property.

He can't tell you anything if he's dead. Was that Lek? It couldn't be. Lek hadn't been there. *Then you'll never know. Langsarik Station sees a lot of Bench Intelligence Specialist Karol Vogel, by the way. You might want to think about that.*

Vogel *had* been there. But it was the Lieutenant that Robert remembered. The Lieutenant, and his sister, his darling, his Megh, alive—but brutalized. The officer had tended her like his own; but nobody would speak against the Lieutenant on her behalf. He'd found something in the garden. What had it been? A trowel. What was the significance of a trowel in the garden? Why was it at night? What had he been doing there?

Threatening me, are you?

No. Only telling the truth, for your own good. Robert has always been his favorite. Or don't you think he'd be doing this himself? Not a patient man, or very forgiving either.

There was no forgiving what the Lieutenant had done to Megh. It couldn't be allowed that the Lieutenant should walk and drink in the garden while Megh lay broken in the hospital. He hadn't seen the other man. He hadn't known the gardener was there. But Koscuisko had understood the truth.

So give me the computer access codes, and I might be willing to table the issue of that message indefinitely. The others never need to know. I'll keep your secret.

He'd tried to tell Koscuisko that the gardener wasn't guilty. *He* was guilty. They'd told him—when he'd woken up in hospital—that *two* officers had been murdered by Free Government assassins, that night in Port Burkhayden. One year ago in a garden on Emandis Koscuisko had confessed to one of those crimes. Now Robert remembered who had done the other.

The rest of the details—Stildyne was in there, somewhere—remained a cloudy blur of memory muddled together with current agony. Still Robert held on to the puzzle as hard as he could, because being in Burkhayden was in the past, which made it better than being here now. He'd survived Burkhayden. His chances here were much more undecided.

Koscuisko never lets go of a question. Lek's voice sounded threatening and despairing at once. *You'll see. I tried to warn you. I hope you remember that, at least.*

Koscuisko never let go. He'd found out. Stildyne had guessed. Hadn't he? What had Stildyne known? What had he told Stildyne, before the governor had shut him up, and why had the governor shut him up, and when, and why did his memory cringe from the idea of Stildyne bending over him?

The welcome darkness came to embrace him and take him away, even if it was only for a little while. Robert was having a nice nap, minding his own business, when someone came up to him and woke him up. He was sorry about that. Rudeness was always regrettable, but more than that he was awake again now, and remembering why he'd prefer not to be.

"You've had a day and a half." Someone was very angry with somebody. Who was that? Deputy Sorsa, maybe? "And what have you got us?" Someone came near, and lifted Robert's head for him, one hand at his jaw. "Nothing. Worse than nothing. We're getting nowhere. What's your excuse? Are you not trying hard enough? Have you forgotten what happened to Sternalle?"

"Give me some credit for knowing my business." That was Mathin, the renegade Inquisitor. "This man is different. He's been under Bond, trained by the best there is, Andrej Koscuisko's own. Imagine the market premium on something like this."

"There'll be no money for either of us here, Doctor. We'll be lucky if we can recover from this disaster with our fish and fins in working order." Fish; what Dolgorukij called their colts. Robert felt his head drop down onto his chest again: so Deputy Sorsa had walked away. "You're off the assignment. If I were you I'd clean this man up and make him comfortable. You're in much, much more trouble than you can imagine."

"What are you talking about?" Mathin demanded. He sounded angry, which made Robert nervous. Bad things happened when Inquisitors were angry, even renegade ones. And renegades didn't have to observe the Protocols. "It was his idea, the great man himself. I'm sure *he'd* have just put through one of his magic doses, but he couldn't be bothered, could he? So leave me alone to do the job."

That reminded him. Lek was around here somewhere. Robert had heard him, from time to time, always in the same place, off to one side. Robert worried whenever he heard Lek's voice, because that wasn't the tone to take with an Inquisitor; never mind the totally inappropriate language. He was surprised Lek even had it in him.

"Shut up and do as you're told. He's asked for a tour, do you know what that means? I mean to give him one. You don't want him seeing *that*, do you? Because I'm reliably informed that he's temperamental, as well as inclined to anarchy. I'm going to have enough of a challenge coming up with the right approach to him as it is. Get started."

"With respect, Deputy Sorsa, you're talking complete gibberish," Mathin said scornfully. Undernote of fear. That made Robert even more nervous, because people went to extremes when they were afraid, to hide it from themselves.

Mathin's voice was coming closer, now. "You won't make a fool out of me," he said—to Robert, Robert thought. "What is your message?" And something hit him in the face, suddenly, a neural rasp shoved up hard against his cheekbone from beneath. His head exploded in a blizzard of malign stars; Robert lost track of things, because trying to breathe was suddenly altogether too difficult for words.

When he came back somebody was talking. "What in the name of all Saints did you hope to accomplish with that little trick?" Something happened with a dose-stylus that made Robert whimper, and there was no shame in that. But this was not a wake-keeper, or an amplifier. He didn't feel the least bit sharper or more focused or awake. Instead he felt increasingly foggy around the edges, and it was a very pleasant sensation, after the others.

There was another dose, one Robert didn't mind a bit because he was starting to not-hurt all over. Not even the fact that he couldn't see out of one side of his head could touch it. "Tell me," Mathin insisted. "The message."

"Don't know what you mean," Robert said, and hoped Mathin could understand because he sounded a little slurred and garbled to himself and he wasn't sure that he was speaking Standard. "What message." *Pay attention now*, he told himself. *It might have been a speak-serum.* He could hope to be resistant to speak-sera, because he'd learned to get around his governor a little bit before it had gone terminal, and the two concepts were not dissimilar. Koscuisko had bought his life with a speak-serum. That had been a long time ago.

"Last chance, Mathin." The Sorsa voice was cold and deadly. "Clean up your work and get out. I'm not telling you again. The man who authorized this was not Andrej Koscuisko."

Mathin hadn't repeated his question; Robert sincerely hoped it wasn't because he'd inadvertently answered it. He looked around him, trying to focus his eye and his mind alike. There was Mathin, the renegade Inquisitor. Deputy Sorsa. Lek in an open-faced cell along the wall staring hard, as though he could get Robert down by main force of will.

Over to the right, a door, which was opening; and

through that door, pushed with great force and enthusiasm by two station personnel Robert assumed, someone who looked like the officer. "What's happening?" Mathin said, obviously bewildered. The "Koscuisko" looked mostly unbruised to Robert, but he'd been stripped naked, and then re-dressed by other hands. Robert knew what that looked like. So they'd found Cousin Stanoczk out.

Sorsa didn't bother to answer, giving Robert a little push. Didn't shift him much. He wasn't going anywhere. "Take him down," Sorsa said. "What a mess you've made, Mathin. Koscuisko isn't going to like this, not at all."

"If the Deputy please." That was Lek, and Robert was relieved to hear that his tone of voice was perfectly correct this time. There was still that speaking-without-being-spoken-to problem, but nobody but Robert seemed to have noticed. "This troop has extensive experience in prisoner management. Request permission to remove the prisoner to cells, your Excellency."

Was Sorsa an Excellency? Dancing-masters weren't. Dancing-masters were "Dancing-master." In a pinch, they would usually answer to "please." Not "help me," though. "Help me" crossed a line between a request and a demand, and bond-involuntaries didn't take that tone of voice with anybody if they didn't want a prompt correction from their governors.

Cousin Stanoczk was in the cell north of Lek's, now, his wrists still bound together behind his back; facing the wall, with his head bowed. As if he was waiting to be unshackled. That didn't seem to be on the agenda.

"Well, not even a Sarvaw could do worse than you

have, Mathin," Deputy Sorsa said. "All right. Let it out.
Mathin, take its advice, and then come see me in my office
immediately. If I'm not there, wait. I'm going to do my
best to save your life, but it may be difficult."

Security held him steady as Lek unfastened the
secures on the tee-post, supporting his weight, letting him
down gently. "The officer would administer pain-ease,"
Lek said, to Mathin. "What may I say, your Excellency?"

That was a risk, there, telling the officer what to do.
Maybe less of a risk, when it was merely an officer rather
than the real one—Himself, as Stildyne sometimes put
it—and Lek would know as well as Robert did by now that
though Mathin might be a Ship's Inquisitor he wasn't a
very good one. None of them really came up to the
Koscuisko benchmark.

Mathin had come to kneel down at Robert's side,
which could only make him very, very nervous. Robert
didn't like Mathin anywhere near him. It was bad enough
when Mathin was in the room. "No worries, Robert," Lek
said to him, low-voiced and confident. "These'll be only
good doses."

Lek put his hand to Robert's face as he spoke, a tender
caress, not usually the sort of thing Robert expected from
Lek; but it was in order to pass finger-code. *Or else.*
Robert understood, though he couldn't respond. His
hands were probably swollen from hanging by his wrists
for however long it had been; he couldn't move his
fingers. And he didn't want to.

"Oh, very well," Mathin said ungraciously. Robert
thought he heard an under-note of fear in Mathin's voice.
It was true that his brain was muddled, but working with

Andrej Koscuisko gave a man a very practiced ear for fear in men's voices, and maybe it wasn't so much of an undernote as a strong thread in the weave. "Three units of hannerdoi." Robert felt the pressure on his skin as Lek pressed the doses through. "Half-a-dozen local of chipermum for shock and swelling."

His knees hurt. They did. Mathin hadn't liked his knees. Robert didn't know what his knees had ever done to Mathin to earn his resentment, but so long as Mathin was going to be using neural rasps he'd considered himself relatively lucky that it'd been his knees that had annoyed Mathin and not his shoulders. More weight, and crozerhinges, so more to hurt.

"Very good, your Excellency. Thank you, your Excellency." He'd done hannerdoi before. Hadn't he? It was the officer's anodyne of choice for Nurail. Robert remembered that from Burkhayden. The officer had opened a clinic there, and run pharmacy stores dry while the Bench was still responsible for replenishing them. "This troop thinks he may have heard the officer call for vixit as well, if the officer please."

Robert wasn't sure he'd ever heard Lek use so many "this troops" and "if the officer pleases" all at once in the many years of their acquaintance, but Lek was clearly doing everything he could to wring what he wanted out of Mathin. If Mathin had been any good at medicine he'd have known all of those things already, which just fit the picture.

"Vixit? Really? At these prices?" Robert wanted to smile, despite himself. Just let Mathin ask a question like that where Koscuisko could hear him, and he'd learn a few things about himself that he might not appreciate. There was another dose, even so; and taken all together Robert as was relaxed as he could remember feeling for the past little while.

"Thank you," Lek said. "I'll let the officer know. Not to Infirmary? Together with me, then. The officer will take it into account." A blanket would be nice. Maybe a pillow. But Lek clearly felt he'd gotten all he was going to be able to wrangle out of Mathin, because "this troop" and "your Excellency" had become suddenly conspicuous by their absence.

Picked up and moved again, well, he'd known it was going to happen and it hurt anyway. One of those doses had been something for bloodless hands; it needed to be done—fingers needed a blood supply, after all, or they started dropping off, one by one—but with luck he'd be well out of it before returning circulation started to get really difficult.

"Thanks, put him down." Since Mathin hadn't been using a whip Robert could lie on his back without worries for the waking; and because he lived in an age of wonder Lek had managed to get him some warming blankets as well. They were clearly very concerned indeed about what the officer was going to say, and they were right to be.

Where was the officer? Here? Next door? No. That was Cousin Stanoczk, trying as hard as he could to look like the officer. Confusing. It was all too much for a man in his condition. Robert put his trust in Lek to look out for him, and went to sleep.

Fiska sat at the table in the executive dining room on

Canopy Base, still struggling to fathom the magnitude of the disaster that had overtaken them, keeping to his role with careful attention.

"I can't wait to show you, Andrej," Iosev said, reaching across the table draped in spotless linen to lay his hand on the wrist of the man who sat opposite him, and give it an emphatic shake. Andrej Koscuisko. All of their careful planning, all of these years of struggle, and for nothing? "You'll be as impressed as I was. I promise you."

Taking a lefrols-case out of his blouse Iosev offered one to his brother, who declined with a shake of his head. Iosev selected one regardless, as though he were the elder brother. Fiska leaned forward with a fire-point; Iosev puffed away contentedly in silence, and the stink of lefrols filled the air. Disaster piled on disaster. From the worrisome problem of *Fisher Wolf* to complete ruin; all because of Iosev's egotism.

"I am already impressed." This was not a Malcontent. This was *the* son of the Koscuisko prince, not *a* son of the Koscuisko prince like Iosev; and he did not seem to be unreservedly glad to see his brother. "But tell me, Iosev. How did you come to find this opportunity, what it is that you do here?"

He interfered, Fiska thought bitterly. He made elaborate plans to impress Sorsa by delivering Andrej Koscuisko like the lordly wheat-wreath of the saga that defined the patron-client relationship and established his supremacy. He'd lied to Pravel Plebach. He'd as good as murdered Cousin Stanoczk, who had been his own cousin in blood before electing the Malcontent. Iosev didn't know what he had done.

"Well. Andrej." Iosev settled his forearms on the edge of the table, tipping lefrol-ash into the remains of his after-sweet. "Thou knowest, eldest and firstborn. A man in my positon must not complain if he lacks for employment. Through my own fault, yes, I confess it freely."

False humility, Fiska thought, savagely. Andrej Koscuisko had not been pleased by the public scene Iosev had staged. There was little chance, Fiska believed, that Andrej Koscuisko had forgiven his brother anything; rather the contrary, from indications Fiska had seen. He had been living for five years with people who would kill him if they found his secret out. He had no illusions. It had made him very sensitive to non-verbal communication; so he knew Deputy Sorsa was furious, too.

"And yet—" Iosev lifted his hand to the ceiling, as if appealing to the Holy Mother to be his witness. "A man wishes to be of use. Nothing I took in hand challenged me for long, alas. Still, I must have been doing something right with my poor efforts, because one fine day this fellow—" Deputy Sorsa "—asked for an interview."

Andrej Koscuisko turned to Sorsa, seated at his right hand. "Freight forwarding and infrastructure development, Deputy Sorsa?" Koscuisko asked, with polite interest. There was a little tinge of relief in Koscuisko's voice; was it because he was talking to someone else beside his brother? "I haven't heard of your enterprise before now, but I beg you to consider that a reflection of my isolation at Safehaven, merely."

Sorsa nodded deferentially, but spoke with confidence from his position as the man responsible for the operation of Canopy Base. "Celestial Heights is a new company, lord prince," Sorsa said. "Unlikely to have crossed the threshold of his Excellency's consideration. I'd be surprised, had his Excellency heard of us before now." There was just the whisper of a rebuke for Iosev, there, in Sorsa's voice. *Because the son of the Koscuisko prince is not involved in the minutiae.*

"And now here's the thing, Derush." It couldn't be said that Iosev actually interrupted, because Sorsa had stopped talking. Iosev moved quickly to regain control of the conversation, though; willing to use a personal name, a pet name, for his brother in front of people who were all but strangers. A power play. *Notice that I call Andrej Koscuisko "Derush," he is my brother, after all.*

Had Cousin Stanoczk ever called Koscuisko that? He never would again. Would Sorsa win Koscuisko over to interrogate Cousin Stanoczk? And if he did, was it possible—oh, Holy Mother, was it possible—that Koscuisko would help?

Andrej Koscuisko nodded, his expression that of a weary man being polite. Iosev took one cue, but not the other; and continued. "What we have here, Andrej, is nothing less than an entirely undeveloped market, a huge new opportunity. Sorsa is a man of vision, Andrej! Of genius! No, don't blush, Ichens, I won't go on. If we can get a foothold, Ichens says, we can be first to provide services uniquely valuable to Gonebeyond."

Koscuisko's expression changed, immediately wary. He looked to Sorsa, clearly about to ask a question; Iosev as clearly wasn't about to let that happen. "Uniquely *lucrative* services," Iosev said, flinging his arms wide in an extravagant gesture. "An immense resource is opening up before us, unlimited, unprecedented, it will never happen again in our lifetimes. And no one was out there trying to develop it! No one! The field is absolutely open."

"Only because the Bench proscribed any extra-territorial activity, surely," Koscuisko said. "And I have been a year at Safehaven, in the Nurail octant. I have seen signs—small ones, but they are there—of developmental activity, from within, slow and from the ground up, the sort that lasts."

Casting both hands up to heaven in his excitement Iosev scattered lefrol ash in a broad arc across the tablecloth. "But we will be first, with the most to offer. And the genius of it is that we will pay ourselves with resources otherwise useless to them. We earn their trust, their gratitude, we attach them to us firmly. Once we have shown them clearly enough where their best interest lies, we'll be the most powerful organization in Gonebeyond space."

Koscuisko pressed his lips together, as if against the taste of something unpleasant. "Then you will be offering security and defense, I expect?" Koscuisko said. "That will be the best way to develop a relationship and protect your own interests as well, no doubt. There are pirates and night raiders at prey in Gonebeyond. We treated some survivors of the Oak Leaf massacre at Safehaven."

Iosev blinked. Sorsa didn't move a muscle—Fiska admired his self-control. "Oh," Iosev said. "Oak Leaf? Surely that's one of those wild rumors. I heard there'd been a misunderstanding of some sort, yes, an incident—nothing more." No, they'd found Oak Leaf surprisingly well-prepared. It hadn't made any difference; their raiding party had still taken three years' yield of ephemere gems and left the station to burn.

Koscuisko said nothing. Iosev made up the lack. "Anyway, we're just getting started here, Andrej. Ichens asked me to be the face of Celestial Heights, to show that we are Dolgorukij, that this is an Aznir enterprise, Aznir power. The Koscuisko name. Respected and admired throughout Jurisdiction space, and who better to step up to the need in Gonebeyond?"

"The Holy Mother bless all such gifts of grain for goods," Koscuisko said. Fair and balanced contracts, in other words; mutually beneficial ones. "I look forward to seeing your facility, Deputy Sorsa. Do I return to *Chornije* tonight, or go to guest quarters? I'm tired. I would like to sleep."

Did Andrej Koscuisko know? Had he seen something in Iosev's eyes, on Iosev's face, that revealed the truth to him, that it had been the Angel of Destruction at Oak Leaf, and that Iosev was in a position to know the truth of it—whether or not Iosev turned a resolutely blind eye?

Iosev jumped to his feet with a look of dismay. "Surely there's no rush to say good-night, Derush. It's been so long. I hoped that we could have a talk."

But Koscuisko was clearly talked out, and Sorsa would want to be able to concentrate on his own problems. There was the problem of Cousin Stanoczk to consider. "Tomorrow," Koscuisko said. "After the tour, perhaps. You shall tell me all about the challenges you face, and how you mean to overcome them, and what our family strategists have to say."

Some pertinent and pressing questions, then. Sorsa

had stood up when Iosev had. He bowed to Andrej. "Fisner Feraltz is my confidential aide, almost my Tikhon," he said. "Fisner, please escort the son of the Koscuisko prince to the guest suite, and make sure all is arranged for his comfort."

Tikhon to Sorsa's Dasidar: that was heady praise indeed. It was more than the most powerful model of romantic masculine friendship in the entire Saga. It was as good as adoption as Sorsa's trusted councilor, above all others—within the rank-hierarchy of the Angel of Destruction, the acknowledged surrogate. "It is so good to see you, Derush," Iosev said. "And to know I am forgiven. Sleep well, firstborn and eldest, and most beloved brother."

"It will be this way, lord prince," Fiska said, mind and heart full of misery. "If the lord prince will condescend to follow me?" Cousin Waclav was on the *Chornije*. If Wishka were here, on Canopy Base, instead—

Maybe there would still be nothing left of the great endeavor. But the presence of his Reconciler would give Fiska comfort, if no hope. And there would be hope. There was always hope. If Andrej Koscuisko caught the secret out, if Iosev and Sorsa had made a mistake, then perhaps Koscuisko could be that hope, and help them find a way out of this disaster.

CHAPTER FIVE

Labyrinth

The first order of business, Andrej decided, was a drink; a very large drink; perhaps two. There was a well-stocked bar in the guest quarters to which young Fisner Feraltz had escorted him, and the cortac brandy was of even better quality than that Iosev had sent to him at Safehaven, good though that was, especially for men who had been forced to subsist on hospital home distillation product.

He'd never liked Iosev. He'd tried. Even before what Iosev had done, there had been a layer of distance between them that was unlike that which separated him from his other brothers. Mecha he liked. Leo he liked, though he didn't know him very well. Nikosha he loved, but Nikosha he knew less well than any of his brothers; Nikosha was only a few years older than Andrej's own son Anton. Whom he didn't know at all.

Canopy Base was hip-deep in horror. Pravel Plebach was a racist, all the more corrupt for being an otherwise apparently decent young man. Deputy Sorsa had recruited Iosev, but was not to blame for the flaws in Iosev's character; Andrej had seen it, he was sure he'd seen it, a minute flash of understanding and recognition in Iosev's eyes when Andrej had spoken of Oak Leaf, layered over in an instant with willful ignorance. So Iosev knew, or guessed, that the people to whom he had lent his name—Andrej's name—were connected, in some way at least, with the night raiders. And had countenanced the enterprise.

What was he going to do about it? According to tradition, Andrej could kill Iosev if Andrej thought Iosev needed it. It wasn't fratricide under law unless it was the younger brother who killed his elder, to whom he owed deference and obedience.

The Malcontent frowned on such behavior, however, in these modern times; which reminded Andrej that he wanted another glass of cortac brandy, and to seek out his cousin Stanoczk as soon as he could get away from here. Because Plebach's racism might not be an unexpected anachronism but a symptom of something even uglier than that. No. Not a symptom. A corollary. Canopy Base was at least complicit in piracy of the worst sort. Was this what Waclav had warned him about?

There was a signal at the door. A woman, perhaps, veiled and escorted, to be offered for his use. Andrej didn't want a woman. He'd had more than enough women coming to his bed over the past year. He'd be able to refuse her, that was a point, but there was still protocol to be considered; so it was a relief, almost, to hear the polite announcement coming over the talk-alert. "Ichens Oxeievitch Sorsa requests the favor of a few moments of your time, lord prince."

Well, that would be all right. What did Sorsa want? "Ichens" was an archaic name, very old, very traditional, seldom heard in these modern times. Andrej keyed the entry mode, and the door opened. "Step through," he said. Sorsa had something on a tray, a glass of wine; and he was alone.

"His Excellency has been on Safehaven for a year, alone amongst alien races," Sorsa said. "And the conversation at dinner tonight, I hope to be excused for saying this, did not seem entirely to your taste, lord prince. I have brought an offering to rinse the taste out of your mouth."

The wine was thick and wound-red in the glass. Its fragrance once encountered could not be mistaken for anything else: caraminson wine, a high-level relaxant and euphoric, and available—at least legally—only by prescription, from a restricted number of health care professionals. Masseurs licensed to work in service houses. Like the one who'd prescribed a glass for Andrej in the hours after Joslire's death in Port Burkhayden; the first, and last, time Andrej had ever tasted caraminson wine.

Sorsa put the tray down on the side-table and straightened up. He gave the impression of competence, intelligence, perceptiveness; Andrej needed to be careful. He should find out everything he could about Canopy Base: so much was clear. But any suggestion that he join the enterprise—on what grounds, under what conditions, in what role—had to come from Sorsa, before Andrej could decide how he should respond. He had a feeling that the suggestion might be coming soon.

"'How many facets of what rare gems would I not give,'" Andrej said. It was one of the idioms in common use on Azanry from the saga of Dasidar and Dyraine; but also, of course, there was the cost of caraminson wine, with explicit reference to the plunder—ephemere stones—taken from Oak Leaf.

Sorsa shook his head. "We were offered, lord prince," he said. "There was too great a variance between the value of the goods and the price asked. I sent them away. Then we heard that there'd been an attack, and gave prayerful thanks to the Holy Mother who shielded us from having any part—howsoever innocent—in what had been done there."

Andrej was diverted, but not convinced. Sorsa had taken Iosev's words and found a story that would reconcile two ends of the loaf with the middle, leaving the midmost slice pure and savory for consumption. Sorsa was going to be difficult, but a challenge could be fun—the contest of wills, the grappling of minds, the final crushing victory. He was Andrej Ulexeievitch Koscuisko. He always won. And, oh, how he missed the struggle.

Loosening the collar of his under-blouse Andrej sat down, considering the wine. Chilled; little drops of condensation were forming on the glass. He took a sip. Yes, delicious.

"Iosev could ask the familial corporation for warships to combat piracies," he said. "Why has he not done so? Is his presence here a secret from his family, what is he hiding?" He declined to ask Sorsa to sit down. He was tired. He was unhappy. He wanted to be left alone to wash, to put on one of those soft clean night-shirts that he'd found in the bathing-room, and go to sleep.

"Questions which the lord prince would but direct to his brother, your Excellency," Sorsa said. A very neat evasion. "For myself I can only wonder, lord prince, how it is with you, to sit in a poverty-stricken hovel of a charity hospital amidst people prejudiced against you. When you still hold a Writ to Inquire, and all of the power that such a thing entails."

Well, technically, yes, he still held the Writ. He'd been about to surrender it, to be free, to go home and live at peace with his bride and their son and his memories, before circumstances had intervened.

Sorsa apparently took Andrej's distracted failure to respond as permission to proceed. "Might one presume so far upon the lord prince's condescension as to ask whether his Excellency ever thinks back to the days in which he was the rule of Law in his own person, with absolute license to seek out truth as he saw fit, with none to challenge him or interfere?"

Why not. It was a personal question, but a pertinent one, because he did think about the days. There had been accused after accused, meat to his knife, souls to his savagery. To be Captain Lowden's whore; and not die of shame, because of the terrible transcendent joy of it. To surfeit on suffering.

"It's an addiction." One he hadn't understood until the day he'd made up his mind to starve the wolf within him, since he couldn't kill it. It was part of him. He couldn't pretend it wasn't there. He could only shut it in a room and turn around, looking back over his shoulder as he fought to walk away. "And yet I have no longer the license to execute. I am a man much reduced in compass, Deputy Sorsa."

Pent, managed, trammeled. Prisoner. Held in confinement, not close, but confined none the less, unable to reach out to people he loved and missed and needed, alone in a city full of men and women with the best of reasons to hate him. He had no one to talk to. He was alone. He wasn't expected to enjoy it.

"It does not need to be that way, lord prince," Sorsa said, and there was something so peculiar about Sorsa's choice of words that Andrej's attention snapped into sharp focus. "Your genius is a gift within your power to bestow, should you see fit to accept your destiny and defend the rule of Law. Our ancestral law, Aznir law. There are enemies of the Blood, lord prince, and you have been marked by the Holy Mother as her special instrument."

Standing up suddenly Andrej turned his back on Sorsa's insinuations to put his mind in order. He didn't have much time. Sorsa was not to be underestimated; Andrej had learned that much watching him, listening to him, watching him watching Iosev. He found his truth, and spoke from it. "These are hard things to say to me, Sorsa. I go back to Safehaven to be among the Nurail, who may use me as they wish."

He knew how much they needed him, but it was frustrating. Safehaven had hardly enough carpets to cover the public floors, let alone the luxury of a runner of deep

blue edged in silver-white that could be held waiting in
reserve in case one man whose feet were not to be soiled
by contact with alien ground should step down from a
ship. *Chornije* had reminded him of how much he had
given up to come here; and yet at the same time—in a
sense—*Chornije* had also reminded him of why he'd
come.

He'd been raised as his father's heir. The blood of an
autocrat ran strong in his veins—never so strongly as when
he had souls to take for his own, in intimate dominion.
Then he was Koscuisko indeed: but he had turned away
from that power, and denied himself the most intense
sensation he had ever known.

"I overstep," Sorsa said. Andrej turned back to face
him; Sorsa had lowered his head, but still watched Andrej
keenly. "It's not my place to say his Excellency need have
no shame in doing as he was meant and made. I beg his
Excellency's excusing of my fault. The Holy Mother
knows I mean no disrespect."

All the same he said it, didn't he? Not unlike the man
who said *I probably shouldn't tell you that your father
was seen eating fish in the city three days ago*. Andrej
decided how he would play his role, whether or not he
understood it.

"We do not discuss it further. The days are gone and
it troubles me to speak of it.—There is a kitchen-master
with *Chornije*, Deputy Sorsa, can he be brought here to
cook for me?" Sudden shift of topic. A common trick.
Andrej was interested in what Sorsa would make of this
ploy.

"It is already done, lord prince." Meaning, of course,

that it would be done directly. Sorsa sounded pleased; when a man reverted to the diction of a prince, it meant he was falling back upon a younger self, and could be manipulated. "His Excellency is aware that this man is Sarvaw?"

Andrej snorted with unfeigned disgust, though more at Plebach's remembered ugliness than Waclav's nationality. "Do you imagine I am unaware of that? I have known Sarvaw, I am familiar." To say *with the smell of them* would be gratuitous. Iosev would say that. "And still he is a very good cook. You would gratify me by seeing to it."

These were not the words of a guest to his host. This was the language of an autocrat; but it was even more. It was something said by a prince to a man whose service he would graciously consent to accept. Conditionally; on probation. So long as he continued to give satisfaction.

"I will send Fisner to wait upon his Excellency's pleasure in the morning," Sorsa said. Of course. "May I be excused, lord prince, to further all things that might bring honor to his Excellency and his noble house?"

Andrej nodded. "I drink this wine with pleasure. Thank you, Deputy Sorsa, I will see you tomorrow." *Good night.* "Prosper all Saints." *Go away.*

"And the Holy Mother bless his Excellency to Her purpose, in all things." Sorsa sounded subtly gratified. He was supposed to be pleased; Andrej had granted him standing. Andrej hoped it was more than that. Sorsa had passed Andrej's test; had Andrej passed Sorsa's?

Something was wrong, here. Waclav had warned him, though of what exactly he had yet to understand. He had to stay on his guard. He had to go with care. For that he needed to be rested and alert. Lifting the glass of wine from its tray Andrej raised it to the light to admire its color. It represented a certain degree of risk; it had been eight years, perhaps, since he'd last tasted it, and peoples' reactions to such medications could change with age.

He didn't know who had prescribed it, or what their qualifications were; still, on balance, he judged the risk worth taking. He drank the wine; he treated himself to a long hot shower in scented water; drying himself with towels as thick as his thumb he selected a sleep-shirt—one embroidered with lapped duck-wings—and went to bed.

When Karol Vogel touched down at Langsarik Station he saw no signs of small Dolgorukij freighters in geosynch orbit, which was a disappointment—he'd entertained fantasies of finding Koscuisko there. Switching off, setting the courier's status to "stand-by," he deployed his passenger loading ramp as soon as the tarmac's thermal sink capacity would let him; because Hilton Shires was waiting for him on the other side of the safety line and Karol was anxious for good news.

Shires met him close on, loping along down the guide-path with a hitch in his gait so minor it was almost not even there anymore. Karol knew why Shires limped in humid weather. Shires had told his family that it'd been an accident, something to do with a speed machine; and that had not been strictly untrue. "Good-greeting, Bench specialist," Shires said, but not loudly, and coming rather close. "You got my message?"

"You sent one?" Karol asked, by which he meant *no*.

"Did you get mine?" *Hold all outbound commercial traffic from Safehaven, until my arrival*. He'd known there was the chance he would outrun the message. *Helva* was the fastest courier Poe Station had; and the communications relay stations across vectors in Gonebeyond space were inconsistently reliable.

"Thank you, Bench specialist." Shires mimed pleased surprise, but subtly. *Man invited into newly arrived and unfamiliar ship for a tour*. They'd done this before, once, years ago, when he and Shires had first worked a common problem together, at Port Charid. "I *would* appreciate a chance to look around inside, yes. Will it be this way?"

"Up the ramp and to your right," he agreed. "*Your* right, Shires." That was an old joke. "Mind the totally non-existent rug." Following Shires back up into the courier Karol palmed the communications secures, as if absent-mindedly. Confidentiality in effect. Reaching the wheelhouse Karol keyed the doors closed, and sat down.

"There are five Pashnavik-class warships standing on the Line at Poe Station, commanded by one of Andrej Koscuisko's younger brothers," Karol said. "Safehaven lost track of Koscuisko not long after a Combine freighter departed en route to Langsarik Station, and they're very annoyed about it, too."

Picking a sheaf of flatfile flimsies up out of the co-pilot's seat where Karol had tossed them, Shires sat down. The body language was not encouraging. Karol could see Shires look to the tell-tales on the communications board before he spoke, checking the security status. "Well, Koscuisko's been here. Then he left. Then Koscuisko arrived, and *he* left, too."

Folding his hands across his chest, thumbs tip-to-tip and his elbows resting on the arms of the chair at the primary pilot's station, Karol waited. Shires nodded, *yes, I know, it's confusing*; and went on.

"Andrej Koscuisko came through my office six days ago. Our Malcontent liaison had asked for the thula to come for him, so I did rather assume it was Cousin Stanoczk, at first." Shires had worked with Cousin Stanoczk before, but the Malcontent used a number of liaison agents at Langsarik Station.

Karol himself hadn't seen Cousin Stanoczk for months, not that that meant anything. The fact that he'd maintained a relationship with Cousin Stanoczk was apparently a bit of an anomaly, but for all Karol knew so was Cousin Stanoczk himself. "Undivided attention," Karol said, encouragingly, to keep the flow of information coming.

"Took the thula, left the station, we looked the other way. You know. The way you do." Karol nodded. Yes, he knew. Langsariks knew their business, and how to mind their own. "Then what, two, three days ago, here comes another Koscuisko."

"Combine hull *Chornije*," Karol suggested helpfully.

"Perfect and precise, Bench specialist. The physical presentation was very similar, but my friend Kazmer— remember Kaz?—thinks it's the man himself. And Kaz knows Cousin Stanoczk better than I do."

And was in a better position to judge on the relative Koscuisko-ness of any given Koscuisko accordingly, Karol presumed. That would be Shires' point. "Tracks on the *Chornije*?" Karol asked, but it was for form's sake, really.

Shires shook his head. "Vector control reported the
Chornije in queue shortly after departure from station.
Our people at Neshuan weren't watching it closely
enough to try to guess where it was going to exit."
Attempting to calculate destinations from the observed
characteristics of a vector spin was an imperfect science,
even with the best equipment. So they only had one real
avenue of approach.

"If the thula hadn't made the vector someone would
have noticed it, though, it being the sexy little beast that
it is. Somebody must have let somebody know to watch
for it." There was a question implicit in Karol's suggestion;
Shires took him right up on it.

"Very discreet inquiries confirm that *Fisher Wolf*
hasn't come off any mapped vector drop in Langsarik
space. We're not staffing all of them, of course, and the
Ragnarok keeps on turning up new ones. It's been
mapping in our quadrant for weeks."

As per its assigned mission. There was no comfortable
place for a Jurisdiction Fleet ship in Gonebeyond, where
it was as much of a symbol of what Gonebeyond had
escaped from as Andrej Koscuisko himself; but its
Captain, ap Rhiannon, wasn't going back until she got
official vindication and immunity from prosecution for her
crew. That could take years to sort out. The *Ragnarok* was
hardly uppermost on Fleet's to-do lists.

"We need to find at least one of those ships. I really
want to find them both." He was going to need a good
story. If *Chornije* was taking Koscuisko home, Captain
Leo could leave; but Karol did not think that was going to
happen. Koscuisko wasn't going home until he'd done

what he'd come for. Stubborn, but Karol liked that in a man, even if that man was Andrej Koscuisko.

Which brought him back to the thula, because Koscuisko had come to Gonebeyond to apologize to his Chief of Security, and the thula was where Security Chief Stildyne was to be found. Someone was masquerading as a ranking Fleet officer in custody of a Writ to Inquire, and Inquisitors had been disappearing.

If Captain Leo found out that two different Andrej Koscuiskos had come through Langsarik Station and disappeared, there'd be no dissuading him from moving out with vigor and dispatch to investigate for himself. That was what Karol would do. They'd have no option then but to defend the integrity of Gonebeyond space by force of whatever arms they could muster.

And that would be insane: because Pashnavik-class warships laughed at armed freighters, snickered at heavy scouts, and would only sneer contemptuously at the best-armed smugglers that Safehaven could throw at them. There was always a chance that they could incapacitate the Pashnaviks by surrounding them with Gonebeyond's finest fighters and sending them into helpless giggling fits, but even then the odds were not good.

"Double-diamond switch-back," Shires said. "Chevron trace. We've got practically nothing to go on, Vogel." But that was exactly what they had to look for, nothing. Somewhere there was a recently cleared line of flight where a ship had passed, collecting and consuming all the tiny bits of rock-debris with which the deepest space was dusted to fuel its voracious conversion engines, leaving nothing behind.

Somewhere there was a trace of the residual energy dissipated by the thula's propulsion stream. A ghostly wake. All they had to do was find it, a single herring-bone in a stew-pot sized to feed a multitude.

"And call out for the *Ragnarok*," Karol said, standing up. "Ask them for anything that might bleed off from Neshuan to parts unknown. Pulse the stations on all of Neshuan's exit vectors, whether it's in Langsarik space or not. We can use the courier's comms to supplement Langsarik Station's resources."

It was little enough to start with. But he had no choice. Because there was nothing else that he could think of that had any chance of stopping Captain Leo's warships from crossing the Line and invading Gonebeyond, ending Gonebeyond's autonomy before it had had its first real chance to assert it.

"Two" was the only one of her species on the mobile cave *Ragnarok*, which was sometimes of aggravation because it did not fit itself well to her. There were issues of communication. They were very poor at it, very slow; and frequently wrong. For instance, she was not a giant bat. She was a proud Desmodontae, and it was not to be blaming that the world-caves under Jurisdiction had populations of very small similar species that well below her thinkingness were having.

She liked puzzles. She had always liked the puzzling out of things. She was in her office, Intelligence and Communications, listening to data streams run correlation patterns while the dynamic chart-plot graphs scrolled across her goggles where she could see them, when the talk-alert chimed. Annoying. She could only do three things at one time.

"Two," the talk-alert said. It was the Captain-person, the cave mother. Not exactly, no, but the mapping worked for Two. "Data calling from Langsarik station, skein in braid."

But from courier *Helva*, with Karolvogel. She'd seen the call come in, hadn't she? To the cave mother she was expected to respond, however, so Two reached across to the far side of the room and keyed the speak-back with her wing-finger. "Yes hearing, Captain." What came out of her translator was not her responsibility. She knew what she'd said.

She could hear the transmission gates talking to each other, channeling data through; and scratched her muzzle, irritably. They always took so long to say anything. It was a continuing wonder to her that such an admirably large puzzle as the *Ragnarok* or the Jurisdiction could ever have been constructed in slow motion; but a constant frustration also.

Speak, she urged the Bench specialist of Vogel, in her mind. It was perfectly clear that the channels were open; what was he waiting for? "Thank you, your Excellency." It was a beginning, at least. She could tell by inflection that she was not the "Excellency" person he was thinking, though, so there was yet more delay. "I'm pulsing some traffic through, two items of interest. *Fisher Wolf*. Combine freighter *Chornije*."

There were more words than that, but the actual information was very small. "And yes you are wanting what?" she asked. *Fisher Wolf* she knew; she talked to it from time to time. It had a bad attitude. Freighter *Chornije* was clearly from the Desalt family built at Barend shipyards twenty-three and twenty-five years ago, and there were maintenance records about the coolant systems, but otherwise its biography held little of interest. She went to look at the initial equipment issue, and wondered why there were no records of nourishment though it should be past depleting; but Karolvogel was saying something again, now.

"Neshuan exit, other vectors, unmapped any," he said. More or less. That was not very interesting either; and she was playing a much more diverting puzzle which the Captain-person probably did not mean to describe so Two would not mention it. Maybe she could play both puzzles at once. That could make it more interesting, because more complex, and would not take away from the important puzzle.

Hominid children were not Desmodontae babies. But they were babies. And in a cave everybody looked out for all the babies, because babies belonged to the cave. "These," she said. "I will calibrate." He would naturally want Neshuans that went away from Langsarik Station. She had two or three that went in to Langsarik Station, but there was one Neshuan that had gone out with several dead pings. She would pull on that thread while her primary resources worked the larger issue.

"Thanking," Karolvogel said. *Of course yes*, Two thought crossly, wishing he would go away. There was a new puzzle. Maybe one that was actually inside the other puzzle. She wanted to hold it in her mind and admire it for a moment or two before she launched herself into its cloud-field.

"Away here," the Captain-person said. Finally.

"Langsarik Station to target area, any," Two said to her comm, because it could speak Desmodontae. "Recent traffic origin Langsarik Station any, produce." Then she gave herself a little shake and settled back into cave-perch meditation posture to see what the cross-correlation would turn up, smiling happily.

Fiska had seen Sorsa at fast-meal; had swallowed only the courtesy-morsels, along with his dread. Now of all times he could not let his mask slip. He had orders to relay.

If only he could cover his head with his two hands, and crouch down to the ground beside his desk, and howl in agony—but he could not. There was always hope. And he had a tone on his scheduler; not Sorsa, not Iosev—Iosev did not call on him, but on Sorsa direct, no matter how trivial the matter—but from the night-attendant, the one who'd sat the watch at the guest suite. "Yes, Yeharl?"

"Prosper all Saints," the attendant said, sounding very worried. "The lord prince does not accept his fast-meal, firstborn and eldest. He demands the presence of the one who has cooked it. And also a Sarvaw from *Chornije*, I have relayed the message, you should know."

He wasn't the oldest of Yeharl's brothers, nor the first-born of Yeharl's siblings. But Yeharl was clearly at a loss as to what the correct form of address should be, to report a fast-meal crisis in progress. "Thank you, I come directly."

He knew Canopy Base; he knew its short-cuts. As he made the last turning, opened the hidden service-door, stepped into the corridor outside the guest suite in which Koscuisko had spent the night, Fiska could see three other people hurrying toward the same set of double doors, from the other direction. Someone from the kitchens. And Cousin Waclav.

Fixing a stern scowl on his face Fiska addressed the attendant, not feeling sure of his ability to hide his relief at the sight of his Reconciler. To whom he owed his life, his soul, his understanding of the Holy Mother's mercy. What was Waclav doing here? Yes, Yeharl had said "Sarvaw from the *Chornije*," but why? "I will go in," he said. "Everybody wait."

He signaled at the door. "Fisner Feraltz, as it please the lord prince," and received his permission to enter, Koscuisko's "Step through." Koscuisko sounded annoyed. He shouldn't be annoyed. Sorsa had carried a glass of caraminson wine to Koscuisko, last night. It was supposed to make Koscuisko cheerful and good-humored in the morning.

Koscuisko hadn't started to dress. He was sitting at the fast-meal table that had been set up for him in the front room of the suite; Fiska could see that no more than two bites had been taken of the grain soup, one of the rolled meal-cake with its savory filling, one corner of a flaky buttercrust pastry torn and bitten into and discarded. Koscuisko looked up at Fiska with a mild expression on his face that felt like a punch in the stomach, and leaned back in his chair.

"This need not go further than it has already," Koscuisko said. "Last night I spoke to Deputy Sorsa about the services of a particularly good cook, and was highly gratified by his response. And yet I am served this meal, Feraltz, which while by any measure would be very nice indeed cannot touch the meals that Waclav prepared for me on *Chornije*. Between us we must resolve this, Feraltz, you and I."

Koscuisko offered him partnership in a conspiracy, but what was it to be? "The ones you have sent for are outside, lord prince," Fiska said. "Shall I call them in?"

"Send me in first the person who this meal prepared," Koscuisko said, pointing with his hand at his tray as if at some sorrowful failure. "And close the door, you are with me here, of course." Koscuisko meant to have witnesses; but not, as it seemed, to make trouble. He had something else in mind.

When the executive fast-meal cook from Canopy Base's kitchens was brought in and the door closed Koscuisko asked Fiska, "What is this person's name?" but Fiska didn't know. So he whispered to the cook, who whispered back. "Your servant is Shifan Tedorevitch, lord prince."

Koscuisko nodded. But then Koscuisko merely sat for a long moment musing over his grain soup, now cold and congealing, before he spoke. "This is not Waclav's cooking," Koscuisko said; and the cook was so wrought-up he almost trembled.

"No, lord prince."

"Why is this not Waclav's cooking, Shifan? Waclav is a superlative cook. I asked for his service specifically, and Deputy Sorsa assured me that I would have it."

The cook closed his eyes tight shut, clearly aghast at the magnitude of his error. "This person had not realized that the Sarvaw had been called to serve you, lord prince. But could not believe that food from such a hand should be placed before the son of the Koscuisko prince, here, on Canopy Base."

"And yet he has cooked my meals all the way here from Safehaven," Koscuisko said mildly. "I have found them much more than merely acceptable. Do I not know what is to my own taste, and am I not to have it?"

The cook clearly knew he'd made a frightful blunder. It was Sorsa's fault, really, Fiska thought; hadn't he made things clear enough? "Of course, lord prince. I am in error. I should not have presumed."

Surely Koscuisko knew where to lay the blame. "You look familiar, Shifan Tedorevitch." Koscuisko seemed to have shifted into graciously forgiving mode. Fisner was not completely taken in; the interesting question was why Koscuisko had pushed the cook off balance, if he wasn't going to threaten and roar. "Who are your people?"

It was an autocrat who spoke, extending his hand in gracious pardon. "My father is Theodor Illiaronovitch, lord prince," the cook said eagerly, almost franticly. "His mother, Maurievna, her father Heverdus, his mother Tilfragij, her father Shomsirkho. My father's mother's father's mother was once so honored as to see an aunt selected for the sacred wife of a distant kinsman of his Excellency's several times removed grand-uncle Porchivian Libetrevitch—"

Holding up his hand to stop the spate, Koscuisko nodded. "You are from good blood, Shifan. You were wrong to reject my expressed wish, but I will excuse it, because I had not to you my purpose made clear."

Now the cook was back among the living. Koscuisko had recognized his pedigree, acknowledging kinship—if of the most attenuated degree. Fiska waited, curious to see what Koscuisko was going to do next. "My purpose is to ensure that I should continue to enjoy meals of the highest quality, and until there are others as good, it must be from his hand. Yes? For this to happen I wish you to put yourself at Waclav's service, and learn as much as you can. He is the best cook I have ever met."

Holy Mother, Fiska thought prayerfully, with almost overwhelming gratitude. *Waclav will be here. There is hope. We will make hope. Your providence truly surpasses all understanding. Forgive, forgive, forgive my despair.*

"Now, Feraltz," Koscuisko said—and if he had noticed anything unusual in Fiska's expression he said nothing about it. "Ask for me in Waclav, if you please."

Fiska could show no emotion to Waclav either, though his excitement was painfully all-consuming. He opened the door; he beckoned Cousin Waclav in; he closed the door again. "Good-greeting, your Excellency," Cousin Waclav said. "May one respectfully venture to hope that his Excellency's fast-meal has been to his satisfaction?"

"I'm sorry to say not." Koscuisko gestured toward his plate with what seemed to be helpless resignation. "Because someone clearly incapable of letting it pass before him and not tasting of it himself has devoured it entire, as I would have done. I understand, but I remain unfed. And here—"

Koscuisko pointed to the cook, napkin in hand. "This person's name is Shifan Tedorevitch. The fast-meal he presented to me shows great promise, lacking only a truly great teacher to elevate his art. Would you, Waclav, accept his service so long as I am here, and teach him what you can?"

Koscuisko meant to have Waclav in the kitchen, of all places. Where the requirements for meals and provisioning meant that one heard everything about everything. There would be nothing more natural than for Fiska to call Waclav to quiz him on his progress. Waclav would find out about Cousin Stanoczk; and have better hope than almost anybody else of knowing what to do to solve this, to fix this, to complete the mission. If it was not to be Cousin Stanoczk to depart from Canopy Base, surely there would be a way for Waclav to smuggle the precious data-trove out with him when he left.

"I'm sure it's a very well-run kitchen, lord prince," Waclav said. "But, with your permission, I don't know what I could possibly have to offer Canopy Base, I am merely . . ."

But the cook had taken the bait. "It would be a privilege to receive your tutelage," he said, sounding very determined. "I must know how to earn such praise from the son of the Koscuisko prince. Teach me, kitchen-master Waclav, I beseech it of you, I will give my first-born son your name."

For a moment Fiska was afraid that the cook would actually go down on his knees to Waclav, anxious as he was to validate Koscuisko's forgiveness of his error. Koscuisko intervened before the cook had a chance.

"Decided," Koscuisko said. "Shifan Tedorevitch, your kitchen will place all at Waclav's disposal, to seek his knowledge. Waclav, you will look upon Shifan's kitchen as your own, and guide them to improve their craft. To Deputy Sorsa I will explain that it is my will."

And demonstrate thereby that he would not hesitate to have his way with other peoples' employees, with other peoples' resources, in other peoples' establishments as if it was his natural right—because he was Andrej Koscuisko. It was something Iosev Ulexeievitch might have done; or tried to do, and not as smoothly.

Cousin Waclav bowed deeply. Fiska knew Waclav better than anybody here could guess; and it seemed clear to Fiska that Waclav believed Koscuisko was on the Malcontent's side. "Does his Excellency then require a fresh meal?" Waclav asked.

Koscuisko nodded. "Thank you, yes. Send only what can be done quickly, Waclav, I have an appointment with Deputy Sorsa within the hour. Already I look forward to mid-meal. Thank you, Feraltz, I will get dressed now, return for me in an hour, with my respects to Deputy Sorsa."

Now this, this was the man Iosev Ulexeievitch wished to be, the man Deputy Sorsa almost was, a man Cousin Waclav could take into his confidence. This was Cousin Stanoczk's cousin indeed. Fiska's heart was so full of emotion he thought he might die of it; so he bowed and took leave, and stood for long moments in the silence of an empty service corridor to compose his mind before he could trust himself to speak to Deputy Sorsa.

Andrej was feeling mildly self-satisfied, if apprehensive. He'd got Waclav placed in the kitchens, the breathing heart of any organization; and a very adequate second fast-meal on top of it. And he had made his point with Deputy Sorsa. Sorsa's aide Feraltz was an intelligent and conscientious man; he would know how to tell the story. It was a shame that such a man should be placed below Iosev.

The passenger lifts at Safehaven were creaky freight boxes hauled on cables; noisy, drafty, and few. This one was whisper-silent and pristine; Sorsa's aide Feraltz keyed the lift's destination instructions, but Andrej felt no chuddering jerks as the lift set out. "My brother does not join us this morning?" Andrej asked Deputy Sorsa. "I expected to find him in your company."

A flicker of embarrassment passed over Sorsa's face, but Andrej couldn't tell whether it was genuine or whether Sorsa merely meant him to observe the situation-appropriate response. "The prince his Excellency's brother begs to be excused. Matters of urgency demand his personal attention."

Hung over, Andrej had no doubt. "Perhaps this after mid-meal, then. I am anxious to spend time with him, as my stay here must be short." He wasn't going to lie to Sorsa; he wanted Sorsa's confidence. But he was sincere about the shortness of his stay, and it didn't matter if Sorsa knew he wasn't telling the truth about being "anxious to spend time" with Iosev.

He didn't need Sorsa to be completely convinced; just persuaded that Andrej didn't believe he could be blatantly lied to. Were it not for the troubling presence of a Malcontent, Plebach's racism, the attitude expressed by the young kitchen-master, Sorsa's insinuations, it might be genuinely enjoyable, testing himself against Sorsa. Where had such a man come from?

"His Excellency desires an early return to Safehaven?" Sorsa asked. "I'll have my own courier placed on stand-by immediately, lord prince. Fisner, take note." Feraltz bowed, reaching into his blouse for his scheduler. "Permit me, though, to ask, have we given offense in some way?"

Ask me if any inducement will persuade me to remain. Then maybe I'll have a better idea of whether you have offended me or not. "I'm needed at Safehaven, Deputy Sorsa, I am the only surgeon in my specialty. I must not be away too long, or people may suffer for lack of care."

"Perhaps our enterprise can provide services, in time, that would satisfy his Excellency's concerns for staffing there. No price would be too high to pay, in exchange for the honor of his Excellency's patronage." The passenger lift opened up onto a wide and well-lit floor; they'd arrived somewhere. "If it please his Excellency, I'd like to start this tour in the command center, with an overview of the base."

No further mention of Andrej's departure. This was unlikely to be resignation on Sorsa's part; Andrej had second thoughts about returning to Safehaven now in earnest, because Sorsa was clearly offering to actively fund the hospital in return for Andrej's cooperation. They needed a real hospital at Safehaven much more than they could possibly need him.

There was a chart-plot on a broad table in the middle of the command center, an airy octagonal room with clear-wall all around providing a comprehensive view of Canopy Base in whatever direction one cared to look. The atmosphere containment dome was brightly luminous; its starlight catchers had to be powerful indeed, in the absence of a nearby star. Or else they were running on auxiliary power, which would require a very significant investment in small-heavies.

One way or another there was a great deal of money here. Andrej wondered who'd approved the business case, if Iosev was using family funds. He should ask Iosev, and see what happened. "We built Canopy Base when the Selection failed," Sorsa said, inviting Andrej to precede him into the room with a graceful gesture of his hand. "As soon as it became clear that Gonebeyond would no longer be under interdiction."

The Sixth Judge at Sant-Dasidar Judiciary, with the Combine in her purview, was obviously in favor of economic development, especially at private expense. Or had been assumed to be persuadable, at the very least; and if a man waited for all permissions to be granted nothing would ever get done.

Following Andrej as he walked slowly around the chart-plot table Sorsa continued. "This is our showroom, as it were. We bring people here to show them the services and support available, when they accept our offered partnership. A material demonstration of our sincerity, if his Excellency please."

There were five freighters shown on the dome-plex of the schematic, large ones, if Andrej read the scale correctly. Ten more ships, several of them on the ground; freighter-tenders. "On my arrival my debarkation was delayed, Deputy Sorsa," Andrej said. "I see no hint of any disorder. I congratulate you."

"We heartily regret having inconvenienced you, lord prince. One of our ships has suffered a motivation failure. If his Excellency would care to observe—" Sorsa pointed out of one clear-wall toward the launch-lanes with one hand. Andrej saw only a featureless free-standing structure, an enormous box as big as one of the cargo staging areas. "It was necessary to seal the vessel against any danger of explosion before we dared risk his Excellency's person. The blood, with his Excellency's permission, is sacred."

Yes, he knew. In the folk-tales of his childhood, there were no great events in history that could not be traced back to the mystical power of pure Aznir ancestry. As a boy he'd been required to memorize his generations all the way back to Dasidar and Dyraine; and been quizzed relentlessly on the precise details of his blood relations with all of the best families.

That childhood drill had come in useful in the years since; just this morning, as an example, with Shifan. "Would that my Nurail associates held so correct a view. If the spilling of my blood could sanctify, I dare say all of the hospital at Safehaven would be a holy ground."

It hadn't been twelve days since the latest would-be assassin had sliced him across the ribs. Safehaven's people had treated the injury with careful efficiency, either because they'd been embarrassed by Security's lapse or out of the pragmatic desire to minimize reduction of his duty hours; and *Chornije*'s medical stores had been more than adequate to requirements for aftercare. The wound was down to an almost minor irritation.

Which made the intensity of Sorsa's near-curse even more of a surprise. "And it is an offense beneath the canopy of Heaven." Andrej was startled; Sorsa knew about the attacks on him, at Safehaven? Had he spies, and if he did, why hadn't Andrej heard from Iosev before now? "In earlier times the Holy Mother would have known how to put an end to such a thing."

Such a thing, singular, rather than plural. Andrej put his surprise away, but kept it in a shallow store, close to the surface. Plebach had arrived shortly after the incident. He could easily have heard about the attack, and passed the information on. "Who knows if that would be a good thing, or not?" Andrej tapped the dome of the chart-plot. "These are large ships, Deputy Sorsa, what do they carry?"

"Supplies in." Sorsa looked around him with evident pride. "Good-will gifts from potential partners out. We are developing markets, lord prince. There is a great future for the Blood in Gonebeyond space, may I not give offense by saying so."

The arcane folk beliefs of the Dolgorukij Combine were of some sensitivity in this modern age, primitive, a little embarrassing. And tainted, to a significant degree, by their prominent role in Chuvishka Kospodar's regime during the reduction of Sarvaw, that led to his death in solitary confinement. Andrej examined the chart-plot, looking for something intelligent to say about it; Sorsa saved him the trouble. "But not without cost, lord prince. We have enemies."

"Enemies, or competition?" While the Combine was restrained by the superior power of the Jurisdiction's Fleet they'd been forced to abide by the Bench's trade regulations. Where would it go now that no single authority remained to hold all nine Judiciaries equally to one standard? "Without wishing to be rude, Deputy Sorsa, have you not my brother Iosev recruited to provide market advantage?"

Because he's useless, really, for anything else. Curious, Andrej tapped the floating image of one freighter with his index finger, and called up the status. *Combine mercantile ship* Petrofij, *Aznir registry, Aznir port of origin, Arakcheek shipyards. Small arms sixty-four units two hundred and fifty-six each. Field pieces fifty-six light installations.*

Sorsa tapped the freighter-trace again, but without haste—as if careful with potentially sensitive details rather than attempting to conceal the information. "Enemies, lord prince. Their malice has no cause but history, they seek no profit, no advantage, make no investment in the welfare of the less fortunate, only to thwart and prevent our enterprise. There were six people of ours killed at Oak Leaf, and of pure blood."

The story was shifting, then. Tapping the freighter manifest again, deliberately, Andrej held Sorsa's gaze, daring him to close the list and deny Andrej the information. Stun gas. Tearing agent. Riot control. Personal armor. An over-abundance of ammunition, or at least so it seemed to Andrej.

"This is not as you led me to believe, Deputy Sorsa." The settlement at Oak Leaf had not been armed. The people Andrej had treated were lucky to have survived. "Perhaps you care to explain to me how defense of hearth and home against armed extortion makes a man your enemy. And why you lied to me."

It was true there was no complete casualty count for

the other side. People could be telling the truth and mistaken at the same time. And yet—a freighter manifest that would equip a small army, and not a defensive one—

Deputy Sorsa bowed his head deeply. "His Excellency is right to ask." He sounded somber, but not ashamed. "Our offer was good, it was fair, it was generous. But someone else was moving amongst the people there, spreading lies and slander. The deaths on both sides are at their feet, not ours."

Andrej tapped the freighter manifest display off. "Explain." Was he beginning to believe, or perhaps only imagining, that he smelled the direction in which Sorsa was going?

"If his Excellency would consent to walk," Sorsa suggested, with an expression that said *not in front of the staff if his Excellency please*. All right; Andrej could accept that, and had no particular need to challenge Sorsa's authority by calling him to account in as public a place as his own command center.

Sorsa's aide Feraltz coded a new instruction as Andrej stepped into the lift, with Sorsa following. Feraltz seemed to be uncomfortable; understandable, Andrej thought. Feraltz had just heard Andrej call Deputy Sorsa a liar.

When the mover began to descend Sorsa spoke, facing the door, not looking at Andrej. "I said we were a new firm, lord prince, and I would not dare insult his Excellency by telling an untruth. It *is* new. But our funding comes from an old and powerful religious order, one whose divine Patron has suffered from octaves of relentless persecution by a concerted enemy."

Sorsa was Malcontent? That would be astonishing.

Waclav had said two others, and there were two men in
the lift beside Andrej. But the Malcontent didn't have an
ancestral enemy, to Andrej's knowledge. It was treated
rather as beneath contempt, by the rest of the Dolgorukij
religious establishment; that was one of its strengths.
Andrej waited.

"Since the days of our great work we have been
hounded, with no regard for how faithfully we have served
the Holy Mother's purpose. That is the enemy responsible
for the deaths of our people at Oak Leaf, yes, and for the
deaths of innocent people misled by deceit and armed by
treachery."

There'd been no hints of anybody "arming" the people
at Oak Leaf. Men and women—and children—had fought
with mining equipment, smelting equipment, kitchen
equipment, anything they could find. "Please continue."

"We will not allow it to happen again. Our enemy has
come to us, sending a man disguised as one we must
revere as the exemplar of one of the purest bloodlines that
remain to us in this degraded age. It's our chance to
avenge our dead, lord prince, to root out this
contemptible treachery, to stop the poisoning of
Gonebeyond space before it can go any further."

The lift had stopped, its tell-tales stabilized. The door
opened and Andrej stepped through into a quiet and well-
furnished office, Deputy Sorsa's perhaps. A beautiful
desk; several well-padded chairs; a rug of understated
quality, a rhyti-service. On the wall behind the desk there
was a framed image Andrej had seen before, one he
recognized even from across the room. One of his
ancestors. Chuvishka Kospodar.

Deputy Sorsa's voice had become urgent, confidential, intense. "His Excellency has spent a year serving as the chief medical officer in Safehaven, and is known throughout all Gonebeyond as the Nurail's friend—the champion of the Domitt Prison. Do I speak the truth, lord prince?"

Andrej nodded. He felt he was on ice so thin that he was afraid to guess what might be underneath the fragile surface that was fracturing beneath his feet. "This have I always hoped to be," he agreed. "With obvious qualifications." How could it be true, what Sorsa seemed to be saying? If the Malcontent were behind the night raiders—unbelievable as that was—would Waclav be working undercover? No. It was not possible.

Sorsa stepped up to address Andrej indirectly from the side, apparently not presuming in this crucial moment to engage him face-to-face. "No, lord prince, without qualifications. You are revered for your sense of justice, admired for your passion for the truth, honored for your leniency."

That was a highly creative restatement of the facts. Had Andrej not been so disturbed by the trend of Sorsa's words he might have admired its sheer effrontery; but there was more. "We need your assistance desperately, lord prince. We can restore to you the dominion that is yours by birth and blood, for which the Holy Mother Herself has fit and shaped you."

All right. It was out in the open. Andrej knew what Sorsa wanted from him. It all came down to torture. Sorsa offered him a cell that held a prisoner to be subject to his will, and praised the wolf that was starved for the sweet smell of blood as a sacred instrument of the Holy Mother's will.

"And yet she did not so shape the world," Andrej pointed out, not bothering to conceal the hunger in his voice. "You speak of things which are criminal, outside of Fleet. There is no authority in Gonebeyond that can lawfully direct my Writ."

But Sorsa waved this objection aside, albeit with exquisite respect. "How can the service of the Mother of all Aznir ever be unlawful? She Herself has set you apart from other men. The divine order in which I serve offers you its protection, lord prince, fields for the reaping, forests for the hunt. Accept your destiny. We kneel before you, pleading for your help—in this time of our greatest need—to combat our ancestral enemy."

Only one religious order under the Canopy of Heaven could make so categorical an offer with such absolute confidence. "The Malcontent?" Andrej said, slowly, struggling to understand. What use had the Malcontent for a torturer, when the saint's mission was that of reconciliation, not enforced obedience? And yet who else could speak to him of his passion for the pain of captive souls, without shame?

Sorsa nodded slowly, with an expression of deep compassion in his eyes. "Yes, lord prince," he said. "The Malcontent. That is the enemy. We beg you, the Holy Mother Herself intercedes with you on our behalf. Help us root out and punish those who murdered the victims of Oak Leaf as surely as if they had themselves wielded the weapons that their evil placed in deluded hands."

And Sorsa sank down onto his knees at Andrej's side,

bowing his head. To the ring Andrej wore, Andrej realized. His thrice-great-grandfather's ring, a family heirloom, sigil, seal. Not the Malcontent. Then who? Who was the Malcontent's deadly enemy, when the Malcontent was despised and contemned precisely for opposing itself to no moral failing, no personal degradation, howsoever vile?

"Help us," Sorsa repeated. "We beg for your assistance. We will see you satisfied for it, lord prince, we have it in our power to give you everything you desire in abundant measure, and with the Holy Mother's merciful blessing."

Who. Canopy Base. The Canopy of Heaven—where angels dwelt. Waclav was "unredeemed." The portrait of Chuvishka Kospodar. *Sometimes there is foulness that can only be spat out.* The mad dog, to speak the name of which was to spit. The Angel of Destruction. And Sorsa waited.

"Get up," Andrej commanded; and with a haughty gesture of his fingers granted Sorsa permission to kiss his hand. It was beyond belief. It was insane, impossible. And still the Malcontent was here, in the person of Cousin Waclav; so the threat was real, and the Angel of Destruction offered him a place in its organization. He would accept it. The Angel of Destruction had to be destroyed. "But don't toy with me. I'm hungry. No one could possibly understand how much I thirst."

Rising gracefully to his feet Sorsa stepped forward and away to face Andrej with another deep bow, one of what Andrej knew he was meant to believe was deep and heartfelt personal gratitude. Perhaps it was. He'd let Sorsa kiss his hand. He was engaged to this enterprise, now, on his sacred honor; and he would sacrifice that willingly, even any hope he might still cherish of redemption, to see this evil stopped.

"Indeed not, lord prince." Sorsa nodded at Feraltz, who moved to open a door at the far side of the room. The man who came in was uniformed, shockingly so: Ship's Inquisitor. A renegade, then, a deserter. "We are holding the enemy's agent here on site, hoping for your aid. Time is our enemy. Dr. Mathin has been of assistance, but you are heaven-sent to us in our hour of greatest need."

"Who did you say?" Andrej demanded. The skin of his hand seemed to blister where Sorsa had touched it with his lips. Andrej apologized prayerfully to the knife he'd sheathed along his forearm for placing it in such close proximity to this corruption, knowing that it had been Joslire's knife, holy steel, shield and defender and sacred legacy.

"Chief Medical Officer Mathin," the man said. Clearly nervous, his voice only barely sustaining his show of confidence. "Lately of the Jurisdiction Fleet Ship *Margidap*. May I say how great an honor it is to meet you."

"*Margidap* has a Brief for Gonebeyond?" Andrej asked mockingly. "I don't think so. You are not Chief Medical Officer of anything, you are a deserter and untrue to your oath, let us be clear on this. It's no surprise that Deputy Sorsa seeks out a better man."

He'd obviously thrown Mathin into confusion, as he had intended. Mathin dropped his eyes. "Ah, recruited," he repeated. "Serving the greater good, filling a need—"

Whoring for specie. "Report." Andrej didn't care to hear the rest of Mathin's transparent self-justification. Sorsa had said there was a prisoner. If Mathin had made a start Andrej had something to work with. He'd have to make an examination; then he would find such fault with Mathin's work that he could not go forward until repairs had been made. It was going to be difficult. He smelled blood. He wanted more.

Pulling himself together Mathin bowed with exaggerated precision. "Three sessions, fourth to fifth level," he said. "Failure to comply. On orders the exercise was terminated prematurely, prisoner is stable in cell—"

An irritated sound from Sorsa stopped Mathin before he got any further, but Andrej's interest had already been aroused. There *was* an Inquiry in progress, then, and it had been initiated without him. All of Sorsa's talk about needing him—had that been based only on Mathin's failure?

"Excuse him, lord prince," Sorsa said, with an angry glare at Mathin. "Mathin, the *special* prisoner, the one with whom we so particularly need his Excellency's assistance." Oh, so there were at least two for him. *All to the good*, his passion whispered in his mind, his body already stirring to obscene interest. It had been so long.

"Ah," Mathin said, covered in confusion like an atonement-cake in bitter herbs. "Yes. Your pardon, your Excellency. Class six hominid, Aznir national, system of origin Dolgorukij Combine. Adult male of approximately thirty-seven years of age Standard. Physical health apparently good, no measures yet initiated, in custody for a little less than one day."

"Aznir," Andrej said to Sorsa. Because he had to know. He was the one who had brought Waclav into the kitchen. But he'd seen Waclav not four hours ago; and there was no way in which these people would call Waclav any sort of Aznir. "An Aznir Malcontent is responsible for this?"

Sorsa took a deep breath. "Worse even than that, lord prince," Sorsa said. So Sorsa had been holding information back even yet, releasing it bit by bit as he grew confident of Andrej's compliance. What test could Sorsa hold still in reserve, before he would trust Andrej, and let him start to work? "Best bring him in, Mathin."

The door at the far side of the room opened again. Three men came through; one in advance shackled and bound, two behind to manage him. The man was familiar. Shockingly so. One of the guards prodded him in the back; he raised his head, and met Andrej's stunned gaze straight on.

"This object was once his Excellency's kinsman," Sorsa said, carefully, clearly testing for Andrej's response. "Who gained entrance to our base and our confidence by a masquerade. Had his Excellency's timely arrival not exposed the deception we might not have discovered the imposture until it was too late. Truly the Holy Mother watches over us."

It was Stoshi. Andrej's cousin Stanoczk.

He had very little time to decide how to react. Crossing the room to where Stoshi stood guarded and trammeled he searched Stoshi's face, his mind racing. Two more Malcontents, Waclav had said. They meant for him to torture his own kinsman; and not just any kinsman but a man he'd loved all of his life. The companion of his childhood, separated from him by circumstance, so recently restored to him by the Malcontent's mercy.

"Stoshi." It didn't matter if Sorsa read his voice. Sorsa would expect a reaction. But for it to work he had to yield; he had to let the hunger in him speak, and be sure he kept the wolf's leash in a steady grip because he could not afford a single mis-step. "What are you doing here?"

That was the way. His voice was familiar in his own ears from times gone past, a life he'd thought behind him; slightly mocking, with a whisper-slim sliver of anticipation, and the promise of punishment. The hunger was strong in his heart and in his body. The wolf struck hard against the barricade he had built up to contain it, but he had to stand firm.

"I might ask of you the same question, Derush." There was no message for him there in Stoshi's voice, nothing to hear and take heed of. There couldn't be, Andrej realized. Sorsa was here, Sorsa was good, and neither of them could risk showing their tiles. Andrej had no idea what tiles were even in play.

But Stoshi had come here, into a place where he was hated. He had surrendered the protection of the Malcontent, the red ribbon that stamped him as the Saint's property. Any man could profane Stoshi's person with impunity. He had come in the person of Andrej Koscuisko on the Malcontent's business; then Andrej had arrived, and put it all at risk.

"You do not speak to me in such words." Andrej spoke softly, gently, so that Sorsa would have to strain to hear him. "To impersonate an officer of my rank is a Tenth

Level offense, under Jurisdiction. But to impersonate *me* is even more serious than that. Why have you come?"

It felt like a very long moment, as Stoshi searched his eyes. Then Stoshi spat on the floor at Andrej's feet. That was the message; that was the charm; that was the final thing that Andrej needed to know. Stoshi had the water in his mouth to spit, the courage in his heart to prosecute his purpose—whatever it was—no matter what it cost. *Do what you must, Derush, do not fail me. There will be a way.*

So he drew back his arm and struck Stoshi across the face so hard that he could see the white track of his fingers on Stoshi's cheek, the skin reddening.

"Manners," Andrej said. One more thing he was going to have to do, because he had to be convincing. He couldn't just pretend, not with himself, and not with Sorsa. He had to resurrect the worst in himself. He would have to unleash the wolf and let it feed. Whatever Stoshi had come to do, Andrej could not let it come to nothing. He needed time to understand, to plan a way out of this. He knew how to find it.

Turning to face Deputy Sorsa—who had come near, and stood now, watching, listening—Andrej took a deep shuddering breath, emptying his face, opening his heart, closing his eyes. "Oh, it has been so long," he said. When he opened his eyes again Sorsa's face had changed; he'd paled, but stood his ground, if with an evident effort. "You have suitable arrangements made? Show them to me."

Was it possible, he wondered, that Sorsa had second thoughts, face to face with the monster that Andrej knew himself to be? No. It was mere shock, but gratification followed after. He stood confirmed before Sorsa now as a man with a passionate weakness. Such men could be managed, and—with the heightened awareness that the scent of prey had always given him—Andrej knew that Sorsa meant to manage him.

It wouldn't work. Andrej had had four years of being managed by Captain Lowden, and there were no bond-involuntaries here for Sorsa to hold hostage against Andrej's best behavior. "Ready and waiting, lord prince," Sorsa confirmed. "We have also the Controlled List in inventory, should his Excellency wish to make use of it—"

"Drug assist?" Andrej interrupted, scornfully. "You do not advise me, Sorsa, I am master in this. Cousin Stanoczk will not have come without preparation, training, development of relative immunities." The Controlled List? Poison. Wake-keepers. Pain-maintenance drugs. Lethally powerful hypnotics, sedatives, addictive drugs. Several of his own formulations were there. "Also, you have promised me. I will have dominion. I take it by force, and by my own hand."

"You do not dare, Andrej, the Malcontent—" Stoshi's voice behind Andrej's back was stopped mid-sentence; Andrej could guess the cause. He held up one hand, and all sounds of sentence-interrupting activity ceased. Turning around he took Stoshi's face between his two hands, tenderly.

"I am very sorry, my dear," he said, and kissed Stoshi between the eyes, standing forehead-to-forehead with him for an achingly long moment. He was utterly sincere. The flesh beneath his hands was his. A man he loved, his. One he had known from childhood, his. He knew what

Stoshi was afraid of, where he hurt best and most. They were both Aznir Dolgorukij. Dolgorukij wore like iron, in Secured Medical. "You have brought this on yourself. You are no longer my kinsman."

Then he stepped away, nodding to the Security behind Stoshi to take their charge in hand. It was going to work. He could do what needed to be done to work this through. He would enjoy it. He knew all of these things; because what Stoshi held for Andrej in his eyes was a gift of inestimable value.

Andrej had opened the door in his heart to lust and savagery, because that was the only way he could move forward. And Stoshi with breathtaking courage opened his heart in turn, and let Andrej see that Stoshi was afraid of him.

His life, Stoshi's life, Waclav's, who knew how many other lives, depended now on his ability to play the role of the man he had once been. And on Andrej's ability to hold on to the man he had become, in the face of a hunger-maddened passion that could blind and deafen him, absorb him and consume him with the transcendent ecstasy of inflicted pain.

The Holy Mother only knew where the doorway was, that would lead them all safely out of here; but only Andrej could buy them time in which to find it.

CHAPTER SIX

Walking Between

Stildyne woke suddenly, squinting and blinking, trying to make sense of what he was seeing. They'd been dismantling the quarters in which they'd been shut up, looking for a way out; and after a day's labor they'd found a way into the space between the ceiling and the floor above them. There'd been something. Godsalt had said something about gas, Godsalt could smell it, the rest of them hadn't. Then there was nothing.

This ceiling was not the same as that in guest quarters. More cell-like. Probably because it was a cell, by all appearances. "Wakies." That was Pyotr's voice. "Good news, Chief. We've found Lek and Robert."

Taking the hand that was offered him Stildyne lurched gracelessly to his feet. The cell was an open-faced model, barred on one side but otherwise offering a clear field of vision; its shutters were there, but not deployed. So someone wanted them to be able to look around. So Stildyne did.

The room was too big for a clinic. He didn't see any medical equipment, apart from a few standard resuscitation machines; so they weren't in Infirmary. There were monitors everywhere, and a tee-post in the middle of the room. Right. Torture palace. Were they expected to be intimidated?

"Talk to me," Stildyne suggested. Of course he was intimidated. He knew what went on in places like this. It didn't need Koscuisko to make it Hell; Koscuisko only ratcheted up the intensity to truly transcendent heights.

Pyotr didn't answer. Someone else did. "Chief." That was not someone in with them; someone outside. But not in the main room, in another cell. And it was Lek. This was good, Stildyne told himself, firmly. "Report, Mister Kerenko."

"One troop down. One disgusted. They have their own Inquisitor, somebody named Mathin." He wasn't sure he was getting Lek; it sounded like he'd said there was an Inquisitor here. His brain was obviously still fogged in. "They've been at Robert, but they laid off, sometime yesterday, I think. Going by the doses. We get doses. Doses for Robert, I mean. Commercial enterprise, Chief."

Lek sounded a little fog-brained himself. Stildyne put his forehead to the bars. No shock field. All of those monitors. If there was an Inquisitor there was a Record, but this couldn't be Fleet. If it was, Robert wouldn't be tortured. He'd be re-implanted with a governor; then they wouldn't need to exert themselves to torture him.

Closing his eyes Stildyne listened carefully to Lek's voice. How long had they been separated now? Two days? Longer? "How bad is it?" Stildyne asked. Going by the sound of Lek's voice he was holding together fairly well; but the strain was showing, for people who knew how to listen.

"Level five, augmented, pushing level six." Stildyne controlled his involuntary wince as best he could. "Supportive medication in effect. No gross bodily injury to critical systems. Worried about his face, though, may have lost his boyish beauty. Neural rasp."

And hadn't that been fun, for both of them? "You?" He thought he knew the answer, but the question needed asking all the same, because he couldn't see Lek's face.

"Front-row seat, Chief, being softened up. Wouldn't hand over the comp-keys, all upset, can't remember them at all."

"No harm done, then." It was all he could think of to say at the moment. "Anything else you can tell us?"

"Yes." He heard a little grunting from next door; he didn't think it was Lek. After a moment's delay—some words low-voiced that Stildyne couldn't quite catch—Lek's voice was back. "Sorsa called it off. Threatened Mathin. 'Wait till he sees what you've done,' that sort of thing." This was good. This would imply that Cousin Stanoczk had intervened. Wouldn't it? "But then they brought our cousin in and threw him into his own cell. We haven't talked."

This was getting worse again. If these people had suspended Robert's torture on Stoshi's say-so, why had Stoshi been arrested? And if Stoshi's disguise had failed, why let Robert off the hook, who were they threatening Mathin with?

"They took him away just as you were coming to." There was a touch of humor in Lek's voice. Emotional resilience was the hallmark of a bond-involuntary, well, that and a governor, of course. "Nice long naps, all of you. What hit you, anyway?"

"Ah." The others could fill Lek in just as well, but they'd all clearly caught those hints of Robert stirring, and were leaving him to it. "We were breaking out, but they had sleeping gas. Are they going to feed us? Because I'm thirsty."

"Four, five times," Lek said, but he was clearly guessing. "Maybe six. I forget. And Robert's just taking doses and going back to sleep, so I've had plenty."

"Is he moving much?" *Or will we have to carry him*, an unspoken question and a promise. *Because we're getting out.*

"Probably not walking, Chief." There was that note of desperate amusement. "Just be knocking into things anyway. Really unhappy about the look of his left eye." Not good. They'd need to factor in a dead weight. Stildyne had expected that, but it was still bad news.

"You rest," Stildyne said. Lek had enough on his plate. "We'll come up with a brilliant plan. We'll let you know." Maybe there wasn't one this time. Maybe they weren't getting out of this. Maybe somebody had set it all up just to get the thula. Except that the Malcontent didn't have to come up with a plot diabolical and arcane to recover the thula, it was the Malcontent's thula, and everybody knew it.

The door to the torture-room slid open. The quarantine wall fell across the face of the cell, but they could still see out, of course—just not be seen. Someone short and blond and probably Dolgorukij went sprawling at full length onto the floor with the force of the shove that had propelled him; someone whose obvious peril wrenched Stildyne's heart, because he didn't know which one of them it was, and loved them both.

Needed them, too, either or both, to get them all safely out of here, and then explain the entire mess to him either over a game of tiles or between the sheets. The man on the floor started to raise himself, pushing himself up, looking back over his shoulder with an expression of undisguised apprehension at the people who'd followed him in. Station security. A man Stildyne supposed might be Deputy Sorsa.

And, closing in on the man on the floor with a keen and feral hunger that Stildyne knew all too well, a man about whose exact identity there was no possible ambiguity.

Andrej didn't know what time it was, or how long it had been. He remembered that, from the old days. Time and again he'd been surprised by the appearance of his mid-meal, or his fast-meal, when he hadn't realized that any time had passed since Security had brought—and he'd ignored—the last one.

His only regret was that he hadn't had time to set Joslire's knives safely aside. He did his best not to bring them into the torture-room, out of respect; when he did, he generally passed them to one of his Security. He didn't have access to his Security. He wasn't supposed to know that they were there, but he'd seen the quarantine wall descending as he'd entered the room, and everything else followed necessarily.

Stoshi lay half-stripped and shuddering on the floor in front of him. Andrej sat in his chair and smoked his lefrol, admiring the view. He knew the shaking in Stoshi's body; it was fear, not pain, that made Stoshi tremble there with his arms clutched tightly around his head, his fingers white with the effort of trying to shield himself from something against which there was no defense.

It was only reasonable to be afraid. Andrej appreciated it, in Stoshi, because it had been so long that the beast within his heart was far more easily sated than it might have been. Right now fear was almost as good as pain, which meant there didn't have to be so much pain as long as there was enough fear. There had to be enough pain to engender fear, honest and naked. That was an unavoidable fact. It bound them both.

Listening to his body, savoring the golden warmth of appetite stoked and fed and satisfied, Andrej smoked his lefrol, waiting for Stoshi to recover himself a little. "I will tell you nothing," Stoshi insisted, though Andrej hadn't spoken. Stoshi's voice was unsteady with his struggle to manage his body's terror of known and anticipated agony. "I must not fail.—I want something to drink, Derush."

Stoshi was supposed to talk to him. He couldn't do that if his mouth was dry. Hours ago he'd been able to spit; now he could hardly speak. "Who's there?" Andrej called out over his shoulder, at the now-closed door.

Someone was watching, or at least listening, or he'd know the reason why. It wasn't his Security's fault that they couldn't come when he called them.

The door opened; Sorsa's confidential aide stepped into the room, closing the door behind him before he spoke. "I serve you at this time, lord prince," he said. "His Excellency requires?"

If Feraltz wasn't Security, he was the next best thing. He gave no sign of either revulsion or gloating in the presence of his ancestral enemy reduced and suffering. "Bring to me a large pitcher of merbar juice. You have it in stores? Yes?" It had been Stoshi's favorite, when they'd been children. "Good. I want it well-sweetened. Two glasses. Ice."

Stoshi was in shock, and needed glucose. True, doses would deliver glucose as easily, but there was comfort in a glass of fruit juice that would serve as its own insulation against the emotional insult Stoshi's mind had sustained from the pain and fear in Stoshi's body. What had Stoshi said? He would not fail? But he *had* failed. It had been Andrej's fault, not Stoshi's, that his arrival had laid bare the imposture; but wasn't it Stoshi's fault that Andrej had come at all?

Andrej had only wanted to meet with his Security, and apologize to Brachi Stildyne. That was why he had come to Gonebeyond. If Stoshi had bothered to arrange it in good time—rather than leaving him to stew for a year at Safehaven—Andrej would never have come to Canopy Base. He pushed Stoshi over onto his back on the floor, and leaned in close.

"You will tell me everything," Andrej said. It was a

plain matter of fact. "Start with the names of those within the Angel's organization who led you to Canopy Base. You create only difficulties for yourself, Stoshi, should you not accept your defeat, and spare yourself more suffering?"

Andrej didn't bother to pretend that he was sincere. Stoshi would not believe him; and Sorsa would expect him to conform to expectation, to jeer, to mock. "Do not pretend." Stoshi sounded bitter. But not as bitter as he was going to be. As carefully as Andrej had managed him Andrej knew, as Stoshi could not, how much more intense a fear Stoshi had in him, and how well-founded. "You are enjoying this."

No, I am enjoying you. But Feraltz had come with merbar juice and glasses, and a table and a tray followed behind. Was he hungry? No. Did the sight and smell of food entice him? Yes. Physical exercise required fuel. Andrej poured two glasses of juice and moved up out of his chair, sitting down on the floor beside Stoshi's head.

"Come up," he said, and lifted Stoshi off the ground, to lean on Andrej for support and drink a glass of cold sweet merbar juice. "Go slowly, my dear, you'll give yourself a cramp. You may have more. Only don't drink too fast."

The room was kept warm, to stave off the partial insulation that shock might provide the prisoner. Andrej appreciated the ice-chill of the juice. Excellent juice. Someone had mixed a kiss of extract of dawn-flowers into the drink, so subtle that it intensified the flavor of the ripe fruit rather than tasting of itself. Waclav's doing, perhaps. There was a message there, then. *You are not alone*. And who was Waclav's other cousin, then? Or had Andrej misinterpreted the necessarily oblique reference, two more bites of soup, two more Malcontents?

Stoshi drank with the exhausted air of a man who had forgotten where he was, a sort of drunkenness Andrej recognized. He refilled Stoshi's glass half-way, because while Stoshi needed the glucose it would all come right back up again if he had too much too quickly; and it wasn't reasonable to demand that Stoshi remember what Andrej had just said.

When Stoshi had finished his half-a-glass Andrej offered him some savories from the plate and Stoshi took them, bit by bit, as Andrej shared them out. For a while they sat together peaceably on the floor, leaning up against one another, eating from a common dish with their fingers just as they had when they'd been children together.

Then Stoshi's breathing changed. He was recovering himself. Letting Stoshi's weight slump slowly back down onto the floor, Andrej stood up. Where were the people that should be here to pick up plates and glasses for him? For all the excellence of Sorsa's establishment this was still an informal environment. He would see some changes made.

"It is time for you to talk to me, Stoshi." Stoshi shook his head. Andrej knew what that meant. It was the gesture of a child trying to cling to comfort and tranquility—in vain. "You must face up to it, my dear, you've lost. You've failed. And you will tell me everything I ask."

Stoshi shook his head again, but with more emphasis, frowning, staring at the ceiling. There were touch-points in the ceiling that Stoshi might want to avoid noticing, if he knew what they were for. Suspensions. Not always an option with taller men, unless one made adjustments, but Stoshi and he were very much of a height. That would have been among the critical elements in attempting the imposture with good hope of success.

If he stretched Stoshi from the ceiling, though, it would be that much more difficult to shield poor Stoshi's body from Stildyne's eyes, if Stildyne was still there, if Stildyne was still watching, and Andrej was convinced that he was.

"Take away, here," he called, because he didn't want tables standing where they could be tipped over. When Feraltz came in Andrej had orders for him. "What time is it? Come back in three hours, with third-meal. I may have something of interest for you then." Or maybe not. It didn't matter. He wasn't sure he cared. Stoshi had had a little rest, a little sustenance; but Andrej had had rest and sustenance as well.

Now he was ready to begin again.

Stildyne stood at the front of the cell watching it all through the one-way barrier of the quarantine wall. He knew why they let him watch; prisoners were to see what horrors awaited them, hear the anguish in the voices of tortured souls, learn to watch the torturer with the hungry fascination of a beaten animal who knew there was only one possible source of solace and release and it was the same man who would brutalize them.

He'd been living in torture-rooms for more than ten years. He could tolerate the duty; he had the stomach for it, if not the taste. Once he'd proved that, any prospects for reassignment had diminished to almost nil; and when he'd been offered the promotion that would have removed him from Secured Medical he had turned it down, because it would have meant leaving Andrej Koscuisko.

He'd thought he'd known what suffering was when he'd found his sister's dead body and known what his father had done to her, and her not eight years old. He'd been fifteen. But he'd been big for his age, toughened and hardened by life in the streets, and when he'd gone to the recruiting station there'd been no questions asked. He'd washed up before he went. There'd been no blood on his hands or his clothing.

He'd thought he'd known despair when he had watched, week after week, the corrosive effects of Captain Lowden's management on Koscuisko's sanity, as the prisoners in Secured Medical kept coming one after another; and every day—it seemed—could be the one on which Koscuisko's ferocious struggle to hold fast to his own humanity might fail, finally and forever.

He'd thought he'd known what guilt felt like during that long night in the waiting room outside the surgery in Port Burkhayden, as the staff struggled to extract a dying governor—insane and vengeful—from the brain of Robert St. Clare and save his life. He'd been the one who'd deliberately pushed it into its final fits of unimaginable torture to shut Robert up before he could incriminate himself. And he'd done it just so Koscuisko wouldn't have to execute a man he loved.

All of those times he had been wrong. He couldn't avenge Stoshi on Koscuisko as he had avenged his sister on his father, because although it was Stoshi who suffered it was Andrej Koscuisko who made him suffer. He couldn't reach out to Koscuisko to steady and support him because he couldn't reach, he was behind a quarantine wall, and the prisoner who tested Koscuisko's sanity was Stildyne's friend and lover. There was nothing he could do but stand and watch and suffer.

He'd shaken off the hand on his shoulder before. When someone put a hand to his shoulder a second time he tried to shake it off again, but failed. Raising his hand he tried to push it away, but its grip just tightened. He couldn't see what Koscuisko was doing. Koscuisko had his back turned, and there was the chair between them. But he could hear all the same.

There were two hands now, one on each shoulder. Two people, taking him by the arms, turning him around. They pulled him into the back of the cell as far from the quarantine wall as they could get and clustered around him closely, fencing him in with their arms around each others' shoulders so that he had to stretch to see. It was no good. They were as tall as he was, and their heads were in the way.

There was nothing left for him to do except the one thing he hadn't, the thing he'd never, the thing he couldn't. The thing he hadn't done when his sister had died from his father's brutal rape or when Lowden had sent Koscuisko back to a fresh prisoner or when Robert lay dying in agony because Stildyne had needed him to stop talking.

He bowed his head against the nearest shoulder, and wept.

⊕ ⊕ ⊕

"I came here to gain the trust of the senior leadership," Stoshi repeated wearily, rolling his head back and forth restlessly where Andrej held it cradled in the crook of his arm. "Sorsa is well-placed, but still working up in the hierarchy. This we infer. It's a good point of entry. I've told you."

"And you've lied," Andrej admonished him, gently, bringing the shock-rod he held in his other hand up in front of Stoshi's face to remind him of why he was talking. "We both know that's not true. Why did you present yourself as me? What is so important, Stoshi? You'll have to do much better than that."

Stoshi struggled in his arms, but Stoshi was tired, and Andrej could control him. He let the uncertainty of the moment draw out; then he laid the shock-rod to Stoshi's unprotected belly. Not the most obvious target, no, but there was a place midway between a man's hip and his genitals where the nerve bundle connected with the trunk line that when shocked induced a full-body spasm that could persist for long, long moments after the stimulus was removed.

A shock-rod didn't inflame the nerve as badly as a neural rasp would do, or burn a bloody hole through flesh and blacken living bone as quickly as a fire-point might. It was convenient and appropriate, in that sense. Andrej sat and held Stoshi for a long time as Stoshi struggled for his breath.

"Well, think about it," Andrej said, and kissed Stoshi's forehead. "I'll come back to you in a little while. I think we've made a good start, don't you?"

Eight hours, nine perhaps. It would have seemed like much, much longer to Stoshi, and that was too bad, but couldn't be helped. It seemed like no time at all to Andrej: but there were things he needed to do, and Stoshi was going to lose his ability for coherent thought sometime soon.

There was a danger, small but real, that Stoshi's breaking point was closer to the surface than Andrej believed it to be. Stoshi's despair—his anguish over the failure of his mission, so easily transformed in a man's mind to guilt—resonated in Stoshi powerfully, increasing his vulnerability to pain and fear. If he was not very careful, Stoshi might say something neither of them wanted him to. Andrej didn't know what it was; which made it all the more important to be careful.

Laying Stoshi down onto the floor Andrej stood up, and walked a few paces in the general direction of the rhyti-brewer. "Feraltz." It was time to try something. Somebody had been watching all this time; there was no reason for there to be monitors if no one was using them.

There were a few moments of silence before the door opened and Feraltz came in. He had people with him, carrying another table covered with dishes presumably of food. Promising. Andrej was hungry. He'd been working hard.

"His Excellency's third-meal?" Feraltz asked. The others with Feraltz were keeping their eyes carefully lowered, but—Andrej told himself with amusement—it would do them no good. Stoshi lay on the floor. His posture was expressive enough of the torture he had suffered.

"Thank you, I'll take it in quarters." Walking past the

place where Stoshi cowered on the floor Andrej found the waist-high shelf on the back wall and started to move some of his tools around. Lowering his voice he spoke to the wall, keeping his back turned deliberately. "Let me see. Leaf-cutter? Peony, oh, yes, it's been a long time, I wonder . . . "

"I beg your pardon, lord prince," Feraltz said, loudly, from near the door. "His Excellency requires—" Of course Feraltz couldn't quite hear him. Andrej glanced over his shoulder with an impatient scowl.

"I said I want . . . " He turned back to the equipment shelf as he spoke. " . . . this. No. Maybe that. I'm tired. I need to rest." *Keep talking. Make him come to you. Show him no mercy.* None of them but Stoshi deserved it; and Stoshi would have none from him. He couldn't afford to extend any.

"Begging to be excused," Feraltz said, quietly—not wanting to expose subordinate staff to Andrej's temper, perhaps. He'd stepped up very close to Andrej now, which was right where Andrej wanted him. The habit of a lifetime, of generations past, the blood of the wolf in his blood—Andrej let it speak.

"Mister Feraltz." He hissed it with as much savagery as he felt in his body for his poor cousin. "You are between me and my prisoner. Never do that, do you hear me—" Turning on his heel he spun around suddenly to the attack, viciously. "Do not. Ever. Step between me and my prisoner." Everybody could hear him, now. His rebuke struck Feraltz like a kick in the belly—as it was meant to; Feraltz backed up hastily, all bowed head and paled face and apologies.

"Yes, lord prince, of course, I sincerely regret my ignorance, I have no understanding of—of the protocol, in such matters, I crave instruction—" Feraltz was off balance, Andrej saw, with a sense of satisfaction. He hadn't lost his touch. Only part of it was practice, of course; the rest was pure instinct. He was Koscuisko, and he would be master here.

"What do you mean by that? Are you uncomfortable, Feraltz? Do you wish you were not here?" He let the question stand on its own for a moment, because he didn't think Feraltz would be able to muster an answer. "I need people who know what they're doing, to take charge of my prisoner."

Moving forward as he spoke Andrej backed Feraltz toward the door, deliberately driving him toward where Stoshi lay. It worked. Feraltz tripped over Stoshi's body and fell over backwards. Andrej reached for Feraltz and pulled him bodily up off of the floor, snarling at him ferociously.

"Nor are you to strike my prisoner, nor indeed to touch him, unless and until you are bidden to it, what's the matter with you people? I thought you already had an Inquisitor here, what has he been doing with you, to leave you all so ignorant? You are useless, all of you. You are worse than useless."

The point was worth emphasizing. Loosing Feraltz with an impatient shake and a hard shove Andrej glared at him, and Feraltz continued his retreat. He was handling himself well under Andrej's assault, Andrej noted; maybe he had prior experience with abusive autocrats—Iosev, perhaps.

"Again I ask for your pardon, lord prince. Security will be here shortly. With respect, Doctor Mathin has a different style, we are—as you justly state—ignorant, we seek only to know your will to do it."

All very satisfying, submissive language. "I'll have none of your Security." There was a risk associated with letting anyone examine Stoshi. Someone might notice how carefully Andrej had tried to minimize the damage, if not the suffering, he'd inflicted.

No one who reviewed the monitors could doubt he'd hurt Stoshi excellently well; Andrej's entire body resonated pleasurably with its physical reaction to Stoshi's pain, and yet he'd been so very careful. Stoshi might never be able to understand or to forgive, but he would not be a cripple, he would carry no reminder in his body, not if Andrej was lucky and the Saint could grant his agent any protection.

"If his Excellency will direct us, we will unfailingly—"

"Release Stildyne to me." It was an order. Andrej made sure of his tone of voice, *I will tolerate not even so much as a single moment's hesitation*. Turning his back he returned to Stoshi to glare down at him, his hands on his hips in his best "imperious and irritated" manner; and waited.

"'Stildyne,' lord prince? I don't understand."

"This is Cousin Stanoczk, a Malcontent. He came here in the person of Andrej Koscuisko, who stands before you. Mere personal disguise would be insufficient to put over such an imposture. Therefore he must have arrived in a manner consistent with my rank and identity. On the thula."

He didn't turn around. Eye contact would give Feraltz a connection that Andrej meant to deny him. "I stopped at Langsarik Station to see my people; they were not there. So the Malcontent brought them to Canopy Base as part of his disguise. Do you refuse me the use of them, Feraltz? I am accustomed to intelligent service in Inquiry."

Leaving poor Stoshi where he lay Andrej walked over to the left side of the room to stand in front of the quarantine wall, folding his arms over his chest. Somewhere behind there were the crew of the thula. One of them might have been tortured on Sorsa's orders by that hack Mathin. Why was that? Why would that have been considered necessary?

Sorsa had said that Andrej's landing had been delayed because there was a ship that had to be contained. The containment structure hid the ship completely. So the ship was the thula, and it was locked. So Sorsa had been having one of the crew tortured. So they were here in cells so that they could watch and take the usual lesson.

He'd try this, then, he'd considered it more than once during the past hours when he'd a moment to catch his breath; and put it off each time as inopportune. He knew what a control panel should look like; a man expected to have the means to raise and lower the quarantine wall as he wished. Toggling the switch with an impatient gesture Andrej turned his back to the wall, sure of his point—and wanting above everything not to have to look at the reproach, if not hatred, he would at last see in Stildyne's eyes, after so many years of deserving it.

He heard the quarantine wall lifting, behind him.

Feraltz had sent the men with the table out of the room; to call for Sorsa, perhaps. Now through the open door to the torture theater Andrej heard people hurrying to approach.

The noise stopped. Sorsa would want to catch his breath before he came in. Andrej risked a glance over his shoulder; Pyotr, Hirsel, Garrity, Godsalt. Stildyne. He made it the briefest of glances, because he dreaded what he might see in their eyes, and because Lek and Robert were not there.

Of course. Lek would be the primary suspect in any motivation problem. But where was Robert? Andrej walked past the front of one cell to the next. Kerenko was on his knees near the back, with Robert in his arms; and Robert's face was badly bruised. He had that looseness of limb that betokened deep sedation—the kind required after torture. Mathin.

Fourth to fifth level, Mathin had said. That seemed a little light, to Andrej; and to judge from the look on Lek's face Lek concurred. Lek would know. What Andrej didn't see was hatred in Lek's eyes, for Stoshi's torturer; Lek showed him the bond-involuntary's mask of professional detachment, but there was something important underneath. *Good. You're here. Now let's get out.* So they understood.

"Gentlemen," he said, moving back to look into the cell with Stildyne. "I trust I find you well. I have work for you."

They'd had time to compose themselves, masks in place. Professional bond-involuntary troops, painstakingly taught to give no sign of pity for a tortured man in Inquiry.

Stildyne was not a bond-involuntary. Stoshi had told him once, however, that he might as well be, and left Andrej to decide which of several impertinences Stoshi might have meant. "Indeed well, your Excellency, except for St. Clare," Stildyne said. "With respect, you'll want to look into that, sir."

Andrej knew how to hear the suffering in Stildyne's voice, as Sorsa would not. Sorsa was coming into the room now; Andrej ignored him. "I'm surprised to see you here." Surprised, dismayed, but also deeply hopeful. Where there were his Security, his gentlemen, where there was Brachi Stildyne there was hope. "How did you come to be misled by—" he gestured at Stoshi contemptuously, for Sorsa's benefit "—this object?"

"He wore an armature cloak, and kept to his cabin. We know how to stay out of your way, your Excellency." There was more there, but Sorsa wouldn't wait patiently forever, and Andrej needed this interview on record; if for no other reason than to establish Security's innocence of any involvement in the plot.

"And you were led to take his identity on faith. I understand." He had to look at Stildyne. He had to. Whether it was simply the amnesia of long absence or the effects of the stress of these past few hours, Andrej found Stildyne less ugly than he had ever been in his life; which was strange, because Stildyne's face was drawn and pale.

Looking Stildyne in the eye Andrej was overwhelmed, for one brief moment, by how ashamed he was of how he'd treated Stildyne, how glad he was to see Stildyne, how much he'd missed Stildyne's company. "We didn't understand why you would deny yourself to us, your

Excellency," Stildyne said. "But you're the officer, and we were glad to be of service. Until a few hours ago we believed him to be you."

Nodding slowly in a token of acceptance—a public signal for Sorsa and Feraltz, *he's telling the truth, they had no part in it*—Andrej turned slowly to face Sorsa, who bowed deeply and stayed at the bottom of his bow for a long moment. Acknowledging his fault. "Deputy Sorsa."

Only now did Sorsa straighten up. Andrej had to admire the perfection of his manners, as much as he wanted to despise everything about the man. Sorsa was intelligent, quick, all too insightful. "I apologize deeply, lord prince. I should have told you that we had the thula and its crew in custody. I feared awkwardness that would end my chances of enlisting his Excellency's vital assistance."

"It would have been better had you told me, yes." But, yes, it would certainly have impacted Andrej's ability to convince Sorsa of his own willingness to be persuaded, so he was glad—on balance—that he hadn't known going in. "But I understand your decision." Rebuke; followed immediately by dismissal of the error. Forward from there. "Since they are here I can use them. I wish them to take charge of the prisoner after I have examined him, can it be done?"

Meaning, of course, *it will be done*. Sorsa's quite reasonable concerns were to be expected nonetheless. "Are you sure of this, lord prince? They've been crewing the thula, a very valuable resource—which speaks of a close relationship with this Malcontent. Might not their sympathies work to the frustration of his Excellency's purpose?"

"Deputy Sorsa." Taking Sorsa's arm, Andrej walked with him toward the door. *Our interview is very soon now over.* "They have been with me for six years, Robert even longer. They know better than to have sympathies. They know I will find them out, and what to expect when I do. Is this not adequate assurance?"

And I have directed that it be so. In a perfect world that should be all there was to it. But he'd let Sorsa kiss his hand. He was obliged to at least hear the best counsel Sorsa could offer; though not to take action on it.

"As best suits his Excellency's good pleasure. Yes. Of course." At the doorway Andrej released Sorsa's arm; Sorsa lowered his head, speaking softly. "May one inquire as to the progress of your inquiry, lord prince?"

A reasonable request. "He's made his first false report. Tomorrow he'll try the same again, and hold to it for as long as he can. To tell you the truth I expect a second false reading, he has trained very thoroughly. It adds to the pleasure of the contest." Perfectly true. Also convenient, in case Stoshi lost track of himself, and he might. "But it is only a matter of time before he offers all the evidence we wish. He may well surrender to me tomorrow. It may be the next morning."

Sorsa had said he was in a hurry. But Inquiry could not be rushed. It took time to get past the layers in a man's mind and will and heart. The more complex the information was the longer it took to bring it to light.

"Thank you, lord prince." Raising his voice Sorsa spoke to his aide, waiting at the door. No sign of the dinner-table, Andrej was glad to see; his third-meal would have gotten cold, and that would have been a terrible way to treat one of Waclav's dinners. It was a pity to put Waclav to two meals within one evening, but Andrej had had a long day and was prepared to be selfish. "His Excellency is to be obeyed in all things, Feraltz. See that he has no cause to find fault."

Nodding to Andrej with a final almost-bow Sorsa left. Andrej turned back to the room, Stoshi still unmoving on the floor, Security in cells. "In all things" probably did not extend to handing over the thula and playing a cheerful march as he left with Security, Stoshi, and Waclav to cook for them all. More pity that. He would work with what he had for now, and see what he could do with it.

"My prisoner and my gentlemen, they all go to Infirmary this moment," he said to the air, because Feraltz would be listening carefully. "I will make examination myself. The sooner you for me these things accomplish the sooner I will get my third-meal, and I'm hungry."

Stoshi needed medical attention, and Andrej couldn't afford anybody else looking at him, because they'd see things they were not to see—or would not see things they would otherwise expect. Stoshi also needed a clean bed to lie in, and someone who cared for him to watch at his side—it was powerful medicine, just that. Andrej knew. He remembered. Waking in the near-dark, and Stildyne there to ask him if he wanted a glass of rhyti, a clean shirt, a game of tiles. Never again.

But he would do his utmost to see them all safely out of here, no matter what the cost.

Stildyne watched Cousin Stanoczk sitting quietly on the shower-bench in the corner of the examination room with his head lowered, shoulders slumped. Godsalt and

Pyotr had run him through the shower in wash-and-prep because that was what they were supposed to do with prisoners in Infirmary, and Infirmary was where Koscuisko had sent them.

It wasn't going to be so much of a problem to break out of here as from the cells in the interrogation room. Robert was here; the team was here; Stoshi was here. All they needed was some way to get to the thula, some way to get away with the thula, and some way to communicate with Andrej Koscuisko.

Koscuisko had apparently won acceptance by Deputy Sorsa, but what was the game? Koscuisko had conducted his interrogation in High Aznir, so Stildyne hadn't been able to grasp all the details. He had only a few words of high Aznir; mostly vulgarities, some obscenities, one or two interesting suggestions, some little general conversation.

There were a few things he knew to be facts. One was that Koscuisko had been careful not to press too hard, while preserving the illusion. Stildyne had been with Koscuisko on field assignment. He knew what it looked like when Koscuisko had decided to get a prisoner out from under the Bench.

And Koscuisko was struggling harder than Stildyne had ever seen him to contain his own lust for pain and power against a hunger he'd denied for more than two years, ever since he'd murdered Captain Lowden in Port Burkhayden. The interrogation Koscuisko had aborted on that night—of some guiltless gardener, accused of a crime only Stildyne knew that Robert St. Clare had committed— had been the last of Koscuisko's interrogation exercises; until now.

Third, and last, Stildyne knew that Stoshi had come on a desperate enterprise, something so important that he'd sent Robert to Mathin to keep the imposture intact. Lek believed that Stoshi had understood Robert's plan, and had put it forward; that was what Lek had said. Robert had been protecting *him* from torture, because Lek was the thula's primary pilot.

The door to the treatment room slid open, and he centered his energies to address the immediate situation. Which was Andrej Koscuisko. Stoshi flinched away when the door opened, raising his hand in a warding gesture as if from a sudden flare; nor was he just pretending to be afraid.

"I have only a few moments for you, Stoshi," Koscuisko said. Advancing on Stoshi, Koscuisko stood with his hands neutral at his sides, looking down on his cousin's bent head. Stoshi straightened up on the slatted shower-bench abruptly, lifting his head; it was a gesture of defiance that Stildyne recognized as having a specific Dolgorukij component. Not showing his bared neck. Since Stoshi was naked there wasn't much else Stoshi could do.

He'd had his body hair bleached and thinned, for the imposture. Stildyne had seen Koscuisko sitting hopeless and defeated on a shower-bench in a lavatory, overcome with guilt and grief and drink, and he appreciated the effort it had taken Stoshi to make his gesture of defiance.

Koscuisko brooded over Stoshi's face as he spoke. "You put Robert to the fire, Stoshi," Koscuisko said. Stoshi looked away; he was trembling. The initial doses Koscuisko had ordered were probably beginning to wear off. "Perhaps we can talk about it tomorrow, after you give me names and dates and places."

"We have nothing to say to each other, Derush," Stoshi said. His voice was shaking. "I have told you. There is no point. Leave me alone, you are in enough danger for your soul already, you do not need to earn further damnation."

Mistake. Koscuisko put his hands to his thighs, leaning down close to his cousin's face. "Answer as you are asked, Stoshi," he said. Stildyne didn't like the note he could hear creeping into the sound of Koscuisko's voice. "Did you not study the protocol of such things, when you undertook to steal my identity? You must learn better manners."

There might be monitors here. They didn't know. Koscuisko had to keep up his own end of the deception. "Does his Excellency wish the prisoner secured?" Stildyne asked carefully. He could help them both best by helping Koscuisko keep his balance; he'd gotten good at it, over the years.

"No, not yet. First you may apply topical analgesics, no, I'll get them, I know you cannot read." Yes, he could; not much, but he'd been studying Dasidar and Dyraine—because Koscuisko played tiles, and a man couldn't play a serious game of tiles without some background—and Koscuisko knew it. So Koscuisko wanted him to play ignorant.

"Yes, here, take these," Koscuisko was back from the dose-cabinets with a double handful of medicaments, dumping them into Stildyne's cupped hands. "And remember, Stildyne. Symmetry."

Why? Stildyne could see that Koscuisko had not been so thorough with Stoshi. But he had to be close to Stoshi's naked body to see that. Koscuisko wanted his help to preserve the illusion that he'd done much worse to Stoshi than he actually had; when what he'd done had been bad enough. "According to his Excellency's good pleasure," Stildyne said, and bowed.

Now Koscuisko put his hands up to his face and dragged his palms down, as if to restore some feeling. "Stoshi, I'll see you in the morning, after my fast-meal. Think on your sins, and pray the Holy Mother grants you grace to loosen your tongue before your suffering goes too far."

Turning toward the door, Koscuisko left, beckoning Pyotr and Godsalt to come with him. "You have to help me, Stildyne," Stoshi said, after a moment. "You have to get me out of here. He's coming back, isn't he?"

Stoshi was speaking to him slowly, carefully, reaching out a trembling hand to clasp Stildyne's own. It was the artless gesture of a man whose judgment was handicapped by torture and fear; but that wasn't why Stoshi did it, Stildyne knew. It was for reassurance—and Stoshi was the one who was trying to provide it, as much if not more than soliciting.

Stildyne hadn't really understood how deep Cousin Stanoczk went before this. He knew Koscuisko had hurt Stoshi, he knew Stoshi was afraid to the point of having been terrified; but still and always would put the mission forward. These were fighting people. Stildyne had thought Koscuisko himself was fighting enough, but maybe the intensity of purpose was a family trait, and had only gone off in the wrong direction where Andrej Koscuisko was concerned.

"I can't help you." He kept his voice flat and level, not hard, just resigned. "Yes. He's coming back in the morning. You're going to tell him sooner or later, you know you will." An observer would expect him to work on a prisoner's will, encourage a sense of helplessness and despair. Stoshi knew that as well as he did. "You'd better tell him what he wants to know. Spare yourself the suffering, you've already lost."

"I can't." Stoshi's cry seemed to come straight from the heart, and by the pain Stildyne felt in his gut he knew that it was too close to true. "There's too much riding on this. Get a knife, you do it, if I can't. For the love of the Holy Mother."

He would be expected to pick up on that. Stoshi meant him to, as much as would any unseen auditor. "Why is that?" He was free to make his touch as soothing and tender as he wanted, now. "What's so important, that you can't—"

"Said too much." Stoshi's voice sounded strangled in his throat. "Kill me. Do it now. With your hands. Kill me."

"You know I can't," Stildyne replied, regretfully. "Save your breath. Try to get some rest. It will be time to start up all over again, before you know it."

And finally with the exhaustion of agony Stoshi seemed to fade, and let himself be moved onto his back on a level without speaking. Starting with the burn patches Stildyne began to work his way down his lover's body, patch by patch, certain they would get out of this, not knowing how.

Lek Kerenko and Garrity were here to help Andrej

with Robert, because as reluctant as he was to expose them to the insult that Robert's body had sustained he did not trust Canopy Base's orderlies. And at least it could be said that Lek had seen it all already.

Godsalt was assigned to waiting at the main entrance to the medical suite for their meals to be delivered. Pyotr's job was to stand outside the door in the corridor in case Andrej wanted him. Stildyne was with Stoshi. To meet up with Stildyne again, and then have it be under these circumstances—

So Stoshi was as safe as possible, and there was Robert. Andrej had worked Stoshi hard, and the cyborg bracing on his right hand had become increasingly less useful over the year he'd been here in Gonebeyond. Usually he was all right. But usually he didn't spend as much of his time knocking the wretched thing against living flesh as he had today.

Lek and Garrity maneuvered the transport shell with Robert on it from the mover—jacked up to the height of the examination level—to the diagnostic bed. What limited awareness Robert had was clearly of a very basic sort; Andrej checked the blood-scans to see what drugs Mathin had used, and found them inadequate for his purposes.

On to physical examination, then, with the diagnostics on scan for gross skeletal displacement and tissue necrosis and body core internal damage. Lungs all right. Heart strong, still. Stomach bruised, liver intact, kidney function normal within temporary perturbation caused by the drugs of Inquiry and the fact that they'd allowed Robert to become dehydrated.

A moderate degree of dehydration could be useful in Inquiry, contributing to mental confusion and lowering internal editors. Judging by what Andrej had seen of Mathin's work on Robert's body, however, Andrej decided that such subtlety was beyond the man. He simply hadn't been paying attention.

Significant insult at Robert's knees, his pelvis, his hips; nothing wrong with what Robert called his personal necessaries, Andrej was glad to see. Saving genital trauma for later, perhaps. Still, there was something wrong; Andrej couldn't put his finger on it, but he knew there was a problem, a big problem, why couldn't he see the problem?

Robert's left eye, bulging a little out of the eye socket. The organ itself did not seem to be compromised; there had to be a reason, and there was a very young bruise beneath Robert's left cheek-bone. As though someone had struck at Robert's face from below and put a sudden shocking amount of force up against the cheek. Hard enough. Savage enough. To do what? To shatter the bones of the occipital orbit.

Lek met Andrej's sickened gaze with a subdued nod of understanding and resignation. "Yesterday," Lek said. "At the end, before they brought Cousin Stanoczk. Mathin used a neural rasp like a blunt instrument, trying to get Robert to talk before Sorsa could pull him off the case. I didn't realize."

There was no way for Lek to have known; and what could Lek have done? It wasn't Lek's fault. "It is not on you, my dear," Andrej said. "I promise you that. Will you call for Feraltz, and for the infirmary supervisor?"

There wasn't much on Canopy Base by way of medical support. Andrej supposed anything serious was just evacuated; which meant there was at least one vector that gave access into developed Space, probably the Dolgorukij Combine. He couldn't risk letting them evacuate Robert. They would all leave together.

Here was Feraltz, and the shift supervisor. Standing at Robert's head with his hands braced to the levels Andrej cut off any polite greetings, and came straight to the point. "Who is on your surgical staff, here? You have a surgical staff? You can perform an emergency reconstruction before this trauma results in the loss of vision, cranial swelling, destruction of the inner ear's structures by gross physical deformation?"

Feraltz was pale. He should be. The shift supervisor, however, did not seem to understand the serious nature of the situation. "We have out-patient surgical support, your Excellency," he said. "Emergency triage, resuscitation, baseline clinic staff. Everything else we send back to the hospital in Stork's-Nest. We have a standing agreement."

Andrej was sure they did. He filed the name away; when they got out he would add it to Stoshi's information. And they would get out. "Then you at least have the medication I will require. And medical equipment maintenance for your population. Ocular stabilization. Cyborg bracing." His hand hurt, and he was going to need his hand.

When Garrity had lost an eye the Bench simply excised the damaged organ and installed a cyborg equivalent. Andrej did not believe that a replacement eye was available at Canopy Base; neural component mapping would be impossible anyway, Dolgorukij and Nurail were wired that differently.

The shift supervisor shook his head. He was beginning to look a little uncomfortable. Andrej raised his voice and shouted, slamming a clenched fist down on the frame of the level on which Robert lay. "Then you have at least an operating theater! With a sterile environment! And someone who is not completely useless in supporting an emergency!"

"Ah, yes, lord prince," the shift supervisor said. "Sterile field available in this room. But, ah, no member on staff qualified to assist in surgery—"

"Then send to me your two least useless people. See it done now. Your pharmacist, or whatever passes for your pharmacist, immediately. Garrity, you will secure the door. Lek, I will tell you what you must do.—Why are you still here?" he roared at the supervisor, with such savagery that the man fell back to the doorway. "This man is worth sixteen of you, and you stand there, wasting time."

Nothing to be done about the pain in his hand, after all. He could not afford to set a temporary neural block for fear of losing even the slightest degree of control, control which was going to be difficult anyway. He had no business even attempting this without qualified support, without a surgical machine.

But there were no cyborg eyes in all of Gonebeyond. If there were they'd be in stores at Safehaven, and he would know. The bone had to be restored, the tissue pressure relieved, blood flow restored. It was not just the loss of Robert's eye, his hearing in one ear, possibly several teeth in his upper jaw, his sinuses. Bone chips could migrate. Robert could not have come so far, survived so much, to lose his life to a massive stroke.

Only one more thing had to be done before Andrej shut the world away, and focused all of his attention on an almost impossible task. No, two things.

"And you, Feraltz," he said. "You will give Stildyne an orderly, and that orderly will do exactly, I emphasize exactly, whatever Stildyne says. If there is even the slightest hint of any failure, I will flay that orderly alive, I swear it. And Mathin. I want Mathin in a box. A very small box, Feraltz. I want him ready for me also, when I have time to discuss with him his grotesque mismanagement of a prisoner in Inquiry."

There. Now he felt a little better.

The shift supervisor sent in two orderlies and a pharmacy technician, but did not dare present himself. Maybe he'd decided he had better place himself at Stildyne's disposal, Andrej supposed. Or maybe he was just a coward.

Andrej called up his doses: for himself, for Robert. He had to be alert, now, he had to have all of his knowledge—skill—experience at his command. The rest of his examination would have to wait. Lek was gentle with Robert, Lek had years of listening to Andrej, Lek did as he was told and did it perfectly. The sterile field was in place. Andrej himself was suited up and sterile: the bright lights shone, the magnifying goggles responded to command; the detail of the damage was sharp and clear and crisp.

One last thing. He could not trust the cyborg bracing. Not for this. He stripped the apparatus off of the back of

CHAPTER SEVEN

Desperate Measures

In the name of Haystacks.

"Permission to join the Engineering bridge," Jennet said. Wheatfields turned around, clearly startled; in the years she'd been on board the *Ragnarok* Jennet didn't think she'd ever actually been down in Wheatfields' command center. On the observation deck, yes. On the floor—no.

In the name of Oak Leaf and Twisbee.

"Attention to the Captain," Wheatfields said, standing up hastily. The rest of his staff followed, except for the technician on status and propulsion. That station was exempt. Jennet nodded her thanks and crossed the threshold. She had Ralph with her, and Rukota; Two came behind.

"As you were." Wheatfields nodded to his people. They all sat back down, and turned to their boards, and pretended to be doing what they'd been doing when she came in. Wheatfields didn't sit down. She wasn't going to sit in his chair; she'd look ridiculous, with her feet hanging down. But she appreciated the gesture. "Two has something to show you, Serge, if she can borrow your on-ship monitor."

In the name of Lammergau and Gearanger and Tahumos.

Jennet assumed that Wheatfields could read Two's display better than she could; she didn't speak Engineering. Two had already told her what it meant, so she waited for Wheatfields to draw his own conclusions—in part to make sure, to make absolutely sure, to make sure without the whisper of a shadow of a doubt, that it was the same conclusion.

"But we're already on the Kamishir vector," Wheatfields said, his tone frustrated. "It's going to be another three days before we can come off at Derideten and hit Shoallens."

"There is no time." That was Two. And she could still sound cheerful. There was no situational adjustment to her translator protocol; never had been. "Look, there."

It was just noise, the kind that signaled a depot or rendezvous or settlement of some kind. But there was more of it than there should be, for a vector that hadn't sent a ping-back. Clearly there was something there. Clearly something was going on. The conclusion was obvious; and she was the Captain.

"I say it looks like someone may be massing for departure," Jennet said. "I say that therefore we need to catch them before they have a chance to hit another vector we haven't crossed yet. We need to drop vector at Scanner Five." The working name for that vector, hitherto unassigned. "I can't wait for us to come off Kamishir, Serge. Let alone acquire Shoallens."

In the name of Carstairs, Jenchou, Chorb, Aberclad.

"Captain, I've never forced a vector drop in mid-transit," Wheatfields said. Jennet thought she might actually have surprised him; on the other hand, maybe his mind had already taken hold of the challenge, and was calculating how he meant to attack it. "I've never even heard of a mid-transit vector drop, not from anybody who survived to talk about it. We could get cut to pieces in the cross-shear."

"'Could,' you said, Serge. Not 'would.' Are you on board for this, or aren't you?" It was a simple question. Was a vector drop mid-transit impossible? Or merely almost so?

"Cassie?" Wheatfields asked. "Jans? Allerb? Manshie?" One by one they turned, and looked at him. One by one they nodded, slowly. But with increasing conviction. Wheatfields nodded too. "At your command, your Excellency," he said.

Two years ago she'd given the crew the chance to leave the *Ragnarok* if they didn't want to join what had been euphemistically described by a man who was dead now as a "mutiny in form." She'd given them a chance to take shore leave at Emandis Station, more than a year ago, with the understanding that if they didn't come back she wouldn't blame them.

This was different. There were no contingencies. Their lives were in her hands. "Put me on all-ship," Jennet said to Two. Wheatfields spun the chair of his command station toward himself and sat down with emphatic force, keying some initiates. She could hear him talking, behind her, as if to himself; *alert, alert, all stations, stand by for vector calculation, alert, alert.* She didn't pay much attention to what Wheatfields was saying. She had to concentrate on this.

"Attention all crew." All-ship went out to duty stations, but it also went out to quarters. Everybody. Everybody had to hear this. "We believe that we have identified a possible location for base of operations, night raiders. There is reason to believe that an evacuation is in progress."

It was by no means certain. Communications across vectors was one thing; but sensor readings across a vector barrier were much less reliable. She was operating on instinct. Risking the ship and all souls on it, on a guess, a gamble.

"Our only chance of interception is to drop vector in mid-transit. This is a hazardous attempt with an unknown probability of success. I take into consideration the oath we swore to protect and defend all souls, to uphold the rule of Law and the Judicial order. Therefore. In the name of Haystacks, Tahumos, Jenchou, and all the rest. I have directed Ship's Engineer to drop vector at Scanner Five, to confront and contain whatever we may find there."

Or die trying. "This is Captain Jennet ap Rhiannon, Jurisdiction Fleet Ship *Ragnarok*, commanding. Stand by for vector drop. Away here."

There was no more Judicial order, not as it had been when each and every soul on board this ship had sworn to Fleet. The rule of Law would condemn the entire crew to death for the crime of resisting the judicial murder of five people. Fleet did more protecting and defending of its revenue streams and tax income than of people and property. She had lost her faith in the verities of duty and honor.

But if they could find, fight, destroy the night raiders none of the rest of it would matter, and she would be as sure as she could ever be that any sacrifice of the lives for which she was responsible was worth it.

Hours, hours, hours. And yes the swelling of the tissue at the back of the eye-socket would have strangled the life out of Robert's eye within the day. And yes the tiny structures of the inner ear, the tympanic membrane, the oscillating bones, the vestibular apparatus were already deformed in place, but Andrej felt hopeful that with adjustment to the vascular swelling it would all sort itself out. If it didn't he would call on the Malcontent to send a specialist to Safehaven who would put it right; and leave them there.

If there were chips of bone fragments left in the tissue after Andrej teased each and every bit that he could find back into its place on Robert's cheek-bone, eye-box, face, Andrej could not see them even at maximum magnification, and the micro-probe came up negative for bone-dust. There was nothing else that Andrej could do. If he was lucky he'd stopped the course of deterioration, he'd stabilized, he'd won a few hours or days till they could all get out of here. If he was not lucky, there was still nothing more that he could do.

He kissed Robert's forehead, for luck. Kissed Lek, for thanks. Kissed Garrity as well, for being with him, for lending strength. Then he retrieved the cyborg bracing,

and issued final instructions, and called an orderly to
escort him to guest quarters so that he could go to sleep.

When Andrej stumbled across the threshold of the
guest suite at last Iosev was there, waiting for him. Iosev
jumped to his feet as the door opened; Andrej had never
seen an expression on Iosev's face quite like the one that
greeted him. Respect? "I'm sorry," Iosev said, and bowed.
"I know you've had a long day. I just wanted to see you."

That was no excuse. "What is it, then, Iosev? I'm tired,
and your torturer-for-hire has very nearly harmed my
Robert past redemption." The hand on which the cyborg
bracing was not helping burned like fire.

"You should know," Iosev said. "Sorsa didn't take me
into his confidence, or I could have told him you were to
be trusted. To think we used to receive that object in our
own house."

That object? Stoshi. Iosev had been watching? Closing
his eyes as weariness overwhelmed him Andrej sat down
heavily in the nearest chair. This went beyond all horror.
"We did not merely 'receive' him like some cadet, Iosev."

They'd played together. They'd chased through
cloisters, barns, mazes, libraries, even if almost always
under the indulgent gaze of minders of one sort or another.
They'd practiced archery. They'd learned to ride together.
They'd studied their first dance-figures in the same classes,
and played tricks on choir-masters together until Andrej's
increasing dignity had put more distance between them.

"No, of course not," Iosev agreed, apparently
chastened. "Not one from so humble a family." That
hadn't been the point. And Stoshi's family was intimately

connected with their own, through the maternal line; did Iosev really mean to scorn his own mother's quality in such a way?

It had probably been a harder blow to Iosev than to anyone else when Andrej had married Marana and established Anton as his heir, Andrej realized. So long as Andrej had no acknowledged son, if he died, Iosev would have become the prince inheritor.

And if that had happened their father would have found a way to de-church Mayra and enfranchise her. Nobody would ever have put Iosev at the head of the familial corporation, not ever, but did Iosev understand that? Or understand it all too well?

"I've watched some of the others," Iosev confided, leaning close. Andrej kept his eyes shut, because after everything else he'd been through today his ability to process outrage was almost exhausted. "One is almost embarrassed. There is no feeling, no artistry. Then there is you. Truly the Holy Mother has made you for Her purpose, Andrej, and blessed you to the work. I am not fit to call myself your brother."

The others. Oh, Holy Mother. Torture on demand, for profit and for persuasion. Sorsa's people didn't bring people here to show them wide streets and strong buildings. Sorsa brought them here to threaten and torture them, for information and compliance.

"How many others, Iosev?" He could no longer entertain a hope that Iosev was a deluded pawn, ignorant of Sorsa's true agenda. He'd wanted to believe in Iosev's foolishness. But what Andrej heard in his brother's voice was bell-toned evil.

"Only one more here, Andrej, Doctor Mathin, you've met him." And seen his work. That Robert was not to be crippled was no thanks to *him*. "Two more elsewhere, that I know of. The market has opened up wonderfully, in this past year, but—if only the world could see what I saw, today—"

If he'd had anything in his stomach he would have pitched it. As it was he had to swallow four times, six times, until the water of revulsion stopped flooding into his mouth. "You are heart and soul of the Angel of Destruction, then, Iosev." He heard no denial. Opening his eyes he saw Iosev draw himself up as tall as he could sit up in his chair, and gesture toward his chest proudly.

"Heart and soul. I alone had grace to find the truth, Andrej, but I am proud, more proud than I can say, to have made smooth the way for you to be enlightened. This is a day of manifold blessings. That is what I wanted to say to you, Andrej, firstborn and eldest. I am so proud."

"Then listen to me." He had to say this, whether or not anybody was listening in. "Stoshi is more of a man than you could ever be, Iosev. I am in a position to tell. I'm repulsed by the sight of you. Do not presume to come before me ever again, do you understand? Now you may say 'yes, lord prince' and leave."

Iosev stood up, white-faced with shock. With evident fury, taking him by storm so that he trembled with it. "You have been corrupted, brother," Iosev said. "You have spent too much time with the filthy scum of alien worlds. I will pray for you, Derush. I will pray that the Holy Mother grants you grace, to work Her will and serve Her purpose."

Then Andrej was alone. He didn't understand how after all the things he'd seen and heard—and done—today, this revelation of Iosev could be the worst. He could not even weep. He could only stare at the now-closed door, red-eyed with horror.

Give me strength and I will bow to you. He had nowhere to go for help. He would compromise Waclav, endanger Stoshi, place his Security at risk if he sought deliverance of anybody here. *Help us get out. Help us escape. And we will put an end to this atrocious evil. In the name of the Malcontent. Take me as yours in name, as I have been in spirit, only give me strength, and see us through.*

Someone signaled at the door, and Andrej could have shrieked for mercy from a relentless stream of blows that came one after another. "His Excellency's third-meal, if it please his Excellency."

It was a sign. "Step through." Because the voice could be anybody's, but the meal would be from Waclav. They *would* get out. They *would* escape. And now he'd eat as much as he could manage, and take a dose to still the pain in his right hand, and go to sleep; because he had so much to do, in the morning.

It was so late it had come around to early. In Sorsa's office the rhyti brewer sat half-empty because they'd been drinking steadily all night, Sorsa, and Fiska, and now Iosev Ulexeievitch. There was a depleted tray of pastries, because Sorsa had wanted to know what Koscuisko thought so exceptional about Cousin Waclav's cooking; and had declared it fine indeed, but denied himself more than one—for no other reason than that Waclav was Sarvaw, Fiska thought.

"I'm telling you, Sorsa." Iosev hadn't been invited. But he'd come storming in anyway, and very untimely. "I watched him. He's up to something. I should know my own brother."

Security surveillance indicated Iosev had come from the guest suite, where his brother lodged. He did not seem to be satisfied with whatever words he'd had with Koscuisko: what had he meant to accomplish, at this late hour? Koscuisko had been tested and tried today, and had shown himself an autocrat indeed. One whose instinct for mastery Iosev lacked; Iosev had the desire, but not the will bred into the bone.

"Perhaps you should have left him alone," Sorsa said. "He hasn't eaten all day. And a complex surgery on top of his hours of hard work on that Malcontent—did he not welcome you as a brother, lord prince?"

Iosev flushed angrily. "It is a private matter," Iosev said. *So no*, Fiska told himself. "But I once again tell you. Remember that I, and not you, grew up with him, Sorsa. I know him better than anybody here. He is in collusion, somehow. I swear it to the Holy Mother herself."

Sorsa declined to rise to the bait. In Fiska's estimation Sorsa had had about enough of Iosev Ulexeievitch. Iosev had lost his value as a trophy the moment Koscuisko had let Sorsa kiss his hand; and Iosev's resentment of his older brother was reason enough to discard his insights as motivated by malice. "I must thank you again, lord prince, for bringing your brother here, regardless," Sorsa said. "We know by your discovery of the imposture that our enemy knows where we are. We are leaving Canopy Base. We have already begun."

Hours ago. The evacuation order had been given soon after Sorsa had learned of the imposture. Such lukewarm validation was clearly not good enough for Iosev, however. "And should you not have consulted me, Sorsa? It may be only one Malcontent has the secret. We should prepare to defend Canopy Base, not run away like cravens. Stand. And fight. The Holy Mother will grant us victory, are you with me?"

Sorsa did not bother to so much as acknowledge Iosev, this time. No one told the Angel what to do; Canopy Base was Sorsa's responsibility. Iosev might not have realized that before. He could not give orders unless by Sorsa's permission, and certainly not *to* Sorsa. "We'll have to abandon the thula," Sorsa said. "Destroy it. If we can't have it at least we can be sure the Malcontent will never enjoy it again. A shame."

The subterfuge Iosev had practiced to induce *Chornije* to take on his secret mission had been irresponsible, even if it had turned out to be in Sorsa's favor. Iosev could not know how truly devastating a blow he'd struck against the Malcontent, doing what he'd done. There was a certain bitter irony in that.

Iosev stood up, with a great air of having made a decision. "So I learn the truth about you," Iosev said. "How you have used me. The Holy Mother will requite you for it. I will be in quarters when you need me, I give you good-greeting, Deputy Sorsa. Fisner Feraltz."

Sorsa responded with the barest nod. Couldn't Iosev see how deeply distracted Sorsa was by the dangers and

difficulties of evacuation? Sorsa would lose everything.
Yes, he would bring back Andrej Koscuisko, and a
Malcontent prisoner; but even that might not be enough.
He had lost the thula. The Angel set high standards for its
officers: the more responsible the officer, the higher the
standard.

"Koscuisko must travel with us on *Buration*," Sorsa
said. "Let him sleep as long as you can, Fisner, and escort
him to *Buration* when the time comes. It won't be long.
The first freighters are already loaded and queued up."

There was something, here. Canopy Base would be
evacuated. No one left. Two people would remain: one to
initiate the self-destruct sequences that would blow up
Canopy Base and destroy any incriminating evidence; and
one to shoot the first man if he didn't, and do the job
himself. What if he volunteered for that mission?

Or what if he, Fiska, stayed back? What if he took
secret refuge in one of those little-used service corridors,
shot both of those men, and took over Canopy Base's
significant communications systems?

It wouldn't be like the thula. But it was a chance. He
could shoot the data-stream out, and if there was little
hope the signal would get through Sorsa would not be
able to stop it. And would never know if it had reached its
target. That would be something, at least.

The Holy Mother would be merciful. He could only
do his best. He would send the hard-won data out; and
die in peace.

Hearing voices over the open comm between the
clinic room and the outside corridor, Stildyne was awake

immediately. *The son of the Koscuisko prince waits for you all at the thula. You must come at once.* Stoshi had not stirred, strapped to the table for show, though Stildyne knew he was awake as well; he couldn't leave the prisoner unguarded—that would be out of character—so the best he could do was wait until one of the others opened the door. It was Pyotr.

"We're called for, Chief." There were some station personnel behind Pyotr, but they were keeping well back and showed no sign of being armed. "His Excellency directs us to report to the thula immediately."

How had Koscuisko managed that? Did it matter? Koscuisko *had* apparently managed it. "We'll need medical transport." For Robert. Koscuisko wouldn't leave him behind. That Stoshi would come with them went without saying; Koscuisko wouldn't be separated from his prey.

"Medical transport is being provided. There's a mover for his Excellency's prisoner." Pyotr wasn't giving anything away. He never had, not once in all these years. Stildyne rubbed the side of his face to improve the blood flow to his brain, in order to ask the obvious question.

Straight? Finger-code. Pyotr stood respectfully at a position of modified attention-rest, and Stildyne didn't want to be too obvious about looking at Pyotr's hand, so he coughed and wiped his mouth with his white-square. Standard item of uniform, a clean white-square, though the uniform itself was Langsarik rose-gold these days rather than Security grey. Pyotr rubbed his thumb with the side of his index finger as if his thumbnail annoyed him in some way.

Can't tell. Then Pyotr hadn't caught a smell, at least.

If it was a trick to move them out of Infirmary the station staff would have to answer to Koscuisko for it. If it was Koscuisko he wouldn't want to be kept waiting, and station staff was within its rights to expect that they'd execute in a brisk and expeditious manner.

"Move out." Stildyne made up his mind. "Garrity and Kerenko, secure the prisoner for transport. Godsalt and Hirsel, see to Robert. Let's go." He'd have felt better if Koscuisko were here to give the order directly. But any movement back toward the thula was progress. He had to trust Koscuisko. In all their years together, when had Koscuisko ever let him down? The once. That didn't really count. He hadn't given Koscuisko the chance to explain himself before he'd left Jeltaria.

Comparing labels in the dose-racks against those Koscuisko had pulled last night Stildyne fitted a carry-pack with fresh supplies to spare the thula's limited medical stock the draw-down. While Garrity and Kerenko moved Stoshi into the upright mover with its straps and secures Stildyne crossed the corridor to collect doses for Robert as well, stowing everything that looked likely in the gurney's storage compartments.

Robert was completely unconscious. The bandaging on his face was a surprise, and Stildyne knew that—unlike the job of work he'd done on Stoshi—none of Robert's dressings were for show. There was a waiting escort, but of only three men—none of them carrying any obvious weapons. No threat there. "Look smart," Stildyne said. "The officer's waiting."

It could be a trap, but if it was, why wouldn't they just lock Infirmary down? The only way to find out was to go forward. As they left, Infirmary staff in white tunics hurried past them into the treatment rooms, starting to pull modular equipment cases away from the walls and close them up.

Stildyne could see transport crates stacked neatly against the walls of the corridor just outside. Evacuation. They were leaving. So that was why Koscuisko wanted them at the thula.

They'd get away. They would escape. Koscuisko had something planned. And once they'd gotten safely out of here he and Koscuisko would have a long quiet talk, because Koscuisko had a lot of explaining to do.

Andrej lay on his side in the bed, trying to remember where he was and why he couldn't remember getting here. It was a nice bed, soft and wide, clean-smelling and lightly perfumed with musk and night-blooming peppery grains-of-grace; linen sheets, finely spun and closely woven. Home? No, he wasn't at home, because if he was someone would be coming in with rhyti and a plate of hot pastries to tide him over until fast-meal, to kiss the back of his hand and put him on notice that it was time to get up. *Holy Mother, bless this child to your work.*

"His Excellency's pardon." There was someone at the door, instead, speaking respectfully. "His Excellency's attention very much to be appreciated, sir. May one presume to enter?"

Now, who was that? No one he was related to. So, not Iosev, though why that thought should relieve him and turn his stomach at one and the same time escaped him just now. Whatever he'd been drinking last night must have been good—but no, he hadn't been drinking, last night. He'd had reason not to. He'd needed to get to sleep, sleep soundly and deeply, and wake within hours ready for the worst; because something horrible was happening and he was part of it.

"It will be one moment." Bed-dress lay waiting for him on its rack, the night-slippers and short sashed-robe that a man belted over his night-shirt when he was at ease in his private quarters. He'd worn the harness of Joslire's knives to bed, why had he done that? It was a hint, though. He'd wanted to arm himself first thing on waking.

He usually didn't carry the five-knives to clinic, so that was another hint. He'd laid them out on the table and covered them with his white-square, inviolable code in a decently run Dolgorukij household, *you do not touch this*. He'd slept with the most important one beneath his pillow. Sheathing her between his shoulder-blades where Joslire had first placed her so many years ago he tied the sash of his robe around his waist. "Step through. I hope you've brought fast-meal."

He'd left two dose-styli on top of the white-square, as well, and that was yet another hint. He put one through, the one coded as a high-end restorative specific for Aznir Dolgorukij. There were few high-grade anythings at Safehaven; and what there were had to be restricted for the patients' use, not that of half-mad Inquisitors. Taken all together he was certainly not in Safehaven.

The door opened on Fisner Feraltz, Sorsa's aide, the one Sorsa had detailed to monitor Andrej's interrogation of—of Stoshi. Now that Andrej's mind was clearing, sharpening, focusing his thoughts, he remembered more than he wanted and less than he needed to know. Yesterday he'd left Stoshi in Stildyne's personal care, and Iosev in desperately urgent need of a quick garrote. What else? Turning away from the door Andrej put the second dose through. Maybe the answer was there.

"I beg to be forgiven for the lack thereof, lord prince." Andrej picked up the rest of his five-knives from the table, still enwrapt in the fine linen; but where was he going to put them? He tucked them into the sash of his short-robe. "The morning meal must be delayed. I have urgent news."

That was too bad. Andrej was hungry. It had been hard work, yesterday. Torture. Name of all Saints. Stoshi. Loving it, while he was hating it, because the only way he felt he could act his part convincingly—as he had to be, convincing—was to remember and recall, to open up the door again and let the heir of Chuvishka Kospodar come out to play.

Closing his eyes Andrej waited for the wave of nausea to pass. He wouldn't have been able to eat anyway. "What news, then?" Perhaps he was meant to be gratified by Feraltz' personal attendance. And yet he wasn't, because Feraltz was one of them, and they were corrupt, and had to be destroyed. Iosev—Iosev was his brother—

"The spy was, as his Excellency knows, discovered, but his presence signifies that the enemy knows we're here." That meant Stoshi, who had known where to direct the thula. "The danger is immediate. We must leave."

"Where are we going?" He should get dressed. Where was his clothing? In the closet, yes, taken away by silent and invisible hands after he'd washed, cleaned and returned to be ready for him in the morning. He had hurt Stoshi in this clothing. He didn't want to so much as touch it again.

"His Excellency is to travel on Deputy Sorsa's command vessel. We seek to know his Excellency's pleasure with regard to whether the prisoner should be available to him in transit." For his entertainment, perhaps. He did need Stoshi with him, to ensure that nobody else tried to molest him; but that led to the next question, inexorably.

"I will rather take the thula. With my prisoner. And my people." Had the Malcontent answered his desperate prayer, and brought him deliverance in the form of an emergency evacuation? "Once I have had a look at Robert and my cousin you will bring us all to the thula. And send fast-meals."

There was a subtle hesitation in Feraltz' manner that caught Andrej's attention like a shout. "His Excellency's people have been called to meet Iosev Ulexeievitch at the thula. They have brought the prisoner with them."

Whose idea was that? Did Iosev mean to travel on the thula, Sorsa's prize, the very valuable token of their significant coup, a treasure robbed from the Malcontent who'd delivered it into their hands at Canopy Base?

Iosev would be preening, anticipating praise and increased prestige. Andrej smelled it. It was an entirely understandable impulse, but Andrej needed ship and crew to himself, in order to make a clean escape. He didn't want to be on the same ship with Iosev, to breathe the same closely recycled air.

"How does Canopy Base mean to move the thula if not on my instruction, or has the code been extracted from Lek Kerenko? Do not, I warn you urgently, reveal that someone interferes with my Security again." Pulling the blue wool short-coat from its hanging frame as he spoke—Feraltz hurrying to hold it for him, while Andrej found the sleeves—Andrej shook it straight across his shoulders, turning on Feraltz.

Feraltz backed away nervously. "Deputy Sorsa gave strict instructions that his Excellency was not to be disturbed in any way. The prince his Excellency's brother only wishes to smooth away all obstacles, to make ready to receive his Excellency, the pilot can hardly refuse to serve his master—"

But Andrej knew things about Iosev now that he never would have guessed just yesterday. His mind was still clearing; Feraltz' words only now caught up with him. Iosev had taken Andrej's people and gone to the thula, with Stoshi. He would be determined on getting his way. Iosev clearly felt for the first time in his miserable life that he was in control here.

"We are going there at this immediate moment." His collar wasn't fastened and his trousers weren't bloused, and he didn't care. Pushing at Feraltz' shoulder to turn him as he spoke Andrej struck Feraltz between the shoulder-blades to get him started, driving Feraltz out of the room before him, furious to avoid a catastrophe.

It was with feelings of sheer frustration that Stildyne stood arguing with the traffic officer on the tarmac at the foot of the thula's loading ramp. "This is not the son of the Koscuisko prince." He pointed, and he used the entire length of his outstretched arm in deliberate invocation of

Koscuisko being autocratic. He didn't care if it was rude, ignoring the shocked expression on the faces of the station's flight crew who stood waiting to be let on board.

Fisher Wolf sat silent and sullen, determined and detached. The thula would not move. Stildyne was determined on it: at least partially because their enemy, Canopy Base, was so determined that it should. "This is *a* son of the Koscuisko prince. Did you think we wouldn't know the difference?"

Stoshi had taught him the Aznir of it one afternoon when they'd had nothing better to do and were trying to catch their breath. If Stoshi had been less ragged he might make a face, Stildyne knew, but he couldn't spare a glance at Stoshi's expression to see whether his accent was still bad enough to cut through the layers of drugs Koscuisko had given him last night.

It clearly wasn't Koscuisko, standing there. One of his brothers, then, but not the priest Stildyne had met at Chelatring Side, who'd worn some sort of clerical robes rather than this man's blue-and-silver-grey coat with the brilliantly shining almost certainly animal leather boots and the bloused woolen trousers. And all of that bunched and gathered lace.

"This is the brother of your master, who speaks with his voice and commands your obedience." The traffic officer wore much simpler clothing; no bloused trousers, no lace. Simple, respectable coat and some white linen showing beneath the little upright edge of the coat's collar. "We must evacuate Canopy Base. The son of the Koscuisko prince travels on the flagship. Issue the orders to release this ship to his Excellency."

But the traffic officer was blustering, because he was in the wrong and knew it. "Our officer has issued no such orders," Stildyne said firmly. How easy it was to fall back into "our officer," when Koscuisko himself had denied them that status—out of his obstinate conviction that he knew best what was good for them all. "We are unable to comply with your demand."

As if Robert's torture, Lek's torture by proxy, what Koscuisko had done to Stoshi was to be cast aside because Iosev Ulexeievitch was Koscuisko's brother. Did he remember something about Iosev, something unsavory?

Walking casually forward at a leisurely pace the brother paused in front of the imaginary line along which Stildyne had formed up the thula's crew, one to each side of Robert on the gurney, one to each side of Stoshi on the mover, Pyotr anchoring the far end of the line.

"My brother is served well by such as these," he said, with a hint of a question at the end of his strongly accented Standard. Clasping his hands behind his back in a genuinely Koscuisko-like fashion Koscuisko's brother paced the line, as if inspecting the crew; who stood stone-still in perfect order.

There were no finer troops under Jurisdiction than those men. Stildyne would set them against the best Canopy Base had at its disposal; but he'd noticed a relative absence of Security around them, and there was information in that fact. Why was there an order to evacuate?

Reaching Stildyne at the front of the line Koscuisko's brother tilted his head back to look down his nose at Stildyne. He *had* to tilt his head back, because Stildyne was as tall as he was. "And yet there is a difficulty, do I understand?"

Backing away to give Koscuisko's brother a respectfully wide berth the traffic officer started to speak in apologetic tones in Aznir. Stildyne could only grasp the occasional phrase, *Sorry, will not. Can't. Forgive; please*.

Koscuisko's brother silenced the traffic officer with one majestically contemptuous glance over his shoulder: *I am having a conversation with this man. I do not require your assistance.*

"This ship has been entrusted to us by the Malcontent, its lawful owner," Stildyne said. One of whose representatives half-lay, half-stood, secured in a semi-upright position in the mover, with only the thin white fabric of a patient's garment to cover him. "We are his Excellency's—ah, sworn-men." Subject to Koscuisko's authority alone. It was a technical term from the saga, the closest Stildyne could unearth from his limited store in a hurry to take the place of "Security assigned."

No, we're not going to give the thula up on your say-so. Koscuisko's brother turned away and took a few steps up the loading ramp, looking up into the thula's currently dimmed interior. He was welcome to look all he liked. Doubtless Canopy Base had had people through the thula from top to bottom since their arrival here, trying to get its attention. Stildyne hoped they hadn't disarranged Hirsel's logic-board, because Hirsel had been in the middle of a multi-tier puzzle and he hated it when people moved his markers around.

"And yet the ship accepted our stores and refresh. We were very generous." Before it locked itself off to even that much of an intrusion, once it decided its stores were adequately refreshed. Standard operating procedure. "Tell me, can that be respectful? Now, if one wanted so much as a cup of rhyti, one requires the command access keys. It seems ungracious."

Stildyne didn't need to answer that. *Only your fault for poking around too long* was true, but a waste of breath. The standard operating procedure for Security was to speak when they were spoken to and even then only if the situation seemed to demand it; and Stildyne liked to practice what he preached.

Koscuisko's brother clearly didn't expect an answer, either, because he was still talking. "Which makes it most inconvenient. We are evacuating Canopy Base, after all. Our medical equipment is surely being packed for transport."

Koscuisko's brother reached into the side closure of his coat, a gesture so familiar that Stildyne could have smiled. Going for a lefrol, here, of all places. Koscuisko's brother was right-handed, though, not like Koscuisko, and he was clumsier as well. Or his lefrol-case was bulkier. "What would happen if there was an emergency?" Koscuisko's brother asked.

It wasn't a lefrol-case. It was a projectile weapon, an Edeslok gun, pointed straight at Stildyne. Pivoting on the ball of his foot Stildyne started to lunge for it, flat-out at full length, to knock Koscuisko's brother down before he could do anybody harm; he felt the impact at his hip tearing into the fleshy part of his upper thigh, and guessed—but only just, with the last thought he had—that he'd been shot.

⊕ ⊕ ⊕

Feraltz had snagged a passenger car, steering it as swiftly as he apparently dared through the crowded corridors, explaining almost desperately as they went. "The enemy knows where we are, or the Malcontent wouldn't have been able to come here. We must get away. They have the power to destroy us, and they mean to."

The slowness of their progress was maddening. He wasn't the least bit interested in what Feraltz was saying, but that fact seemed to have escaped Feraltz' attention, somehow.

"If the scope of our operation is revealed the consequences could set the purpose of the Holy Mother back for years. We might never recover, and it will be the ruin of our enterprise—his Excellency's brother would be very deeply compromised by the economic failure, not to speak of the shame—"

The passenger car barreled onto the platform of a freight-lift, descended to the ground level, crossed out of the building and into the artificial overhead light of the launch-lanes. It was a scene of controlled chaos, people, pallets of equipment, mobile fueling stations, shouted orders with an edge of urgency that seemed to waver on the near edge of panic.

Feraltz wove through the traffic expertly, the passenger car picking up speed now that they were out of the building. They were running straight at the side of a freighter-tender in load-out. Did Feraltz mean to drive up the loading ramp and close the doors on Andrej to keep him from the thula and his crew? He wouldn't sully Joslire's knives, bundled in his waistband. He'd kill Feraltz with his bare hands.

Closer and closer, but the tender had begun to move, its crew running alongside fastening its cargo-bay ramps, swinging themselves aboard the crew loading ramp at the rear of the tender as it swung into the approach to a launch-lane. Andrej felt the hot breath of the tender's exhaust wash on his face as Feraltz steered past it, still bearing straight ahead. He could see the thula. It was out in the open, now, the temporary walls that had concealed it cleared for departure.

There was someone standing on the passenger loading ramp, and there were his Security. He knew those men on sight even from behind and at a distance, and counted them swiftly in his mind. Pyotr. Garrity. Upright mover, that was probably Stoshi. Lek. Godsalt. Gurney, that would be Robert, and there was Hirsel, and then Stildyne. It was Iosev, on the ramp.

"His Excellency's brother," Feraltz said, starting to slow down as they approached. "Your prisoner, and your crew, lord prince. And my most deeply sincere apologies for having given his Excellency a moment's cause for—"

Suddenly Stildyne moved, a flying leap at Iosev as Hirsel broke left to flank the ramp. Andrej saw the arc of Stildyne's body trajectory kick out of true and heard the distinctive report of an Edeslok gun. Stildyne was shot.

Andrej couldn't wait for Feraltz to stop the mover. Flying dismount, something he'd learnt as a boy, how to fall off a moving horse; it had been more than a year since Stildyne had had him practice the tuck-and-roll, but Andrej went over the side of the mover anyway, trusting to muscle memory to do the job. He was on the ground at Stildyne's side in an instant, cutting open the leg of

Stildyne's rapidly soaking trousers with the knife from between his shoulder-blades.

There was some shouting going on in the near vicinity. Andrej ignored it. He found the damage, white tendon and sinew, the cartilage covering not-quite-exposed bone shining in the light. The projectile path furrowed deep into dense fibrous muscle—Stildyne was bleeding, but there was no fountain of blood. No arteries compromised. It was venous leakage, that was all, and that was bad enough.

One of his people handed him a compress comprised of a torn and hastily wadded-up under-blouse. He pressed it deep to staunch the flow of blood, waiting until he could be sure he was right about the source of the bleeding before beckoning to whomever to step in and take over. They were all cross-trained. They knew how to handle a medical emergency.

Godsalt crouched at Stildyne's head, waiting to catch Andrej's eye. Andrej nodded. Yes, there'd be shock attendant on blood loss. Yes, Godsalt needed to stabilize the wound and replace fluid. Standing up, Andrej took stock of the situation.

Gurney; mover. Stoshi. Iosev standing by himself on the pavement with an Edeslok gun held loosely in his right hand, gazing around him proudly with an air of triumphant defiance. Fisner Feraltz was there at Iosev's back, and there were station personnel behind Feraltz, clearly poised for intervention. Lek and Hirsel stood at the foot of the thula's passenger loading ramp, watching and waiting—for an opportunity to strike, by their body language.

There'd be emergency medical equipment on the thula. Why hadn't they fetched it out by now? Because that was why Iosev had shot Stildyne, and they were trying to decide whether to let Iosev get away with it. Blindingly obvious.

Andrej started for the thula's loading-ramp; Lek and Hirsel gave way. Iosev had started to say something, but Andrej wasn't interested. "What is the delay, Mr. Kerenko?" Andrej asked, but without hostility. He was only making a point, and went on without waiting for Lek's reply. "Thula, I am Andrej Ulexeievitch Koscuisko. We are acquainted. I need access to stores, kindly oblige at once, because I'm in a hurry."

He didn't stop to wait for a response, striding up the ramp into the silent ship as he spoke. The interior lights were brightening by degrees; behind him he could hear Lek Kerenko, singing to himself or muttering under his breath, Andrej couldn't tell which.

"Acknowledged," the thula said. Andrej knew where to find the thula's medical stores—cargo bay, below. He'd been there. Hirsel scrambled ahead to open the cargo load doors as Andrej unshipped the medical pallet and pushed it out ahead of him toward where Godsalt and Garrity waited over Stildyne's body.

Stildyne was not going anywhere. Fisner Feraltz was standing between Iosev and the passenger loading ramp, most inconveniently for Iosev, repeatedly apologizing in broken phrases as Iosev berated him savagely. Station security were standing off, clearly wary of getting between them. Fine.

They lifted Stildyne onto the medical pallet and clamped in a standard fluid patch. Stildyne and the others had crewed the thula for more than a year, from what

Robert had told him; there was good hope that its medical stores reflected that.

Going down on one knee beside the medical pallet he turned Stildyne's face toward him with a hand at Stildyne's jaw, looking for signs of consciousness in Stildyne's narrow eyes. He was even uglier than usual, with his lips turned the color of clay. With an apparent effort Stildyne raised his one working eyebrow; and Andrej—feeling much more cheerful than he had any business being—had to grin.

"Shot in the fundament, Brachi," he said. "You may never live this down. We will talk later. Gentlemen, secure our casualties in passenger cabins, but lock up first." Looking back over his shoulder Andrej could see the gurney on its way up the thula's cargo loading ramp, and caught sight of Stoshi—strapped into the upright mover— deep at the back of the cargo bay, pale-faced and grim of countenance. Pyotr had come out to stand at Andrej's shoulder, since Stildyne was not available for the job; waiting for Andrej's orders.

The gurney was safely within. The medical pallet with Stildyne on it was moving. Garrity would secure the cargo loading ramp, and then everybody would be inside except for him and Pyotr, with no one between them and the passenger loading ramp. Andrej at last had time to attend to his brother.

"There," Iosev said, with satisfaction. "Just as I thought. I could have gotten us into the thula all along, Feraltz, if you and Deputy Sorsa had bothered to ask, and then my brother would not be so angry with you. Your own fault."

Shoot a man to force the crew to unlock the thula to gain access to its medical stores, or let one of their own die before their eyes. It was actually well-conceived, more so than Andrej would have expected, coming from Iosev. Had he misjudged his brother so badly, for all of these years? That was a shame. Because it was too late to make any difference.

"Deputy Sorsa did not dare to inconvenience your Excellency," Feraltz said, sounding a little desperate. "It is very much to be regretted that his Excellency felt called upon to take independent action, we have offended the son of the Koscuisko prince, we can only beg for pardon—"

Iosev cut Feraltz off with a short, sharp, ugly laugh. "I will speak with my brother." His emphasis was on "my" brother, a reminder of rank and presumption of privilege. "I thought I'd spare you the annoyance, Andrej. I'm sorry it had to go this far. Stubborn mongrels, aren't they? But Deputy Sorsa will be relieved to know that the thula has been reclaimed."

Looking over his shoulder, Andrej spoke to Pyotr quietly. "Can you move the thula without Robert and Stildyne?" They'd had a short crew when they'd been fighting their way out of Taisheki Station's minefield, if he remembered correctly.

"We'll need course and communication, your Excellency," Pyotr replied, looking at Feraltz. Right. Feraltz was Sorsa's officer, but there was one of him, several of Security, and no reason for Feraltz to make trouble.

"Send down someone to take charge of Feraltz," Andrej said. It was about time *he* made some trouble. "I'll just have a word with my brother. Nobody else gets on board of the thula, Mr. Pyotr." Andrej raised his voice as he said so, in order to be sure that Iosev heard him. Pyotr bowed.

"According to his Excellency's good pleasure," Pyotr said. Andrej imagined he could catch a note of grim satisfaction in Pyotr's voice, howsoever deeply buried. He'd caught Iosev's attention either way. Andrej joined Feraltz at the foot of the passenger loading ramp, nudging him aside by sheer force of proximity. Feraltz took half-a-step to the right, keeping his hands carefully quiet at his sides. There was a coded message there. *I'm staying out of this. All yours, lord prince.*

"You have assaulted my chief of Security," Andrej said mildly, switching to Aznir now that Pyotr knew what he wanted. "You have shot a man to whom I owe both my life and my sanity. How do you explain this, Iosev Ulexeievitch?"

He could see the emotions passing through Iosev's mind by the changing expressions on his face as he spoke. Proud satisfaction gave way to aggrieved surprise; and then, finally, to anger. "You are loyal to them, Derush, but I am your brother. And he was in our way." Shifting his weight Iosev raised an accusing finger, pointing it at Andrej for emphasis.

"I have done what nobody else at Canopy Base was able to do. I have gained entry into the thula. For this I deserve praise, and not reproach. I should have known better. You have been jealous of me since we were children, you who have everything and I nothing, and by a mere accident of birth."

This was insane. "Go to Sorsa, Iosev," Andrej said. "Say that I will take the thula and follow him." Iosev hadn't gained access to the thula. Lek had. Iosev had had no part in it. "Seek your reward from Deputy Sorsa. You will have none from me, for shooting Brachi Stildyne."

That was all Andrej had to say to Iosev, because *thank you for this excellent excuse to have the thula to ourselves* would not be well-received. Turning to go Andrej started up the passenger loading ramp—no hand-knotted runner of fine wool this time, just the bare traction surface underfoot—but Iosev seized him from behind, pulling at the collar of Andrej's coat. "You do not send me away like a servant, I am the master here!"

For one long shimmering instant sheer surprise paralyzed Andrej. In that moment the force of Iosev's imperious fist clenched in his clothing pulled Andrej off balance; he staggered back against his brother, who took him by the shoulders with both hands to spin him around. Almost by the throat.

The moment didn't last. Blind fury rose in Andrej's heart. Iosev had set Andrej to torture Stoshi, and had watched with pleasure. Had shot Stildyne. Iosev had given himself to the Angel of Destruction, to speak the name of which was as to spit.

Iosev could not hold him. Breaking Iosev's grip with ferocious force Andrej spun on his heel to punch Iosev in the diaphragm with explosive savagery, all of his collected outrage concentrated on the blow. Iosev stumbled back and Andrej followed him, on fire with contempt and outrage and thirst for revenge. He had been trained to fight by the same Brachi Stildyne whom Iosev had just shot, casually, carelessly, like a man would shoot a target on the range, just to force an issue out of boastful pride.

Andrej struck his brother across the face and it felt good, so he pulled Iosev back up onto his feet and hit him again. Iosev had the Edeslok gun, pointing it at Andrej with a trembling hand. Andrej believed that at this moment Iosev was capable of firing; but—consumed with furious contempt—Andrej didn't care. Now Station security had seen the gun, though, and swarmed on Iosev, struggling to gain control.

Iosev fell to his knees under the weight of their onslaught with a look of pure hatred in his eyes, and in that moment Andrej felt any residual fraternal affection for his brother die out of his heart and mind utterly. It was just as well for Iosev that those men had come between them, Andrej realized. If they hadn't Andrej would have hit Iosev again, and then again, and again after, and the odds were good that he would not have stopped after that until Iosev was dead.

"Take him to Deputy Sorsa." Let the Angel of Destruction deal with a man who raised his hand against his elder brother. "I will wait on board the thula. I require nothing else from you at this time, you are released."

Once he was up the loading ramp into the ship, once the thula was sealed for departure, they'd won half the battle. If Lek couldn't get them out, even against all odds, no one could. Without a backward glance Andrej walked up the ramp into the thula, hearing it start to retract behind him—sealing them away from Canopy Base, and everything it stood for.

CHAPTER EIGHT

The Flight of the *Fisher Wolf*

Robert St. Clare's brain swam slowly and lazily up to the surface of his consciousness, bypassing a large comfortable-looking bed invitingly made up with flannel sheets and a smiling brown-haired woman with a regretful apology. *Sorry. Someone is talking. I should probably listen.*

"You begin to come into focus, Robert, can you hear me?"

The officer. Robert blinked; where were they, he and his brain? It appeared to be the wheelhouse of the thula, and he appeared to be sitting at his station. He didn't seem to be able to move his legs; half of his field of vision appeared to have gone on vacation. "Anders." Wait, had he said that out loud? Maybe he wasn't dreaming so much as drunk, and of as little use to a woman either way. "Your Excellency. Sir."

"One or more of those. Yes. How do you find yourself here, at this moment?" As his working eye found its focus Robert could see Koscuisko's face in front of him, appraising and watchful. Yes, he was at his station in the thula's wheelhouse, with its familiar low ceiling, the quiet murmur of its comps, the gentle glow of the read-outs from its monitor screens. He could hear voices, coming around to the right side of his head where his ear was still on duty.

Not all the voices were ones he recognized, though. "Fisner Feraltz, voice identification, confirm. *Fisher Wolf* to command ship *Buration*." Turning in his chair with some difficulty Robert saw a man bending over the boards on Lek's left, coding a communications array; Pyotr was somewhere else, then. Lek turned casually away, toward Robert, to capture the code stream with a few keystrokes. Robert didn't catch Lek's eye and Lek didn't wink; it was probably better that way.

"I'm confused, your Excellency," Robert said. That was the least of it. "How did we get here? What's happening?"

The Koscuisko prince is on board? Status, please. That would be *Buration*. "Where to start," Koscuisko said. "We are on the thula. Canopy Base is to be evacuated. You arrived ahead of me with my cousin Stanoczk and put yourself between Lek and an ex-Inquisitor. You have suffered some dilapidations."

Oh. Yes. Right. Robert began to imagine that he remembered this. Had it worked, then? They were on the thula, and he could hear Lek. So far so good. "I can't move, your Excellency." Not much. And the sense he had of his body was oddly removed, as though his limbs were in the next room and ignoring him.

"The son of the Koscuisko prince intends to travel on *Fisher Wolf* with his crew and the prisoner." No, that wasn't Koscuisko. That wasn't even a very Koscuisko thing to say. "Please transmit course and schedule, *Buration*." Who had they said they were, earlier? Fisner Feraltz? Not one of theirs. Station personnel, then. Was that a problem?

"You cannot move because you have been injured, and I forbid you the use of your legs." *That* was Koscuisko. "Nor can you see nor hear out of the left side of your face. You may sit at your station, but touch nothing." As if he could. "Discomfort will increase as sedation wears off. I'm sorry. But you may be needed, we're down one of the crew."

Well, which was it? *Touch nothing*? Or *you may be needed*? Touch nothing until he was awake enough for it to hurt to move, maybe. That actually made sense. He would rather it hadn't.

This is Buration. *Please re-confirm, course and schedule to be transmitted to* Fisher Wolf, *transporting the lord prince Andrej Ulexeievitch with prisoner and crew.*

Buration sounded a little hesitant, but Feraltz displayed no uncertainty whatever. "Personal direct instruction, lord prince Andrej Ulexeievitch Koscuisko. Confirmed."

And from beside Robert Koscuisko said, "Is there a problem, Feraltz?" in the sort of tone of voice that indicated strongly that the only acceptable answer was

No sir of course not sir no problem your Excellency, no problem at all.

Fisher Wolf, *this is* Buration. *Stand by in place for course and schedule, on your mark.*

"No, lord prince," Feraltz said. Koscuisko had given him no option. Robert saw something on one of his monitors, the proximity viewer; Koscuisko had told him not to touch anything, though. What to do? It was a dilemma.

Robert cleared his throat. "Hem. Someone outside, your Excellency." Waiting on the tarmac below the now-closed passenger ramp, a shortish someone with a big nose and two significantly hefty trundle-carts. The kind installation kitchens used to move people's food from where it was prepared to where it was to be eaten.

He had a data stream monitor on his board, too, and it showed him information passing from *Buration* to Lek's boards, though not what the details were. It was coming dense and deep, too, but that was how the thula liked it.

Koscuisko leaned over Robert's shoulder and left his hand there, turning his head. "Feraltz." His voice was considerably more neutral, which Robert was glad to hear for Feraltz' sake. Whoever he was. "Why has Waclav come? Do you not evacuate your Sarvaw? Because I will be very glad to have him, if he is not wanted elsewhere." That was an odd thing to say. Lek was Sarvaw, and they were evacuating Lek. That had been an issue, though, hadn't it? Lek being Sarvaw?

"I'd taken the liberty of directing his Excellency's fast-meal be brought here, with provision for his Excellency's

people as well. It may please his Excellency to permit
Waclav to travel with him, and provide such services en
route as his Excellency might require."

"You do not come?" Koscuisko sounded a little
surprised. "My brother was to travel unescorted?" Feraltz
had turned away from Lek's comms to answer Koscuisko's
question. Robert laid his left hand casually down over the
tell-tale on his board that might betray the signature
capture Lek had initiated. That wasn't touching much, just
shifting a weight, really. Feraltz had probably called
Buration on a secure channel, in which case Feraltz didn't
need to know that the thula was still listening. Quietly.
Not interrupting. Not bothering anybody.

"He was expected to travel on *Buration*, with an escort
suitable to his rank. An officer will be detailed
immediately if you wish it, lord prince, but I have other
duties which necessarily deprive me of the honor."

By themselves, then. "Godsalt, open the passenger
ramp, if you will," Koscuisko said. "That man is a genius
in the kitchen. It will be a distinct privilege to have him
on board, Feraltz, even if he is Sarvaw, and unredeemed."

No, something was being not-said, and unless Robert
was mistaken Lek's shoulders had taken a distinct twitch
at that word Koscuisko had used—"unredeemed." Robert
could catch only the vaguest hint of it, like the deep bass
vibration of his uncle Hams' singing. But if he could hear
it the others could hear it too, and better, because they
were not under the influence of Koscuisko's medicinal
compounds and both of their ears should be on shift.

"You shouldn't be needing me, your Excellency, if I
may be excused?" Feraltz asked. Robert saw Koscuisko

look to Lek, who turned at his station to look back over his shoulder at Koscuisko and nod. Koscuisko nodded back.

"Granted," Koscuisko said. "Good-bye, Fisner Feraltz, you have dealt honestly with me. You have leave to depart." Robert keyed a few sweeps as the ramp deployed, touching as little as possible; and watched his monitor until the cook was on board, and the passenger loading ramp secured once more.

Something smelled delicious. Robert hoped he was going to be able to manage a bite to eat, or several; his right knee was starting to warm up in an I-am-irritated sort of way, and he seemed to have a headache. Fast-meal would probably come as a useful distraction. "Trundlers clean and clear," Garrity announced, but Garrity wouldn't have let them on board any other way. "If his Excellency is sure about this?"

"Mr. Pyotr, are we secure?" Koscuisko asked. Robert turned his hand on edge where it lay: they were still listening to *Buration*, but nothing was going out. "Thank you. I believe Waclav is to be trusted, even though he is not at this time actually wearing the red halter."

That meant something. What? Cousin Stanoczk wore a red ribbon around his neck, and that was what he called it, a halter. The Malcontent's halter. So that was what Koscuisko was saying. Waclav was a cousin of Cousin Stanoczk. What about Feraltz? "I'm going aft unless you need me, gentlemen," Koscuisko added. "Stoshi and Stildyne to be seen to."

"We can use Chief if you can get him up, your Excellency," Kerenko said. What? Stildyne not in duty trim? What had been happening around here, while he'd been away from the wars?

Then Robert smelled something, something with a rich malty fragrance that had undertones of milky sweetness, something speaking subtly of cream and honey. Cold-meal mush? Could it be? Cold-meal mush was always so much better when it was hot, and here was a bowlful with steam rising to fill Robert's brain with a transcendent greed that drowned all other considerations. He was under the influence, Robert told himself. He wasn't responsible for his actions.

"Let me help you with that," the Waclav-cook said, sitting down at the place next to Robert's station. "I'm told you're still coming to full command of your arms and legs."

Waclav put the bowl in Robert's hand as he spoke, wrapping his own two hands around Robert's one to hold the dish in place. Robert held it close to minimize the damage should he lose control of the shallow broad-basined spoon on its way twixt the cup and the lip, and supped a dish of cold-meal mush more ambrosial than anything he'd ever tasted in his life.

Exactly precisely what had happened was something of which Stildyne could not be entirely sure. There'd been the thula; there'd been one of Koscuisko's brothers. The next thing he knew he'd been dumped into a berth like a replacement issue of hygiene flimsy, and abandoned here.

Shot in the arse, someone had said. Someone was coming into the cabin now, wrestling with some equipment—and clumsily, by the sound of it. Things were clearly happening. They'd gained the thula, obviously, since he was on it. Now they only had to get away.

"I'm coming forward," Stildyne said to the ceiling, because they'd laid him on his back and he couldn't overcome the dead weight of his right leg-quarter to sit up. "Little help here. What's going on?" He was missing a crucial element in the situation, he knew he was.

"We are all on board," the someone said. It was someone who was generally Stoshi-sized and Stoshi-shaped, but that wasn't Stoshi's voice. So it was Koscuisko. And he'd watched Koscuisko—and Stoshi—"Lek is receiving course and vector information. We expect to depart soon."

The noise Stildyne had heard was Koscuisko bringing up the walking exoskeleton. "We've got Stoshi?" Of course they did. Koscuisko wouldn't leave without Cousin Stanoczk. "How is he?"

Koscuisko was angling the posterior bracing beneath Stildyne's back, working around the field compression dressing that Stildyne knew without feeling it must be there. "You first, Brachi. I will see to my cousin once you are on your feet, because you are needed to fly the thula, and I don't know which of you I am more ashamed to stand before."

No standing was going on around here. There was lying on his back like a discarded underblouse on a berth on the thula while someone fastened together a walking-brace. Stildyne couldn't really remember the last time he'd been shot; never, with a projectile weapon. "Ashamed, your Excellency?" He didn't know if he wanted to call Koscuisko by his name. Habit came to his rescue. Reaching for Stildyne's right arm Koscuisko strapped it into the support structure.

"To have not spoken to you in time. At Emandis. All of this time trying to reach you, and not escaping from Safehaven." Clearly Koscuisko understood that his shame with regards to what he'd done to Stoshi needed no explanation. He could feel Koscuisko working at the brace's knee joint, pulling the extenders apart to fit Stildyne's height; he could feel pressure below the middle of his thigh, but not much else. "I came to Gonebeyond to say that I was sorry. But I've left it too long."

"Sorry," Stildyne repeated, stupidly. "Of all the things you have to be sorry about, sorry for that?" He'd run simulations in his mind during idle hours from time to time, trying to imagine what he would say to Koscuisko when or if he ever saw Koscuisko again. None of his projections had involved Koscuisko apologizing; but there was such a sense of recognition in his heart when Koscuisko said it that suddenly Stildyne couldn't imagine what he might have wanted to hear more.

"Yes, I know." Koscuisko's smile was very quick, there and gone in an instant. "But it is of a different nature of regret. I've wronged you deeply. And for that I am deeply sorry." Koscuisko stepped back. "See if you can sit up."

Stretching out his left hand for Koscuisko to take Stildyne pulled himself up, sitting on the edge of the berth and catching his breath before he hove up onto his feet. Back-and-shoulder bracing was its own distinct kind of awkward, and having no feeling in his buttocks left him with no sense of his center of gravity. Stumbling forward Stildyne headed for the door: the bracing had a machine intelligence built in, and would adjust to the way his body was trying to move as it learned him.

"Adequately well, your Excellency." He caught at both sides of the open doorway to steady himself. He could get the hang of this. He needed to get forward and find out what was happening in the wheelhouse. "We can talk about it when this is over, Andrej, you'll be checking on Stoshi next. He had a restful night. Relatively speaking."

A night Stildyne had spent at Stoshi's side as so many vigils in years past with Koscuisko drunk or deep in some sort of psychotic fugue state. Just like old times. Nothing like old times. He'd think about it later. Right now they had to figure out how to break away from Canopy Base and escape pursuit, before he could afford to meditate on what it felt like to be apologized to by Andrej Koscuisko.

They'd moved Stoshi into the cabin farthest from the wheelhouse, still secured to the upright mover. There were only four sleeping-cabins on the thula; Andrej wondered who bunked where, because there were seven crew, six once-bond-involuntaries and Stildyne. Now that he'd gotten Stildyne up and moving he could delay this no longer. He had to go in, and face his cousin.

Stoshi was awake, but clearly somewhat confused, by his expression; and watched Andrej's approach with glittering eyes, half-fearful, half-consumed with something different. Dread and remorse. Andrej didn't understand. He'd think about it later.

"I'm going to set you free of these secures." Stopping a good pace in front of the upright mover Andrej reached for the mover's vertical angle adjustment, carefully and deliberately, so that Stoshi could track his every movement. "But first you must pledge me something, Stoshi, in the name of your divine Patron himself, may he wander in bliss."

It was difficult trying to decide what oath might carry weight; Malcontents weren't people in the legal sense, but the personal property of a Saint under Canopy. But what the Malcontent affirmed the Malcontent performed. "Speak." Stoshi sounded half-strangled, and there was a tremor in his voice. And this was Stoshi talking. "Or I cannot give my word."

"You will very much want to assault me, Stoshi, if you do not want to hide yourself above all." Fear made a man lash out against the enemy who made him feel afraid. "Stay your hand until we are safe and away. Pledge me on this."

"Not to strike you down for what you have done to me?" Stoshi seemed to be considering the idea, carefully.

"Until later." It was all Andrej could ask. Stoshi nodded; Andrej stepped close, but kept to one side of the mover, unfastening secures. Ankles. Knees. Thighs. He had to take a nod as a spoken pledge. There were limits.

Andrej was careful to touch only the restraints, and not Stoshi; but when he loosed the final secure across Stoshi's shoulders Stoshi collapsed against him, falling forward. Andrej caught his cousin in his arms, staggering back beneath the sudden burden of the all-but-dead weight.

The berth was right there, close alongside, made up to welcome a tired crewman; he maneuvered Stoshi into a seated position, with his back leaning up against the cabin wall. He wanted Stoshi to lie down, because the drugs in his system would still be affecting his balance and muscle tone. At the same time Andrej knew how important it was not to tell a recently tortured man what to do, once he was rescued, freed.

There. That was done; he could leave. He was halfway to the door before Stoshi spoke in a voice resonant with horror. "I could never have understood, Derush, how terrible you are, when a man comes before you."

Stoshi chose an old word, "terrible," something that creates terror. Andrej paused, looking back over his shoulder; what could he say? "I am so sorry, Stoshi." No, that didn't begin to touch it. And he wasn't sorry, either. There was that in him that wasn't sorry at all. "Only that it seemed to be required. And there was only the one way that I could do it."

He wasn't going to plead for understanding, to ask for forgiveness. He would not pretend to be a passive victim of his own flaws when it had always been his choice, no matter how long it had taken him to understand that, and to admit it.

"You must understand." Stoshi's voice had so much changed that Andrej turned, startled, to see Stoshi slumped against the cabin wall where he sat on the berth, looking straight into Andrej's eyes with neither contempt nor disgust on his face. "None of this was meant to happen. You have confounded the Saint himself, Derush, and I would not have thought it possible. There will be a signal from Canopy Base, and the thula must carry it forward, with all the power that it can provide."

Dropping his eyes to his hands resting on his knees

Stoshi put his head back against the wall. There was a curious dullness in his voice. "It will be a dense signal, and it will come very fast, and above all else it must not be interrupted. Do you understand, Derush? Above all else. It must go through. On this everything depends."

Andrej stared at his cousin with disbelief and dawning comprehension. "Of course," he said. "There is another of you." Waclav had told him as much. Who? Who else? Fisner Feraltz had woken him, warned him; left a secure channel from *Buration* negligently open where Lek could code and capture it, and then left, because he had "other duties to perform." "It was all for a data stream?"

Buration would detect the transmission. One so powerful as to require the thula's comps to handle would leap screaming to anyone's attention; Sorsa would know it could not be in his best interest to allow it to continue. Sorsa would try to put a stop to it, using all of the weapons at his command.

"It wasn't meant to happen this way," Stoshi insisted, still looking at his hands. "All was arranged. I would arrive. I would retrieve our resources. We would leave with Fiska, with *Fisher Wolf* and your gentlemen. We would be away before we were discovered and pursued, and we would have the data. Why did you come? All depends on this information, Derush, all, and it is I who am sorry."

Sorsa would not stay his hand to spare Andrej Koscuisko if the survival of his enterprise was at stake. This was the Angel of Destruction; history had already shown the horrors of which the Angel was capable. Stoshi was right. The Angel had to be destroyed. The signal had to go through.

"We have been years getting this close," Stoshi said, when Andrej didn't answer. "And we find the mad dog thriving. We must not fail. You don't know what it's cost already."

The thula would come under attack. It would have to defend itself for as long as it could. Andrej could only guess at what information there might be, names, locations, plans, passwords, security codes. "You ask them for their lives. And they owe you—what?" Andrej demanded, in disbelief. Stoshi shook his head wearily, *no, it is far worse than that.*

"*You* ask them for their lives, Derush." This was the final horror. This was the ultimate betrayal. "You ask, Derush, and they will give, because you and they already have, years and years ago, did you but notice. My Patron is at fault. Only, I swear this to you, Derush, we did not guess that you would come to Canopy Base."

He couldn't. They owed him nothing. He owed them his life, his sanity, his soul. "How can I. Truly, Stanoczk. As a question in pure fact. How can I?"

"Well, you must find a way." Turning his head Stoshi met his gaze once more, his eyes pitiless and utterly forlorn at one and the same time. "Because you must. Go away, Derush. I must sit and contemplate my crimes against you all, but my last crime is one that you must commit."

And that was clearly all Stoshi had to say. His mind blank and numb with desperation Andrej pushed his way past Waclav in the corridor and fled the cabin for the wheelhouse where his people were, who—because Andrej had sought them at Langsarik Station, and come to Canopy Base—were now condemned to die.

⊕ ⊕ ⊕

The cook with the cold-meal mush from Heaven had left the wheelhouse, because things were getting busy. Robert was much clearer in his mind now that he had something in his stomach, though it came with a price. He hurt all over. No surprise there, because he remembered some of what he'd had from Mathin; and he could remember some other things, too, things that had come to him whilst he'd been busy not talking. He'd think about whether he was going to speak to Stildyne about it all later.

Stildyne was not operating from a good refresh either, shot in the rump Robert understood, strapped into a walking-brace and webbed in to his usual clamshell in the middle of the wheelhouse where he could watch things and stay out of the way. They were among the last to clear Canopy Base. Canopy Base had resigned itself to abandoning *Fisher Wolf* to the general destruction, Robert supposed, since they hadn't been able to get its attention; and the flight formation had apparently been too carefully calculated to update on the fly.

"Clear," Lek said, and Pyotr tapped his boards. Robert watched the station fall away from them; further out from Canopy Base the ships were leaving, one after another, arrayed against the background starfield in a tightly spaced convoy grid.

In the near position Robert could see Canopy Base's command ship *Buration*, a medium-heavy freighter with enviably sexy sensor arrays and a beautiful docking bay all clean and shining under its hull lights, holding—he assumed—to ensure that everyone got off. "We need to leave, Lek," Stildyne said, from his clamshell. He was obviously a little potted; Stildyne had never been a man to waste words on the obvious. Robert appreciated that.

"Departure sequence in process," Lek said patiently. "Another few minutes, Chief. Destination unspecified. We've got the coordinates, but the thula doesn't know where they take us. Unmapped vector. Doesn't matter, anyway." Because wherever it was, they weren't going there. Sorted.

Pyotr had *Buration's* traffic on feed in the background, translation engaged; its syntax came out strangely, in Standard, but the thula was out of practice. Lucky bit of business, Feraltz forgetting to close his secure feed before he left.

Canopy Base was apparently in Langsarik space. They could back-engineer the vector transit they'd come in on, and retrace their steps to Langsarik Station. If there was a ship the thula couldn't outrun they hadn't met up with it yet. Most of the evacuation fleet would be on vector and unable to turn back when the thula started its vector spin, and by the time *Buration* realized that the thula was not coming it would be too late.

"*Fisher Wolf*, this is *Buration*." It was one of the few communications in the clear they'd had, *Buration* making contact. Pyotr muted the background noise to avoid giving the clandestine feed away; Lek waited for Pyotr's nod before he replied.

"*Buration*, this is the thula. Your instructions?"

On the over-screen Robert could see the command ship wheeling in the sky, a long slow somersault that would bring it face-to-face with the now-deserted Canopy

Base. It was a beautiful ship. "Stand clear, *Fisher Wolf*. Canopy Base will be destroyed. Shield from debris and take precautionary measures."

"Heard and understood, *Buration*," Lek replied. Robert supposed he did understand; an emergency evacuation didn't leave much time to sanitize an abandoned base. Destroying it was probably the only way to be sure they didn't leave any compromising information behind.

Pyotr had cut the *Buration* out of braid and brought the clandestine strand back to the forefront of the communication stream. "In eight, seven, six is the initiating of detonation," it said. Canopy Base grew smaller by the moment on the over-screen; the thula was approaching *Buration* rapidly, wheeling to one side as *Buration* turned.

It suddenly seemed that there was a problem. "No— Deputy Sorsa—has occurred none detonation." There was a hitch, then.

"We will a little while wait." Robert didn't think he recognized the voice, but to be fair he'd only had the one interview. Maybe one-and-a-half. "There may be a mechanical malfunction." The longer Robert listened to *Buration*'s stream the less he noticed its syntax. "His blood is pure. He will prove true. We give him chance to complete his assignment."

Robert's board sounded an alarm, and he turned to its tell-tales in an instant, howsoever clumsily. Something was coming through on one of the thula's channels, and there was an auto-relay in effect. He couldn't tell where it was going, but as for where it was coming from—so much was perfectly clear. Mindful of the importance of watching his fingers very carefully he tried to channel the signal to find out what it was.

The clandestine feed from the *Buration* crackled with a voice raised to a shout of alarm. "Canopy Base transmitting, high-density message, encrypted, not in my experience so heavy. Fast too. Catching only nothing."

"Signal destination?" Robert wished Sorsa luck with that question. *Fisher Wolf* didn't know, at least not yet. And what *Fisher Wolf* couldn't figure out nobody could.

"Cannot detect. Out of system. There is no authorization code. Who is sending, when it comes from Canopy Base?"

Sorsa didn't bother to answer the question, not directly. *Buration* had almost finished its spin, was almost true on a direct plane with Canopy Base. "Destroy it," Sorsa said. "Warn the thula. Say there's sabotage. Stop that feed."

The formal channel from *Buration* came in on alarm, now, in plain Standard. "*Fisher Wolf*, this is *Buration*. Emergency. We're under attack from Canopy Base. Get clear."

"*Buration*, check, out and away for evasive action." Pyotr was working quickly; the *Buration* was settling into a firing position. But now here was the officer, Anders son of Ilex, bursting into the wheelhouse at a dead run. Robert hoped he was going for a clamshell to strap in, because he thought things might be about to get a little unstable.

"I have much to say, and not much time to say it," Koscuisko said. "There will be a signal. We must port it through. The Angel of Destruction must be destroyed, and this is why the Malcontent has brought the thula to Canopy Base, though we were not intended to die here."

Not strapping in to an observer's clamshell as he ought to have done, but stopping himself with an effort with one hand to the back each of the central stations, Pyotr's, Lek's. "We" were not intended to die here. Interesting. Old habits of thought died hard; or hadn't sickened at all in the past mere year, which Robert considered to be much more likely.

"Stoshi didn't come here to get in. He came to get something out, with the information to destroy the entire organization." Robert had never heard Koscuisko sound so desperate in his life, and it unnerved him, even more than Koscuisko did when he was wearing the wrong set of hands. "We cannot let it all have been for nothing. You have seen what these people will do. Please, gentlemen."

Pyotr stood up, turning to face Koscuisko. He certainly had their attention, Robert thought, admiring; Koscuisko was good at that. Robert kept working to channel the data stream, listening. "Mystery transmission going hell for overload," Pyotr said. "*Buration*'s going to destroy Canopy Base. We need to get out of here, but we'll lose the feed, and why?"

Reasonable question. Robert looked back over his shoulder, awkwardly, he couldn't help it; nor was he the only person. Koscuisko was looking around him, making eye contact, man by man. "Because they are the night raiders. And also because you have seen the torture room, and Mathin in it. If we don't stop them there will be more raids, more rooms, more people in them."

None quite like Anders Koscuisko, maybe, but the

point was well taken, and since Cousin Stanoczk was not here—in the back, Robert supposed, sensibly keeping out of the way—it was probably up to Robert to speak for the people in those rooms. They already knew how Koscuisko felt about it.

"I like it." It wasn't that Robert wanted to die; only that Koscuisko had saved his life at Fleet Orientation Station Medical, and was the only man who could ask for it back. Also they'd all seen the sorts of things that the night raiders left behind. "Yes by me." It would close to kill his sister to lose him again, but she owed her life to Koscuisko as well.

"Thought I'd never get my chance to die in battle," Pyotr said, and sat back down. *Buration* hadn't stopped moving, but the noise from its feed was getting more anxious by the moment. *Why hasn't the thula moved. We need to get them out of there. I want that ship, and it's the son of the Koscuisko prince.* "At least he asked this time. I'm in. Let's do it."

And, in the background of the *Buration* feed, another voice, *I also am the son of the Koscuisko prince, and I say my brother has betrayed the Holy Mother.* Godsalt laughed, from the weaponer's station; an honest laugh, cheerful and happy. "Better than what we had under Jurisdiction," he said. "Pyotr, weapons are on line. Stildyne, left lateral guns, and you need a head start, go. Hirsel, right laterals. I've got the main battle cannon, Lek, on your direct."

Stildyne moved surprisingly well in that brace, Robert noted, pulling his leg behind him, staggering awkwardly out for the lower weapons bays. *Buration*'s profile on scan was changing rapidly; it was the thula that was moving now. Robert was going to miss the thula when he was dead, but at least it—and he—would die well, and for the good and true.

"Component class indicates weapons distribution on horizontal axis, offset six," Pyotr said. "And we already know they've got money, so we have to assume the worst. Hit it as hard as you can. Gentlemen, your targets."

Reaching across himself—left hand not working well enough for complicated actions—Robert keyed a subsidiary channel so he could track the main screen and his board at the same time, reinforcing the comm feed from Canopy Base with everything the thula could spare from Lek's maneuvering. He had to hurry, because most of the power he was using would redirect when the shooting started, and then the signal would be on its own. If they were all going to die for that signal, it was up to him to make it count, and get it through.

That wild spin on the screen as *Buration* tumbled— that was the thula, skimming swift and nimble into an attack attitude. The aperture he could barely make out opening across *Buration*'s skin, that would be a gun-port, but he had no time to see what the gun looked like when it was deployed because the screen blanked in a flash of white as the thula fired on it.

"*Fisher Wolf*, this is *Buration*, what are you doing, have you gone mad—" The protests were predictable, the response as well. *Buration* fired on the thula without waiting for a reply, but Lek had the ship in hand, and spun out from underneath *Buration*'s plane of fire so that the energy packets sped away into empty space and were gone.

It didn't solve the problem, no. Their problem was only now beginning to present itself in all its true and daunting complexity, because *Buration* was showing its teeth, a wide slice dropped down from the leading edge of its forward hull to reveal an array bristling with guns.

Robert felt an impact that shook him hard in his clamshell, but Koscuisko had webbed him in securely and he had to stay on that data feed no matter how much it hurt. "Sorry about that one," Lek said. "Stildyne, I'm trying for auxiliary. Then I'm going to flip for the main port, hang on, everybody."

Buration hadn't stopped trying, even while it turned to pursue its attack. "*Fisher Wolf.* Lord prince. Andrej Ulexeievitch." That was Sorsa; there was no fear in his voice, and no uncertainty. "We can give you everything you want, everything you need. You need our help and our protection. Call off your attack. Do not spill your brother's blood."

Koscuisko's brother? How had it been for Koscuisko to find his brother here, and mixed up with these people? Koscuisko hadn't webbed in; he'd gotten knocked against the floor, which was a hard one. Now Koscuisko pushed himself to his feet.

"Iosev Ulexeievitch is no longer my brother." It was a terrible thing to say, and for Robert to hear—all of his own brothers were dead. Maybe Koscuisko was just making sure they all knew he knew that his brother was on *Buration*, and would fight anyway. "And we will not call off the attack."

"You cannot prevent us from destroying Canopy Base. The Holy Mother grants us absolution, even if we shed the blood of the Koscuisko prince." There was someone babbling in the background, crying out in disbelief and terror. *Andrej, no. Derush. Don't shoot. One father, one mother. You can't.*

Robert cut the *Buration* out of braid on Lek's signal, focusing on the data stream from Canopy Base. The thula shuddered horribly; Robert hoped that would remind Koscuisko to strap in to a station and secure himself, but Robert had other things to worry about. "We're hit," Lek said. "Garrity. Damage report."

"Last chance, your Excellency," Pyotr said. Maybe, Robert thought, he wasn't the only person here who'd been unsure about the family thing; but Koscuisko wasn't a man to let anything stand between him and what he believed he had to do. Robert had always liked that about Koscuisko.

"We must protect the transmission," Koscuisko said. He hadn't webbed in; he was still standing behind Pyotr and Lek. He was going to be sorry, too, the next hit they took, probably soon. "For that we must defend Canopy Base. We fight."

Facing the *Buration* dead on, nose-to-nose on the overscreen, the thula's armament spoke, loud and firm. Main battle cannon, cruiser-killer class destroyer. Had Sorsa's people understood what it was, when they'd searched the ship? Or had the thula locked off its bay and refused them access?

"Good one." That was Garrity, raising his voice to be heard through the roaring sound that filled the ship's braid. "A little close. Hang on."

The thula rolled head over heels in uncontrolled reaction to the blowback from the impact of the cannon's energy-packet projectile. Shaken at his station but secured by the webbing Robert vaguely noticed Koscuisko's body flying clear across the room, fetching up against the wall. There was an element of humor in that, really; but Robert had a data feed to protect, and a desperate struggle ahead to keep it channeled as the thula fought for Canopy Base and its own survival.

Serge remembered helping his Uncle Tomi rinse the bean-curd for the autumnal equinox. For weeks it would ferment in clear-crock, ten to a barrel, blanketed in sea-weave patiently braided in place by the younger boys. When the time came Serge and his brothers were all enlisted to help—every boy born to clan Wheatfields, within an eight-year span. Serge himself had been in the middle of his age-cohort so he was neither strongest nor the weakest among his brothers; but he had always loved his Uncle Tomi best, and tried to make himself useful.

Serge would strip the dry fibrous sea-weave coverings away from the clear-crocks so that Uncle Tomi could inspect the contents, the milky bean-curd broth, the shining white pearl-like marbles of the curd itself. After final inspection Uncle Tomi would break the seal—if the curd met his approval, if he judged it fully fermented—and the brine-salt stink of bean-curd would fill the rinsing-shed.

Uncle Tomi would pick up a crock, an entire crock, tall as one of Serge's younger brothers and heavier by half again as much, and—with a strong grip on the narrow mouth—upend it over the filter-hoop atop the lees-barrel to let the ripe curd out and drain the brine.

The contents of the crock would drip and gurgle, at first, in a war between gravity and a compression-plug of bean curd in the mouth of the crock. Slapping the side of the crock smartly with the flat of his hand to dislodge the plug of soft ripe bean-curd, Uncle Tomi would start to rotate the crock base-uppermost, and within moments what had been a chaotic slosh would start to spin into a vortex that grew stronger and stronger as brine and bean-curd alike whirled out of the mouth of the crock into the waiting filter-screen.

And that—Ship's Engineer Serge of Wheatfields told himself—was as good metaphor for a vector transit as any. One entered the displacement vortex by matching speed and spin to that of the vortex itself. One exited by flying out of one of the vector's mouths in a circular pattern, adjusting speed and spin to give steady course.

The process was simple in concept, but required precision in execution. One never knew what bit of bean-curd would consistently exit the vector where until the mathematical characteristics of the vector had been fully mapped, and even then there was always the chance that one might be flung out of the mouth of the clear-crock at an unexpected time, toward an unmapped destination.

The Kamishir vector was new-mapped. They knew next to nothing about it. But they knew they were a lump of curd of certain dimension. They knew what their position was in the vortex, and where they could expect to come out—Derideten. They knew that somewhere out there, outside the vector, was where they wanted to be, the point in space they had named Scanner Five. All they had to do was break out of the vortex, one soft tender cube

of bean-curd, and make it past the wall of the spinning
energy field without being whirled to a slurry: and then
find the trajectory that would drop them on top of that
disturbance Two had located. Yes. That was all they had
to do.

He didn't pace. He'd learned it made people nervous.
He didn't look up at the observation deck on the
mezzanine; he didn't need any help from any other officer
on board ship whether they were watching from the
observation deck or not. And his people didn't need any
help either. The hardest thing about being Ship's
Engineer was staying out of peoples' way.

But he didn't want to sit in his command chair and
calmly receive status reports. He needed to be closer, in
the middle of it all, in the center of the wheel of data-
stations, where he could look over anybody's shoulder
without them noticing. For that all he had to do was
crouch down in the middle of the floor, and occasionally
stretch his neck for a better view.

"Skein in braid," Cassie said. "On station. Sela, one.
Pumet, two. Allerb, four." There were ridges and valleys
in the vector spin. They needed to find a promising ridge,
one that would spin them to the right place along the
inner wall to drop straight down through the hollow throat
of the vortex and out into normal space.

They had to stay on the inner wall. The sea-weed that
Wheatfields' Uncle Tomi still used to set off the
coagulation process was never completely free of grains
of sand and tiny pebbles; when those bits of gravel spun
out to the outside of the vortex wall they could too easily
drop onto the inner shoulder of the crock and come to

rest there, to be rinsed out later. If that happened to the *Ragnarok* they could end up as one of the ghost ships that rode the vector forever. Serge wasn't interested.

"Taking the ridge, your Excellency," Cassie said, without turning. "Jans, next run, check line three. Pumet, take four. Manshie, you're six."

Once you were riding a ridge you could find ridgelines within ridgelines, because a vector carried multiple streams that joined and dropped on their own schedules, contributing their own energy, riding the collective power of the vector. They didn't need the fastest one; they needed the one that would bring them to the innermost eddy of the roiling wall at just the right moment. "Six," Manshie said. "Take it in twelve, Pumet."

"Concur," Pumet said. Cassie and Jans agreed too. Wheatfields nodded.

"Go, Manshie," Wheatfields said. "Sela, how are we doing on time?" He could sense the shift in the power of the ship's great conversion engines as Sela adjusted their speed to gain the strand of the vector skein they needed. They had to pick up speed. He could see how much more velocity they needed on the monitors that lined the walls, that tiled the ceilings; *more speed*, he urged Sela, in his mind. *More power*.

"Jans, we need redline," Sela said. "More speed." Serge kept his mouth shut. The right word in the right place, that was all they needed from him. He was in a sense completely superfluous to this process, except that it was his process, he was the one who owned it, he was the one who had trained it, and he was the one who would be to blame if it failed.

"Coming up on it in four," Jans said. That would be their drop. This was where he said something; so he stood up from his crouching position in the middle of the floor.

"Wheatfields," he said, knowing he had all-ship, reveling in the moment. "Battle stations, battle stations, brace for turbulence."

They hit the wall. He could see sensor displays, the shearing force through which the *Ragnarok* staggered, the onboard systems struggling with gravitational fields, the thickening of the plasma membrane that protected the hull against impact with any foreign object. Something negligibly small in normal space carried enough momentum to crater the hull, on vector.

The conversion engines' statistics kept edging up, into the red-line, deeper. Toward the black. Toward the point of failure. If the furnaces went black they wouldn't have to worry about where they dropped vector.

"Through," Jans was muttering. "Through, through, through, through, through—drop! We have vector drop!"

"Stay on it," Serge said, encouragingly, warningly. Yes, they had the drop. They'd be off vector in moments. Sela had to calibrate the line of departure, and she didn't have a moment to spare. Manshie had to locate the target area of space and calculate seventeen different ways to get there based on what Pumet could give him. And he, he should probably issue a status report sometime soon.

"We have vector drop, your Excellency," he said to the observation deck. If the Captain wasn't there she should be, and since she should be, she'd be there. He'd learned that about her. He liked it; predictability was a good thing, in senior officers, even brevet ones. "Into arrival calculations."

No answer, but he didn't expect one. And things were starting to get exciting, on the engineering bridge. "Your Excellency!" Allerb said, his attention riveted on his screens. "Small armada, arms at twelve-to-twenty-four by analysis. Apparent station evacuation in process."

Armed. Not a commercial station; not a civil population. "Light freighters?" he asked. "Landing craft?"

Allerb nodded. "Ship's signature analysis, stand by." The waste residue from the landing fields. The chemical components of a ship's energy exhaust on landing, taking off again, their holds full of plunder. The forensic evidence they'd collected from Haystacks. "It's them, your Excellency. Night raiders."

Suddenly Serge's eyes were full of salt that burned with ferocious intensity. Tears of sheer joy. "Shield all comms, close at speed, and prime for hostile contact," he ordered, pointing at the visual display on screen, his body resonating with fierce intent. "On 'em before they know we're coming, stand by to crush their comps to powder!"

Maybe he should have asked first. That was supposed to be the Captain's job, wasn't it? So maybe he'd violated protocol, and maybe he didn't care. The Captain wasn't saying anything. Then she did.

"Your action, Engineer," she said. It was all he needed to hear. They would be there. They would take those ships, cripple them with darts of energy that would target ship's comms and deprive them of any chance to get away. And then they would have a word or two with the night raiders about murder and plunder and driving little children out to stumble through the cold woods in their bare feet while their parents burned.

The emergency sulphurs had come on. Stildyne found himself thrown clear of the weaponer's station, lying awkwardly on his side on the floor; the place was lumpy with debris, but that was all right, because it gave him traction as he struggled to stand up, dragging his unresponsive leg in its brace.

Godsalt had fired the main battle cannon. They'd scored a hit, and it must have been dead at the *Buration*'s primed cannon, because they'd clearly had backsplash.

"Status," Stildyne called. Clawing his way to his feet he staggered into the thula's narrow corridor to go forward. Fire suppression was in effect, inerting foam clearing off from the ceiling as he went. He'd got some in his hair. It made his scalp itch. If he didn't get it rinsed away before too long he'd be getting a rash.

He heard the allship clip into braid, but it wasn't anything he didn't already know. *This is the Malcontent's thula* Fisher Wolf. *I have damage sustained. Assistance requested, ten souls in custody.*

The corridor behind the forward weaponer's station was even more cluttered with shoals of stores and wrack. The sulphurs were fading fast, which meant ship's onboard lighting was coming back up. He hadn't heard the hull breach alarm yet, which was good, because they didn't have survival gear for ten. Maybe the alarm had gone off while he'd been unconscious, but it was hard to sleep through the klaxon. He knew that from experience.

Scrambling through the corridor-panels and the ceiling-tiles that were in his way Stildyne fought his way through to the weaponer's station, encouraged by what seemed to be an echo of his scrabbling sounds coming from up ahead. Godsalt, cresting the frozen wave of shock-tossed kit-crates like an aquatic mammal in heavy surf. What kind of mammal exactly Stildyne couldn't remember, but he'd seen a presentation on the educational track once, in his few years of Bench-mandated juvenile programmed instruction.

"I'd *completely* forgotten how much fun that is," Godsalt crowed. Stildyne had to grin. If they didn't make it out of this at least Godsalt would go out on a high note. Behind him, now, Stildyne heard more commotion; Hirsel had gotten himself extricated without any help from them. But they hadn't heard from the wheelhouse, where the others were—

"Reporting," the allship said. Pyotr. That was a relief. "Power down by six, shields damaged, aft nav may be compromised. Koscuisko's unconscious, no news from cousins Waclav and Stanoczk. Topside now. You're needed."

As a status it left too much to the imagination for Stildyne's entire satisfaction—where were they, what had happened, was somebody going to start shooting at them again, was Canopy Base intact?—but the best place to get answers was the wheelhouse. Stildyne pulled himself up the emergency ladder between decks as quickly as he could, hauling the dead weight of his braced leg up out of the floor-well to clear the way for Godsalt and Hirsel.

The wheelhouse lights were up, but they were still dim. Someone had strapped Koscuisko's limp body into an observer's clamshell, in the rear; Lek had the over-screen working, murky and undefined. Stildyne could just make out Canopy Base's atmosphere containment dome, glowing serene and milky-white in the middle distance. It was still there; so they hadn't been out for too long.

"*Buration* is apparently disabled," Lek said over his shoulder. "Five light freighters with serious weapons profiles are turning back out of convoy. Maybe to take souls off *Buration*. Maybe to fire on Canopy Base. Almost certainly hostile in intent."

"Have we got anything for them?" Stildyne asked. Godsalt had hurried to the weaponer's station, and was working fast. Unfortunately, what he did was shake, not nod, his head. "Main battle cannon is operable, but only at cost," Godsalt said. "We can blow them up but we'll go with them. We'll have to get close." The enemy was unlikely to allow that to happen. "And what did you do to your station, Chief? Completely useless."

Stildyne could see ships coming nearer. They didn't look like they were coming straight for the thula, though. Maybe they'd decided the thula was not an immediate threat; if so, Stildyne was inclined to agree with them. But Koscuisko had asked them to protect Canopy Base.

"Swivels?" he asked. The swivels weren't good for much, and there were only two of them. But there were only five heavy scouts. If they caught them in exactly the right spot maybe they could slow them down.

"We'll only annoy them, Chief," Godsalt said. "Do we

feel like being annoying? They'll just blow us up sooner, rather than later, on their way to Canopy Base."

Probably. "Robert?" It was all about the data feed, the signal, the information Stoshi had come for. If Koscuisko wasn't unconscious there were good odds he'd tell them not to let the thula fall into enemy hands, but they didn't need Koscuisko's help to come to that perfectly obvious conclusion.

"Data feed carrying forward." He was running ragged. Stildyne could hear it; but Robert was on task regardless. "Not slowing down." So Canopy Base was still to be protected.

"Well, I vote we continue to annoy them, as much as possible." He was their chief by consent now, not by rank, and they were the ones who were running things. He could suggest, but not mandate. "Have we got feet?"

Little thula feet, suitable for running around enemy ships. Lek nodded. "We can give chase, or we can get clear." Maybe they could outdistance pursuit. Stildyne knew from experience that the thula was capable of astonishing speed, even with the battle cannon on board. "But not far away. I say we go after. It'll buy some more time for the data feed, at least."

"Good answer," Garrity said. "I'm in. Let's go."

He wouldn't get the chance to say good-bye. Not to Stoshi, in one of the rear cabins with his cousin Waclav Stildyne supposed. Not to Koscuisko, because he was unconscious. It didn't matter. Stoshi would understand; he didn't know what he could say to Koscuisko; and they'd all be dead as well, so what difference did it make?

And the other people here, the thula's crew, Andrej

Koscuisko's stolen bond-involuntaries, they didn't even have someone to say good-bye to. Not anywhere near. Robert had a sister in Burkhayden, but that was a long way away.

The lights pulsed with the drain of new demands on the ship's power. Lek had tapped into life support. When the lights stabilized again they were much dimmer, and the emergency sulphurs tinted the shadows yellow-brown. Spinning on its axis the thula moved to intercept the foremost ship on its trajectory toward Canopy Base; they'd taken the enemy by surprise, which was good, but the surprise didn't last long, which was less so. The other ships diverted to flank them as Stildyne watched.

"Hirsel, station," Godsalt said. Stildyne took Hirsel's place on the boards, falling into the clamshell half-in half-out. Sensors and cartography; near situation in space. One of the enemy ships had outpaced the others, which could be a mistake and Stildyne hoped it was. They were in too much of a hurry—and also, apparently, in range.

"Swivels, Godsalt," Lek said.

The thula bloomed. The enemy ship bloomed much more prettily, and spun back and away. It was apparently intact, but they didn't need to destroy it, only to disable the ship. Had they? The ship behind that one increased its speed, closing the gap in the line as the others drew up in array. If the interval worked in their favor they could take three of them out, between one shot left from the main battle cannon and the predictable shock-and-debris waves that would spread out after it.

Suddenly Stildyne missed Dierryk Rukota. Rukota was an artilleryman; he would have enjoyed this duel. On the other hand, he would be dead within minutes if he were here, so maybe Rukota wouldn't so much mind that he'd missed it.

There was a distortion field of some sort on the overscreen as Stildyne spun the global status sphere to check on vessels approaching from further out. There was nothing any closer than the enemy, and yet there was a signal-shadow rising across their seventh gradient. Godsalt fired the swivel gun again, but the enemy evaded, and now they wheeled closer, surrounding on four of the eight axes, each one with its own clear field of fire.

"Yes," Lek said. "That's the way to do it. The Holy Mother wants you to come home." If they could only lure the enemy just a little closer, they could all go together—

The lights went. All they had left were the emergency sulphurs. With the wheelhouse's last remaining power Stildyne tracked the sensor shadow in the sky. It was approaching from the fifth octave, as if it had just come off vector.

"Wait," Stildyne said. "Lek. Hold your fire. Godsalt. Use the swivels, keep them clear." Sensor shadow. Big. Huge. Getting bigger all the time. It wasn't alone. There were much smaller blips hiving off, Stildyne could see them, now. He knew what they were, and he couldn't believe it.

Another shot, but contact this time—on both sides, unfortunately. They weren't going to make it work. They barely had power to maintain contact. At any moment the klaxon would sound hull breach and it would be over. Then the only thing left for them would be to fire the main battle cannon and blow themselves up, to keep the

Fisher Wolf from falling into enemy hands. "No time left," Lek said, regretfully, but resigned. "No regrets. You've been good to know. Thanks, Chief."

"Wait!" Stildyne insisted. "Stand by. We have company." *That's an order*. But if he said that, Lek might remote-fire the cannon now, just to make a point. "Look who's come—"

He didn't get to finish. The sensor shadow's blips were in the display range, now, where everyone could see them. Wolnadi fighters. In Gonebeyond space that could only mean one thing.

The power of the comm signal that came through was almost more than the thula could process into intelligibility, in its weakened state. "This is the Jurisdiction Fleet Ship *Ragnarok*." It couldn't be anything else. That sensor shadow was the black hull technology, experimental, the first of its kind and—now that there was no Jurisdiction-wide Fleet to fund building any more— the last. "Keep your hands off that ship."

They were that ship. That was the *Ragnarok*'s Chief Engineer, his Excellency, Serge of Wheatfields. He'd wanted the thula for his own from the moment he'd first set eyes on it.

And the thula already knew the *Ragnarok*'s comm channels. "*Ragnarok*, this is the Malcontent's thula *Fisher Wolf*." Was it Stildyne's imagination, or was Lek putting the emphasis on "Malcontent's," in that hail? "We're porting a data stream from Canopy Base by direction, Andrej Ulexeievitch Koscuisko. Carriage requested."

"Confirmed, *Fisher Wolf*.—JFS *Ragnarok* for *Buration*." The *Ragnarok* had run the registries off ship's auto-idents, clearly. "Abort any further hostile action immediately. Return to holding array and stand by. Acknowledge."

Stildyne pushed magnification; the *Ragnarok*'s hull filled the overscreen. They knew that ship. They knew her maintenance atmosphere, her docking slips, her crew quarters, her mess. Her infirmary. Secured Medical.

The first of the Wolnadi fighters had closed with the enemy, facing off with the one closest to Canopy Base. Stildyne waited. So did the enemy; so did the Wolnadi. There were more Wolnadis arriving moment by moment. Stildyne knew each one, and the people who crewed them. It had been a year. He was suddenly, painfully, intensely homesick for the *Ragnarok*.

"*Ragnarok*, this is the private commerce freighter *Buration*." The signal was faint, as if they'd only just now gotten enough auxiliaries scraped together to get anything out. "We were attacked. No contact with. Our senior officers all. Other souls dead. Assistance. Criminal act—"

Slowly one of the armed freighters turned back toward the line of convoy, proceeding at a carefully controlled rate of speed to resume its place. Then another. "Stand by, *Buration*," Wheatfields said. "*Fisher Wolf*, your status, report."

But Stildyne had nothing to fear from the *Ragnarok*, more than condemnation to death as a deserter. The others here were Security slaves, their governors illegally extracted; they were Bench property, and wasn't the Captain—Jennet ap Rhiannon—going to want to return them to the inventory?

Nobody spoke. Waiting for him. Reverting, under the

influence of the reminder of where they'd come from and who they'd been. He wasn't going to cooperate; they were free men now, and he was determined not to say or do anything that would compromise their status in the least.

"*Ragnarok*," Lek said, after a moment's pause. "*Fisher Wolf*. We have sustained potentially critical damage. Ten souls in custody, injuries of unknown extent and severity. Seven members of Langsarik fleet security, three unaffiliated Dolgorukij nationals. Senior officer on board Chief of Surgery, Safehaven Medical Center."

Their lives were saved; but what were they going to have to give up, in exchange?

CHAPTER NINE

Souls in Transit

General Dierryk Rukota stood on the glassed-in mezzanine observation level of the *Ragnarok*'s Engineering bridge watching the forward scans as one by one all five freighters disengaged from the thula and returned to an appointed place in convoy array. They were Combine hulls; so why had they been firing on the Malcontent's thula?

"*Fisher Wolf*, your status," the Ship's Engineer said. Serge of Wheatfields sat below the observation level, in the heart of the Engineering bridge, where he could exercise command and control directly. "Report."

Most of the rest of the *Ragnarok*'s officers were here on the observation mezzanine as well—the Ship's First Officer Ralph Mendez, the Intelligence officer "Two," and Captain Jennet ap Rhiannon. Dr. Mahaffie had gone down to the maintenance atmosphere to wait for casualties, medical teams on line and at the ready.

There was a waiting silence that dragged on. Rukota could see out of the corner of his eye the colored lights of Two's earpiece process so swiftly that they blurred into an irregular pulse of blue and white, but Two gave no hints about what she was hearing, hanging by her strong little feet from the anchor in the ceiling and swaying gently to and fro with an occasional rustling of her great black leathery folded wings.

"*Ragnarok*," the thula said; and then, just to be tiresome, repeated its identification, to make the already-annoying point that Wheatfields couldn't have it. "*Fisher Wolf*. We have sustained potentially critical damage." Standing beside Rukota Mendez snorted, but kept still; *well, obviously*. "Ten souls in custody. Seven members of Langsarik fleet security."

Langsarik fleet security, was that what they were calling themselves these days? Kosciusko's stolen bond-involuntaries. This was going to be a challenge for ap Rhiannon, Rukota knew. She was ferocious in husbanding Fleet resources; yet she'd apparently known what Koscuisko had planned for those troops and done nothing to stop it. Theft of resources of significant value, considering how much it cost to train and condition a bond-involuntary; and she'd put no obstacles in Koscuisko's way.

"Three unaffiliated Dolgorukij nationals. Senior officer on board Chief of Surgery, Safehaven Medical Center," the thula said. Oh, really? Well, why not? It was the thula, it was crewed by Koscuisko's once-bond-involuntaries, so who else would be there but Koscuisko?

Wheatfields at his station on the bridge below was

looking up at the glassed-in windows of the observation deck, where he knew they were watching. Ap Rhiannon toggled into braid, and Rukota waited, curious to see how she was going to play it. Wheatfields could have issued standard rescue and relief orders on his own authority, that was true enough; but the situation was far from standard. It was going to have to be her call.

"*Fisher Wolf*. This is Jennet ap Rhiannon of the Jurisdiction Fleet Ship *Ragnarok*, commanding." It was the issue of Fleet ownership that made this situation different and interesting—though maybe "interesting" was too mild a word, at least for the Bonds. Wheatfields couldn't speak for ap Rhiannon on the disposition of Fleet property. "We can take you on for repair. The use of our medical facilities will be extended to Chief of Surgery, Safehaven Medical Center, as required."

She could grab them and drag them in. She had the authority, and the *Ragnarok* had the power. Rukota already knew she didn't want them by force, but allowances had to be made for the natural apprehensions of embattled men with wounded crew.

The silence lengthened; *Fisher Wolf* had started to drift—all power diverted to life support. There was an active weapon on board, to go by Wheatfields' boards; Rukota frowned. Was that what he thought it was? What else could it be? Who on board this ship knew that signature better than he did? Soliciting permission with a glance, Rukota keyed into braid with an urgent question. "*Fisher Wolf*, Rukota here. Respond. Is your cannon stable? Do you require emergency evacuation?"

"Cannon stable, standing down. But we do need

medical assistance." Rukota didn't recognize the voice; but he hadn't known those men as long or as well as the others here.

"Captain, if I may," Mendez said. "Pyotr. Good to hear from you. We'll lower a slip. You don't have to leave the thula if you'd rather stay, and I wouldn't blame you, everybody knows Wheatfields has got sticky fingers."

"If you knew what we had to go through to get it back—" That was the sound of muted desperation in a man's voice. Rukota recognized it; so, apparently, did ap Rhiannon, and it seemed to make up her mind for her.

"Mister Pyotr, if that's who you are, and I make no official assumptions as to your identity." Good one, Rukota thought. They had no reason to trust her.

"On my honor, and that of this ship. Your crew in whole or in part may debark temporarily for maintenance and medical services. We will not interfere with your departure at will. I urge you to accept our assistance for your crew and your craft."

There was a long moment. Jennet could see Wheatfields conferring with some of his people— arranging for emergency maintenance, and preparing to deploy the tractor, clearly enough. When response came it was determined and decided.

"Then on the honor of the *Ragnarok* and Captain Jennet ap Rhiannon we gratefully accept your offered assistance. Thank you, your Excellency, and if you could collect as many of those other ships as possible. They're the night raiders."

Well done. Rukota wanted to say it out loud; but he didn't think he dared. The trust of such men was a rare honor, not easily earned, not lightly bestowed. "Thank you, *Fisher Wolf*," she said. "Wheatfields, your action."

And that was, in the end, why he was here, unauthorized, self-assigned, his career in ruins and his family under the protection of another man. It was because the *Ragnarok* and Jennet ap Rhiannon understood. An officer held his honor inviolable so that anybody, no matter who or where or when or why, would know that it *was* inviolable. They could afford to gamble on her, because what she put on her honor—and that of the Jurisdiction Fleet Ship *Ragnarok*—was no gamble at all.

All of which meant, apart from re-affirming what he was doing here, that he couldn't have that cannon. The one on the thula. The main battle cannon that they had no business having. It wasn't his; he'd taken his back—the black-market cannon that ap Rhiannon had confiscated fair and square, and used to good effect at Taisheki Station. But it couldn't possibly be theirs, either, because it was Fleet-issue, and the expense of a commercial procurement contract—

Was probably well within the means of the Malcontent, since they'd bought a thula out of pocket. Maybe if they wrapped those convoy ships up in a sufficiently tidy package the Malcontent would give them a nice tip for rescuing their ship. A pretty little armed courier of their own, maybe.

"Medical on alert and in route," Two said, suddenly, making Rukota jump. He wished she'd put a tone-alert on her translator, and give a man warning. "Courier ship *Helva* on its way from Langsarik Station with our friend Vogel, estimated time of arrival seven hours. Consult in your office, your Excellency? Of course. I am meeting you there."

She had the dismount of a gymnast, hooking the flange-talons hinging from the primary joints of her great black wings into the ceiling anchor before she let go with her feet, swinging herself to the floor, scuttling out in a flurry of wing-tips and forward momentum.

Ap Rhiannon stood watching on the forward scans as the tractor and three tugs coaxed the crippled thula carefully into alignment, guiding it up and into a mobile docking slip lowered from the maintenance atmosphere. Rukota knew they were moving as quickly as possible; still it seemed a slow and painful process. Finally the mobile slip docked; the thula opened its passenger boarding ramp, and someone came down onto the platform. Pyotr Micmac, yes, of course. He hadn't recognized the voice, but the figure was memorable.

Sighing deeply, ap Rhiannon closed her eyes. She'd been worried. They could see Wheatfields and Mendez down on the main slabs now, waiting, with emergency medical and mission-critical maintenance crews standing by. Everything under control. "Let's go talk to Vogel," ap Rhiannon suggested, turning away at last. "It's always interesting, where Vogel is involved."

And hands off the battle cannon. "Wouldn't miss it," Rukota agreed, and followed her out of the room.

Transmission complete, the status ticker said. *Confirmed receipt, in the name of the Saint. May he wander in bliss.* It was the chapter house at Firnova; so it was done and he was over. No. Wrong. It was over and he was done.

He had to lean on the console to support himself, his knees suddenly weak. He remembered. It had been there, then. They'd shot the station-master; then they'd shot him. He had sent the message. *This is Okidan, Feraltz, we're raided, dying, help.*

All in the service of the Angel of Destruction; all in the service of the Holy Mother, no, of a perversion of the Holy Mother, who had led him into captivity among his enemies, who had brought him to understand the fact of his crimes—gently, gently. Who'd sent Cousin Waclav to him, to nurse him through the soul-shattering realization of what he had done.

Now he felt nothing. He'd thought he would feel relief, triumph: years of successful imposture, living as a servant of the Angel, thinking and speaking and acting only as a postulant in that religious order, entering whole-heartedly if not with a will into crimes and atrocities. All for the data. The information. The things the Malcontent needed to know to understand the organization, to find each operative and active sympathizer, each revenue stream, each officer.

But what if he was wrong?

He'd been there, on the raids. Haystacks hadn't been his first. He knew what he'd done. The Angel tortured and murdered in the firm conviction that its mission was sacred. He'd committed atrocity right beside them, as fully convinced that anything he had to do to put his mission forward was as holy.

Had he played a pivotal role in excising an ancient evil from the world?

Or had he merely helped the Malcontent destroy the competition?

"Fiska." There was a signal on his open communication line. Waclav. He hadn't dared pass the information on to Cousin Wishka. They hadn't known in time whether Waclav would get away or be executed as a man who had seen things no Sarvaw could be allowed to see, much less report. Only at the last minute had Fiska figured out how to get Waclav to the *Fisher Wolf*. "Fiska, in the name of all Saints. I will be there soon. Wait there for me, Fiska. Say that you will wait."

They had not been able to transfer it to Cousin Stanoczk, because Stanoczk was in the hands of Andrej Koscuisko. He'd known what he had to do. Now he had done it. Now he was alone.

Look to the fruit, Waclav had told him. *By the fruit of the branch will you know the worth of the tree.* The Malcontent had saved the Langsariks despite the best Fisner Feraltz had been able to do. The Malcontent had come to put an end to the night raiders in Gonebeyond, and Fiska was in a position to know how urgently those horrors needed to be stopped.

And there was Waclav, who had never asked anything of him, never made any demands on him, only inspired him—enabled him—helped him to lay bare the guilty shame in his heart that had led him into things he'd always known would not withstand the full light of the Holy Mother's radiance.

"I will meet you on the launch-field, Cousin," Fiska said; and used the most passionately positive Aznir word for "cousin" he could call to mind. "I have so much I need to say to you."

Waclav, who knew Fiska's heart. Who had guessed his

despair before Fiska himself had seen it coming. Fiska felt better now. He would talk with Cousin Waclav. Waclav wouldn't tell him what to think or how to feel, or what he had to do to atone for his complicity in the Angel's crimes. He would lead Fiska to a clearer sense of what he knew already, and leave it to Fiska to decide what he should, and what he could, do.

"You have such wonders accomplished." And yes, there was relief in Waclav's voice. "I'll make us dumplings. Cousin Waclav away, here."

"Fiska away," Fisner acknowledged; and set the comms to auto-forward so that he could go out to the launch-field and demand dumplings of his Reconciler.

Andrej Koscuisko sat in a chair in the meeting pit of the Captain's office on board the JFS *Ragnarok* with his head in his hands, because he had a headache, and had never thought to be in this place again in his life. He had associations with the Captain's office and none of them were good. No, he felt no need to assassinate Jennet ap Rhiannon, but the memory of the years he'd spent whoring for Captain Lowden cast a shadow over her in his mind that had nothing to do with her.

"We'd triangulated off no-pings on new vectors," ap Rhiannon was saying. On the display screen on the wall facing the meeting pit was a low-grade scan from the courier ship *Helva* with Bench Intelligence Specialist Karol Vogel, and a man Andrej recognized from Langsarik Station—the Provost Marshal, Hilton Shires. "When Two came up with a possible intersection in Scanner Five we dropped vector."

Which was, to judge by the sudden silence from the on-screen Karol Vogel, a remarkable thing for her to have said. Sitting down beside Andrej the now-Chief Medical Officer, Gille Mahaffie, quietly placed a flask of rhyti at Andrej's elbow, close at hand. The fragrance of hot milky rhyti with plenty of sugar did not overpower the perfume of the cortac brandy, and some more clinically effective analgesics besides.

"Ah, hadn't realized there was a drop from Kamishir to Scanner Five?" Vogel replied. "I'm thinking there's more to it than that, your Excellency. Looking forward to hearing it. First things first, might you have located Andrej Koscuisko?"

The sooner Andrej took his doses the sooner his head would start to clear. He'd collided with the wall of the thula at speed and whilst airborne, from what they'd told him. Why was Vogel asking? Vogel had done him favors, some significant, but Andrej had never felt that Vogel liked him.

"With us." Oh, Andrej thought. He should sit up, so that Vogel could see him. Ap Rhiannon sounded as though she was as uncomfortable with him being there as he was to be present. "We found the *Fisher Wolf* engaged in a firefight, and intervened. We have it on board. You know Cousin Stanoczk."

Stoshi had declined to sit in the meeting area with Andrej. That hadn't surprised him. Cousin Waclav had moved a chair out of the cluster for Stoshi, behind Andrej, where they could both sit down and neither of them had to look at the other.

"Cousin Stanoczk," Vogel acknowledged. "That would

explain two Andrej Koscuiskos. There are five Pashnavik warships standing off Poe Station threatening to invade unless we produce Leo Ulexeievitch Koscuisko's brother. What's going on?"

They couldn't produce Andrej's brother. Andrej's brother was dead. Andrej had killed him. He'd asked the crew of the thula to fire on Iosev's ship. *Buration* was lifeless and adrift, because it hadn't been built to withstand a direct hit from the main battle cannon that had torn into its weapons banks. *Good luck explaining that, Stoshi*, Andrej said to himself. Whatever Mahaffie had put into his glass wasn't working: Andrej's headache was getting worse, not better.

"I'm sorry to hear that, Bench specialist." Stoshi sounded remarkably composed. Dr. Mahaffie had probably dosed Stoshi, too. Did any of these people know what had passed between them? "It comes as a surprise, if not a complete one. The family has been collecting news through its own channels. We believe another brother is responsible for the breach in their security; we counseled patience. It compromised our entire effort."

Another brother? Oh. Iosev. But if Leo wanted Iosev retrieved from shameful involvement in a criminal enterprise, why had Vogel asked about *him*? "Explain," Vogel suggested. "I get lost in Koscuisko brothers."

Andrej half-believed he could actually hear Stoshi take a deep breath. Maybe it was only Two, shifting on her perch; ap Rhiannon's other officers—Mendez, Wheatfields—were engaged down in the maintenance atmosphere with the thula and its crew, though Rukota was here. Andrej hoped Stildyne and Robert were in

Infirmary. Stoshi should be. He'd be wishing he was there himself, if his head didn't stop hurting soon.

Stoshi didn't sound quite so sure of himself, suddenly. "I would rather not, but if I must. Captain ap Rhiannon, I solicit your confidence, and that of your officers as well. Particularly your intelligence officer." Maybe ap Rhiannon nodded. Andrej didn't hear anything, but Stoshi continued.

"Ever since they surfaced at Port Charid we have been hunting the Dolgorukij terrorist calling itself the Angel of Destruction, to speak the name of which is as to spit. We came to understand that they had established a presence here in Gonebeyond space. Now we have what we need to hunt them down and destroy them, but we must have their convoy ships. None must be permitted to escape, and give the alarm."

How did Stoshi expect to contain them? The plan Stoshi had explained to Andrej had been simple: get in, retrieve data, get out. Where was taking the station's personnel into custody, in that? *Well, it is obvious, Andrej,* he told himself. *They meant to give no alarm until they returned in force. They did not anticipate that Canopy Base would take alarm, and order the evacuation. That was your fault.*

"How many ships are we talking about, Cousin?" Vogel asked. "We can't get a good scan at this distance, not and tell the difference between the *Ragnarok*'s and theirs."

Ap Rhiannon's voice, now, again. Andrej sat back in the chair, very cautiously, to see whether or not the top of his head was going to stay where it was supposed to be.

It hurt much worse for a long moment: but then the fog of pain started to resolve, and he could hear what she was saying. "—neutralization, but it's a tedious process. And we're going to need somewhere to put them all. Guards. Facilities."

He'd clearly lost some of the conversation. Putting one hand very carefully to the back of his neck Andrej risked turning his head to one side and the other. Mahaffie pressed a dose-stylus into his other hand; Andrej put it through.

"If Leo wants to see me he can come here," Andrej said, his voice echoing unpleasantly in his skull. His face hurt. Quite possibly he'd spoken out of turn; maybe he'd lost the narrative thread again, somewhere, but he had several good excuses. And a headache. "Is that not what you said, Specialist Vogel? Five Pashnavik warships? Send them to me, here. Tell Leo I direct it. I will tell him myself."

"Pashnaviks," Vogel said thoughtfully. "Under Gonebeyond pilots, under Gonebeyond command. All right, Shires?" If he squinted, Andrej could believe he saw Shires nodding his agreement. "Very well, I'll hold you to that, Doctor Koscuisko." Oh. That was him. It was good to have clarification. "Estimated time of arrival three hours, Captain. Do you have further instructions at this time?"

"They'll wait," the Captain said. "*Ragnarok* away, here."

"Away, here," Vogel agreed, and the view-screen blanked.

"It's not working, is it?" Mahaffie asked Andrej, squatting down on his heels to study Andrej's face intently. He'd be looking at Andrej's eyes, Andrej knew, to see whether or not they were tracking together, whether or not the pupils were inappropriately dilated given the medications Mahaffie had given him, whether or not they were the same size. Andrej shook his head. Mahaffie was going to insist he go to Infirmary as well as Stoshi, and maybe that was only fair.

There was a signal at the door. "Transport teams from Infirmary," Two said—the first Andrej had heard from her in all this time. "I will send them back if you don't want them." She was talking to Mahaffie, Andrej assumed. It was a little strange to think of Mahaffie as Chief Medical Officer; but they no longer had any use for a Ship's Inquisitor, and Mahaffie was much more qualified over-all than Andrej had ever been.

"*Fisher Wolf* is too badly damaged to risk on shuttle duty," the Captain was saying to somebody. Was that Waclav? Because Stoshi was in no condition. "I can send you on the shallop." Here were some orderlies to escort Andrej into a riding-chair. He didn't want to sit in a riding-chair, but if that was what Mahaffie had called for he would simply have to swallow his pride, and submit to be scuttled through the hallways into what had once been his own Infirmary like any other patient incoming for triage and treatment.

Once he sat back in the riding-chair he closed his eyes. And once he closed his eyes he fell headlong into a comforting pain-free fog too pleasant to admit further thought of any kind, so he gave up the effort as useless and went to sleep.

⊕　⊕　⊕

Andrej filled the lavatory basin with warmed static micro-spheres to rinse his face and stood, leaning on his forearms against the edge of the counter-top, lifting handful after handful to his face in his cupped palms, letting the tiny things cascade down through his fingers like water.

He'd hit the bulkhead wall head-first and knocked himself out, Mahaffie had told him. So his body had been sufficiently relaxed that he hadn't done himself more injury than deeply insulted muscles and several very sore joints.

Not like the other casualties, Stildyne shot, Robert tortured, Stoshi shut up in a room by himself and refusing to talk to anybody for reasons Andrej didn't need to guess at.

Robert was going to be all right in time and was mostly asleep, which was sensible; by the grace of the Holy Mother Andrej had managed to do him more good than harm when he'd performed emergency surgery. Mahaffie had been very complimentary, but Andrej suspected him of simply trying to talk Andrej into coming back to handle the documentation that the position of Ship's Surgeon entailed.

Infirmary had replaced his dilapidated cyborg bracing, with many a horrified glance; so it was all good. He was keeping clear of Stildyne while he worked up his nerve to propose his solution to the problem of their lives, if only it was not too late. Stoshi—who knew? Andrej dreaded to ask.

He'd been released from Infirmary to guest quarters. Main room, small bedroom, tiny lavatory; not as spacious as the quarters he'd once occupied, but Mahaffie was Ship's Surgeon now and welcome to the accommodation suitable to his rank.

He was alone, and that suited him. His gentlemen, the men he'd stolen out from under ap Rhiannon's nose while she declined to take official notice, were busy working on the thula; insulating themselves from who they'd been when last they'd been here. They'd been to quarters, as he understood, and retrieved their clothing; underwear, boots, whitesquares. Uniform trousers could be dyed, uniform blouses similarly altered.

He had also personal effects to retrieve from the *Ragnarok*, crated and delivered and stacked up against the wall. He had no intention of resuming his uniform, but a man needed his under-linen. He was going to have to make do until he could call on Leo for civilian dress: because what he'd been wearing when they'd left Canopy Base was simply out of the question.

He heard a signal at the door, but it took him a moment to summon up the energy to straighten up from the basin and call out for whomever to enter. Whomever didn't wait. When Andrej raised his eyes to the mirror above the basin to adjust his attitude before receiving company he saw a peculiar double image reflected back, but of course it wasn't him; it was Stoshi.

Andrej felt the blood sink from his scalp into his boot-stockings. He didn't turn around. "We should talk," Stoshi said. Andrej wasn't interested. What he had done to Stoshi had shamed him more than he'd ever been ashamed in his long life of shameful actions; and more than that, Stoshi didn't know what had happened himself. Not yet.

Not in terms of his own psyche. How could he? Stoshi had never been tortured before. Andrej was in a position to make a professional call, on that.

How could Andrej pretend to understand what Stoshi was going through better than Stoshi did, when his role was to torture people, not rehabilitate them? "It's too soon," Andrej said. Whether for him, or for Stoshi, Andrej declined to specify. "You will only say things that you regret. And I will regret having heard them. I am over-fed with regrets already."

Reaching out his hand with deliberate care Stoshi took him by the shoulder; snatched his hand away as though he'd felt the bite of a static discharge, but took hold of Andrej again with firm determination. "I have it in mind to relieve you of one or two, would you but let me," Stoshi said. "Or perhaps I seek relief for some of mine, selfishly, but I will exploit yours to assuage mine without shame. Because I must. And you were right. I do want to hit you."

They'd been evenly matched as children, and their occasional boyhood tussles had never settled into a consistent advantage one over the other. Things would be different now. Andrej had been trained to defend himself by Brachi Stildyne, who had been especially relentless after the assassination attempt Andrej had survived at Chelatring Side.

But Stoshi was a Malcontent. There was no telling what training he'd received. Andrej suspected that as a class Malcontents were superlatively dirty fighters; but then Stildyne had taught him to be one, too. *No such thing as a dirty fight*, Stildyne had explained, patiently. *Only*

*ones you do, or don't, survive with your fish still attached
and in working condition.*

"Then let us by all means put a table between us." One
that had liquor on it. Stoshi looked back into the main
room at the table, its two chairs; the remains of Andrej's
mid-meal, and a pile of fried pastries provided by people
on what had once been his staff, out of concern for his
metabolism. It had been kind of them to remember.

Stoshi chose the place that let him put his back to the
door, so that he had a clear escape lane. Without speaking
Andrej poured two glasses and took one. He would not
suggest that Stoshi drink. Stoshi would have to make his
own decision.

"You in all inadvertence placed our entire enterprise
in jeopardy," Stoshi said in a meditative manner, looking
at the glass Andrej had poured. Andrej took a swallow;
cortac brandy, and it was good. Stoshi had brought a
case or two with him the last time he'd visited the
Ragnarok. "You cannot be said to be at fault. But you
are to blame."

Only in the sense that he'd been presumed safely out
of the way. "I do not apologize," Andrej said. "You know
why I came to Gonebeyond. My purpose has been
consistently prevented." Came to see Stildyne;
quarantined at Safehaven. "Had you not called for the
thula, Robert would not have come to see me. And you,
you sent him to be tortured, Stoshi."

Maybe he shouldn't remind Stoshi of that, with the
other thing lying bleeding there on the table between
them. Or shuddering in pain, if not bleeding very much.
Nodding thoughtfully Stoshi picked up the second glass.

"That was his idea." True, from what Andrej had been told by Lek Kerenko. But no excuse. "And yet beside the point. Which is this."

Stoshi reached forward for the open bottle. Andrej extended his glass; Stoshi refilled it, both of them careful to take no notice of the chiming of the lip of the bottle against that of the glass as Stoshi's hand trembled. Stoshi drank deeply before he spoke again.

"The point is this. What you did salvaged the mission I thought lost; and saved us, the fruit of Fiska's daring above all. The Malcontent is indebted to you, Derush. *I* am indebted to you." Stoshi said it with a clear note of disbelief in his voice. Andrej shook his head, *no*.

"This time has not been the first that I have cried out in my heart to the saint for intercession. It was he who brought us all out from that place, not I. I claim the Malcontent's halter by election, Stoshi, because I was never so desperate in my life, and the saint heard me."

There'd been no thunder from on high, no. No divine executors robed in awesome splendor had descended bearing weapons of unbearable brightness with which to confound and dismay miscreants and sinners. But his prayer had been answered. They were here safe and alive, the Angel of Destruction confounded; Stoshi, however, laughed.

"You do not seriously intend—no, Derush. The saint does not accept. Our rescue was your doing, do not joke." That Stoshi laughed was good; that Stoshi answered back was good also; but that Stoshi didn't take him seriously was less so.

Andrej scowled. "If the saint is to me indebted, should

I not be granted what I wish? How else should the Malcontent discharge its obligation, if as you say there is a debt owed?"

What was interesting about this conversation was how it had slid by the central problem that confronted them without catching a thread against the jagged truth of it, so far. Stoshi grew serious. "For you to say, except we do not take a man on the strength of an unwitnessed vow. Nor do I accept the task of speaking to your mother to explain. No, Derush. How can the saint make this right for you? We must know."

"Can the saint make it right between *us*, Stoshi?" What he'd done, and how he'd done it; and, oh, the pleasure he had taken. How he'd fed of Stoshi's suffering.

"There is no 'us,' Derush." It *was* too soon. Hadn't he said so? "The saint knows, and you are as the Holy Mother made you. But I—"

That was altogether too close to what Iosev had said to him, *truly the Holy Mother has made you for Her purpose*. The memory of that horrifying interview surfaced too quickly for Andrej to dissemble; Stoshi stopped talking, looking at him.

It wasn't true. The Holy Mother had made souls with hunger in their hearts for blood and pain; that was Her providence. "She did not make me to glory in it," Andrej said. "But to recognize my nature, and not yield to what in it is criminal."

It was a crime to implement the Protocols. Whether a man did so well or poorly, with revulsion or rejoicing, it was an offense beneath the Canopy of Heaven to torture captive souls. And he had lost his friend, his cousin Stoshi, the man the Saint had taken away from him years ago and then restored; now lost forever, their bond severed irrevocably by the unimaginable violation Andrej had committed.

Stoshi was waiting; Andrej tried to explain. "Iosev was watching us, Stoshi. He was proud of me, he said. And how could he say such a thing of you, of me, of us—"

"And so we made you to see things in your brother that you were not meant to see. In time we could perhaps have rescued him. What are we to do, Andrej. What are we to do?"

Build me a hospital in Safehaven. Shelter my son and Marana, because the thought of going back amongst my own people sickens me and I mean to make peace with my life amongst the Nurail, so long as I am sent lefrols and linen.

Andrej had learned things about his cousin Stanoczk, in the past days; he knew that Stoshi had the heart and mind and will of a hero. If anyone could do this Stoshi could. And if anyone could demand it, it was he, himself, Andrej Koscuisko, and no other, because the Malcontent had put him in this place and he had done what he needed to do to put the Malcontent's purpose forward, just as Stoshi said. He had killed his brother.

"I can pardon the saint if you can me, Stanoczk." It was unfair to ask, unreasonable, and insane. Indecent. But Stoshi had asked. "I loved you more than ever I did Iosev."

It was a hard truth, but truth was like that. Stoshi sat silent for a long moment. Andrej could see Stoshi's fingertips gone white against the dark matte barrel of the flask of cortac brandy; but then, very slowly, like a man approaching a venomous snake with a mind to seize it and milk its fangs of poison, Stoshi leaned forward.

He tipped the neck of the flask against Andrej's glass, again, and poured until the liquor spilled over the lip of the glass and overflowed, puddling on the table's surface. It was the universal Aznir code for *let's get drunk*. "We're going to need more cortac," Stoshi said.

There were only four flasks on the table. Stoshi didn't have Andrej's years of experience with killing quantities of overproof wodac; finally, a contest in which Andrej could be confident that he had the advantage. "My drinks-cabinet is somewhere here, in these boxes." Andrej nodded at the array of crates against the wall, the things that Engineering had packaged up to clear the way for Mahaffie. "It will not escape."

They'd pour cortac brandy over the problem until it was stupefied, and sank into the floor beneath the table. And that would be a start on getting past it.

Karol Vogel sat at a luxuriously appointed conference table in what had apparently been Canopy Base's elite meeting room, observing the proceedings of a select committee convened to determine what was to be done about the night raiders. About the Angel of Destruction.

"The Combine will build a replacement hospital in Safehaven," Koscuisko said. "Safehaven Medical Center. A teaching hospital, and the Combine shall build it, and fund it, and staff it, with Nurail oversight and control, in perpetuity."

"From revenue streams the Malcontent recovers from

the Angel, to speak the name of which is as to spit," Bench
Specialist Erenja Rafenkel replied. Karol was glad she'd
agreed to travel from Chilleau Judiciary to chair the
negotiations. "Agreed. Next. Safehaven will not refuse to
accept Combine legal counsel for the accused without
good reason."

She was uniquely qualified to manage the challenge
that Karol saw before them; because she was a Bench
specialist, she was neither Sarvaw nor Aznir but Kizakh,
and there were hints that beneath her trim and proper
over-blouse she wore the scarlet halter of the Malcontent.
There would be little fear of partisan sympathy creeping
in around the edges of things, with Rafenkel. The
Malcontent had issued no objections.

"We get two challenges for each defender proposed."
Hilton Shires had been hastily delegated speaking
authority for Gonebeyond space, because he was here,
and because Canopy Base was in the Langsarik sector. He
had five proxies all told; and for any proxies outstanding—
they hadn't heard from all of their polities, in
Gonebeyond—they'd figure it out as they went along.
"The Combine will pay all expenses for the defense, and
six in every eight parts of the net administrative costs."

At Cousin Waclav's insistence they had gathered here
at Canopy Base. Hostile territory, in a sense, for the
Combine, as represented here by Rafenkel. Captain Leo
Koscuisko sat quietly minding his own business at one side
of the table. He and his brother Andrej had viewed Iosev
Ulexeievitch's body earlier today, and agreed that it was
in fact exactly that.

"Until resources recovered from the Angel of

Destruction's organization are exhausted, then to be negotiated," Rafenkel said. Shires held up a forefinger.

"No. Until resources are exhausted to include reparations paid in full by the Dolgorukij Combine for terror raids on Gonebeyond settlements. And specifying. Those resources to include everything recovered within Jurisdiction space."

On one side of the table: Shires, Karol, Rafenkel. Facing them, Cousin Fiska, Cousin Waclav, Cousin Stanoczk. Along one side, Andrej Koscuisko. Facing him, his brother, Flag Captain Leo Ulexeievitch Koscuisko. "We call upon Safehaven for the services of Andrej Koscuisko for development of evidence fit for Record," Rafenkel said, and Koscuisko scowled.

"Stipulation," Koscuisko said. "Drug assist only. And I retain complete control over my process, and how I choose to prosecute my interrogations. Also I will have the option of scheduling around my medical responsibilities." Koscuisko was apparently unhappy, if in a beaten-down sort of way. Karol wasn't worried. He'd seen Koscuisko fall under far worse than what had happened to him at Canopy Base and come up from it with his spine, his bad attitude, and his lefrols-case intact.

On the other hand Karol didn't know exactly what *had* happened on Canopy Base, but with one man and one Malcontent sustaining injuries consistent with torture it wasn't likely to have been pleasant. Wait. What? "Agreed," Rafenkel said.

"To be subject at any time to review and protest," Shires said. "Agreed, Doctor Koscuisko. Now. The Malcontent Cousin Fiska has earned the undying gratitude of all souls in Gonebeyond for his pivotal role in bringing the night raids to an end. His testimony will be taken off-site at a place of his choosing. Not to be required to return to Canopy Base."

Not allowed to return to Canopy Base, that was what Shires meant. Because he'd recognized Cousin Fiska as well as Karol had: Fisner Feraltz. Who had been the Angel of Destruction in port Charid all of those years ago; whose acts of terrorism had broken the amnesty the Bench had granted the Langsariks, and sent them into exile in Gonebeyond.

Karol didn't like it any more than Shires did. But the Malcontent occupied a unique place in the Dolgorukij church, and it had the Judicial exceptions to cover it. Whoever Cousin Fiska had been, he was only Cousin Fiska now.

And there was no diminishing the courage he had displayed, playing a precarious double role as a Malcontent infiltrating the Angel of Destruction. History had shown what the Angel was capable of doing to souls it condemned as traitors. It didn't excuse what he had done. But it did set significant weight in the balance of Fisner Feraltz' crimes.

"Accepted," Cousin Fiska said. He didn't look well; now that it was safe for him, now that he had completed his mission, Karol expected there would be some significant debriefing time required before he would regain his balance in turn. Another good reason for Cousin Fiska to go off-site, to seek sanctuary in a Malcontent chapter house. Cousin Stanoczk meant to have no part in the trial and sentencing of the Angel of

Destruction at Canopy Base either; Karol thought he recognized the haunted look in Cousin Stanoczk's eyes, and was sorry for it.

"And that should keep us for now," Hilton said—taking the initiative to end the meeting. "Specialist Rafenkel? Your action." Hilton Shires. Giving instruction to Bench specialists. It was an age of wonder.

Standing up Karol hunched his shoulders, stretching his back; and followed Hilton, Rafenkel, and three Malcontents out of the room. Andrej Koscuisko rose politely and respectfully, but he and his brother Leo stayed behind; as the door closed Karol could see Koscuisko sit down again, carefully. Well. Who knew what brothers had to say to one another, with the corpse of another brother waiting transport to Azanry?

Karol put the speculation away into a small drawer in his mind and hurried to meet with three Malcontent agents to strategize the future of Canopy Base.

CHAPTER TEN

New Orders

"Derush, please come home," Leo said quietly. Andrej had watched him play his role; it had been up to him to secure orders directing the surrender of command and control of five Pashnavik warships, placing himself—howsoever nominally—in a subordinate position to Gonebeyond senior representative Hilton Shires. Diplomatic gestures could carry disproportionate weight at critical times in the lives of new states. Leo had done his part to secure Combine cooperation.

"I don't think so, Leshik." Uniformed or not, Leo sat across the table as Andrej's brother, and to be addressed with intimate language would help soften the impact of what Andrej had to tell him. Speaking Aznir helped as well. "I am in a place where I can be useful. I like it there." That was a bit of an exaggeration, maybe; or maybe not. "I will not go back."

Turning his head to one side Leo slumped where he

sat, in an attitude so familiar to Andrej's heart that it tore away at his resolve. "We heard of Inquisitors disappearing, and feared for you," Leshik said. "We should have left it with the Malcontent. Our mutual father has never reconciled himself to your absence, as your mere brothers must."

"Someone in position of authority then thought to make use of the pretext," Andrej suggested. He heard a trembling in his voice; "mere brothers" was a phrase that struck him to the heart, coming from Leo. "To force a confrontation. That was not well done. And our brother Iosev is dead."

"It is still difficult to understand, Derush. How could he have gone so wrong? And how are they to reconcile themselves, the lord prince our father, and our lady mother?" Andrej waited for Leo to fight his emotion down and wipe his face. He had no tears for Iosev.

"They have nothing for which to blame themselves." Perhaps. But Iosev was not the son that had gone the most wrong, not the most criminal of Leo's brothers. "I'm serious about a hospital for Safehaven, Leo. Our family also owes reparations." And a sauna. He would insist on having a sauna.

"I have heard something in addition, about an event," Leo said reluctantly. From the tone of his voice Andrej could guess what it was. "I would have been as glad if I had not been told. Is it for this reason you will not come home? They say you came to Gonebeyond out of good lordship, to see your men were well. They are all here, you have seen them, they are well. Please come home, Derush. Do not abandon your son."

And once he'd thought it might be possible. The last time he had gone home his father had forgiven him for his unfilial behavior; his mother had blessed him. Marana had re-admitted him into her bed, and Anton Andreievitch had embraced him with a whole heart—or at least Anton had embraced in him the idea of a father, an idolized hero to be adored and admired as all Dolgorukij fathers were to be adored by filial sons. Now he knew better. It had been self-delusion from the very start.

"He is my child, and I love him." He didn't know Anton; he'd had so few days with him. But he had discovered in himself a parent's heart, and knew what it demanded of him. "Therefore he must grow up without me. I have placed him in good hands. You know who I am, Leo, how could you bear the day when he should learn, if you were me and he was yours?"

Cowardice, plain and simple. There were more practical considerations, however. "And consider this." Leo might not know. "I am the guest of the Nurail. There is no place in known Space where I can be as safe, outside of a small box." Suddenly Andrej wondered where Dr. Mathin was. He'd told Cousin Fiska to put Mathin in a very small box; but that was all right, then, because Cousin Fiska knew where he was, and would have let him out. Andrej hoped so, anyway.

Leo was looking perplexed, even resentful. "You will be better protected on Azanry. Think of who you are." Not *what you are*. Andrej couldn't go back. The moment he had found within himself the ability to see Stoshi as prey, any lingering fantasies he'd had of going home, being husband to his wife and father to his son, resuming his life as if it had had no Inquiry in it had been destroyed.

He was what he was. He was better off by far among people who understood that about him. "No, I will not have it. I am determined, Leo." Safehaven needed him, whether he was wanted or not. He could be useful there. On Azanry he would be the master of the Koscuisko familial corporation; he wouldn't be a doctor. He'd wanted to be a doctor, and his father had sent him to Inquire. The Koscuisko familial corporation owed him at least ten years of being left alone to practice medicine.

"You abandon your natural debt to your own blood," Leo said. He was angry, but sorrowfully so. "You turn your back on your duty and your destiny. Was it for this that our sister Mayra went to cloister, Derush? I beg you to reconsider."

Leo was right. He *was* abandoning his duty. He *was* turning his back on his destiny. Or, rather, he had redefined his destiny; it had been altered, permanently and irrevocably. It had been reset at Fleet Orientation Station Medical. That duty he had done. That destiny he had fulfilled. He was free to make up his own duty and destiny now.

It was a cruel thing to do to Anton Andreievitch; but if Anton grew up to understand that a man could make up his own mind and find his own way, Anton would be the better for it. Anton need not love his father for Andrej to love him. Andrej stood up. "I have considered and considered again, Leo." Deeply, and long. "I will remain. I will have a new hospital for Gonebeyond. I will write to our parents."

Since he'd stood up Leo had to stand up also. "I don't know when I may see you again," Leo said. There seemed to be no further argument in him. Andrej was his eldest brother. "May we part as brothers, Derush?"

Andrej embraced Leo with a full heart. He didn't know if Safehaven would keep him on when they had a choice, though a new hospital might buy him room. He only knew that he was not going back. He was needed at Safehaven, he, himself, his personal skill and abilities. It had been too easy to forget who he was, Dr. Andrej Koscuisko, not the "lord prince" Andrej Ulexeievitch.

"Take my love with you wherever you may go. And share it out generously, with the rest of our family. Good-bye, Leo, I wish you all the best. Come and see me if you like. But leave your armed ships at Poe Station next time."

"I may come back as your brother and be welcome?" Leo seemed to accept Andrej's decision as final, at last, because his expression was calm and resolved as he stepped back. "Good-bye, then, Derush, firstborn and eldest, almost." It was a private family joke, brother-to-brother only. Firstborn and eldest son, yes. Firstborn child, no, that was Mayra, and she never let Andrej forget it. "I'll send lefrols."

Then Leo bowed and left the room, to return to *Direwolf*. That was that. That was settled. And now with all of the other business of his family life cleared away it was time for Andrej to make his peace at last with Brachi Stildyne, and—if the Holy Mother could be merciful, even to such a sinner as he was—perhaps a partnership as well.

⊕ ⊕ ⊕

Stildyne remembered Infirmary. He remembered the treatment rooms; he remembered it all. "Now stand on the other foot," Dr. Olfs said. He remembered Dr. Olfs, too. Gross skeleto-muscular structures. "Flex your knee. Deeper. Any pain?"

Constant pain, to be reminded. He was standing half-naked on one foot in a treatment room doing one-legged deep knee bends with the walking-brace to which his wound had condemned him laid aside, for the moment, so that he had to hold on to the edge of one of the levels to keep his balance.

"All the way from here to there," he said, but decided against providing additional details. It hadn't been ten days. On the other hand he wanted to escape from the walking-brace as soon as possible, because simply hopping from place to place on one leg was much less of an annoyance.

Olfs nodded cheerfully. "Good. That's good. Range of motion is improving, Chief. You can get dressed.—Ah." The door to the treatment room had opened without a signal, but the man on the other side wasn't wearing whites. Wasn't wearing any kind of a uniform, actually. Was Andrej Koscuisko, in clothing that had been issued to him from *Direwolf*'s stores; because otherwise he'd still be walking around in the same suit of clothes he'd escaped with. "Good-greeting, your Excellency, we're just finishing up, here."

Koscuisko smiled. "Your pardon, Dr. Olfs. I came looking for Chief Stildyne. I did not expect to see quite so much of him." This was no longer Koscuisko's infirmary, and he'd been careful to stay out of the way. Doing his best not to fuss about Robert's injuries. Seeing Stildyne only once or twice at physical therapy, and then only in order to make jokes about assignment of laps. Politely declining the offered opportunity to provide expert advice on his cousin Stanoczk's therapy and prognosis, in order to not blur the lines of responsibility. It was very delicately done all around.

Dr. Olfs smiled back. "Not at all, your Excellency." They all called Koscuisko that, and why not? He'd been one, and it was harmless enough. "I'll leave him to you, sir."

Delicately done, yes, but with an effort that Stildyne knew took its toll on Koscuisko; because his instinct was clearly to examine Stildyne all over again himself, right now, and he couldn't, not without giving offense. And he would doubtless have liked to quiz Robert's treatment team twice a day.

And he would almost certainly have wanted nothing better than detailed reports from Stoshi's doctor, and had had to make do with several hours' worth of drinking with Stoshi a few days ago, instead. Mahaffie himself was looking after Stoshi. Stildyne didn't know if Mahaffie knew anything, and he didn't care to find out. It was none of his business either way.

"You came to see me?" Stildyne prompted, because they were alone in the treatment room now and he wanted to get dressed. Koscuisko handed him his trousers, pointing at the level with a nod that was an instruction; Stildyne shrugged. Fine. He'd sit down and put on his trousers.

"I have not yet begun to apologize to you," Koscuisko

said. That was right. Stildyne remembered. Just as the thula was leaving Canopy Base. "I thought to invite you to a game of tiles, and a discussion."

It was hard being back on the *Ragnarok* for all of them, in one way or another. For Stildyne part of the problem was that it had been here that he'd met Koscuisko, come to know Koscuisko, and become a part of Koscuisko's life in a way that he would never be again. He couldn't wish it back; the intimacies he'd shared with Koscuisko had been forced by circumstance. He could only mourn his loss even as Koscuisko himself went on to better days without him.

"Tiles sounds good," Stildyne said. "But. The thula. They need me." They did not. He just didn't know if he could manage a game of tiles with Koscuisko without succumbing to maudlin self-pity. He didn't want to take the risk.

"Underblouse," Koscuisko said, and tossed it to Stildyne. "There is one sheaf out of the reaping in particular that has been much on my mind, Brachi. And I have no one with whom to discuss it. Nobody at Safehaven can be tempted. My life is a much lonelier one without you."

Stildyne stopped in mid-shrug, putting on his underblouse. Shaking the fabric straight he started to work on fastening the secures, wondering how he was supposed to respond to that. What was there to say? *I love you, and I want nothing more than to share your life, if only there was a way?* "Mine as well." It was true. Not because the rest of the crew didn't look after him as they looked after one another. They were a team. It wasn't the same. "All of that effort put into the saga gone to waste, no one to practice with. May I ask what sheaf it is?"

Andrej. Koscuisko had said Brachi. Stildyne didn't know if he had an "Andrej" in him any more, and after all the years it had taken him to get that far. Koscuisko leaned his back up against the doses-cabinet on the wall and folded his arms across his chest, his eyes fixed on the thumbnail of his left hand; which was apparently suddenly deficient, in some sense.

"Well." Koscuisko spoke with reluctance, apparently unsure now that he had brought it up of whether or not he really wanted to discuss it. But once Koscuisko had determined on his course he was not a man to turn aside from it. "How is it with you and my cousin, Brachi? You are close."

Not what Koscuisko had been about to say, Stildyne was sure. He started to tuck the long tails of his underblouse beneath the waistband of his trousers. "He's struggling." What did Koscuisko need to hear? "It'll be a while. I think he may go away for some time." Maybe back to Azanry; maybe somewhere else. Maybe bury himself in debriefing the Angel's operatives.

"It is too late for us." Koscuisko shook his head. He spoke slowly and carefully, as if with every word he stopped to seriously consider whether he truly meant to say the next or not. "And yet, had I not laid such cruel hands on my cousin, whom you love, I might have wondered whether we should not after all these years join our destinies together, you and I, as did Tikhon and Dasidar. Or if we already had, only I had never the wit to understand."

Reaching for his blouse Stildyne froze, stunned and silent. Of all the things he'd ever imagined Koscuisko saying, to him—

He let his hand drop to his side. "I have loved you— as Tikhon did Dasidar—for a long time," he said, at last. "You already know that." As Tikhon did Dasidar; of course. The Dolgorukij ideal of passionate masculine friendship. "And, may the Holy Mother of all Aznir forgive it, not even what you did to Stoshi, what I heard and what I saw, could alter that, for long." It was a terrible thing to say about a man he loved, if not as well as Koscuisko. But it was true.

Which had been the Hell of it. But maybe hope. Maybe there was hope for him, as well. Straightening up from where he'd leaned against the doses-cabinet Koscuisko closed the little distance between them to reach up and put his hand around the back of Stildyne's neck, as Stildyne had seen him do with Robert and the others, as he had envied bitterly.

But this was going to be different. "'Then be my friend and walk with me as I with you, because you are a man tested and tried. To be held close, as I would hold you close.'"

When Koscuisko put his hand to the back of a bond-involuntary's neck it was one signal, master and man, because the Bonds had been subordinated to Koscuisko by law and it was the ancient road of respect and affection between Koscuisko and men who'd been condemned, enslaved in his service. In the famous scene between Tikhon and Dasidar, however—

Gripping the back of Koscuisko's neck Stildyne leaned

his forehead against Koscuisko's forehead. Tikhon and Dasidar had met on equal ground, though wealth and blood and circumstance had stood between them. "'I would with all my heart that I may, now and forever. And may all Saints keep us both, to aid and comfort one another. Your ills my ills. Your joys my joys.'"

Those were the words. He'd had cause to remember them. He didn't have them in High Aznir; but Koscuisko recognized them in Standard well enough. There was only one more thing.

For the first—and almost certainly the last—time in his life Stildyne kissed the man he loved, with perfect chastity and a whole heart that overflowed with gratitude. It was a long moment, but it passed without awkwardness; until Koscuisko dropped his hand, and stepped back. "For this I thank you, Brachi," Koscuisko said. "From the bottom of my heart. Come and see me, perhaps, when the thula does not require your company, and play a game of tiles."

Yes. *Fisher Wolf*. Going to work on the thula was a good idea. He needed time alone, to let his astonishment sink in. "According to his Excellency's good pleasure," Stildyne said. "As in all things."

They'd know something had happened, Lek and Pyotr and the rest. They'd know something had changed. But they'd leave him alone to process for himself, and let him be the one to tell them what it was, or not tell them at all.

Something for which he did not have a name had sealed this moment in his heart forever; and he'd never known till now his heart could sing.

⊕ ⊕ ⊕

Robert had escaped from Infirmary. He still couldn't move around much; his joints ached and his face hurt; but the drugs were good and he was much more comfortable here on the floating slip with the others than he'd been in Infirmary, with people always peering at him.

So there he was quietly and peacefully lying on his back on a flat trundler on the floor of the cargo bay working on a set of servo-caps that had been thoroughly disjointed by one of many recent and unfriendly impacts when something caught his eye, and he looked up, and there was trouble on the horizon.

"Incoming," he called, to alert the others. "Favorite cousins on approach mark point aught nine, proximity—zero." Because Cousin Stanoczk had arrived. Robert keyed the riser on the trundler so that he could sit up at eye level, and the rest of the crew gathered around the open cargo loading ramp. Pyotr, Garrity, Lek. Hirsel. Godsalt. Stildyne.

Stildyne would be leaving them soon, and that was a shame, because he was a good Chief and a good man; but he and Koscuisko had worked something out between them—obviously not the most obvious something, but something none the less—and Stildyne had decided to go back to Safehaven.

"Cousin Stanoczk," Pyotr said, wiping micro-shell gel off of his fingers with a strip-cloth. "Good to see you ambulatory." Robert had been wondering what Stanoczk was going to do about them, now that the Malcontent had a major issue to work at Canopy Base.

"Thank you," Cousin Stanoczk said. He was considerably haggard and haunted, but he was looking a little healthier over-all. His hair was gradually darkening, his eyes were the color they were supposed to be, and if he was still walking a little slowly—it was the sheer weariness of the psychic shock he had sustained, the others had had to watch and Robert was just as glad he'd been unconscious—his general posture and demeanor was very nearly normal. "I need to talk. Is this a good time? I don't want to interrupt."

Almost a joke. There was never a bad time to take a break. "We can spare a few minutes, I guess," Hirsel said, after a quick look around. Robert was perfectly willing. After all, he was already sitting down. "What have you got for us, Cousin?"

"I am in a situation," Stanoczk said. Well, yes, Robert thought. They knew that. Cousin Stanoczk was frequently in a situation, with Stildyne. Would that change, now that something had changed between Stildyne and Koscuisko? It would be interesting to find out. "I have to an extent exploited your unique position, to your cost, placing you in unintended jeopardy. And yet I would like you to accept a change in mission assignment, at least for the near future."

Ferry duty. Malcontent debriefing teams to Canopy Base and back. Glorified transit service. It would be stress-free and easeful; but Robert wasn't sure any of them were really suited to a life of peace and quiet. They'd been Security for too long, and though it was true that the *Ragnarok* had had no combat mission they'd all come to the *Ragnarok* from somewhere and Andrej Koscuisko had been a combat mission all by himself.

"What did you have in mind?" Robert asked, because

Cousin Stanoczk was not getting to the point, which was unlike a man usually so cheerfully blunt. Dedicating the thula to Canopy Base seemed to be the obvious thing to do, but it would be boring, and a little depressing. "Back to Langsarik Station, maybe? We know some people there."

Female people. He'd seen many old friends amongst the female people here on board the *Ragnarok* and it hadn't been an experience of unalloyed cheer. He was a changed man; there was a sense in which none of them seemed to understand that, just because he looked as he had before.

"Canopy Base was only one of the mad dog's outposts in Gonebeyond space, though it was the control center. There are more, and we do not know where all of them are yet, only that they have acted mostly in the Nurail octant. So you see my situation is of two kinds of awkwardness."

No, Robert didn't see, not yet. There was a chance that Cousin Stanoczk would start making plain sense soon; but Robert wasn't going to hold his breath.

"Angel hunting? How is that awkward?" It was Lek's turn to ask a question. "Oh. Of course. You probably want them alive. Oh, well. We could promise to do our best. Accidents happen." Robert had feelings of his own about Angels, so he didn't call Lek on it. Cousin Stanoczk made a face, as if wincing away from something embarrassing in a slightly less than serious manner.

"An imposition, given the trouble the mad dog—to speak the name of which is as to spit—has already caused you all. We do not forget your willingness to put yourself between *Buration* and Cousin Fiska on Canopy Base, to protect the data stream."

Stildyne shrugged. *It's our job. It's what we do.* All right, maybe it had been more than that, but the basic idea pertained, and since no one spoke up to relieve Cousin Stanoczk of his apparent perplexity on that score he was left with no choice but to continue.

"And since it must be hunted amongst the Nurail we must detach the thula from the Langsariks among whom you have lived and with whom you have formed what I am reliably instructed have been mutually agreeable relationships, and attach it to Safehaven instead. There." Cousin Stanoczk took a deep breath and let it out with the air of a man who was relieved of a disagreeable chore. "We would like you to take the thula and pursue our enemy under Nurail liaison. *Fisher Wolf* also hates."

Out of Safehaven? That would maybe mean keeping Stildyne on, or at least close. And a good chance of maybe some fighting and shooting. That always entailed risk; but it would be in a good cause, as well as a welcome outlet for pent-up aggression that might otherwise be turned inward. Or even against each other, the one place where above all it should not be exercised.

"I see a downside," Pyotr said. "Cold-meal mush. Nurail cuisine. I don't care for it." Robert shook his head, but quietly, and to himself. People didn't know how to appreciate the finer things in life.

"Flat meal-cake as well," Robert admonished. "Don't forget the meal-cake. I had good meal-cake at Safehaven the last time I was there." Except that if he hadn't gone Koscuisko might not have found out that the thula was at

Langsarik Station. So he wouldn't have tried to reach them at Langsarik Station; so he wouldn't have accepted an invitation to go to Canopy Base in order to get to Langsarik Station; so none of this would have happened. So maybe it would be more prudent to just keep quiet about the fine dining choices available to a man in Safehaven.

"We'll discuss it," Pyotr said, to Cousin Stanoczk. "Take a vote. Give you an answer in what, two days?" Pyotr looked around him; one by one they all nodded, *agreed.* It probably wasn't going to take that long to decide, but there was no reason to make things too easy for Cousin Stanoczk.

"Two days," Cousin Stanoczk agreed. "I hope for your agreement. I'll let you get back to it, then, thank you for your time." *Carry on.* Stanoczk couldn't say that, because he wasn't their officer. They spoke for themselves, now. They got to keep the thula. Maybe they got to keep Chief Stildyne, too.

"Back to work," Stildyne said. "Hirsel, do you want any help on the swivels' targeting systems? There are several people in Engineering who are convinced that you do."

Robert keyed his trundler down to a good working level and lay back to resume examination of his servo-caps, well satisfied with the world and his place in it.

A ship had been taken on board for repairs, and medical assistance provided its crew. Now it was ready to leave the *Ragnarok* at Canopy Base and proceed to its newly assigned mission, at Safehaven. By itself this would ordinarily be unremarkable; but the ship was the

Kospodar thula *Fisher Wolf*, the new assignment was hunting Angels for the Malcontent, and Karol Vogel thought he'd just go on down to the maintenance atmosphere and see what was what.

There seemed to be more people than usual there. Karol took advantage of his ambiguous rank to join the ship's officers on the maintenance slip; the thula was there, fueled and ready to go. Its crew was there as well, drawn up in formation; Koscuisko stood with them, but apart—passenger only.

"Eight days ago we took on board the Malcontent's thula *Fisher Wolf*." Jennet ap Rhiannon stood on the platform in facing array, with her officers. And Karol. "At that time four souls on board required medical assistance. Are those men here and now present?"

The man who stepped forward to reply was Pyotr Micmac, not Security Chief Stildyne. The thula had been rearranging its own crew; they were free men now. "Present, your Excellency."

More people in the maintenance atmosphere. People clambering up to sit on the broad backs of ships in dock. People clustered on the gangways with cups of cavene in their hands. Ap Rhiannon started to pace, slowly, between the line of the thula's crew on one side, and that comprised of the *Ragnarok*'s officers on the other. "And has everybody and everything that came off of *Fisher Wolf* been restored to you, to your complete and unreserved satisfaction?"

"Yes. And more besides." The thula had enjoyed the almost undivided attention of *Ragnarok*'s engineering and maintenance crews since they'd been brought on board, as Karol understood it. "The *Ragnarok* has honored its promise in every detail."

More people, Karol noted. Where were all of them coming from? More to the point, where were they all going to sit, or stand, or crouch? There were more than seven hundred crew assigned to the *Ragnarok*. It was beginning to look like the majority of them had decided to just go down and check out the maintenance atmosphere.

"Thank you. Now hear this." Ap Rhiannon's pacing had brought her back to a central position, facing Micmac. "You remind us all of people we once knew. They were part of us, and we admired and respected them as such. Those men would be welcomed back at any time, but we understand that they may no longer be available to return to their previous employment."

She wouldn't admit to knowing who they were, not in so many words, not in public. They'd been property, if property of a peculiar sort—except for Stildyne and Koscuisko, of course. Had she been in on Koscuisko's theft? Probably not; she was crèche-bred, and they were notorious for inflexibility. Karol sometimes wondered how the crèche system could have failed so spectacularly with ap Rhiannon: who was coming to her point.

"You would be welcome to take their places, among us. They're missed by those who knew and worked with them. But since your other responsibilities may preclude that action on your parts I will just say that on behalf of JSF *Ragnarok*, I wish you all the best in your future endeavors, and hope that we may see you again some day."

Then there was an animal, a visceral roar of approval and applause whose full-throated spontaneity took Karol by surprise. And not just him. It went on; and then it went on some more, and in those cheers Karol heard everything a man separated from his command could want to hear.

Those men had been Security slaves, isolated from the crew by their Judicial sentence and their governors. But every single soul on the *Ragnarok* was glad that they were free: and there was nobody to whom they would not be welcome back as free men and fellow crew.

That included Andrej Koscuisko. Karol had personally witnessed several attempts to recruit Koscuisko back onto the *Ragnarok*'s medical staff, and they'd come from enough different people to convince Karol that they meant it. It hadn't done them any good, but the impulse had been genuine and sincere.

"On behalf of the *Fisher Wolf* and its crew I sincerely thank your Excellency, your officers, and your crew," Micmac said. He was clearly moved; so were they all. And he didn't mind showing it: that was a victory over indoctrination if ever there was one. "We look forward to that opportunity. Now requesting clearance to depart."

"Carry on, *Fisher Wolf*," ap Rhiannon said, acknowledging Micmac's salute with a crisp nod.

It was the hail-and-farewell they'd never had, Karol realized. To the accompanying noise of renewed cheering the crew of the *Fisher Wolf* and its passenger boarded the ship, while the Captain and her staff—and Karol Vogel— left the platform so that the thula could be on its way, to whatever its future might bring.

"Cleared through to set down, your Excellency. You're to be met, and escorted to the hospital. An officer named Dawson expects to be greeting you."

"Yes, very good," Anton replied, with more confidence than he felt. This would be a great day. Construction was complete; the hospital was fully staffed; the budget pledged to maintenance in perpetuity had been negotiated and agreed upon; Anton had grown a beard. His mother thought it was handsome. What would his father think? It helped him in his meetings with the business people, because it made him look a little older.

The city grew larger on the view-screens as the *Temujin* continued its descent. The city had grown up around the launch-field at which he was to be received; but it had been a working sea-port, once upon a time, and the organic way in which it seemed to have developed from the seed to the flower showed it.

From the air the chaos of its streets made it look much older than it actually was, with its buildings crowded higglety-pigglety together. The Port Authority was bringing him into the old docks as a mark of special privilege, but they'd have to drive through the core of the city to get to the hospital. How Anton's security had been persuaded to allow it Anton didn't know; but since Security *had* agreed, Anton had to trust that it would be all right.

There were few green-belts left in such a city, and few parks; but there was one of which Anton felt he could be justly proud, because he'd built it. As parks went it wasn't over-large, and by comparison with his own parks—at the Matredonat, for example—it was little more than a garden with an over-high opinion of itself. But it was something.

His father had made clear his intention to stay at Safehaven for the rest of his life. Because of his history, because of who he was, he couldn't go from the hospital grounds without security arrangements made in advance; so it had been important to Anton that his father have all a man might need or want there, close at hand, and convenient.

His father's residence was hidden within a perfect jewel of a garden, the best of Chigan landscape design— the illusion of limitless space, within the compass of a few city blocks. Anton had toured the scale model, and approved the plans. There were public areas, a bereavement sanctuary, places for hospital employees and patients to walk; a system of ornamental lakelets, with Chigan fishes red and cream and white. That might have been a Chigan joke, but they were traditional, and a prudent man did not dispute with artists of their caliber.

When *Temujin* had landed and Anton debarked, he found people waiting for him at the foot of the exit ramp. The bare pavement was cold and hard underfoot, once he stepped off the carpet that had been laid on the passenger loading ramp to cushion the footfall of princes. One of those waiting—a tall man whom Anton judged to be in his thirties in Standard years of age—stepped up to him, extending his hand.

"You are Anton Andreievitch," he said. "Andan, son of Anders. My name is Chonnie of Darmon-that-was, called Dawson, in these days." He was meant to take the offered hand, and clasp it. Anton found the experience novel, but not disagreeable. "I'm your escort captain. On behalf of the Port Authority I affirm that you're welcome here among us."

That was the story, anyway. "Well met, Ishifan Darmonevitch." If Darmon was going to put Anton into Nurail, he'd put Darmon into Aznir Dolgorukij, and see how it sounded. "Thank you, and I'm honored. How do we go to see my father?"

"Ishifan, is it?" Dawson turned to walk beside Anton down the double row of security that stood at attention, making an aisle for them between the *Temujin*'s passenger ramp and Port Receiving. There didn't seem to be a mover waiting. "But I can't call you Koscuisko, because we have one of such here already. Permit me Andan Ander's son, and you can call me Chonnie. Let me introduce you to the Provost Marshal, his name is Sangriege, but we all call him Beauty."

Because the man's face was scarred, of course; but his hair, still thickly curling though now iron-grey, must have once given even such a face an attractive frame. Beauty wasn't much taller than Anton, and he looked into Anton's eyes for a long moment before he smiled beautifully and broadly—which only contorted his damaged face the more.

"Pleased," Beauty said. "And when we first met your father our Chonnie was younger than you are. Our lives are owing to him, did you know that? Chonnie's, and mine." Beauty had something in his hands, a scrap of cloth, a long pin. As he spoke he raised his hands to Anton's right shoulder. "And therefore, this. Walk safely among us, a ward of my weave, Andan son of Anders, Koscuisko."

It was more than a mere scrap of cloth. It was the scrap of a weave, a little piece as broad and deep as the palm of a man's hand. Darmon had one too, and was about to pin it to the upper shoulder of Anton's coat when Anton raised his hand to interrupt the gesture, and made Darmon pause.

"Not like this." He thought he understood. If he had it right, this was too important to be done half-way. "With your indulgence. When Ealith was received by Senanij's people he came to them naked, and alone." Much as the Nurail had come to Gonebeyond, really. "May I receive this honor in like manner?"

Unpinning Beauty's weave from his shoulder he took off his coat, with its full sleeves and its modest allowance of flat-braid trim, and handed it to the nearest Security before he re-fastened the weave to the yoke of his under-blouse. Now he stood beneath the sky in his shirt, which if it was not "plain pieced weave with sorrow and strife stained, torn in many places, and no proof against the weather" was still as close to naked as he had any intention of being under Safehaven's skies.

For a moment he didn't know whether he'd just insulted the very people he had to rely on for his father's safety and well-being; but then Dawson laughed.

"You're more politic than your daddy, Andan Ander's son." And still, somehow, Anton got the feeling that he'd done something right, because Beauty's own grin seemed to be one of approval. "Here, wear the weave that was my father's, that would have been lost had not your father saved it. Beauty. Let's go. There's a lot of ground to cover."

And they were going to walk. Anton swallowed back his nervous trepidation. He'd had a big meal before *Temujin* had made port; it would be good to take a little exercise. He'd wanted to get a feeling for the port? He was to be privileged to receive a ground-level familiarization course.

The streets were lined with people, orderly, and in abundant number. Beauty walked to one side of him and Dawson on the other, and Security made no move to hinder the people who come through the guard-lines into his path to gaze into his eyes with unreadable expressions and pin more bits of weave to his shirt.

It was granting-of-leave to walk among them, as had been given Ealith in Senanij's city. There would be bread and milk and a warm place by the fire, or he mistook the meaning entirely—which was, of course, entirely possible. So it was safest to suffer himself to be covered in scraps, and keep silent.

A woman came out of the crowd to stand in the road, and she brought a child with her. A very young girl not yet begun to bloom, blonde hair, blue eyes, who reminded Anton of his Aunt Zsuzsa. When the girl came forward at her mother's urging Anton went down on one knee, so she wouldn't have to reach up too far to pin her bit of weave on his shirt; which gave him the chance to look at her more closely.

It was true that among the Nurail he had met there'd been people who might have passed for Dolgorukij in a darkened room, but he had yet to meet one that put him so strongly and immediately in mind of two of his aunts— at once. Two of his aunts, and his father's mother. He'd heard some remarks; but was he guessing right?

He could find out. "Where is the man with my coat?" he asked one of the Security. "And a pocket-knife." His tailor would make him pay dearly for what he was about to do, but there was no other way to test his theory. He cut a piece out of the sleeve of his coat, not without effort—the wool was fine, and the lining layered with gossamer silk and fine-spun goat's-hair.

Now came the tricky part. The girl had gone back to her mother, but the woman hadn't melted back into the crowd as the others had done. She stood there hand-in-hand with her daughter, watching to see what he was going to do.

Land-pledges. Once on Azanry the lord of fields and farmlands lay with a woman in a new-plowed field, to make a contract with the earth and the people who worked it; hard work indeed, Anton had always felt, because new-turned earth was clammy and cold before the spring sowing. Each village thus became his family, its elders with standing to demand good lordship as from a nephew or a grand-daughter's husband.

When Anton had heard about the Nurail blood-price, the taking of a child from the body of a murderer to replace a soul robbed from the weave, the cultural resonance had seemed imperfect but still comparable. Now, would this work?

He went ahead. Beauty and Darmon let him, apparently curious about what he had in mind. He wasn't taking a child on as an honorary ward. He was asking permission to claim kinship. Would the woman have sent her daughter to him had she been unwilling to grant him that privilege?

It was a question well worth asking. Anton knelt on both knees, offering the woman the piece of the fabric cut from his coat. *Let me consider that she is my sister, although I have no right to make a claim.*

The woman stared hard at him for a long moment. Then she reached out and took the piece of Anton's coat with a nod of agreement, holding the scrap high overhead for all to see. Public acceptance. *Very well.*

Anton bowed his head, on his knees in the street, overwhelmed by a sudden rush of unexpected emotion. He'd been an only child. That was unusual in his extended family; even his uncle Iosev's unfortunate orphans had been several in their number. Cousins, yes, in plenty, but he had no siblings of his own—until now.

Then he stood up and walked on. Darmon put his hand to Anton's shoulder, but carefully, because of the pins. "That was prettily done," he said. "What is in your mind?"

"This is an unexpected gift." Though now was not the time to savor it. "But tell me, will I be allowed to take an interest in her schooling, and her welfare?"

"Beauty" Sangriege leaned in close to speak confidentially in Anton's ear, not without a certain note of amusement in his voice. "Wait and discover how many of you there are, before you fly into speculation," Beauty said. "Walk on. We've got a further while to go."

How many? His father had been in Safehaven for eleven years. There might be a small army of half-siblings for him here. He could found an autonomous enterprise under the aegis of his family name, and place in its charge all of the investments of the Koscuisko familial corporation in Gonebeyond space. He hoped that some of them would like accounting.

But first. And even more important here and now. He was Anton Andreievitch Koscuisko. And he was going at last as a proper Aznir son to meet his father, and be named and claimed.

This was the day. Andrej Koscuisko stood at the top of the ramped stairs in front of Safehaven Medical Center's headquarters building, the administrative heart of the hospital he and his son Anton had built over these past years to serve as the foremost medical complex in Gonebeyond space. At any moment Anton Andreievitch would arrive, on foot, with the escort Safehaven had provided; Beauty Sangriege, and Chonnie Dawson himself.

"Nervous?" Stildyne asked from just beside him, his voice pitched so low only those clustered close would be able to hear. Robert St. Clare, a married man, several children, his own battle squad. Lek Kerenko in instructor's uniform, who led a strategy program in the war college; only they didn't call it that in Safehaven, but "commerce regulation," like the much-reduced cadre that was all that remained of what the Jurisdiction Fleet had once been.

There was Godsalt, greying and gaining a little weight, with an export firm trading in medicinal herbs; Garrity, a spokesman for the "Locator" office that had been funded by public subscription to develop resources for Nurail refugees to seek out what remained of their families—or at least find out, at last, what had happened to their kin.

Next to them, Code, who'd been with him at Rudistal that black night when Joslire had been shot, who'd lived to claim the Day and come to Gonebeyond to make himself useful. Hirsel was here, in hospital administration, always pushing for efficiencies and documentation. Especially documentation. Pyotr, who'd gone into literature, gradually becoming a recognized expert on the Gelizar poetics.

"How could I not be nervous, Brachi?" Of course he was. He'd seen his son Anton from time to time, yes, on visits to Joslire's family on Emandis, for example; but he had no real father's claim on his own son. Other people had raised Anton, loved Anton, shaped and formed Anton, and—most importantly—kept out of Anton's way as he'd grown up into the man that he was, his own man, with his own notion of who he was and what he would and would not do in the service of heritage and tradition.

With his courtesy nieces and nephews in Joslire's family he could be at his ease, because they were not Dolgorukij. There was nothing Andrej could do wrong within that family because they all knew he was no kind of Emandisan, except in his custody of Joslire's five-knives. He was wearing them now. Joslire Ise'Ilet was still an important part of the life of his heart; so Joslire had to be here, to stand with the others and greet Andrej's son on his first official visit to Safehaven.

Andrej's father, the old prince Alexie Slijanevitch, had stood as Andrej's proxy for all of the rites and rituals that surrounded the growing-up of inheriting princes. Sons had left grandsons to take their places before. But Andrej had not been dead, merely absent. For such cases there were no precedents. They'd all had to do a very great deal of improvisation.

He wouldn't have had it any other way. Gonebeyond space was all about improvisation, the self-aware melding of proud old traditions into a new polity that could take in everything that its citizens could contribute and make out of it a new way of doing things. The nations of Gonebeyond, confederate, unique and distinct, and yet all one people.

There were people here, a lot of them, hospital staff and local residents lining the wide avenue between the main trunk line from the old launch-field to the hospital. There were no cars on the ground today; foot traffic only. It had an Aznir resonance, though Andrej didn't know whether the port authority had understood or intended it; sons were to come on foot to kneel to their fathers.

"Here they come," someone murmured from behind: Caren, one of Stildyne's several step-sons, who had survived all improbably the difficult years of his adolescence to step into Security himself. The widow who'd claimed Stildyne had had four sons, of varying ages, and three more had found their way to Safehaven to claim foundling-rights from their mother's sister's family. One from their father's brother's wife.

Watching Stildyne, of all people, learning to gentle wild angry boys at the most difficult times of their lives had been a revelation—to them both, Andrej knew, him and Stildyne alike. Stildyne's wife had known what she'd been about when she'd annexed Brachi Stildyne to herself. *Sons need a father, and you have no sons. Your maister it was who bereft me of theirs, so the claim is a true one.* She'd been right about most of it, Andrej had to admit; except the word "maister." Robert had laughed, when he'd heard.

Andrej couldn't see anybody, not yet, but the crowds on either side of the access road had quieted to silence broken only by the inevitable cough without which a crowd did not truly exist. Heads were turned. Andrej squinted. He could see Sangriege, the grey in his hair catching silver in the sun. And there was Dawson, with someone else between them.

Was that his son? That blond bearded fellow in his shirt-sleeves with scraps fastened every which way, fluttering as he walked? He'd grown since Andrej had seen him last. Marana was a tall woman. Anton would never be as tall as his grandfather, but he would over-top his own sire any day now.

Halfway to the ramp-stairs where Andrej waited someone stepped out of the crowd. Pirascon, Andrej thought, someone from infectious diseases, though he couldn't be sure at this distance. Something was passing between them; Anton half-turned his back, and Pirascon pinned something onto Anton's shirt amongst all of the other tags and tatters.

"What is this?" Andrej asked the world, in wonder; Robert answered, with a note of gleeful mirth in his voice, as though he were in possession of the best joke in the world and was now about to deliver the punch-line.

"Adoption papers," Robert said. All of these years and Robert had never quite gotten around to calling him "Andrej," but at least it was "Doctor," rather than "Excellency." "It's weaves, the ones you brought out from the Domitt Prison, and other ones beside. He's ours, now, no one will raise a hand against him. Megh's brought mine."

Robert was moving as he spoke, breaking from ranks to jog down the stairs in a measured sort of a run, bearing in mind the dignity of his position. He met Anton at the foot of the stairs. There was a moment's confusion as both of them sought a place to fasten one final tag; then Robert came back up, but Lek went down now, with a sudden "by your leave, lord prince," in a very rusty sort of Aznir Dolgorukij.

"This isn't in the protocol," Stildyne's son muttered from behind, in a tone much like that of his step-father. Andrej turned his head slightly, to set Caren at ease.

"Tradition," Andrej said. "Anton is expected to be terrified. Lek takes upon himself the role of the one who walks with him to face the ogre, which is me." Lek had met Anton at the Matredonat, years and years ago. They'd made some sort of an emotional connection there that had only deepened over the years, *right trusty and well beloved I greet you well* and *young lord of fields and flocks the Holy Mother hold you in Her heart*.

The moment of recognition was poignant, the exchange of kisses restrained and queerly formal; Lek had children of his own and Safehaven was far from Azanry. "You could have told us, Uncle," Caren said, but he sounded much calmer. "Sorry, sir—" to Stildyne, who had given him a very soft paternal growl, *pay attention*. "Shutting up."

Andrej was glad Lek had gone ahead even so, because it gave him the extra moment to fill his heart with the sight

and sound of his child. "Is that what you'd look like, with
a beard?" Stildyne asked suddenly. "It looks well on him."

"Maybe twenty years ago, Brachi." Anton was not so
very much younger now than Andrej had been when he'd
left home for the Mayon teaching hospital. It was a
thought that came unbidden, and not entirely welcome.
But Anton had had to be more his own man; and in that
much, at least, was more of a prince in fact than Andrej
had been, at his age.

Anton climbed the last few steps to stand three precise
treads below and in front of where Andrej stood waiting.
There was a cushion there; Anton knelt. "My lord the
prince my father," Anton said, but he said it in Standard,
clear and strong and carrying. "I beg that I may be allowed
to serve you, sir, and be admitted into your household as
your son."

There was more to it than that. But Andrej had had
enough. He took a step down as Lek helped Anton up—
not because Anton needed help, but because that was how
it was done—and put his arms around Anton to hug him
fiercely. Then hug him again. He was pin-pricked in the
process; and put his son away from him at an arm's length,
critically. Little dots of blood, where he had hugged
Anton, but Anton hadn't seemed to notice. Why should
he? When fathers met their sons there were pin-pricks
between them, no matter how much they might love each
other.

It was a small thing, in the end. "What is this thing on
your face?" he asked, because tugging gently at the short
blonde beard that Anton wore let Andrej touch his child's
face and cup Anton's cheek against his palm.

"Do you like it, sir?" Anton leaned into Andrej's caress, not enough to be seen at a short distance's remove. "Just say the word and it's gone. I'm overwhelmed to see you." Yes. That made two of them. He'd completely forgotten his lines.

Raising his voice Andrej said the words, because they were the words, whether or not he and Anton and Lek—and Stildyne, by oath and association—were the only Combine nationals here who shared the common expectation.

"I am your father, and I claim you as my son; who is to inherit. You have been born to my sacred wife, my first and oldest child." This was true. Andrej had been too carefully protected, as a young man, to have engendered any others by misadventure, accidentally diluting the blood that was his heritage with an inferior strain in doing so; which was a pretty good joke, really, in light of what had become of him in Safehaven. "You are Anton Andreievitch, Koscuisko."

One more part of public ceremony and Anton could go and get changed, and have a drink. Perhaps two. It was a long walk from the sea-docks, and he might be tired. "These men are my household, to stand as your advisors, who you will therefore respect and heed. And this is Brachi Stildyne, my most constant companion and my friend; look to him as your second father, to be guided and advised, and love him as I do, also to be loved."

In fact Anton would be lucky if he found his own Brachi Stildyne; and Andrej could only hope that Anton would have more wit to recognize him, when he did, than Andrej had for years.

Behind Stildyne Caren was making a small restrained whuffling noise, a sort of stifled snort. Laughing. And because Andrej had come to know Stildyne's step-children if not very well, he thought he could hear the thought in Caren's mind; *oh, fine, there's another plate for dinner.*

The moment took Andrej by surprise, and overwhelmed him. These people granted kinship to his son, after everything he'd done to theirs. Yes, Anton had invested in Safehaven, and the hospital was a significant resource. But something about the tags of woven cloth pinned to every bit of Anton's shirt seemed very personal, all of a sudden, and Andrej didn't know how to express the gratitude he felt to these people for declining to hold the sins of Andrej Koscuisko against his child.

"Are we done here?" Caren asked. "You're expected in quarters. We need to clear the steps."

"And to send the shirt to the registry, to be catalogued," Robert said thoughtfully. "Better get young Andan changed. They'll have brought his kit up from the dock by now, surely."

Andrej shook his head. He brushed past Anton on the stairs to go down half-way to the bottom, where he stopped in the grip of the confusion in his mind. "Steady," Stildyne said, from two steps back. Andrej ran his hand up through his hair to set his thoughts in order, and raised his head.

"You do us both great honor." Anton was his son. Nobody knew so well as Nurail how unfair life could be to parents of children, and children of parents. "It is from the bottom of my heart, that I thank you. I will never forget this day."

He was helpless to continue. Bending his neck to
them, to each of them, to all the people gathered now
crowding into the road in front of the ramp-stairs, he
bowed, as solemnly as if they'd all been his father. He was
a little dizzy when he straightened up, but he had his feet
firm on the stair beneath him, and Stildyne at his back.
And people were cheering.

Turning back to join his party at the top of the ramp-
stairs Andrej called Anton to him with a nod of his head,
still moving. Across the wide front apron. Through the tall
doors as they opened for him to pass. Into the welcoming
calm of the reception area, to cross past the banks of
public lifts to one of two secured ones well sequestered
deep within the offices; down to the connecting corridor,
to ride the lift at the tunnel's far end and surface in the
garden.

"You had a good trip?" he asked, as they walked.
"There's a new planting gone in by the guest quarters,
something Chigan, very pleasing fragrance. And tell me,
how is your lady mother, and how stands her
determination to see you married?"

They'd granted him his own weave, years ago; he'd
have to ask Lerat—who kept house for him—to hunt it
out, so he could pin a claim on his own son. It had come
to him as a length of the finest Nurail woolen cloth, as
black as the uniform of a Fleet officer of Ship's Prime
rank; and carried a white bar at three-quarters, as a token
of his rank and his former branch of service, Fleet
Medical.

And the red line running through the white bar that
marked his precise status, Ship's Surgeon, Ship's

Inquisitor, in custody of a Writ to Inquire, was placed within it in such a way as to represent a single sustained note at a certain pitch and in a certain register. The sound of a man screaming.

It was the sort of thing that apparently passed for hilarious, amongst the Nurail. Although Andrej couldn't help but feel that it was in at least slightly poor taste he hadn't felt in a position to spurn the offered courtesy. It was an honor to be granted a weave, they'd assured him. Andrej was prepared to believe that, now.

"Yes, good, and well, lord father," Anton said, with an easy note of affection in his voice that softened the formality of the title into something close to the homely Nurail "da." "And we continue not to agree. My father set for me a poor example." He spoke Standard, out of respect for Stildyne and the others who accompanied them just to make sure they got where they were going. "Frequently she bemoans this fact, and blames him bitterly. I am implacable. She says I am my father's son."

And, oh, how many ways that could be heard. But Anton was not at all his father's son in one great aspect; he was not afflicted in spirit as Andrej had been. No wolf lay in wait in Anton's heart to challenge and betray him. The Malcontent that was his wife's heartmate, who more than anyone had had the raising of her child, had watched and listened carefully, and affirmed that it was so.

So Andrej laughed, and felt joy in his heart. "We will speak more on it, but not right now," he said. "Lerat will be waiting for us, with bread and milk. Then you may change your shirt, and we can finally sit down, and take mid-meal."

There was still horror in the world, cruelty and injustice; but because all Saints were generous to him, a sinner, he was no longer an instrument of suffering. Here he could hold the people that he loved in his heart even as they went their own ways; and rejoice in the daily cycle of administrative annoyances that went together with the satisfaction of knowing that the work of his hands in surgery would have a good outcome.

Stildyne had sons. Anton Andreievitch had grown a beard. Joslire Ise'Ilet's family had embraced him as their own.

Against all odds, in open defiance of all sense and reason, and despite such dreams as did still come to him in the dark hours, he was happy.

The End

Series Time Line

An Exchange of Hostages (Fleet Inquisitor)

After graduating with honors from Mayon Surgical College Andrej Koscuisko reports to Fleet Orientation Station Medical to learn the tools of the trade. He will form alliances with the bond-involuntaries Joslire Curran and Robert St. Clare, and make a dangerous enemy of Mergau Noycannir.

Prisoner of Conscience (Fleet Inquisitor)

Sent on remote assignment to a refugee processing center (the Domitt Prison) Andrej discovers horrors, and must put an end to them. The relationship between Andrej and the Nurail people that will become an important part of the story starts in this book.

Angel of Destruction (Fleet Inquisitor)

Bench intelligence specialist Karol Vogel attempts to salvage an amnesty between the Bench and the Langsarik pirates. The Dolgorukij terrorist organization the Angel of Destruction (to speak the name of which is as to spit) is introduced in this novel, alone with continuing characters Jils Ivers, Hilton Shires, Cousin Stanoczk, and others.

Hour of Judgment (Fleet Renegade)

Andrej has run out of options and strategies. The only thing left to do is to commit a crime that's been a long time coming, and accept the fatal consequences. It is in this novel that Andrej finds out that there is a termination order out on him, even before he commits an act of mutiny.

The Devil and Deep Space (Fleet Renegade)

The *Ragnarok*, suspected of mutiny, shoots its way out of Taisheki Station with the assistance of the Malcontent. The story-arc of Mergau Noycannir that began in An Exchange of Hostages concludes.

Warring States (Fleet Renegade)

Andrej steals his bond-involuntary Security troops, and sends them into Gonebeyond space, out of reach of the Bench. The orderly transfer of power to a new First Judge Presiding fails; the Bench will have to adopt a new, confederacy model.

Blood Enemies

In this, the present novel, Andrej's pursuit of his aim to apologize to Brachi Stildyne leads him into a crucial role in the war for Gonebeyond space's autonomy.

Who are all these people, and where did they come in?

(continuing characters only)

Crew of the Jurisdiction Fleet Ship *Ragnarok*

Dierryk Rukota (supernumerary) (The Devil and Deep Space)

Gille Mahaffie (acting Chief Medical Officer)

Jennet ap Rhiannon (Captain) (Hour of Judgement)

Ralph Mendez (First Officer) (Hour of Judgement)

"Two" (Intelligence Officer) (novella "Jurisdiction")

Serge of Wheatfields (Ship's Engineer) (Hour of Judgement)

Andrej Koscuisko's Security

All of Andrej's security with a major role in this story first appeared in the novella "Jurisdiction;" with the exception of Robert St. Clare, who first appeared in "An Exchange of Hostages."

Garrity

Godsalt

Hirsel

Kerenko (Lek Kerenko)

Pyotr (Pyotr Micmac)

St. Clare (Robert St. Clare)

Stildyne (Brachi Stildyne)

Everybody Else

Alexie Slijanevitch Koscuisko (Andrej's father)
(The Devil and Deep Space)

Anton Andreievitch Koscuisko (Andrej's son)
(The Devil and Deep Space)

"Beauty" Sangriege, an influential Nurail
once-war-leader, now the Provost Marshall of
Safehaven (Prisoner of Conscience)

Chuvishka Kospodar (one of Andrej's antecedents,
a brutal and racist tyrant)

Cousin Stanoczk (Stoshi, Stoshik), a Malcontent
agent and member of Andrej Koscuisko's
extended family (Angel of Destruction)

Fisner Feraltz (also called Fiska) a Malcontent agent,
former member of Dolgorukij terrorist group
"Angel of Destruction" (Angel of Destruction)

Hilton Shires (Langsarik officer)
(Angel of Destruction)

Iosev Ulexeievitch Koscuisko
(one of Andrej's brothers)

Karol Vogel/Garol Vogel (Bench intelligence
specialist) (Prisoner of Conscience)

Kazmer Daigule (Langsarik ally)
(Angel of Destruction)

Leo Ulexeievitch Koscuisko (Captain)
(one of Andrej's brothers)

Lowden (Captain Griers Verigson Lowden)
(novella "Jurisdiction")

Megh (Robert St. Clare's sister)
(Hour of Judgement)

Names and Terms

Azanry (planet)—Andrej's home world

Aznir—ethnicity of Andrej and his family, topmost class of Dolgorukij

Bench (the Bench)—overall term for interplanetary government, government offices, etc.; not operational in Gonebeyond

Bond-involuntary—a Security slave with an implanted "governor," condemned to participate/perform torture of enemies of the Bench; stolen from the Bench by Andrej Koscuisko in the novel "Warring States"

Burkhayden—port city in which most of the action of "Hour of Judgement" takes place

Charid—port city in which most of the action of "Angel of Destruction" takes place

Chelatring Side—mountain aerie of the Koscuisko familial corporation

Chilleau Judiciary—location of First Secretary Sindha Verlaine, long-time adversary of Andrej Koscuisko "An Exchange of Hostages"

Darmon—family name of famous line of Nurail war-leaders; Andrej executed the war-leader of Darmon at the Domitt Prison in the novel "Prisoner of Conscience"

Dasidar and Dyraine—Dolgorukij cultural icons ("Prisoner of Conscience")

Dolgorukij (the Dolgorukij Combine)—system of origin for Andrej Koscuisko, Fisner Feraltz, Cousin Stanoczk, Lek Kerenko, others

Domitt Prison—a notorious death camp for Nurail refugees, exposed/shut down by Andrej Koscuisko in the novel "Prisoner of Conscience"

Fisher Wolf—the Malcontent's thula, currently crewed by Andrej Koscuisko's escaped bond-involuntary Security troops, first appearing in "The Devil and Deep Space"

Fossum—for "Fleet Orientation Station Medical," training facility for Ship's Inquisitors at which the action of "An Exchange of Hostages" takes place

Gonebeyond space—a no-man's-land beneath official Bench notice

Judiciary—one of nine geographical units under Jurisdiction

Jurisdiction—overall term for system of government characterized by legalistic structure, increasingly harsh methods of control

Langsariks—pirates/commerce raiders framed for terrorist acts in the novel "Angel of Destruction" whose relocation/escape to Gonebeyond space was facilitated by Karol/Garol Vogel in that novel

Malcontent—the secret service of the Dolgorukij church "An Exchange of Hostages," by reference

Nurail—ethnicity of Robert St. Clare, and most of Safehaven's population

Ragnarok—Jurisdiction Fleet Ship of assignment for Andrej Koscuisko in the novels "Hour of Judgement," "The Devil and Deep Space," and

"Warring States;" technically mutinous, lurking
in Gonebeyond waiting for its status to be
resolved

Rudistal—port city in which most of the action of
"Prisoner of Conscience" takes place

Sant-Dasidar Judiciary—Judiciary to which
Andrej's home system, the Dolgorukij
Combine, belongs

Sarvaw—Lek Kerenko's ethnicity; bottom rung of
Dolgorukij ethnicity

Scylla—Jurisdiction Fleet Ship *Scylla*, Andrej
Koscuisko's ship of assignment prior to his
transfer to the *Ragnarok*

Taisheki Station—location of Fleet Audit Appeals
Authority featured in the novel "The Devil
and Deep Space"

Thula—an elite courier characterized by its speed,
high-end navigation and interception abilities,
and ability to support heavy armament
(e.g. main battle cannon), first appearing in the
novel "The Devil and Deep Space"